THE TRIUMPH OF BACCHUS

THE TRIUMPH
OF BACCHUS

Douglas Skeggs

ᘓ ᘓ ᘓ ᘓ ᘓ ᘓ ᘓ ᘓ ᘓ ᘓ ᘓ ᘓ ᘓ ᘓ ᘓ

All the characters and events portrayed in this work are fictitious.

THE TRIUMPH OF BACCHUS

A Felony & Mayhem Mystery

PRINTING HISTORY
First UK edition (Macmillan): 1993
First U.S. edition (St. Martin's): 1993
Felony & Mayhem edition: 2008

ISBN: 978-1-933397-99-3

Manufactured in the United States of America

The icon above says you're holding a copy of a book in the Felony & Mayhem "Traditional" category. We think of these books as classy cozies, with little gunplay or gore but often a fair amount of humor and, usually, an intrepid amateur sleuth. If you enjoy this book, you may well like other "Traditional" titles from Felony & Mayhem Press, including:

For more about these books, and other Felony & Mayhem titles, or to place an order, please visit our website at

www.FelonyAndMayhem.com

or contact us at

Felony and Mayhem Press
156 Waverly Place
New York, NY 10014

THE TRIUMPH OF BACCHUS

Chapter 1

The police came for him in the early hours. There were two of them, a driver and a plain-clothes officer who called himself Forsyth. He was polite but brusque, avoiding small talk, wanting only to get on with the job.

The car they bundled him into was one of those un-marked civilian affairs that you can spot as a police car a mile off by the size of its aerial. The short-wave radio was open and as they drove him across the city an irrelevant series of voices crackled across the static.

It was dark outside. Trevelyan sat in the back seat and held his collar to his neck, not so much as protection against the cold as from shock. The news of the theft had hit him hard. He felt a numbness, a sense of helplessness, and he stared out of the window at the cars that were bundled up at the lights in Horse Guards Parade, wondering what the hell anyone was doing out at this time of the morning, while his mind slowly came to terms with what had happened. Only gradually did he start groping for details.

He turned to Forsyth. 'How did you hear about this?'

The policeman didn't appear to have heard him. His hands were pushed down into his overcoat pockets and he was staring at the road ahead. He'd hardly uttered a word since they'd left Trevelyan's Chelsea flat. The police car turned out of Trafalgar Square and accelerated up the Strand.

'There was a call,' Forsyth said after a moment, speaking as though his mouth had grown unused to the sound of words. 'Someone rang one of the stations—Colindale, or Cricklewood, I can't remember which. Somewhere out in the sticks. Told the duty officer that the painting had been taken.'

'He didn't identify himself, I suppose?'

'No, nothing. All he said was that he would be ringing your office at six thirty.'

Trevelyan peered at the hands of his watch in the dark. It was ten to six now. Whoever had made the call had worked out his timing. It would take them another forty minutes to reach the office, set the recording in place. Whoever it was that called would be expecting the line to be tapped, just as he'd be expecting the engineers to try to trace where he was ringing from.

'Did he mention me specifically or just the name of the syndicate?'

'Both. He knew his stuff.'

Trevelyan ran one hand across his face, feeling the stiffness of his skin, the rasp of unshaven cheeks. Sleep was tugging at his mind. He'd been up late the night before, dining with a firm of brokers in some God-forsaken dive off the Fulham Road and his mouth was sour with the memory of Valpolicella and cigarette smoke. It seemed only minutes after his head had hit the pillow that the telephone had jerked him awake again, the police car screeching to a halt outside his home almost simultaneously, scarcely giving him time to pull on his clothes before they were hammering on the door.

'When exactly did this happen?'

'Just after five. The van set off from Burlington House at four fifty and the ambush came about fifteen minutes later.'

'Were they armed?'

'Two of them had shot-guns, sawn off. Very nasty. And gas masks. Bust in with a tear-gas canister. That's about all I can tell you at present. I'll know more when I've had the chance to talk to them myself.'

They were passing St Paul's now, the solid bulk of the cathedral looming above, its silhouette just visible against the sky. 'I suppose there's no chance this was a random attack, is there?'

'None.' Forsyth wriggled his shoulders, shifting up in the seat, his voice becoming more alert with the movement. 'They had a van of their own ready, transferred the painting straight into the back. It was all very quick; well rehearsed.'

'But how could they have known it was being moved at that hour of the morning?'

'It wouldn't have been difficult.' There was a slight dryness to his voice. 'It's hardly been kept a State secret, has it?'

'I suppose not.'

No one, unless they happened to have been testing out a nuclear bunker for the last two months, could have failed to know that *The Triumph of Bacchus* was here in London.

The media had put their full weight behind it. Posters advertising its appearance at the Royal Academy were pasted all over the tube stations, articles had appeared in colour supplements and glossy magazines. It was said to be Titian's greatest masterpiece, the beginnings of modern art, the end of the High Renaissance, depending on who you read.

Trevelyan had seen *The Triumph of Bacchus* twice. Once, briefly, before the restoration work had started, and then again at the opening night. It was an extraordinary work of art, almost hypnotic. He was an insurance underwriter, not an art historian, what he knew about Titian could be written on his season ticket into Bank station, but as he had stood in front of that painting he had sensed something of the quality the experts talked of. It was like an aura about it, he could think of no other word to describe the sensation. And it had left an indelible impression on his mind.

'It's valuable, I take it?' Forsyth's mind had been working along similar lines.

'More than you can imagine.'

'That's what causes the trouble, you know. If it wasn't for the money attached to these works of art nowadays people wouldn't give them a second thought. Leave them to moulder away in the galleries.'

'No, probably not—'

'It's only the money that makes them valuable.' Trevelyan detected the sudden screech of exasperation in his voice and flopped back in the seat. It was unlike him. He was known in the insurance market as a man who kept his head in a crisis. But when you're tired and cold and facing the largest insurance loss of your professional career the last thing you need is to be lectured on the morality of the art market by a snotty young police officer whose only financial problem in life is calculating the results of the football pools. Turning up his collar he closed his eyes and for a moment he pictured *The Triumph of Bacchus*. Not the whole thing, just the face of Bacchus himself. His head thrown back as he laughed, wine trickling from his half-opened mouth. It was the image that had captured the imagination of the public. A strange, diabolical face, half God, half football hooligan, as his wife had described it.

'It's the same organization, you realize that?' Forsyth offered the remark with a little more caution.

'I guess so.'

'The call to a suburban station, another directly to your office. The same routine as the time before.'

And the three times before that, Trevelyan reflected bitterly.

'It gives us an advantage. Knowing what to expect.'

Trevelyan couldn't think how. Here they were being jerked around like puppets on a string. Dragged out of bed in the small hours, driven at high speed across the city to receive a ransom demand on a painting that had been taken at gun-point. He couldn't see where the advantage lay, but he guessed the policeman was trying to look on the bright side, searching for silver linings in a storm cloud.

The syndicate offices were housed in a high steel-framed building sheathed in the smoky glass that film stars sport on their car windows. Two telephone engineers carrying enamelled boxes of tools were waiting by the swing doors, their breath streaming out in the cold air. They greeted Trevelyan as he arrived with the crisp smiles of those who don't wish to get involved.

He led the way to the third floor and unlocked the door. Empty offices are untidy places, useless cubicles of space cluttered with the detritus of working life. This morning they looked more than usually dreary. He flicked on lights to bring the atmosphere alive and as they twitched awake Forsyth made his way down the passage.

'We'll take the call in your room.' He knew the way from previous experience.

The two engineers had a routine worked out between them. Without speaking they dumped their tool boxes on the leather-topped desk and began to lay out their equipment. One unplugged the telephone, wrapping it tightly in its own flex, and set it aside. Forsyth watched impassively, his hands still planted in his pockets. Through the plate-glass window behind him the Lloyd's building was lit up against the night sky, the cranes, the polished aluminium frame gleaming in the beam. To Trevelyan it looked like the setting for some momentous project, a stage on which hope and fortunes were riding.

'Is that thing accurate?' Forsyth nodded towards the clock on the wall. It stood at six fifteen.

'Should be.'

'They'll be punctual.' Forsyth gave them the benefit of his experience. 'If it's anything like the last time they'll come in bang on time. Any chance of some tea? I could murder a cup right now.'

'I'll see what I can do.'

Trevelyan went down to the kitchen at the end of the passage and plugged in the kettle. As it rumbled into life he rummaged through the cupboards until he found tea bags and a leaking bag of sugar. This was alien territory to him. There was never reason to come into the kitchen during normal working hours. Coffee arrived in the hands of his secretary.

'Stall for time if you get the chance,' Forsyth told him as he sipped at the steaming mug. Trevelyan hadn't used the bone china cups. Somehow they didn't seem appropriate to the situation. 'See if you can keep him talking.'

'I doubt if we'll get the chance.'

'You never know.' Forsyth turned to the engineers to ask how long it would take to get a fix on the call.

'Two minutes, maybe less.' They weren't going to commit themselves. 'Depends whether it's local or not.'

Trevelyan sat down in his chair, hearing the familiar creak of complaint as the joints took his weight. If it was the same organization as they'd met before there would be no chance of playing for time, no chance of delaying the conversation. They would find themselves listening to a recording, a cold, dismembered voice that could be neither analysed nor identified.

'Do you know anyone with a Rolls-Royce?' Forsyth asked. He was looking down into the street below. There was a slight lightening outside now, the translucence of night giving way to a sooty darkness that clung to the buildings. 'Someone's just driven up in a chauffeur-driven Rolls.'

'David Ambrose.' Trevelyan didn't have to look to know who it was.

'Does he work with you?'

'He's the Chairman of the Agency.'

'I thought you were the boss here.'

'I'm the underwriter on one of the syndicates. He's the chairman of the whole lot.' Trevelyan hadn't got time to go into the structure of the Lloyd's market. 'How did he hear about this?'

'The Yard would have contacted him.'

They heard the lift doors opening outside, the sound of hand-made Maxwell shoes approaching down the passage. Trevelyan glanced up at the policeman.

'Does the Press know about this yet?'

'If they don't they will do pretty soon.'

David Ambrose paused in the doorway, taking in the scene. He was in his early sixties, a neat figure with a wing of silver hair brushed back over either ear and the swift, direct movements that suggested a military training at some formative point in his career.

'Morning, James.'

'David—'

'Chilly time of day. Could have sworn I saw a touch of frost on the ground as we were crossing the park.' He nodded towards the others in the room. 'So much for the greenhouse effect, eh, gentlemen? If it goes on like this, the boffins will have to come up with something new to scare us with.'

Men who wear Old Etonian ties and immaculate Savile Row suits don't blunder straight into a subject. They observe the niceties of conversation, put you at your ease before cutting to the point.

'Have you heard from them?' he asked Trevelyan.

'Not yet. We're expecting it any minute now.'

Ambrose was removing his gloves, tweaking the tip of each finger before flapping them on to the desk. As he sat down Trevelyan noticed the rose pinned to the lapel of his coat. A small yellow bud, the stem wrapped in foil. How did he do it, for God's sakes? He'd turned up only a few minutes behind them and yet he looked as though he'd been given an hour's warning from a personal valet who'd already run a bath and laid out his clothes. Maybe he'd been up and dressed already. Trevelyan had heard that he only needed a few hours' sleep at night. Startled underwriters had been summoned to his club at four in the morning to find him finishing his breakfast, reading the early edition of *The Times* that was brought to him directly from the press. Crossing one leg over the other, David Ambrose gazed at him with his pale blue eyes.

'Bad business, James.' It was a simple statement of fact and Trevelyan nodded in return.

'What's this painting valued at?'

'Thirty-eight million.'

'And what capacity are you carrying?'

'Twenty per cent.'

A fractional lift of the eyebrows. It was a massive sum to be carrying, much more than most syndicates would have taken on, but it was Trevelyan's policy to grasp the nettle. Undue caution never paid, in his experience. The only way to recover losses was to invest boldly.

'What re-insurance do you have?'

'None. I was running bare on this one. After the last two claims I couldn't renew.'

'No.' Ambrose could appreciate the problem. 'I suppose it's hardly surprising in the circumstances.'

Compared to many of his colleagues in the City, Trevelyan had come to the insurance market with few advantages; no friends in high places, no strings to pull. It had not mattered to David Ambrose. He made it clear to everyone within his influence that he judged a man on his merits, not his background. Five years ago when Trevelyan had applied to set up his own syndicate it had been Ambrose who had backed him, a decision that Trevelyan and his wife had celebrated in champagne a few days later. After fifteen years of struggle it had been the breakthrough, an end to the financial problems that had nagged him for so long.

Now it looked as though the celebrations had been premature. If he failed this time, the best he could hope for was a humiliating retreat back on to the floor, a job as a deputy underwriter. Not bad work in itself but a comedown after you've aspired to greater ambitions. He'd be known in the market as a man who had tried and failed. A man whose luck had run out on him.

Ambrose dropped his voice. 'Can you take this, James?'

'I don't know. No, probably not. It rather depends on what the demand is.'

The engineer came between them, placed a tape deck in front of Trevelyan. 'It's voice activated,' he said, 'so you don't have to worry about starting it. Just pick up the receiver and speak.'

'OK.' Trevelyan felt the first clutch of apprehension in his stomach. He wanted to get this over with.

'We've attached it to a speaker so everyone in the room will be listening in to the conversation. But only you can talk in reply.'

As he turned away Ambrose asked: 'What do you think they'll be asking this time?'

'They've never gone above a million.'

'Isn't this one worth a lot more than the others?'

Trevelyan nodded. 'Four, five times as much.'

'It might encourage them to be a little bolder in their demands.'

'I hope not.' Trevelyan's syndicate was still young, the names who invested in it were new. The annual profits had already been swallowed, the reserves they had managed to build up had been all but eaten away. The market is geared to accept losses—even heavy losses. But this wasn't the first claim. It was the fifth major work of art to have been taken in under a year.

'You've had a rough ride, James.'

'That's the way it goes.' Underwriting is a gamble. Ambrose knew that as well as he did. No one can predict the future. If they could there'd be no need for insurance.

'That should do the trick,' the engineer told them. Picking up the receiver he punched in numbers. 'I'll just check the line, see that it's functioning.'

From the speaker on the desk they heard the clicking of the relays, the sound amplified in the enclosed office. Then a voice shouted: 'On the third pip the time according to Accurist will be six twenty-eight and thirty seconds…'

'Sorry about that.' The engineer reached across the desk and turned down the volume, listened again before putting down the phone. 'That seems to be OK.'

Switching off the tape, he ran it back and played it through again. Trevelyan listened to the voice calmly repeating the time. Suddenly he needed a cigarette. He been trying to give them up, managed to cut himself down to three or four a day, but this wasn't the moment for self-flagellation. He took a packet from the desk drawer and slit open the cellophane.

'You mustn't blame yourself.' Ambrose leaned across the desk, a gold lighter in his hand.

Trevelyan put the cigarette to his lips, saw the smoke waver, and realized that his hands were trembling. 'We should have guessed something like this would happen.'

'Why's that? Every reasonable precaution had been taken.'

'There must have been some way of preventing it. Better security, more planning, I don't know. Anything.'

'Then they would have taken another painting.' Ambrose offered him the truth as consolation. 'The result would have been much the same.'

Across the office Forsyth was talking into a portable phone, one finger buried in his ear to cut out the background noise. The engineers were packing away their tools. It was six twenty-nine. Trevelyan stared at the tape deck in front of him, at the two spools waiting to draw in the words that could finish his career.

Forsyth finished his conversation, pushed the phone into his pocket and came across to them. 'Bloody balls-up, if you ask me.'

'Why do you say that?' Ambrose made the enquiry out of politeness.

'That thing was asking to be taken.'

'Really?'

'Stuck up there for the whole world to see. Everyone telling us that it was the greatest thing since sliced bread. Someone was bound to have a go at it.'

Trevelyan watched the second hand of the clock sweeping down the face. He felt suddenly alone. No one else was watching the time, no one was paying attention.

'In that case, Inspector,' Ambrose was saying, 'I've no doubt you know which painting will be taken next.'

'No, of course not—'

The telephone on the desk rang, the sound breaking into the conversation. A moment's silence and it rang again.

Reaching across to the ashtray Trevelyan crushed the cigarette on its head and picked up the receiver.

'Yes?'

'Who is speaking?' The question was made slowly and haltingly with a pause between each word. Trevelyan knew from previous occasions that this was not a person speaking but a tape, cut together from snatches of recorded conversation. The stuttering voices were all different, some male, others female. It made the words hard to follow, as though they were in code.

The engineer was leaning across the table, watching the needles dancing in the tape deck. He gave the thumbs up.

'Trevelyan,' he said into the receiver. 'James Trevelyan.'

A click at the other end and the toneless voice continued: 'We have taken *The Triumph of Bacchus*, Mr Trevelyan. It has not been harmed. If you comply with our wishes it will be returned to you undamaged. Do you understand?'

Trevelyan glanced across the table to where David Ambrose sat watching the speaker, an expression of grave concentration on his face, fingers meshed together and pressed against his lips.

'Yes,' Trevelyan said. 'I understand.'

'In exchange for the safe return of the painting we will require five million pounds in uncut diamonds. You will be told where to take them in due course. If you refuse, if you attempt to recover the painting yourselves, it will be destroyed immediately. Have you received this message?'

'Yes—I've got it.'

'Then we will contact you again, Mr Trevelyan.'

Chapter 2

'I need five thousand pounds.'

'That's a lot of money.'

'It would only be for a short time, Mr Rinaldi. I'll pay the whole lot back in a couple of months, three at the most.'

The office was on the first floor at the back of the building. In all the time that Shaughnessy had worked at Shanghai Lil's Casino he had only been in there twice. The first occasion had come when he was promoted, the second a few weeks later when he'd handed in his notice. The decoration was pure Hollywood, black panels, golden dragons, and pierced lanterns with red tassels. It was all plastic of course but what the hell, the whole outfit must have cost a bomb just the same.

Maurice Rinaldi faced Shaughnessy across the enormous desk. In keeping with the mood of the casino he was dressed in a black silk dinner jacket that shimmered in the afternoon light as though it was slightly damp. The face above registered no expression, the eyes hooded and unblinking. But through the narrow lids, Shaughnessy could see the chocolate-brown pupils watching him, assessing his motive in coming here asking for money.

He said: 'It'll cost you, Shaughnessy.'

'I know that.'

'Five hundred pounds a week.'

'That's a lot of money, Mr Rinaldi.' Mathematics had never been Shaughnessy's subject but he could calculate the percentage on this one easily enough.

'Those are the terms,' Rinaldi replied quietly. 'Take it or leave it.'

'Two hundred a week would suit me better.'

Something approaching a smile melted the edge of Rinaldi's mouth. 'I'm sure it would,' he said. 'But this isn't an auction, Shaughnessy. We're not haggling over the price of cabbages now. You came asking for money. I've given you my rate. Five hundred pounds a week.'

Shaughnessy gave a shrug. 'OK—if that's the way it has to be.'

'Can you afford it?'

'Sure I can.'

He had a cheek coming here, Shaughnessy knew that. He had only worked in Shanghai Lil's for ten weeks. Now he was asking for twice as much as he'd earned in all that time—not including the tips he'd picked up on the door, that is. But he needed the money in a hurry and when it comes to ready cash there's nowhere like a casino.

Rinaldi was drumming his fingers softly on the edge of the desk. He had small hands, just as he had small feet and small ears pressed close to his head, which gave him the look of a dozing salamander. 'Where are you working these days?'

'I've got a job up at the Shropshire Hotel.'

'Pays well, does it?'

'Not bad. I only work evenings.'

With an imperceptible movement of the head, Rinaldi turned to the bouncer who was leaning against the wall by the door. 'Is this right, Sylvester?'

The man nodded without speaking.

'You've checked?'

'I have, Mr Rinaldi.' Throughout the interview Sylvester had stood watching Shaughnessy with an expression of blank curiosity on his face. It was as though he had convinced himself that Shaughnessy didn't exist and was now having trouble re-adjusting.

'How do I know you can pay?' Rinaldi asked.

'I can do it.'

'You sound confident.'

'It's only for a few weeks. Then I'll have enough to pay the whole lot back.'

Rinaldi reached to his left and picked up the glass of sherry that Sylvester had poured him. 'What do you want it for, Shaughnessy?'

'A bit of business that I have.'

'What sort of business?'

'Now I couldn't tell you that, Mr Rinaldi, could I?'

Rinaldi dropped his eyes to the desk top. 'Get out of here.' There was a weariness to his voice as though he only just realized that they had nothing more to discuss. 'Go to a bank if you want money.'

'It's a dead cert, Mr Rinaldi. Just a couple of months and I can give you back twice what I owe.'

'Sure you can.'

'It's the truth.'

'You're a bum, Shaughnessy.' He found the word he was looking for. 'You've no collateral, no steady pay. You've never held a job down for more than a few weeks and yet you've got the gall to come here asking for cash.' Across the room, Sylvester was listening intently, his mouth gaping open in concentration. 'Why would I want to do that?' Rinaldi asked. 'Giving you money would be like throwing it down the toilet.'

'That's looking on the dark side.'

'You've no respect,' Rinaldi told him. 'I gave you a good job, promoted you above the other boys. You were doing well for yourself. And what did you give me in return?'

'I gave you two weeks' notice.'

'Don't get funny with me.' Rinaldi's lower lip was damp and hanging slack as though anticipating the return of the sherry glass. 'Didn't I tell you that there's nothing I like less than a Mick who tries to get funny with me?'

He nodded to Sylvester who showed Shaughnessy out of the door.

Ahead of him was a short length of passage.

'You must be off your head,' Sylvester said as he pushed past.

'Why's that?'

'Coming here asking for money. You must have gone off your bleeding rocker. Think yourself lucky you weren't chucked out.' At the end of the passage he opened a second door and gave a jerk of his head. 'I could have told you from the start that you were wasting your time. Mr Rinaldi's not going to throw money away on rubbish like you.'

'Did you get it framed then, Sylvester?'

'Get what framed?'

'Your diploma from charm school.'

Sylvester's expression didn't change. 'Piss off,' he

said flatly. 'Show your face around here again and I'll give you a kicking you won't forget in such a hurry.'

He closed the padded door. Shaughnessy heard the bolts slam home on the other side. Rinaldi was a stickler for security. It's an obsession that comes to all men who extract money quickly and painlessly from others.

He walked through into the main gambling room. It was only three in the afternoon but you'd never have known it. There were no windows in Shanghai Lil's, nothing to give any indication of the time of day or night. The only light was artificial: soft and low in the alcoves, gleaming on brass fittings, then sharper spots above the green baize tables where the croupiers in waistcoats and shirt-sleeves were busily dealing.

The cash desk was by the entrance. Behind the thick glass shield was a lean man with sunken cheeks and watchful expression. Shaughnessy took out a handful of notes and pushed them beneath the barrier.

'I'll take two hundred pounds' worth in small denominations.'

The cashier flicked his attention up from the calculator that he was prodding and then back again. 'Your money's no good in here, Tom.'

'Why's that?'

'You know the rules. No staff playing on the premises.'

'I'm not staff any longer, or haven't you noticed? I'm just an honest punter trying his luck on the tables.' He nodded towards the back office. 'Rinaldi knows I'm here. I've just been having a chat with him.'

'It's your money, Tom.' The cashier gave a shrug. Taking the notes he counted them quickly, cracking the stiff paper in his fingers before picking out the equivalent in plastic chips and stacking them on the counter in three neat coloured piles.

Business was good for the time of day, Shaughnessy observed as he moved back into the room. A crowd of people were swarming around the central roulette table. He eased his way into the circle. The croupier was shovelling chips across the bright green cloth before raking back the winnings.

'Place your bets, ladies and gentlemen.' No French spoken here, nothing to alienate the punter who has come to Shanghai Lil's via the high-street betting shop.

Shaughnessy looked at the faces around the table. He knew them all from the way they sat, the way they handled their chips. There are those who gamble out of boredom, sitting back in their chairs, tossing their bets into position, not bothering to count the returns; those who've only come for the occasion, the novelty of it, risking small sums to titillate themselves; and those who play because they can't stop themselves. The addicts. They were the ones that had always interested Shaughnessy most. The ones who played for the kick of adrenalin the game gave them; the ones who couldn't walk away from the tables whether they were winning or losing.

He put twenty pounds on red, won, and left it there, adding another ten elsewhere on the table. Shaughnessy wasn't a gambler by instinct. It was his Catholic upbringing, he guessed, the deep-rooted belief that money must be earned by hard labour. Anything else was a mortal sin. He could almost hear his mam saying it. But while he was working in the casino he had watched the game enough to know that greed never paid. You had to play for small profits, keeping your chances wide, steadily feeding the table, using your winnings to off-set the losses.

For over an hour he worked, moving from one game to another, gradually accumulating the coloured plastic chips in his pocket.

'Christ, you're doing well,' said a girl beside him.

'Seems to be going my way—'

'Do you have a system, then?'

'I just keep the pieces in play. Let them find their way around the table.'

He moved further round the table but when he left it ten minutes later the girl followed him. 'Are you finished now?'

'For the time being.'

'Would you like a drink or anything?' She was wearing a diaphanous blue dress that had been designed for reasons other than warmth, long expanses of arm and thigh left showing at either end. Girls like this were part of the furniture. Shaughnessy knew most of those who hung around Shanghai Lil's from experience but this one was new to him.

'What's your name?' he asked.

'Ingrid,' she told him. 'I'm Swedish.'

'Sure you are.' The blonde hair was dyed, the accent came from within a five-mile radius of Islington. He guessed the nearest she'd been to Sweden was a mixed sauna in a Bayswater hotel.

She was watching him with hungry eyes. 'Maybe we could go somewhere, have some fun?'

'I'll tell you what.' Shaughnessy dug the chips out of

his pocket. 'You take these to the desk and cash them in for me. There's someone I must talk to before I leave.'

'OK.' She accepted the offer readily. 'I'll meet you outside.'

When she emerged ten minutes later and hurried down the steps, her ankles wobbling on pointed high heels, she was wearing a stylish coat with fur trimmings.

'I've got it,' she said breathlessly. 'It's a fortune. Did you know that?'

'I had a fair idea.'

With small hands she pulled out the thick wad of fifty-pound notes from her pocket. 'Where do you want to go then?'

'I'm in a bit of a hurry, love.'

The disappointment showed in her face. 'But you said that—'

'I know, but I've changed my mind.'

'That's not fair.' Resentment flared in her voice. She'd had a few knocks in her time. 'I came out here because you said you wanted to go somewhere.'

'I'll tell you what,' Shaughnessy told her. 'I'll make a bargain. You take these for your time.' He peeled off two fifty-pound notes and gave them to her. Then reaching into the front of her dress he pulled a tight tube of rolled notes from between her breasts. 'And I'll keep these.'

The girl had jumped back as he touched, legs stiff, mouth twisting into an obscenity. Then she hesitated. Whatever he wanted of her it wasn't her body. It must have been those chips. He'd needed her to cash them in for him so that he wouldn't be seen to have won so much money. That was it. He had worked some trick on the casino, used her along the way. In many ways he was no different to her, she realized. Just working his trade in the casino.

'You're a bastard,' she said sulkily. She hadn't lost her pride.

Until that moment she had hardly bothered to look at Shaughnessy too carefully. He had been a punter, someone with money to unload. But now as she stood in the road, cars pouring past, she looked him over. He was a tall man with thick fair hair that fell across his eyes. He was wearing a tweed jacket, patched at the elbows, a blue Guernsey, and well-washed jeans. Out of place in a casino, she thought. Very different to the usual trade with their light-weight suits and silk ties. This one looked as though he would be more at home at a horse auction than a gambling table.

Shaughnessy had turned away from her and was hailing down a taxi.

'Do you come around here often?' she asked as it drew into the kerb.

Shaughnessy paused, the door open in his hand. 'I think I'll give it a miss for a while, love.' He smiled and gave her a wink. 'It's never wise to go back to a place where you've done well. Tends to bring bad luck, if you know what I mean.'

She hugged her coat around her shoulders. Sure, she knew what he meant. 'I'll see you around, maybe.'

❈ ❈ ❈

The gallery was in Dover Street, sandwiched on one side by an Italian bistro with a red plastic awning and a heel bar on the other. Hanging in the window was a Dutch still life, a large brown picture that didn't catch the attention of anyone walking by.

The owner sat at an untidy desk at the back of the single room. He got up as Shaughnessy came in.

'Ah.' A note of genteel surprise in his voice. 'I was beginning to wonder whether you were coming back.'

'I was held up.' Shaughnessy let it be implied that traffic or business had caused the delay and the owner nodded sagely. He was a thin man with a dry, dusty look about him like a piece of furniture which has had an attack of the beetle. His hands were pushed down into the pockets of a fawn-coloured cardigan which had stretched under the weight so that it reached down to his knees. He searched in his memory. 'It was the Venetian capriccio you were interested in, wasn't it?'

He couldn't have forgotten. Selling a painting must be a rare event in this gallery, something to celebrate. But Shaughnessy let him have his moment. 'That's the one.'

'Wait there a moment. I'll bring it up.'

He returned from the basement carrying a large canvas. Padding across the floor he leant it against the wall. 'I have the frame downstairs. I'll fetch it in a minute.'

'Don't bother yourself. I'll not be needing that,' Shaughnessy replied, crouching down in front of the painting and examining it carefully.

Capriccios were a bad habit which certain artists in the past fell into of reassembling the landscape for no particularly good reason. This was a view of Venice with the Rialto bridge connecting directly to the Doge's Palace and the Salute cathedral appearing where it wasn't. The paint had oxidized over the years so that the underpainting had turned the shadows to the colour of cold coffee. It was the sort of picture that is destined to hang in the passageway of some gentleman's club where it won't be noticed.

The gallery owner stood watching with the mournful expression of a man who is selling his daughter for less than the market price. 'It's a fine example of the genre.'

'Isn't it a beauty.'

Taking a measuring tape from his pocket, Shaughnessy checked the dimensions again. The height was right but it was four inches longer than he wanted. One edge would have to be cut down to size. Slightly risky but he had no alternative. And the canvas was early eighteenth rather than sixteenth century but he didn't see that that was necessarily a problem. It would take extensive carbon dating to establish the difference. He ran his hands down the side of the stretcher, feeling the smooth texture of the canvas. It was a fine linen tabby weave with twenty-four threads per centimetre to the warp and twenty-three threads per centimetre to the weft, that was the important point. It was the closest he was ever going to find to what he wanted.

'Two thousand five hundred. Wasn't that what we agreed?'

'Three thousand.' The owner had already been knocked down seven hundred on the asking price. He wasn't going any further. 'Plus fifteen per cent VAT.'

'We don't need to worry about that,' Shaughnessy told him, straightening up and knocking the dust from his trousers. 'I'll be paying in cash.'

'I've got books to balance.'

'You can keep the frame. That must be worth a couple of hundred.'

The owner was dithering on the brink of indecision.

The frame was carved wood, it would fetch at least three fifty but he didn't want to lower the price further.

'Two thousand eight hundred and no questions asked.' Shaughnessy was at his most persuasive. 'What do you say?'

'No, I'm sorry. I can't go below three thousand.'

'Why? Is there a law against it or something?'

'Please, don't press me any further. Three thousand is my bottom price and that's all there is to it.'

'Do you have a van, then?' Shaughnessy changed tack. 'Something I could move this in?'

'I don't own a van myself. We use a carrier service whenever we're picking up large pictures.'

'Then I'll tell you what. I'll make a bargain with you. You get on the phone and fix a van and if you can get it to come round right away I'll give you two thousand nine hundred—cash on the table. That's fair enough isn't it?'

'Oh, very well. Have it your own way.' The owner was shaking his head to indicate that he was robbing himself. From the pile of papers on his desk he extracted the phone and cradled the receiver in his neck as he searched for the number.

'What do you want it for in such a hurry?' he asked as he dialled.

Shaughnessy didn't reply immediately. For three days he had scoured the galleries and sale rooms of London, working his way through thousands of paintings, searching for the canvas he needed.

'It's for a client,' he said after a moment. 'He collects this sort of thing.' It was a vague answer. But Shaughnessy reasoned that if he told the man he was going to paint a fake on it he would probably have had a coronary.

Chapter 3

On the way across London, he sat in the back of the van with the painting and counted through the money in his pocket. There was two thousand four hundred and fifty quid left. Adding the price he had paid for the painting, less the two hundred he had put down as a stake and the two notes he had given Ingrid, he calculated he'd won five thousand two hundred and fifty in the casino. A small fortune, as Ingrid had pointed out, but almost exactly what he expected. Rinaldi was going to be sick as a cat if he found out. He didn't have much sense of humour when it came to money. Shaughnessy tapped the wooden stretcher of the painting with his fingertips and hoped to God that the eventuality didn't arise.

He was going to need every penny of it, he told himself as he stuffed the notes back in his pocket. The materials alone were going to cost him close on a thousand, the travel another fifteen hundred, not to mention the backhanders he was going to have to dole out.

Still, it would do for the present. If he needed more he could always dig it up from somewhere. There was enough here to make a start.

The van had turned in off the Brompton Road and parked in a small square of smart residential houses with bars on the basement windows and bay trees padlocked to the railings. Three children were running down the pavement swinging their satchels about their heads and shouting in high, piercing voices.

Shaughnessy climbed out of the van and slid the painting on to the road.

'Do you want a hand inside with it?' the driver asked.

'Don't you worry yourself with that. I can take it from here.'

He waited until the van had driven away before lifting the canvas on one shoulder and walking back in the direction they had come. It was growing dark now, the sun working itself into a fury as it settled behind the roof tops. Lights were coming on in shop windows and the cold air chewed at his ears and nose.

Inkerman Mansions is one of those seven-storey Victorian blocks of red brick and wrought-iron balconies that are tucked away behind the Cannon cinema in the Fulham Road. The windows are all identical, as are the apartments inside, as though this uniformity will somehow force the residents to lead morally identical lives.

Shaughnessy carried the painting round into the narrow alleyway behind. Despite its heroic exterior, Inkerman Mansions was made up of small, pokey flats. Most of the residents were elderly: retired civil servants and widows with annuities and blue-rinse poodles. The stairs smelled of disinfectant and the drains didn't always work but they put up with it because it's Chelsea and that's a good address.

Scobie's studio was on the top floor.

'You've got it, then,' he said, coming to the door and stating the obvious. Taking one end of the canvas each they hefted it up the last flight of steps.

The studio was a large dusty space set between the chimney stacks. A huge window covered one wall and half the sloping ceiling, so that when you looked up you could see the backsides of the pigeons perched on the gutter. During the war, sticky tape had been crisscrossed over the glass panes to prevent them shattering but only part of it had been removed. The rest fluttered like pennants. A paraffin stove was hissing in the corner, filling the air with a sweet, drowsy scent.

Shaughnessy had no idea why they had decided to build studios on the top floor of Inkerman Mansions. Maybe the architect had been hoping to integrate artists into society, maybe he'd just reckoned no one else would be prepared to walk up so many flights of stairs.

They settled the canvas on a studio easel. Scobie cranked it up to eye level. 'Bit of a stinker, isn't it?'

'Nothing to write home about.'

'What were they asking for it?'

'Three thousand six hundred—plus VAT.'

Scobie gave a little snort. He was standing back from the easel, his hands on hips, face set into the surly expression with which he confronted every work of art. He was sixty-eight years old—sixty-five of which he admitted to—with a wave of grey hair bursting over either ear and a beard that was trimmed short and brushed forwards in a style that had been fashionable in an age when most people in this country hadn't been born. He was dressed in a corduroy jacket and baggy trousers. On his feet were brown boots with elastic side panels that had grown tired so that they now opened around his ankles like crocuses.

'What did you give them for it?' He was still giving the painting the first degree.

'I managed to push them down to two-ninety in cash.'

'Daylight robbery. If I tried knocking up something like this I wouldn't get five quid for it. But wait until it's covered in cracks, the paint flaking off like dandruff, and suddenly it's worth thousands.'

'There's no justice, is there.' Shaughnessy found it best to agree with Scobie's views on the art market. It made life quieter.

In the alcove beneath the gallery was a Welsh dresser decorated with scenes of rustic life. He dug out the bottle of Jameson's whiskey which he'd put there the day before and checked the level before searching the nearby table for a glass.

Scobie's studio was a mess. Not a temporary untidiness but a total, ingrained mess that takes thirty years to establish. Brushes were crammed into jam jars, diseased drapery was piled on the floor between easels and stacks of discarded canvases. Others hung from nails on the wall, along with empty frames and clippings from newspapers.

In his own way Scobie was a celebrity. Not one of the new designer artists who come and go with the speed of pop stars but a solid, dependable portrait painter whose views on contemporary art, politics, and sex occasionally leaked into the Sunday papers. His bread and butter came from three-quarter-length portraits of college masters and company directors—mug-shots as he called them—although he had painted most members of the Royal family in his time. He had two pictures in the National Portrait Gallery and his wartime sketch of Montgomery was rated as a classic in military circles.

Presently standing on an easel was a painting of Princess Diana. Just the head complete, the rest a wash of grey tones. Standing beside this painting were two copies, exact reproductions of the first in various states of completion. Scobie always made copies of his own paintings and sold them to anyone interested. It was good business.

'You got the money, then,' he said.

'Eventually.' Shaughnessy found a glass, ejected some colourless liquid that he hoped wasn't turpentine, and poured in whiskey.

'I'm amazed. I never thought Rinaldi would part with hard cash.'

'He didn't.'

'Then where did you get it from?'

'I picked it up on the roulette wheel.'

For once he had Scobie's admiration. 'You won five thousand quid at roulette?'

'Not exactly.' He thought Scobie better know the truth of it. 'I won about a hundred and fifty at roulette and added in a few chips I'd made myself along the way.'

'You passed off forged chips at Shanghai Lil's?'

'That's right.'

'Are you out of your bloody mind?'

For a man who has bounced cheques all round Chelsea, Shaughnessy felt he was taking an unnecessarily moral tone. 'Why not? He'll never find out if he lives to be a hundred.'

'Never find out? Are you joking? Of course he'll find out. There are video cameras all over that place. The chips are numbered and there's only a limited number of the damned things. He's going to break every bone in your body when he finds out.' He stared around the studio for inspiration before snatching a name from the past. 'Archie Cameron. You remember Archie Cameron? He ran up a debt there a few years back. When he couldn't pay, Rinaldi sent two of his boys round and soaked him in petrol. Threatened to turn him into a kebab unless he came up with the money in the next twenty-four hours. He's a psychopath, a bloody nutter.'

Shaughnessy could picture Sylvester with a lighter in his hand. He would have enjoyed that.

'You shouldn't be such a pessimist, Scobie. You'll give yourself an ulcer. I did a beautiful job on those chips. You should have seen them. Not just on the outside, either, I put the electric tab inside, the lot. They were a work of art. It'll take him an age to work out what's gone wrong.'

'It's your arse, Tom.'

Scobie wasn't seeing the point. 'I got the painting. That's the important part.'

He picked up a sheet that had been white when ration books were around, flapped off the dust, and draped it over the painting, tacking it in place with drawing pins. Scobie switched off the lights and the studio was plunged into darkness, or that silvery approximation that passes for darkness in a city.

Shaughnessy switched on the projector and taking a slide from his wallet he poked it down into the aperture. The beam of white light contracted to a golden rectangle. He adjusted the focus. The golden haze broke into individual colours, the image hardened, and *The Triumph of*

Bacchus appeared on the stretched sheet. He adjusted the projector until the two fitted as closely as possible.

'I need to take off a few inches at the top.'

'The canvas is right, is it?' Scobie asked.

'A couple of centuries too young but not so that you'd notice.'

Scobie examined it thoughtfully, rubbing his thumb up one edge of the stretcher. In the light of the projector dust particles drifted around his head.

Shaughnessy had recruited Scobie from the start. He needed him both for his technical knowledge and as a sounding board for his own calculations. Scobie had trained at the Slade in the days when painting was still a craft that could be taught and mastered. When he wasn't drunk, when he wasn't wearing himself out chasing after his younger, and generally faster running, female students, Scobie knew as much as anyone about the chemical properties and performance of oil paint.

They'd been in the Roland when Shaughnessy first put the idea to him. It was some time back in July, a hot and sultry day, and they were sitting at a table outside in the street.

'They've got it back,' Shaughnessy said. He had a newspaper spread out on the baked wooden table top.

'Got what back?'

'That Gainsborough which was nicked.'

Scobie took a mouthful of Webster's bitter. It left a cloud of foam on his moustache, giving him the appearance of a disgruntled Father Christmas. 'It was just a matter of time.'

The painting, one of the Suffolk landscapes, had been stolen some weeks earlier. The press had made quite a feature of it at the time, not so much because of its value, which was around one and a half million, but because of speculation that this was the fourth theft by a single organization who had been operating successfully in the country. The ransom method that took place in Montreux on Lake Geneva had confirmed this suspicion to the police.

'It says here that before the ransom demand of four hundred thousand pounds in uncut diamonds was handed over, the painting was examined by Thomas Sutcliffe, an acknowledged expert on the work of Gainsborough.'

'I bet he was wetting himself with fright,' Scobie said. He had a low opinion of art historians.

'How long do you think he was given to examine it?'

'Can't have been more than a few minutes. Long enough to see it was the real thing and clear out, I imagine. Where did this happen?'

'On the mountain road above the town. It was night time.'

'I expect he could hardly see it, let alone verify it.'

'That's what I was thinking.'

Something in Shaughnessy's tone of voice made Scobie pause. He filled the interval with a mouthful of beer and wiped his sleeve across his moustache before asking, 'What were you thinking?'

'That it would have been a cinch to pass off a fake on them.'

'It's not possible to fake a picture nowadays,' Scobie said. This wasn't just an opinion but a well-known truth much discussed by the regulars at the Roland.

'That's because of all the chemical tests and checks on the provenance they can do these days,' he said. 'But they all take time. I'm talking about passing off a fake on a man who has a gun pointing at his head and can hardly see what he's looking at in the dark. That's possible. In fact it's more than possible, it's the easiest way of making four hundred thousand quid I can think of.'

Scobie rubbed his fingers into the pits of his eyes and regarded him steadily, trying to decide whether he was titillating himself with idle speculation or making a serious proposal. What he said next was by way of a test. 'It's too late now anyway.'

'You're right; it is,' Shaughnessy agreed. 'But there'll be another in a few months' time.'

'You ready for another of those?' Scobie pointed towards his glass. He wasn't changing the subject, merely preparing the way for further discussion.

'If you're getting them in.'

He waited outside while Scobie disappeared into the ink-black interior of the pub. The sun was warm on his back, the image of the street wobbling slightly in the heat.

'I've got Dave to knock us up some sandwiches,' Scobie said, returning with the drinks. He set the glasses on the table and sat down. For some reason the tables at the Roland were bolted to the ground, the benches part of the fixed structure, making them into a minor obstacle course.

'How can you be sure they'll take another?' he asked when he was in place.

'It'll be irresistible. They're on a winning streak.'

Scobie siphoned off an inch of beer. He always drank when he was thinking. Shaughnessy sometimes thought it was lucky he had such an easy-going nature. Had he been a more reflective man he'd never have been sober long enough to think at all.

'You'd be faking a picture you've never even seen,' Scobie said. 'You realize that?'

'There are ways of pitching it right.'

'It'll have to be good, Tommie. They may send a real expert to look at it. Someone who knows his onions.'

'Do you think we could get away with it?'

The question was interrupted by the arrival of a plate of sandwiches. When they were alone again Scobie said, 'You'll have the police after you.'

'No, I won't. The police will be looking for whoever it was nicked the real thing. That's the beauty of it. Besides, there's more to it than that.'

He explained the background to the idea, filling in the details, leaving nothing out. Scobie listened moodily. 'You're serious, then?'

'Will you help?'

Opening one corner of a sandwich, which had already curled up in anticipation, Scobie examined the contents. Shaughnessy had known him for over ten years but there were times when he could be inscrutable. It was a secretiveness, Scobie said, that came from having lived for forty years with a grasping wife, although why he should say that was obscure. He only saw her twice a year at the most, less if he could arrange it.

'I'll have to think about it,' he said eventually.

Shaughnessy had heard nothing more from him for over a week. Then, when he was beginning to think Scobie had dropped the idea, he came round one evening to say that he agreed. Shaughnessy had offered him a cut of the profit but Scobie didn't want it. Money was of no use to him at his stage in life, he'd said. What he wanted instead was a condition imposed on the agreement. It was a strange request he came up with but not difficult and so Shaughnessy had accepted it.

'How long do you think you'll get to make this fake?' Scobie had asked before leaving.

'I don't know. Six weeks at the most.'

He had shaken his head sadly. 'That's not long. You'd better pray that whatever they take is easy to copy.'

And that, Shaughnessy thought now as he looked at the great painting on the screen, was the first major stumbling block. He had been banking on copying a formal painting, something with a mechanical technique that could be followed like a cooking recipe. Titian was different. He was one of the supreme painterly painters, a magician.

Moving forwards he touched the canvas, running his palm across the surface as though already feeling the dry crust of paint.

The setting was an island. Sun-drenched rocks and an emerald sea. Beyond it the porpoise backs of distant mountains. The party, if that's what this tremendous debauch could be called, was nearly over. Twenty or so figures were lying in the shade of the trees, already stupefied with drink and sunshine. Silenus on his back, a beached whale of drunken flesh; Ariadne asleep, long blonde hair across her eyes. Near by a girl was pouring wine from a cymbal into the mouth of a satyr while a small faun relieved himself against the wheel of the chariot.

Above them Bacchus, the apex of the triangle, the focus. A powerful figure, lazy and insolent, staring out of the canvas with his head thrown back, sensing the spectator like an intruder to his territory. The sulphur-yellow eyes were half-closed, the expression mocking, knowing, the mouth open so that the wine dribbled down his chin as he laughed in defiance.

An art historian would have catalogued the painting as a mythology; the more practically minded would have seen it in contemporary terms, the transposing of a Mediterranean wine festival on to the concept of antiquity. But it was neither of these. There was a violence to it, an urgency that was both sensual and disturbing. Here was cruelty and love in co-habitation; Venetian light trapped in a glass of white wine; the conflict of reason and chaos. It was tangible, vibrant, the invention of a peasant-boy turned painter, the daydream of an artist who has read legends in the shuttered darkness of an Italian library.

'What is there on Titian's technique?' Shaughnessy asked.

'Max Doener, Charles Locke Eastlake.'

'Any good?'

'They talk about his methods. They don't really explain them.'

'A picture like that takes some explaining.' Shaughnessy switched off the projector. 'What's the time?'

'I make it just after five. But I'm fast.'

'I'd better be getting off to work. We'll talk about it when I get back.'

The Shropshire Hotel is hidden away in one of those narrow alleys between St James's Street and the park— when you are small and exclusive with one of the best wine lists in London you don't need to advertise your presence. It has this beautiful Georgian facade with a double staircase that flows out from the entrance to welcome everyone who approaches. Everyone, that is, apart from the kitchen staff. They go round the back.

'You'd better get your butt in there double quick,' Ernie told him in the locker room. 'Gascoigne will go spare if he sees you're in late.'

Shaughnessy buttoned up his tunic. You could tell the day of the week by the state of the white tunics. They were clean on Saturdays, grubby by Monday and filthy by the time they hit the laundry.

He'd been working in the hotel kitchens for five weeks. It was a job like any other. Before that it had been Shanghai Lil's, and a stint in a hamburger joint off Queensway. He didn't mind the work. The pay was a fraction of what he'd been used to in the last few years but there was no responsibility, no mental effort, and he didn't have to wear a suit. That was worth something in itself.

The kitchens were run in the old-fashioned manner so that you could tell a man's rank by the length of his apron and the height of his starched white hat. The tallest belonged to Philip Gascoigne, the head chef.

'What time do you call this?' he asked as Shaughnessy came in.

'There was a cock-up in the store room, Mr Gascoigne. The groceries have the wrong labels on them. It took me a little time to sort it out.'

'We've got a private party in the Blue Room,' he said to no one in particular. 'And a full dining room. I want to see you working. Any slacking and you can whistle for your reference.' Gascoigne had dense black hair on short arms that hung out from the side of his body and tiny fingers that moved with the speed of a concert pianist when he worked. Egon Ronay rated him as one of the best chefs in London but that doesn't make a man any easier to love.

Shaughnessy upended the box he was carrying, spilling the French beans out on to the worktop. 'I hear what you're saying, Mr Gascoigne.'

'Don't say I didn't warn you.'

As Gascoigne moved away, Jake jerked his chin in his direction. 'You want to watch him. He can be a right bastard when he puts his mind to it.'

'He doesn't have to try, does he?' A trolley of crockery trundled past them on its way to the dining rooms, the stacked plates chattering to the rhythm of the wheels.

'Are you off, then?' Jake asked. He had an amiable face, rather flat with a broad nose as though he'd been pressing it against a window pane when the wind changed and it had stuck that way.

'I thought I might move on.'

'Got anything lined up?'

Shaughnessy took a knife from the overhead rack, ran its blade across his sleeve. 'I'll try going it on my own for a bit.'

'I was thinking of getting out myself. There's a place going for a pastry chef at the Cleveland.'

'Nice work if you can get it.'

Shaughnessy had considered walking out the day *The Triumph of Bacchus* was stolen but on second thoughts he had decided to work out his notice. There was always a chance that someone might make the connection. Not very likely, admittedly, but you never knew. It was better to be careful.

Jake said, 'I could get you a place there if you like.'

'I haven't got the experience. The only way I know of making pastry is to ask my mam to do it. And she never got prizes for it.'

'So what? The head chef's a mate of mine.'

'I'll think about it.'

It was eleven that night when he got back to the studio. Scobie was still awake. Getting up from the sofa he stretched each leg in turn, carefully balancing on the other as he did so.

'Bring anything with you?' he asked.

'There's a steak and a few other bits and pieces. Sent back for being over-done.' Shaughnessy took a foil-wrapped package from his pocket and tossed it on the table.

'Cold burnt steak,' Scobie observed. 'My favourite.'

Pouring himself a drink, Shaughnessy took a sip and let it work its way through his veins on its own. Jameson's whiskey is a great democrat. It tastes as good for a kitchen porter as for one of the nobs in the dining room. He switched on the projector and studied the painting once more as though convincing himself it was there, a finite problem that could be overcome. 'We need to make a plan of campaign.'

'What's first on the list?' Scobie asked. He had unwrapped the package and was holding up the piece of steak like a woman who's found a rogue sock in the laundry basket.

'To knock the paint off this picture; strip it down to the canvas and reprime it. But in the mean time I need to start laying in the pigments.'

'I thought you'd already got them.'

'Only a few basics. I couldn't tell which ones I needed until I knew what we were dealing with. This needs some specialist colours, ultramarine amongst others.'

'Not the real thing?'

'It'll have to be.'

'Why not use the ready-made stuff? No one will have time to test it, that's the whole point.'

'Commercial paint has a whole lot of preservatives in it: poppy oil and other crap. It slows down the drying time.'

'Drain it off on blotting paper.' Scobie put bread on the table along with the meat, cutlery, and a bottle of tomato ketchup.

'It's still ground too fine. You'll never get the consistency.'

Constructing a makeshift sandwich from the kit on the table, Scobie took a bite and stared at the painting projected on the screen.

'Holy saints, Tommie. How long's this all going to take?'

'A week, maybe a bit more.'

'You're never going to do it.' He gave his opinion with his mouth full. 'You start farting around grinding pigments and you're going to run out of time.'

He was probably right. It was impossible to fake a Titian in a few days; it just can't be done convincingly. But there was no point in being defeatist about it. Shaughnessy had often observed that the greatest advantage of being Irish is that you're not expected to see sense, and so he said, 'We'll worry about that when it happens.'

Chapter 4

Patricia Drew first heard of the theft of *The Triumph of Bacchus* in Brussels airport.

She'd come in on the early flight from Bogotá where she had spent three days recording an interview for a documentary she was making on the South American arms trade. The schedule had been punishing, she'd hardly slept in the last forty-eight hours, and she was feeling tired and crumpled.

There were only a few other passengers in the first-class lounge, all in pinstripe suits with briefcases opened on their laps, justifying their first-class tickets by poking numbers into their personal calculators. Patricia sat down with the morning papers. They'd been delivered to her room in Bogotá but she'd scarcely registered the contents. For some reason the news had seemed less important over there, like looking at the world through the wrong end of a telescope.

She was twenty-eight, an elegantly dressed girl with the fair-skinned beauty and slightly supercilious manner of the English upper class. Her blonde hair, which was cut and streaked to look both windswept and coiffured at the same time, was collar length. Beneath it, she had startlingly pale blue eyes, the colour of the sky in those faded Italian frescoes, which gave her a wild, slightly untamed appearance. When her portrait by David Poole had been exhibited at the Royal Society of Portrait Painters earlier that year one critic had said that she looked like the young Boudicca posing for the society pages of Vogue. The remark had been intended to be slighting but it was possibly more apt than he realized, for beneath the Armani suit, the carefully groomed exterior, she was as ambitious, as self-seeking, and as motivated as any man.

'Do you have a phone?' she asked the stewardess after a few minutes.

'There's one in the passage, madam.'

She got through to her office in Vanbrugh Films with the aid of a credit card. Suzie sounded surprised to hear her.

'Where are you?'

'Brussels airport. The flight was delayed and I've missed my connection. I should be back around mid-morning.'

'How was South America, then?'

'It's a long story.' Patricia wasn't in the mood to confide in a PA who imagined that the entire southern continent consisted of palm trees and girls in grass skirts. 'I've just been reading about *The Triumph of Bacchus*.'

'Oh, that.'

'When did it happen?'

'The day before yesterday, I think it was.' It hadn't made an impression on Suzie's memory. 'No, it must have been Tuesday. About five in the morning.'

Patricia calculated the hour change, estimated that at the moment she'd been on the way up into the mountains sitting in the back of a truck wedged between two men with automatic rifles cradled between their legs—and feeling pretty scared, if she was honest with herself.

The stewardess was hovering at her elbow, indicating that the flight had been called by pointing at her watch. Patricia nodded her understanding and turned away.

'Look Suzie,' she said. 'Go over to the Royal Academy, could you. Find out what you can about it.'

'OK.' Patricia could picture her scribbling a note with the pen she carried on a leather thong around her neck. 'Anything in particular?'

'All the background information you can find. I want the name of the Lloyd's syndicate that's covering the loss. And get the papers from the day it was taken. Anything else I might have missed while I was away. I'll go through it all when I come in.'

Gus was waiting for her at Heathrow. He greeted her with a fanfare and a little castanet snap of his fingers. 'Hey, good to see you. Welcome back to civilization.'

He had on his wide red spectacles. You could always tell what mood Gus was in by the spectacles he wore: thick black rims for board meetings, the little round ones when he was with his arty friends, square when he was being responsible. These were the ones that said he was successful but still unconventional. A fun guy to be with.

Patricia kissed him on both cheeks, felt him grasp her round the waist so that she was lifted on to tip-toe. There weren't any Press photographers around but Gus never took chances.

'What are you doing here?' she asked as he let her go.

'Suzie said you were sounding down in the dumps so I thought I'd come to pick you up.' He had taken the trolley of luggage and was causing maximum damage as he propelled it through the crowd. "Aren't you pleased to see me then?'

'Yes, Gus, I am.' And she was too, she realized. In the sterilized, impersonal arrival lounge Gus was suddenly very warm, human, larger than life.

When they reached the point where the trolleys had to end, Gus pushed it under the plastic flaps. His silver-green Porsche was parked in the road alongside the taxis. It should have been clamped there but Patricia knew he would have tipped someone to look the other way. He was good at getting what he wanted. It was one of the things that had first attracted him to her.

The bucket seats were lined with thick fleecy wool covers. Gus demanded comfort from all his possessions. He dressed in soft moccasins and the type of Italian suit that looks as though it's been knitted rather than tailored. His shoulder-length hair was tied back in a pony tail in the daytime and loose at night, the silk shirts beneath opened wide. In the three years she'd known Gus she had never seen him in a tie although he did allow a black cravat on formal occasions. The fridge in his double-glazed air-conditioned office held iron rations of smoked salmon and champagne at all times and the carpets sucked in your feet like quicksand. Gus could see no possible point in earning a large salary if you couldn't use it to indulge yourself.

'So what's this about *The Triumph of Bacchus?*' he asked as he nudged the car out into the M4, moving directly ahead of a lorry in the way that you can when there's a three-hundred-and-forty-eight horsepower engine under the bonnet.

'Did Suzie tell you about it?'

'She didn't need to. She's been fizzing around London ever since you rang.' His voice had dropped now that they were in private. Gus had two voices, one very loud which he used to help radiate his personality at cocktail parties and award ceremonies, and this one which was shorter and jerkier and only came into play when he wanted information.

'I thought it sounded promising.'

'Rather a long shot, wouldn't you say?'

'Why's that?'

Gus removed one hand from the wheel and stirred the air. He'd been under the sun lamp, she noticed. It had probably been bugging him that she was going to come back from South America with a tan. He said, 'Art's all about museums and dead artists.'

'Not necessarily.'

'Come on, Patricia. It's an elitist world. You know that. It belongs to little faggots in velvet suits.'

'That's not how I see it.'

'No, you probably don't.' Gus had worked his way up from the bottom rung. He never tired of reminding Patricia that she wasn't representative of public opinion. 'That's because you were brought up to believe that you need a Van Dyck and a couple of Gainsboroughs just to decorate the drawing room.'

'Don't be stupid, Gus. You are always saying we should merge with Arts more than Current Affairs.'

'That's art with a small "a", dearest: theatre, ballet, the what's-on of London. You're talking about fine art—highbrow art.'

'It's a commodity nowadays, part of the international currency exchange. You can't just ignore it.'

'Art doesn't make good TV. Take it from me.' The subject was closed. They'd discussed it and dismissed it. Programme control was his territory and he didn't like her to forget it. She wrote and presented her series but ultimately it belonged to him. 'You're an actress, honey,' he'd told her once when she'd had it out with him. 'You get the curtain calls and the fan mail. But I run the theatre.'

She turned and stared at the motorway ahead. It was safest to let him have his way in these situations. Gus had fifteen years' experience on his side and a reputation for getting the answers right. But she felt patronized.

'You think I'm being impulsive, don't you?'

Gus edged the car forwards in the traffic. He was craning his head to one side to see how far ahead the queue stretched. 'I think you don't always understand that just because something interests you doesn't necessarily mean it interests anyone else.'

'It's a good idea.'

'It might be.'

'Art theft is new; it's different. The public has never come across it before. There's money and scandal involved and we've got the whole field to ourselves. I can't see why you're not interested.'

'Hey, I didn't say I wasn't interested.'

'No?' She spoke in the slightly mocking voice that she only put on when she knew she was gaining the advantage. 'Then you're giving a fair imitation of a man who's not interested, darling.'

'We'll make a pilot, OK? See what the others think about it.'

Brook's Club is half-way down St James's Street. It is a graceful if somewhat spartan-looking building that dates from a period when proportion reigned over ornament.

As James Trevelyan approached, the uniformed butler stepped forward to open the glass inner door. And that was as far as he was letting him go.

'Can I help you, sir?'

'I'm lunching with David Ambrose.'

'Very good, sir.' The butler didn't take his word for it. He consulted the registration book before saying, 'I believe you'll find him in the library.'

A log fire was burning in the grate. Leather armchairs contained members of the club whose legs were visible beneath the opened newspapers. Cigar smoke hung in the air, occasionally flashing to silver in the shaft of afternoon sunlight that fell in through the single sash window.

'So glad you could join me, James.' David Ambrose came towards him, his hand extended in greeting. 'Did you find any trouble parking?'

'I came by taxi.'

'Ah yes.' He said the words lightly, as though he understood them to be a euphemism, before indicating the waiter who stood near by. 'Can I get you a drink?'

'Thank you. A gin and tonic.'

The waiter had heard but Ambrose repeated the order. It showed who was in charge.

'Shall we take it in with us?' he enquired when it had arrived. 'It's steak and kidney today. Rather good usually.'

Was it his imagination, Trevelyan wondered as they went through to the dining room, or was it a polite way of reminding him that he shouldn't take off more than the allotted hour for lunch?

'Have you heard any more of *The Triumph of Bacchus?*' Ambrose asked while they ate.

'Nothing new. The police are still analysing the tape. I hope to have the results in the next few days.'

'So you still have no idea where or when the ransom will take place.'

'Not yet, although I'm assuming it will be somewhere in Switzerland.'

Ambrose nodded briefly to acknowledge that Trevelyan's reasoning hadn't drifted from his own so far. 'And the diamonds?'

'I've warned Seligmann-Schnell in Hatton Garden that they may be asked to acquire them in the near future. I've not asked them to go ahead yet.'

'Why's that?'

Trevelyan pirouetted the two cubes of ice round the base of his glass. 'Because I don't intend to pay them.'

'Really?' Ambrose lifted his eyebrows as he helped himself to more cauliflower. 'Any reason?'

'I want to see how they react.'

'They may react very violently, James. It would only take a few seconds for them to put a lighter under the canvas and leave you with a thirty-eight-million-pound headache.'

'It's possible,' Trevelyan agreed. 'But I doubt that's what they will do. As I see it, the painting has no intrinsic value to them. It's too famous to sell and if they destroy it they have earned nothing for their pains. That's the one advantage we have on our side.'

'So you force them into a stalemate. What good does that do?'

'It gives us a little more time.'

'But not the painting. They still have that.'

On the next table two elderly gentlemen were engaged in a comfortable discussion, leaving long pauses for reflection and digestion between each bout. There was no danger of them overhearing. In a London club there are invisible barriers between each table more sophisticated than any electronic jamming device.

'So far we've played the game to their rules. Everything they've done has been carefully premeditated and carried out on schedule. If we refuse to co-operate it will throw their plans. They'll have to make alterations to compensate. In particular they'll have to make direct contact with us.'

'You think they can be hustled into making a mistake?'

'There's just a chance.'

Chapter 5

Scobie ran up the stairs. By the time he reached the third-floor landing he was out of breath and he had to lean against the banisters. The cleaning lady watched him reprovingly.

'You want to watch that at your time of life, Mr Woods.'

Scobie ignored her and continued on up. He didn't like references to his time of life, particularly from those who are only a few minutes off it themselves.

When he reached his studio he put his hand to the knob and cannoned into the door. It was locked. He was forgetting that they always kept it that way now, even when someone was inside. He fumbled the keys out of his pocket and opened it.

'Have you seen this?' he asked as he came in.

'Seen what?' Shaughnessy looked up from the painting which lay spread out on the work table. The sleeves of his blue denim shirt were rolled back to the elbows and there were flecks of dry paint on his hands and forearms.

Scobie took the rolled newspaper from his pocket and rifled through the pages for the place. 'The Lloyd's syndicate who insure *The Triumph of Bacchus* are refusing to pay the ransom.'

'For what reason?'

'They say they refuse to give in to the demands of extortionists.' Scobie held the paper close to his face to get the print in focus and read out a passage. ' "A spokesman for Lloyd's told reporters that to give in to the demand for ransom would only invite further thefts in the future. The matter has been put in the hands of the police who will now be handling the affair." '

'Is that what they are saying?' Shaughnessy came round the table: and taking the paper he read the article through for himself. When he had finished he tossed it down on the table.

'They're bluffing.'

'Do you reckon so?'

'They'll pay up when the time comes.' He went back to the painting. Pulling it over the edge of the table he pressed downwards so that the ancient paintwork cracked. He ran his hand along the crease, brushing away the loose particles that still clung to the canvas.

'They'll have to,' he said. 'They need the painting back in one piece and there's only one way they're going to get it.'

Scobie watched the flecks of paint fluttering down to the ground and found himself believing him. Shaughnessy had always had that effect on people. In one of her more amiable moods, his wife had once confided to him that he could twist her round his little finger when he wanted. It might have been the reason she had divorced him.

'Do you want a hand with that?' he asked.

Shaughnessy shook his head without looking up. Half the canvas was clean now, a pale grey ground showing where the painting had been removed. Scobie heard the brittle crack of the paint as it bent over the lip of the table, saw the pieces fall to the ground.

'Brings back memories,' he said. 'When I was a student we used to strip them down by the dozen. In those days a second-hand painting in a junk shop up the Rue de Bac was half the price of a new canvas.'

Shaughnessy straightened, ran his forearm over his brow. 'Do you want to make yourself useful?'

'Depends…'

'You could make us something to eat.'

Scobie went over to the fridge and began rummaging through its contents. The machine didn't work but he used it just the same. He felt the contents would still feel cold in there. 'There was one picture I remember ripping the paint off,' he said over his shoulder. 'A small brown thing it was. Looking back at it I'm sure it was an early Van Gogh.'

'And to think you need never have worked again if you'd just kept it.' Shaughnessy could see his cause for concern. 'I suppose you replaced it with one of your nasty little pink nudes.'

'Probably.'

Scobie found a few slices of bacon wrapped in grease-proof paper. He put them in a pan where they spat and wrinkled in the hot oil. The air filled with the smell of cooking.

'I'll make a B, if that sounds all right.'

Taking the bottle of Jameson's from the dresser, Shaughnessy poured two glasses, putting one within reach of Scobie and taking the other back to the table where he was working. He touched it to his lips, as though giving his tongue an idea of what was to come.

'It would sound a lot better if I knew what it was.'

'It's a BLT without the lettuce and tomato.'

He nodded thoughtfully; it was his own fault for asking.

Laying the bacon on slices of bread, Scobie added a top layer and pressed down hard, crushing out any last resistance. Putting the result on a plate, he dumped it down by the canvas.

'How much longer's it going to take.'

'The rest of the afternoon, maybe longer. Some of the thinner paint's a bitch to shift.'

'I'll finish it off when you go to work if you like,' Scobie said. Going over to the cassette player he put in a tape of Rodrego's Concerto de Aranjuez and then picking up a sandwich he chewed it thoughtfully as he examined the remains of the Italian painting.

In the last twenty-four hours a new canvas had been laid over the old. When it was done Shaughnessy had taken four inches from the right hand side of the painting, disguising the cut by fraying the edge slightly with a toothbrush. The newly exposed threads he'd tinted with a little dust which he scraped from the back of the canvas and diluted in water before applying with a fine sable brush.

Shaughnessy chucked his sandwich down on the table. 'These are disgusting.'

'I think the bacon was past its sell-by date.'

'Past its sell-by year, by the taste of it.'

The thin, melancholy music filled the studio. Scobie sat on the edge of the table and whistled tunelessly to the better-known bits. In one of the lulls he asked, 'How are you going to hide the thing while you're painting it?'

'I was wondering that myself.'

'Best to keep it out in the open.'

Shaughnessy fetched a jar of mustard. Prising off the top layer of bread he spread it over the bacon. It was the only known antidote for Scobie's cooking. 'Pretty risky, isn't it? There are always people poking around in here.'

'Make a cover for it out of plywood then stretch a canvas around it. If anyone comes in, you pop it on and it just looks as though there's a new canvas on the easel. I'll rough out a picture on it, work on it from time to time. No one will ever suspect.'

'Won't you see one hidden inside the other?'

'Not with a bit of extra canvas turned around the back.' Scobie seemed to know what he was talking about. 'It works. I know someone who used to run pictures out of South Africa that way.'

'You have some useful friends.' Shaughnessy was considering the device. 'With their combined talents I'm surprised they didn't take over the country.'

'Some of them wanted to.'

'We'll give it a try.'

When he had finished eating he washed his hands in the basin, splashing water over his face and towelling himself dry. Returning to the studio he went over to where a pile of paintings was stacked against the wall and began searching through them.

'Have you got anything here you don't want?'

'What sort of thing?'

'Something that looks as though it might be crummy enough to be a cherished heirloom.' He pulled out a canvas and held it up. It was a small landscape with a lot of green paint and a few improbable-looking cows. 'Do you want this?'

Scobie squinted at it from a distance. 'Not particularly. I think one of my students painted it years back.'

'I'll borrow it if I might.'

'Help yourself.'

Shaughnessy thumped the painting down on the back of a nearby chair. The wooden upright punched a hole through the canvas.

'Jesus Christ,' Scobie said, coming over and inspecting the damage. 'What the hell did you do that for?'

'I thought I might get it mended for you.'

He took the bus into the West End, sitting on the top floor beside windows misted with condensation, the damaged painting wrapped in brown paper on his lap.

If he had taken a survey amongst the passengers on board there was every chance that none of them would have heard the name of Helmut Schalk, but in the trade he is known as one of the foremost picture restorers in Europe.

The studio from which he conducted his business was off Drury Lane. Parked cars were humped up on the narrow pavement, shop signs craning out from the walls. A crack of sky above.

A service entrance cut in much larger wooden doors led through into a courtyard, surrounded on three sides by lean-to buildings, and paved with those round, egg-shaped cobbles that used to rattle the teeth out of coachmen.

Shaughnessy found the reception area and rang the bell. A girl appeared down the short flight of steps.

'Did you make an appointment?' she asked. Her black hair was tied back in a scarf and she wore a white coat over her ankle length dress.

'No, I'm afraid not.'

'I'm not sure he can see you.'

Shaughnessy could hear the doubt in her voice. This was a specialist business. They didn't take trade off the streets. 'Maybe you could make an exception? It's very urgent. And I was recommended to come to you particularly.'

'Hang on there. I'll have a word with him.' She went back inside, leaving him waiting in the entrance.

A few notices were pinned on the wall alongside the fire regulations. Near by, a coffee dispenser that looked as though it had lost its will to function.

'Would you like to bring it in?' The girl sounded more positive when she returned.

Shaughnessy followed her down a short length of passage into the main studio. It was a large, brightly lit room, scrupulously tidy, with the faint tang of solvent in the air.

Helmut Schalk was sitting on a stool before a ten-foot canvas, examining the surface through a magnifying glass mounted on a mechanical arm. Two assistants stood on either side. As Shaughnessy came in he stood up and held out his hand.

'How can I help you?'

'Mr Schalk?'

'That's me.' The grip was firm and dry. He wore stone-washed jeans and a blue Guernsey, the sleeves pulled back to the elbows. Despite this informality he managed to convey a sense of fashionable smartness.

'I was hoping you might be able to do something about this.' Shaughnessy unwrapped the painting, pulled it out of the brown paper. For some reason the public always wrapped pictures in paper, the trade never did. He didn't know why.

'Is this damage recent?' Schalk enquired.

'It happened today. An accident. Just dropped out of my hands while I was hanging it.'

Schalk studied the torn canvas thoughtfully. He had a strong, broad-boned face with a flattened nose and cropped hair. In his eyes the steady, distant expression which would have had any film director worth his salt casting him as a freedom fighter rather than a picture restorer. 'It needs relining, of course,' he said. 'And the paintwork will have to be retouched. With all due respect, the job would cost more than the picture's worth.'

'It's very important to us.'

'I see.' He looked up at Shaughnessy, neither intently or rudely but with a steady, appraising stare. 'Haven't I seen you somewhere before?'

'I wouldn't have thought so.'

Schalk's gaze didn't waver. Then reaching down he rested the painting against the wall. 'Yes, I can mend your painting. Although I'd be interested to know why you've brought it to me.'

'I read in the papers that you restored *The Triumph of Bacchus*.' The two assistants were levering the huge canvas down from the easel. Schalk watched as they lowered it on to the flat worktop before turning back to him.

'That's right,' he said, 'I did.'

'You must have been sorry to have heard of the theft.'

From the long, cool stare that he received in return, Shaughnessy guessed that this was an understatement. But all Schalk said was, 'I dare say it will be returned.'

'You must have got to know it very well while you were working on it.'

'I could recognize that painting in the dark, if that's what you mean,' Schalk replied. 'When you've had your hands on a picture for six months you get to know it. Not just the sight of it. I know the feel of the thing: every ridge, every crack, every texture.'

And that, Shaughnessy thought to himself as he went outside, was exactly what he hadn't wanted to hear.

He ran his eyes around the courtyard, checking the layout of sloping roofs and windows, committing them to memory before going out into the street and closing the service door behind him.

It had twin locks.

Shaughnessy pushed a small stone into the larger of the two before walking away towards Holborn.

When he knocked off work that evening Shaughnessy looked in on the Roland. Scobie was at his usual table in the corner with a redheaded girl he didn't recognize.

He looked up as Shaughnessy joined them, scrutinizing his face for information. 'How did it go, then?'

Shaughnessy took a chair from the next table. The place wasn't crowded. It very rarely was. There was no Space Invaders machine, no microwaved lasagne. The only entertainment in the Roland was a darts board and a donation box for the guide dogs. Turning the chair around he sat down, his legs straddling the back-rest. 'No trouble.'

'You got in?'

'I did.' He nodded towards the bottle of champagne on the table. 'What's the celebration?'

'Scobie's sold one of the copies of his Princess Di portrait,' the red-head said. She had been listening to this exchange with a puzzled expression on her face.

'You know Marjorie, don't you?' Scobie asked. 'No, I don't think so.'

She smiled at him over her glass.

'We were just pushing off down to the Chelsea Arts for a bite of supper,' Scobie added vaguely. 'Care to join us?'

It wasn't like him to celebrate the sale of a picture. Shaughnessy guessed it was an excuse to find out how this girl ran on high-performance Bollinger. He shook his head. 'I've got some work to do upstairs. Who's bought the portrait?'

'Some regiment. The Royal Artillery, I think it was. They want it for their mess.'

'Do they realize they're getting a copy?'

'It'll be different.' Scobie stirred the air with his glass to indicate the extent of his vision. 'I'll put her in uniform, change the background. The whole thing will be different.'

Shaughnessy pushed back the chair and stood up to leave. 'I'll see you later.'

'How long are you going to be?' Scobie called after him.

'An hour, maybe longer.'

He went up to the studio and put a match to the paraffin stove, turning the flame down until it bounced on the wick, gnawing at the cold air.

The canvas stood on the easel, smooth and taut on its new stretcher. Scobie had been working on it all afternoon, flaking away the last of the old painting, removing the final traces with a scalpel.

Putting a saucepan of water to warm on the oven he took the canvas down from the easel and laid it on the table. With a bathroom pumice-stone he smoothed the surface, softening the threads. They had hardened over the years and needed to be teased open again to accept the new priming.

It was a delicate operation and he relied on his touch as much as his eyes, running the tips of his fingers across the canvas, sensing rather than seeing what he was doing. He had known a blind man in Dublin who made a living painting the black doors of the Georgian terraced houses. Polished like mirrors, they were without a blemish. He'd told Shaughnessy it was easier to visualize the world through touch. Fingers were more sensitive than the eyes, he said. They concentrated the mind on to one tiny part of the world rather than the whole.

When the water boiled he stood a jug of rabbit glue in the saucepan. The amber chunks had already been soaking for a few hours and they dissolved quickly in the warmth. He could feel the liquid thickening, gripping the wooden spoon as he stirred.

He added gesso, a mixture of gypsum and anhydride, beating the two together to knock out the lumps. At first the white substance was solid, unmanageable, but as the glue worked in it began to relax, reducing finally to a loose cream-like consistency.

With a wide brush he spread it across the canvas, working it into the weave. He'd made a number of experiments with this priming, trying it out on scraps of canvas, adjusting the water content until he had the proportion right.

It was the absorbency that concerned him. Too thin and the oil paint would sink in and refuse to spread properly across the canvas. Too solid and it would skid around the surface. There'd be no body, no build up of texture. The painting would fail before it had started.

Just after midnight Scobie returned. He had Marjorie and a bottle of wine with him and was evidently intending to make an evening of it.

'Nice place,' Marjorie said in a voice that held reservations on the subject of tidiness. 'Do you live here then, Scobie?'

'Much of the time.' Scobie was getting the cork out of the bottle and not inclined to enlarge on the subject.

'Does it always smell like this?'

'That's Tommie. He's been sizing a canvas for me.' He poured two glasses of white wine, handing one to Marjorie and indicating with the lack of another what he wanted Shaughnessy to do with himself.

'Rabbit skin,' he added. 'It always makes a bit of a stink.'

'Enough to turn you vegetarian,' she agreed.

Shaughnessy left them to it and went downstairs. Two months earlier he'd moved into a flat on the second floor. After the house in Chepstow Road he'd had to re-adjust to the thud of the neighbour's hi-fi, the screech of raised voices through the partition walls, the smell of cooking on the stairs. But in many ways he preferred it there. It was smaller, easier to run.

He turned on the bath taps, went next door, and fished a canvas bag down from above the wardrobe. Setting a 6mm bit into the chuck of a hand drill he put it inside, along with a can of polyurethane-foam filler and a pair of leather gloves. Then stripping off his clothes he lay in the hot bath water.

At half-past one, dressed in jeans and a dark Guernsey, he went down into the street. Removing the chain from his bicycle he pushed it into the road and pedalled up towards the West End.

The narrow lane was deserted.

Shaughnessy opened the door in the wall with a piece of plastic draught-proofing. It was more flexible than a credit card. It curved round the lip of the door and pressed back the catch. The heavy mortise lock below had been left open—a small stone jams in the works, grinds into the tumblers when the key is turned. A locksmith would be coming to mend it in the morning. But for now it was open.

The courtyard looked smaller in the darkness. Derelict without the animation of lights and activity. He closed the door, moved forwards, keeping close to the shelter of the building.

The burglar alarm was set high on the wall, under the eaves of the corrugated roof. He'd marked the place that afternoon, could see it now as his eyes accustomed to the night. It had been put up as high as possible, out of harm's way. But the building was only one storey tall. It was not hard to reach.

He hefted a dustbin across the courtyard, dumped it against the wall, and climbed on to the lid, feet apart, resting on the rim for balance.

The casing of the burglar alarm was yellow plastic, hexagonal, the maker's name printed across the front. Shaughnessy took the drill from his bag, set the tip to one side of the alarm, and cranked the handle around. A tiny hair of plastic sprang up from the hardened steel point, pirouetted with it then fell away as the drill bit in deeper, gouging into the surface, furrowing out crinkled plastic.

He held the handset against the wall, keeping it steady. Applying no pressure, letting the twist of the spiral drill carry it into the casing. An ancient system this one, thirty years old at least. But it still worked, make no mistake about that. There was a trembler nerve inside, a delicate membrane poised between two contacts. It wouldn't take much. The slightest vibration and the thing would go off. The bell shattering the silence. Hammering in the eardrums. The game up, the whole area awake. He'd be down off that dustbin like a shot, running for his life, getting the hell out of it before the squad car arrived.

He felt the drill come through the side of the casing, the resistance giving way. He put his hand on the chuck and turned it in his fingers, edging the tip through the last fraction of plastic. Then drew it back, still twisting the head to clear the hole he'd made.

Still silence in the courtyard. Nothing to break the stillness of the night. Nothing but the thumping of his heart, the pounding of blood in his ears. His breath streamed out of his mouth, visible as it curled around the burglar alarm, warm on his hands as they worked.

He put the drill back in his canvas bag. Twisting around, holding his balance as he tucked it away. The pressurized can of foam filler out in its place. This was the bit that worried him. This was the part he couldn't anticipate.

He shook the can awake, fitted the short nozzle of tubing to the diffuser head, and dug it into the hole he'd bored in the alarm. Gently, very gently, just edging it into place. Then pressing down on the head.

The hiss of release, the jerk of the tube. Foam poured up into the plastic casing. The can was cold in his hand, the metal gripping his palm as the contents flowed into the system, muffling the bell, paralysing the trembler arm before it had time to respond.

Shaughnessy held his breath and prayed that it did the trick. He could picture the thick, viscous substance filling the internal space, finding its way into joints and crevices.

Then the excess leaked out around the edges of the plastic casing—a beautiful sight. Like cream from a crushed eclair. And the mechanism was sealed. Buried. Not even an archaeologist was going to be able to dig that one out.

He jumped down to the ground, moved the dustbin back in place, and stood back. The lower windows of the studio were locked. No point in even trying them. But the skylight in the roof was open. Just a crack. Enough to let the air in the studio circulate, enough to clear away the smell of paint and solvent.

Enough to give him a way in.

Chapter 6

'I've got them.'

Shaughnessy found the table lamp in the dark, fumbled with the switch, and turned it on.

Scobie woke slowly. Turning over, grunting complaints at the light. Then sitting up in bed with a curse of realization.

'What the bloody hell—' His head appeared over the gallery. Hair on end, face pale and still concussed with sleep, gaping down at him in surprise.

'I thought you'd like to see them.' Shaughnessy spread the photos out on the table with the flat of his hand. There were twelve in all. Large glossy plates. The background black, in the centre of each one a bright object streaked with colours. To the inexperienced eye they could have been mineral samples or rock formations. But they were cross-sections of paint, tiny fragments taken from *The Triumph of Bacchus* blown up several hundred times in size.

'See them?' Scobie couldn't think of anything he wanted to do less. 'At this time of night?'

'I would have got here earlier but the chain came off my bike.' Scobie pulled on a dressing-gown, tied it round with a cord, and stumped down the steps.

'What's the time?'

'Two—half-past. Something like that.'

'Jesus Christ, Tommie. You might have bloody told me. You might have said you were coming back here. Bursting in like that. I might not have been alone. Did that occur to you? I could have been occupied.'

'I heard her leave earlier.'

Scobie pushed the hair from his eyes with long fingers; bony hands dappled with liver spots combing it into place. He glanced at the photos, rejected the challenge, and shuffled into the kitchen, plugged in the kettle. A cup of tea: the restoration of normality, compensation for a rude awakening.

'So you got in, I take it?' He returned with the mug in one hand, the other jigging a tea bag as though it were a one-stringed puppet.

'The skylight was open.'

'And the burglar alarm?'

'It was primitive—Anglo-Saxon by the look of it. The sensors only covered the studio. These were in a filing cabinet in a side office. I knocked out the squawk-box for good measure.'

'Knocked it out?'

'Sealed its guts with polystyrene foam.'

'You've got some nasty talents, Tommie. I don't know where you picked them up.' Scobie opened the window, twirled the spent tea bag, and lobbed it outside, a David and Goliath act he'd perfected over the years so that it cleared the roof tops and vanished into a neighbouring garden.

He came back to the table. 'Isn't he going to notice those things are missing?'

'I took out some photos from other files, put them in their place. It'll take him a while to tumble what's happened.' Desecrating Schalk's meticulous system had been a crime in itself.

Scobie took a mouthful of tea and set the mug on the table. For all his feigned indifference he was interested, intrigued by the information of the photos, the secrets they revealed.

The photos were of extraordinary quality. Every layer of paint was clearly visible, the focus so sharp that the individual flecks of pigment could be seen floating in their medium like the chips of gravel in concrete. Schalk was a true craftsman. There was no escaping that. Meticulous in every field of his work.

'Look at this one.' Shaughnessy pulled out a photo, twisted it round on the table.

It was a section through the sky. A streak of brown over the white ground, then a thick band of pale orange—burnt sienna at a guess—a haze of blue over that.

'Ultramarine floated over an earth base.' His finger pointed to the specks of white in the blue. 'Diaphanous by the look of it. One showing through the other.'

Scobie had another. He was counting through the layers, his thumbnail marking them off in turn. 'Five separate drying times, Tommie. Do you realize that? That's eight, nine weeks, minimum. You haven't got that long.'

'I'll have to speed it up. Some sort of lead siccative in the oil, do you think?'

They went through the photos, calculating processes, the build-up of opaque paint, the sequence of translucent glazes that had modified the colour.

'There's an alteration here.' Shaughnessy's finger tapped on a photo.

It was more elaborate than the others, the pale earth construction overlaid with dense streaks of red and black. Then a change. A thick band of ochre had been added, darkened with green-blue glazes.

'He's made a change half-way through.'

'Where's it from?' Scobie was rubbing the cobwebs of sleep from his eyes, then craning forwards again.

'Ariadne's drapery. It was going to be red. He changed it to this light green.'

'That's no problem, is it?'

'He could have altered the drawing at the same time, re-adjusted the design of the whole area. I can't tell without the X-rays.'

'Haven't you got them?'

'They weren't there.' Shaughnessy had looked for them. One of the reasons for breaking into the restorer's studio had been to find the X-rays. The large smoky black plates that showed the skeleton of the picture, the initial constructions of lead white.

'Do you need them? You only have to copy what shows on the surface. It doesn't matter what's below.'

'Maybe—'

Shaughnessy thought of Helmut Schalk, who had worked six months on the painting, who'd said he could recognize every crack and ridge in the paintwork. He thought of the assurance in the Austrian's voice, the experience of those hands. He wasn't going to be easy to deceive. Not easy at all.

'I'll have to think about it.'

'Good.' Scobie took it that the conference was over. 'Does that mean I can go to bed now?'

Patricia Drew was fifteen minutes late for lunch.

The delay was intentional. She had rung James Trevelyan at his Lloyd's office, asked for this meeting, but she wasn't going to appear to be begging. The more you wanted from someone, the less you should show it. It was something her father had taught her.

Several heads turned as she came into the restaurant. She was well aware that her appearance was one of her natural assets and treated it with respect. Every morning she swam ten lengths of the pool and put herself through half an hour of exercises, not the puny flapping of legs and arms in time to music that daytime TV recommends for housewives but hard physical exercises that made her muscles ache.

James Trevelyan stood up as she approached.

She didn't apologize for the delay as she shook hands with him but gave him her full attention instead. 'I'm so glad you could come. I know what a busy time of the year this is for you.'

The head waiter was nuzzling the chair beneath her, flapping out the serviette to lay across her lap, murmuring specialities of the day as she sat down.

'Have you ordered anything to drink?' she asked.

'Not yet.'

She passed the wine list across the table and as Trevelyan scanned the contents she studied him quickly and critically. He was younger than she expected, with wide-framed spectacles, brown hair which looked as though it preferred not to be brushed and a wide mouth suggesting humour. Rather attractive in a clean cut way, she decided, probably more fun as a son-in-law than a lover but certainly better company for a lunchtime meeting than she'd hoped for.

'Any requests?' he asked, glancing up.

'White would suit me better. I'll only be having a salad but choose something you like.'

'A Pouilly-Fuissé '78?'

'Sounds delicious.'

When she'd spoken to Trevelyan on the phone she'd told him she wanted information on *The Triumph of Bacchus* but she waited until the first course arrived—it was so much easier to talk once the business of ordering was over—before coming to the point. 'You say that five paintings insured by your syndicate have been stolen. How do you know it's the same organization each time?'

'The method is distinctive.' He scooped a snail from its shell and chewed it quickly, holding the fork up in his hand as though using it as a baton to hold the conversation while he collected his thoughts. 'In each case the thefts themselves have been different—one painting was taken from a private house in broad daylight, another was burgled from the vaults of a Bond Street gallery—the method has never been the same twice. But the ransom demand is identical. It's like a fingerprint.'

'Is it true that the voice you hear after each theft is recorded?'

'It's several voices, to be more accurate. The words cut out and pasted together.'

'That must sound eerie.' She frowned briefly as she visualized the effect.

'And impossible to trace. The voices all come from radio or television programmes. Yours may be amongst them.'

'With no royalty payment? I must look into that.' She raised her eyebrows in mock horror at this loss of income before reverting back to the subject. She had the conversation already scripted in her mind. 'The demands have all been for uncut diamonds?'

He nodded.

'I noticed that the exchanges have taken place in Switzerland. Why do you think that is?'

'Convenience.' Trevelyan mopped up melted butter with a piece of bread. Brave man, she thought, risking garlic at this time of the day. 'Assuming,' he said, 'that the money passes straight into a Swiss bank, they give us the job of getting it through border control into the country.'

'The painting still has to be moved.'

'They have plenty of time to do that. The ransom has never come directly after the theft. They wait for a while—two months, ten weeks, something like that—before contacting us again. You can keep customs control on high alert for a few days but not that long.'

Patricia moved back her chair, crossed her legs. It was devastatingly simple when you thought about it. Crude but simple. She goaded him with a touch of sarcasm. 'They seem to be holding all the cards.'

'So far,' he agreed.

'Is that why you are refusing to pay the ransom?'

'More or less.' He studied her thoughtfully for a moment, undecided how much to tell her. 'I don't see why they should have it their way all the time.'

'The Italians can't be too pleased.'

'There has been a complaint from the Embassy.' He gave a shrug as though that was to be expected. 'They want us to pay up.'

'Wouldn't that be more sensible?' she asked lightly.

'In the short term, yes. But this way there's a chance we may be able to wrong-foot them.'

He was a gambler, she realized. Beneath that fresh-faced exterior was a man who took risks and possibly enjoyed it.

'I hope you're right,' she said. 'For your sake.'

The waiter was removing their plates. She had chosen this restaurant with some care. It was extremely expensive, the up-market end of Soho with menus the size of Monopoly boards and bills that could only be serviced by gold credit cards, but relaxed and cheerful at the same time. The right atmosphere for the occasion.

'Tell me about the ransoms,' she said as the waiter withdrew.

'There's not much to tell.'

'Do they take place in public places?'

'They have done. The exchange took place in Zurich station on one occasion. Right in front of fifty thousand commuting gnomes.'

'Couldn't you make an arrest?'

'They ran our men around for half an hour. We didn't know where it was going to happen until the last minute and by then it was too late to get anyone into place.'

'Who handles things at your end?'

'We use a team of professional negotiators. Loss and Security Assessment: they're good.'

Patricia had heard of these specialist teams. They were made up of ex-SAS men, members of Special Branch, and the Anti-Terrorist squad, on the whole. Trained operators who'd left their profession and turned their hand to the more profitable business of private security.

'Do they work under the Swiss police?'

'They liaise with them but no more. They're quite independent, as I was telling the Minister for Arts this morning. They take orders from us and no one else.'

'A sort of private army.'

'You could say that.' Trevelyan didn't want her to get the wrong impression. 'It's quite legitimate. In many ways the police prefer it that way. It removes the responsibility from their shoulders.'

'They haven't done you much good so far.'

'They will do.'

In the taxi back to the studios Patricia jotted down the main points that had arisen, the notebook propped on her knee. She never wrote anything during an interview, the sight of a notebook or a tape recorder invariably cramped the conversation.

'Did you get anything useful?' Gus asked her later that afternoon. He was sitting in the armchair of her office, legs crossed, knees parted wide. He must have been reading one of those books on sexual body-language, she thought spitefully as she ran a comb through her hair.

'Yes,' she said. 'I think so.'

'Such as?'

'I discovered that *The Triumph of Bacchus* is probably still in this country. I discovered also that if Lloyd's goes on refusing to pay the ransom there's every chance it will be destroyed.'

She pulled on her jacket and fastened the buttons, turning to one side to check that the effect hadn't changed since she last examined it. Gus watched the performance with detached interest. He wanted something from her. She wasn't sure what but guessed it must be personal because had it concerned her work he would have come straight out with it, started talking before the door was half-closed. But he seemed disinclined to raise the subject.

'Are you going somewhere?'

'I must have a word with Carol about locations,' she replied, and blowing him a kiss she went out.

As he listened to her walk away, Gus felt a stab of irritation. He'd come round on the off-chance that Patricia was in the mood to go out somewhere. But she evidently had got other plans.

Of late she'd had other plans too often for his liking. Whenever he saw her she was busy. He was lucky to get a flutter of the manicured fingers, a quick peck on the cheek in passing. It was reaching the point when he was going to have to make an appointment to sleep with her.

He looked around the deserted office. It was serene and feminine, not to his taste but impressive just the same. Hanging on the wall were various framed photographs, the largest taken on the night she had been awarded a BAFTA award for best documentary. Gus got to his feet and studied it thoughtfully.

Patricia, in a strapless dress and long black gloves, was holding the bauble in her arms and looking calm and beautiful. And she was beautiful, he reflected. Everyone who watched her show knew that. She was also stubborn, arrogant and headstrong. The most desirable woman he had ever met, and the most frustrating.

The first time he'd seen her had been on television. She had been acting as the spokesman for Barclays de Zoete Wedd, commenting on some fluctuation in the Stock Exchange. Recently down from the Fontainebleau business school, which she had sailed through with flying colours, she could do all those things that seem to come naturally to the daughters of the extremely wealthy: she skied, she rode to hounds, and she had proved herself a formidable opponent on the polo field. She had studied the history of art and displayed the irritating ability to speak most of the languages of the countries in which it was created.

Although there can't actually have been many like her, he saw Patricia Drew as an image rather than an individual, a symbol of the elitist, in-bred world of the City, and he'd pressed hard to have her head up a financial programme for them.

The rest was history now. She was good at the job, Gus had never denied that. There was a lot of show-biz in Patricia, which in the circumstances was possibly not surprising. She had once told him that of her two grandmothers one had been a Greek millionairess, the other a chorus girl. Everything, he observed, is in the breeding.

The door of the office opened and Suzie came in. Seeing him there she gave a little start.

'Oh, Gus—are you waiting to see Patricia?'

'No,' he replied drily. 'I've been standing around here waiting to crawl up my own backside.'

'Ah,' she said, as though this was an interesting new pastime she hadn't heard of before.

Gus left and went downstairs. As he reached the second floor he heard a voice from above.

'Gus—'

He turned to see Pete Chadwick, assistant producer on one of their current affairs programmes, hurrying down after him.

'Just the man I was looking for,' he said, pulling a slip of paper from the clipboard he was carrying. 'This has just come through.'

'What is it?' Gus didn't particularly like Chadwick. He had an ambitious wife, bad breath, and designs to become a news broadcaster, none of which Gus found attractive in a member of his staff.

'The Italian government is offering a reward for information leading to the recovery of *The Triumph of Bacchus*.'

'How much?'

'Half a million.'

'They must be out of their skulls.' Gus took the sheet of paper and scanned it quickly.

'That's pounds,' Chadwick added.

'I didn't think it would be lire.'

'I thought you'd like to know.'

Gus handed it back to him and continued on downstairs. 'Show it to Patricia.'

'Aren't you making a programme about it?'

'She is.' Gus had dissociated himself from that project. 'It's nothing to do with me.'

'Lapis lazuli?'

'I ordered some earlier this week. You said it would be in today.'

'Ah, yes. That would have been Mr Davies who took your call. He deals with the orders.' The shopkeeper smiled at his explanation. He had plump red cheeks and a small red mouth, as though he had been blowing a trumpet all his life. Above this he wore steel-framed spectacles through which he looked beadily at Shaughnessy.

'You have it, though?' he asked.

'I'll go and check for you, sir.'

The minute art store was just a turnip's throw from Covent Garden. When Shaughnessy had first known the place, the street outside had been filled with barrows and unloading lorries. Now it had been taken over by wine bars. But the shop itself had escaped the worst effects of this social earthquake. Glass cabinets lined the walls above the counter, beneath them were rows of small drawers with brass handles that fitted flush with the polished woodwork, containing such useful commodities as steel pen-nibs, cobbler's wax, and hand-made engraving tools. The light from the window was obscured so that the place had the dark, intimate feel of an ancient apothecary rather than a supplier of artist's materials.

He heard the shopkeeper coming up from the basement.

'Yes, sir. We have your order ready.'

Shaughnessy always pictured pigments in glass jars with ground lids and brittle labels such as you see in museums. But this was in a sealed plastic container. The shopkeeper prised off the lid and took out one of the crystals.

'Lapis lazuli.'

It was the size of a sugar lump, a dark purple-blue stone veined with turquoise.

'We don't have much call for it these days.'

'I suppose not.' Shaughnessy took the crystal and felt it in his fingers. He had bought the pigments he needed from four different suppliers, just one or two from each to avoid suspicion.

'You know how to prepare it, I take it?' The shopkeeper had the expectant air of those with superior knowledge to impart.

'I've some idea.'

'Wrap the crystals in a cloth'—the man was eager to oblige as he took back the crystal and began wrapping the container in brown paper—'preferably silk, so that nothing gets caught in the weave, and break them up with a hammer. Then grind the pieces on a stone like any other pigment until it is as fine as castor sugar. Mix it with equal parts of stand oil and resin—I would recommend copal or damar—so that it forms into a dough. Seal this up and leave it for several days. That gives the pigment time to separate from the impurities.'

He twisted the wrapped parcel in his hands to smooth out any wrinkles and gave it to Shaughnessy.

'How much do I owe you?'

'That'll be three hundred and forty pounds.' He quoted the price in a small voice as though that would minimize its size.

Shaughnessy thumbed out notes and handed them to him.

'Then when the time comes to make paint,' the shopkeeper continued, speaking confidently again now that the business of money was over, 'you knead the dough under water and the pure ultramarine is washed out. The water has to be slightly alkaline. They used to add wood ash in the past but I dare say there are simpler methods nowadays.'

He opened the till and fed the notes into their respective trays. 'The first time you do it produces the best results,' he added, returning with two pounds change. 'You can leave the dough for a few days and try again. It'll release more pigment but never as pure.'

'That's very helpful.'

'There's nothing like the real thing. So many substitutes on the market these days but none of them have the same quality as genuine ultramarine. Look at any old master picture and you'll see what I mean.'

'I'm sure you're right.' Shaughnessy didn't want too much discussion of the old masters.

'It's the price, of course. No one bothers with it.' The shopkeeper gave him the small cherubic smile that precedes an impertinent question. 'Might I ask what you want it for, sir?'

'Tricky question.'

'What did you say?' Scobie was sitting before the easel, his legs kicked back around the stool as he worked on the background to one of his portraits.

'I told him I needed it for a demonstration.'

'Did he believe you?'

'I didn't hang around long enough to find out.' Shaughnessy tore the wrapping off the container of lapis lazuli and showed it to him.

'How much did it cost?' Scobie asked, taking one of the glittery crystals and holding it up to the light.

'More than the same weight in caviare.'

'Expensive demonstration.'

Shaughnessy snapped the lid back on the container and put it beneath one of the steps leading up to the gallery. The riser board was loose and could be removed to reveal a small triangular cavity. In there, along with a couple of spiders and a rusted woodscrew, were various glass jars containing the dry pigments he'd already assembled. The dull green, verdigris; two copper carbonates, azurite blue and malachite green; a small quantity of vermilion; yellow arsenic sulphide which used to be called orpiment; and a number of basic earth pigments. Fortunately, at the time of restoration, Schalk had written an article in *The Burlington Magazine* describing the colours used in the painting. The only one that Shaughnessy couldn't track down was lead-tin oxide, a bright, rather acidic yellow, but he thought he could approximate the colour by mixing quantities of lemon and cadmium into Naples yellow.

'The little fart in the shop was so pleased with his knowledge of how ultramarine is made he didn't wonder what it could be used for.'

Scobie put down his palette and washed his hands, wiping them dry on a dish cloth.

'Look at this,' he said. With a bend of his knees, he unzipped his trousers.

'I'm not sure I want to.'

Scobie gave a grunt to indicate the remark was uncalled for and tucking in his shirt tails he zipped himself up again and went across to the easel.

He had built a cover for the painting. It was a shallow plywood box covered in canvas that fitted over the other like a lid.

'What do you think?' Scobie was pleased with the effect. He put it on and removed it again a couple of times in demonstration.

Shaughnessy walked around the easel and examined the reverse side. As Scobie had said, with a bit of extra canvas turned around the back it was virtually impossible to see the old canvas hidden within the cover.

'Not bad, eh?'

Shaughnessy tapped the front. Somewhat to his surprise the sound was muffled.

'I put a piece of blanket between the wood and canvas,' Scobie explained. 'It makes it spongier, deadens the sound.'

'What stops the painting inside sticking to the back of the wood?'

'Pieces of cork. I've put them in the corners as spacers.' Scobie had thought it through and now stood, hands in pockets, waiting for the spontaneous applause.

'You're impressed, aren't you?'

'Seems to work—'

'You're just peeved because you didn't think of it yourself.' He wasn't having his good humour dented. Going into the kitchen he plugged in the kettle, holding its handle with one hand to encourage it to function. Shaughnessy looked over the bare expanse of canvas.

'What are you going to paint on it?'

'I thought I'd get that girl Marjorie to pose for me.'

'Why her?' Shaughnessy had to raise his voice to reach the kitchen, which was no bad thing in the circumstances. At the mention of Marjorie he felt like shouting. 'What's wrong with painting a landscape, or a bowl of rotten apples?'

Scobie came to the door. 'Because a nude will keep people away,' he said as though this were self-evident.

Scobie's artful paintings of semi-naked girls in gipsy costumes and Turkish slippers were tasteless at the best of times and reminiscent of a style that died out with London's last epidemic of cholera, but Shaughnessy would never have said they were bad enough to clear the studio. But this evidently wasn't what Scobie had meant.

'No one ever looks at a painting of a nude up close. Haven't you noticed that?' His voice, coming from the kitchen, sounded astonished that this basic fact had passed him by. 'They stand back, view them from a distance. Back there it's art. Come any closer and it suggests you're looking at the wrong thing.'

'It's still an unnecessary risk.'

'It might be a risk if she suspected anything but she won't. She's not the suspicious type.'

Shaughnessy didn't like it, but he had a feeling that this was one argument that he wasn't going to win and so he let it go.

Chapter 7

'Have you heard?'

'Heard what?'

'They've increased the ransom,' Patricia said. 'They were asking for five million. Now they want six.'

'I could have told them that's what would happen.' Gus spoke with the deliberation of a man with half his mind elsewhere. 'You don't have to be a financial genius to see that if you play silly buggers with an organization like that they'll turn nasty and up the asking price. Stands to reason.' He was sitting slumped in his high black-leather chair, one leg cast across the armrest, his attention fixed on his fingers, which were going through the complicated ritual of making a cat's cradle from a rubber band. Gus liked to fiddle as he talked. He had the kind of restless energy that had to be channelled into small and generally useless occupations. On the black stained-oak desk in front of him were various other toys: a silver model of a Ferrari, another of a Lynx helicopter, a lighter set in a scaled-down replica of a .44 Magnum revolver.

'How did you hear about this?' he asked.

'I had a call from Dickie Hughes this morning,' Patricia told him. 'He's in the marine market but he keeps his ear pretty close to the ground in Lloyd's.'

'Could be a rumour.'

'It's not. I talked to James Trevelyan just now. He confirmed it. A tape was delivered to his office yesterday afternoon. They want more money and they want him to stop messing them about.'

'Or else what happens?'

'They didn't say.'

Gus brought his fingers together, picked up a new sequence of links, and parted them again. The rubber band was so tight now the fingertips were turning blue. 'He must be sweating.'

'I don't think so,' Patricia replied. Somewhere there would be a white-haired mother who thought of James Trevelyan as a toddler but everyone else who knew him was aware that there was a ruthless streak in him that was quite out of keeping with his appearance. 'If anything he's rather pleased with himself. These new demands show they're getting impatient.'

'People become irrational when they're angry.'

'Maybe that's what he is hoping.'

'If I tried running this place like they run their affairs we'd be closed down by the IBA.'

Patricia leaned forwards into the mirror and her right eyelid fluttered as she applied mascara with a tiny brush. 'You don't run this place, Gus,' she said brightly. 'You're just one member of the board.'

When Patricia unsheathed her claws it was sudden and unexpected. Gus rolled the band off his fingers and regarded her sourly. She was dressed in a tight black angora sweater held at the waist by a shiny black belt, beneath it a grey worsted skirt reaching below her knee, and wine-red boots. A different image to that which she usually presented in front of the camera. He didn't know the reason for the change but he could be sure that it wasn't unintentional. She would have calculated the effect precisely. Women were light-years ahead on the subject of image.

'Where are you filming?' he asked.

'The Royal Academy.'

'What's to see? There's nothing in the Royal Academy but an empty wall.'

'That's what I want. I thought it would make the point.' She screwed the lid back on the mascara and tucked it back into her bag, her hips thrust forwards, one knee lifted in support, a gesture that was unconsciously erotic.

Gus heaved himself to his feet and came round the desk. He rather resented Patricia's ability to arouse him. It would be so much easier if he could dismiss her from his mind when she annoyed him.

'Isn't there some way they announce a disaster in Lloyd's?' he asked as they went downstairs.

'The Lutine Bell. They ring it once when there's bad news, twice if it's good.'

Gus gave a grunt to indicate that's what he thought. 'Would they ring it if this painting got burnt?'

'Possibly.'

'That would be worth filming.' They came into the car park. It was dark and maladorous, filled with exhaust fumes that had nowhere else to go. Patricia's white Mercedes was parked in one of the reserved slots. 'A bare wall isn't much visually,' Gus said as she unlocked the door. 'But the sight of five hundred Savile Row suits being wetted at the same moment would make great TV.'

'I'll see if I can arrange it.'

'Why don't we have a drink after you've finished? The Ritz is almost opposite. They must be good for a bottle of something fizzy.'

'I'll need to get back home and change, Gus.'

He held the door of the car open. As she got in she paused, turning around, her body brushing against his. It was typical of her to replace one subconscious signal with another. He ran his hand down her spine until it rested on the shiny black belt and drew her close. He could smell the scent in her hair. 'Afterwards then?'

'Yes,' she said. 'If you like.'

'We could leave before this reception is over.'

Her eyelids had dropped; the smile was suddenly lazy. 'Are you needing an early night, then?'

Barry Wesley was one of the best lecturers in London. Unlike the majority of art historians he not only knew his subject, he had the rare ability to get it over to students.

'How are you, Patricia?' he asked, taking hold of her upper arms and kissing her on both cheeks. Then standing back he examined her with that intent interest that homosexuals can show in a woman's turn-out. It was academic but still flattering.

'Well—'

'And thriving on stardom I see.' He was small and lean with the incredible neatness that is often granted to those of diminutive size. His eyes were black, as his hair had been until the flecks of grey appeared at the temples, and his face was a screen on which flickered rapidly changing expressions of humour and sensitivity. He always reminded Patricia of a tiny dormouse, constantly alert, constantly in motion, never relaxing for a moment.

'I'm not a star, Barry.'

'That's not what the papers tell me.' It was one of Barry's boasts that he had never watched television in his life. 'So what can I do for you this afternoon?'

'I need you to tell me about *The Triumph of Bacchus*.'

'Anything in particular.'

'Everything you know.'

Barry raised his hands and rolled back his eyes, a quick gesture of surrender to indicate this might take some time.

Patricia was more specific. 'I want to know why it is such an important painting in the history of art.'

He consulted the shelves, took down a book, and laid it out on the nearby table. The lecture hall was large and dusty with a high domed ceiling and that lingering smell of disinfectant and woodworm that comes to all institutions. In the early years of this century it had been the studio for one of the many artist's societies that splintered off the New English Art Club. Its members were all dead now but their memory remained in the silhouettes of past presidents that were painted in a frieze around the upper wall.

When she came down from the Fontainebleau business course Patricia had spent a year studying in this bare room. Of late, art history has become a trendy way of killing time, and many of the girls with her had been in transit between a cordon bleu course and employment as a chalet girl. But Patricia had carved the time out of her career because she knew very little about the visual arts and that she'd felt was a failing that must be remedied.

'Part of the interest,' Barry said in answer to her question, 'stems from the fact that *The Triumph of Bacchus* has been in private ownership ever since it was painted.'

'You mean absence makes the heart grow fonder.'

'Something like that.' He had found the place in his book now, and smoothing down the reproduction of the painting he laid the billiard cue that he used as a pointer across the pages to hold it open. 'Titian painted it for the library of the Scuola San Antonio and it's remained there ever since. The public hardly ever get to see it.'

'And that's given it a mystique?'

'It happens,' Barry told her. 'But that's only half the reason for its fame.'

'And the other half is?'

'It's a great painting.' He smiled at the simplicity of the reply. Twisting the book around on the table he examined it as though seeing it for the first time. 'It's got energy. That's what Titian did best; creating energy out of chaos.'

Patricia hooked one heel on to the cross-bar of her chair and hugged her knee as she watched Barry's thin hand moving over the painting, tracing out the composition, demonstrating the way Titian had harnessed colour and tone to build his painting. She felt at ease with Barry when he talked of paintings. Once on a trip to Paris she'd spent a rainy afternoon in a cafe pouring out her soul to him, something she'd never done before or since with a man.

'Are you going to make a programme about this?' he asked half an hour later as they were going downstairs.

'I think so.'

'You're not sure?'

'My producer doesn't like the idea.' In the last few days Patricia had begun to realize that art was one of Gus's many grievances in life. Like an appreciation of the countryside or an understanding of which fork to use at a banquet, it was something he felt he'd been deprived of by upbringing and consequently resented.

'Can't you twist his arm a little?' Barry enquired.

'I'm working on it.'

It was ironic in many ways, Patricia thought as she drove across London. Gus probably imagined that her interest in the visual arts stemmed from a contact with beautiful objects at an early age, whereas it couldn't be further from the case. Her father had no taste for the subject. The only paintings at home had been Victorian sporting scenes and the occasional brown landscape that he'd inherited. Admittedly, her mother was mildly artistic. Whenever she was in the Greek isles she was moved to make watercolour sketches but that was only because she felt that seated before an easel in a straw hat and flowing scarf she blended into the scenery better. The paintings themselves were a minor part of the performance.

Patricia parked her car in the courtyard of the Royal Academy. She didn't have a permit but the attendant was indulgent, gave her a wink, and said he'd keep an eye on it. It was the flip side of being recognized, she reflected as she went inside.

The camera crew were waiting in the foyer, just four of them plus the director.

'Do you want to go over the script first?' he asked.

'No, I don't think so.' She could feel the first flutter of butterflies in her stomach. It was always this way when she was about to go on camera. 'I'm going to make some changes. We'll work them out as we go along.'

❄ ❄ ❄

'Did you get what you wanted?' Scobie asked, looking up from the sports page of the *Evening Standard*.

Shaughnessy nodded as he sat down. 'More than I wanted, as a matter of fact.'

The National Gallery's cafeteria is in the basement. It is one of those self-service affairs with hot food in covered aluminium vats, salads arranged tastefully alongside, and drinks corralled into a sunken compound in case they escape.

Scobie was sitting at a table in the smaller of the three rooms which was reserved for smokers although, from the expressions on the faces of the two women on the next table, his home-rolled cigarettes exceeded the brief.

'What's that?' Shaughnessy asked, pointing to the tiny slice of quiche in front of him.

'That's lunch.'

'Only just.'

Scobie thumbed the cork from the bottle of wine and poured a second glass. 'If you want to get a drink here after two thirty you have to have lunch. I've just been discussing the point with a Marxist behind the counter. This piece of quiche was the cheapest thing to qualify.'

Shaughnessy drank its health and said, 'I need to see the X-rays, Scobie.'

'Why's that? I thought you said you could get away with copying the surface.'

'I need to see beneath it.'

'It doesn't matter what's under there, does it? They won't have time to run any tests. That's the whole point.'

Shaughnessy took a pull at the wine. It was Italian and acidic, made from grapes which had suffered a sudden and violent end before being stuffed into the bottle. 'It's not the tests that worry me. It's the texture of the paint surface. The way it has beaded up in places; the way it's cracked. That's caused by the under-painting.'

'It's a fine point. Without the original to compare it to no one will be able to tell the difference. It's just not possible.'

'The surface scumbles are affected by it too. They'll notice that much.' Shaughnessy had spent two hours upstairs examining the Titians in the collection. He pointed to the piece of quiche. 'Are you going to eat that thing?'

Scobie shook his head and pushed it across the table at him. 'Be my guest.'

'You know I'm right,' he said as he ate. 'Maybe.'

Shaughnessy nodded to show that he accepted his unconditional surrender and then pulled a face. 'Jesus, what's this made of?'

'Spinach.'

'Tastes more like seaweed.'

'So where are you going to find X-rays?' Scobie wasn't interested in the culinary details.

'They weren't in Schalk's files when I went through them so I reckon they must have gone with the picture.'

'If we knew where that was we wouldn't be here now.'

'My guess is there'll be a set in the Royal Academy,' Shaughnessy said, brushing the crumbs off his jersey and getting to his feet. 'At least it's worth a try.'

'Who are you going to say you are?' Scobie asked as they came out into the street. 'You'll have to have some sort of authority if you are going to take them.'

'I'll think of something when I get there.'

'What?'

'How do I know what? I haven't had time to think yet.' They walked round into the Haymarket. It was a cold, overcast afternoon, the sort that tourists like to imagine in London but don't like when they get there. A flock of pigeons were pecking at the remains of a hamburger in the gutter.

'Have you noticed the colour of the flesh tints Titian uses for his women?' Shaughnessy asked as the pigeons scattered around them. 'It's got a sort of lustre to it. I can't think how he does it.'

'He probably put a lot of warmth into the shadows.'

'I don't think so. I isolated a piece with my hand and it still looked shiny—like mother-of-pearl.'

'It may be he's run some sort of cold glaze over the surface.' They turned down into Piccadilly. Ahead of them lay the Royal Academy.

'You're not going to say you're a journalist, are you?' Scobie asked.

'What's wrong with that?'

'It's corny. And you can't say you're from the police either. They always ask for identity.'

'I'll think of something else.'

'You're from the National Slide Library?'

'We'd like a copy of the X-rays for our collection, if possible.' Shaughnessy tried to give his smile the sincerity of one who thinks of a pile of yellowing slides as a 'collection'. 'We already have a slide of the painting but one of the X-rays would be of great academic interest.'

'I see.' The girl from the publicity department had a round face, black hair, and the kind of baggy floral print dress that keeps everything else out of sight. She seemed perplexed by the request. 'How long would you need them?'

'A day—an hour if necessary. Just long enough to take a picture.'

'We do have a set,' she said slowly, as though concerned that she might be quoted on the remark later. 'But they are out on loan already to Vanbrugh Films.'

'When are they coming back?'

'I don't know, to be honest. But you could ask them yourselves. They're filming upstairs.'

'Are they just.' Shaughnessy had the look of a man who has finally fathomed the secret of the Trinity. 'My mother always said I'd be rewarded if I ate my greens.'

The girl's smile before she retired to her office was thin sunlight through the mist.

'What's lucky about it?' Scobie asked as they went up the main staircase of the Royal Academy.

'I don't know. At least we know they exist.'

There was a small crowd of onlookers in the doorway to

the gallery. The attendant held out his hand as they approached. 'You can't go in there, I'm afraid, sir. They're filming.'

Filming was exactly what they weren't doing, as is usually the way with location work. The two cameramen were standing in a huddle in one comer of the room; nearby the lighting engineer was sucking his cheeks to indicate that whoever designed Burlington House hadn't taken his problems into consideration at the time.

The gallery had been laid out as it had been when *The Triumph of Bacchus* was on exhibition. A red rope cordoning off the bare area of wall, a vase of flowers on a pedestal. Even the placard explaining the history of the painting had been put back in place. The only thing missing was the picture itself. But it wasn't the rearrangement of the gallery that held Shaughnessy's interest. It was the tall blonde who stood talking to the director.

She could have been a member of the film crew or a representative from the Royal Academy, but he knew instinctively that she was some sort of celebrity. She had the unselfconscious bearing, the cocoon of privacy, that only comes to those who are used to being the focus of attention. It lent her a slight sense of loneliness in the room.

'Who's that?' he asked Scobie.

'Isn't it the one who does those financial programmes?'

'Patricia Drew,' the attendant told them. 'She's making a documentary about art theft. Part of her new series.' An hour holding back spectators had made him an expert on the subject.

'Good-looking girl,' Shaughnessy said. She was standing with one knee resting on a chair and hands on her hips as she listened moodily to what the director had to say.

'Looks like trouble to me,' Scobie replied. They'd never shared a taste in women and since Shaughnessy's divorce he was all the more convinced that his was the more reliable of the two views.

'Aren't you going to ask them about the X-rays?' Scobie asked as they went back outside. The queue for the main exhibition reached across the courtyard. It had begun to rain lightly, only a fine drizzle but enough to make the experience unpleasant. It didn't seem to deter them, however, they stood with their collars turned up, patiently shuffling forwards, waiting for their moment to arrive. There are always hungry people. In Russia it is for bread, here in London it is for culture.

'The film crew won't have them,' Shaughnessy replied. 'They'll be back at their office. We'll have to try there.'

'You haven't got time for this.'

'Then I'll have to make it.'

'It's over a week since the painting was stolen and you haven't even started work yet.'

'And if I start without all the necessary information it'll never come out right.' Time was worrying him too. He could feel it slipping between his fingers as each day passed.

Crossing Piccadilly they turned down a side street and searched about until they found a telephone booth. Scobie waited outside, his newspaper over his head, while Shaughnessy put through a call.

'Any luck?' Scobie asked as he emerged.

'They've got the X-rays but they're not letting them go until they've finished.'

'Who did you talk to?'

'Some sort of private secretary. She wasn't having it. You'd think I was asking for the key to her chastity belt from the way she resisted.' He put his hands in his pockets and looked up at the sky. The rain sparkled on his shoulders and face. 'It's a crying shame. We need to see those plates.'

'You're not going to steal them, are you?'

'No. But I might just borrow them for a bit.'

Chapter 8

When Patricia finished filming that afternoon she went straight back home and took a bath before changing for the evening.

The car arrived promptly at six thirty. It was a black Daimler with a uniformed chauffeur. She would have preferred to drive herself but the preview they were attending was staged by one of the rival film companies and Gus wanted her making a splash when she arrived.

She found him in the crowded bar, studying the credits for the programme that was due to be launched that evening.

'Did you film anything useful this afternoon?' he asked as they went upstairs. Before she could answer he extended his right arm with a growl of pleasure and was away to greet some acquaintance. He didn't say more than a few words before passing on to the next. Patricia watched him as he worked his way around the room, clasping hands, slapping the occasional shoulder, kissing loudly and publicly. If there was a mite of goodwill, ten pounds of coproduction money, a shred of gossip to be found in this excited, twittering crowd, Gus would find it.

A waitress paused beside her with a plate of canapés. As she took a tiny triangle of smoked salmon she was aware of two men standing at her side.

'Miss Drew?'

They were dressed conventionally in dinner jackets and starched fronted shirts. The shorter of the two she recognized as the Minister of Arts. The other was a thin young man. He gave a little nod of the head and continued, 'May I introduce to you Gerald Barraclough?'

Patricia replaced the canapé on the plate and offered him her hand. 'How very well timed, Minister,' she said. 'I was about to eat that.'

'Shouldn't you?'

'Not when there are photographers in the room. If they're going to catch someone with their mouth full I'd rather it wasn't me.'

'I take your point.' Barraclough was a powerfully built man, now running to fat, who stood with his legs planted slightly apart as if expecting a sudden attack. When he spoke it was in short clipped sentences with a Yorkshire accent which she had the impression he cultivated. 'I thought for a moment you were going to say you were on a diet, Miss Drew.'

'Patricia, please—' She felt his gaze flicker down over the smooth sheath of her dress and guessed he was wondering, as every other man in the room had done when she came in, what it was she could be wearing beneath it.

'Drew…' He considered the name. 'You're no relation of Leonard Drew, the chairman of Schneider-Williams, I suppose?'

'He's my father.'

Barraclough said, 'Ahh.' It was a sound she found intensely annoying. All her life she'd heard people saying 'Ahh' like that when they made the connection with her father. It was meant to show that they understood, that they appreciated who she was and how it was she came to be where she was.

He must have sensed the coldness in her reply for he amended the remark. 'You won't find him here, I'll bet.'

'No.'

'Not unless they start making a few documentaries about model railway trains, eh?'

Patricia smiled. Model railways were a private and almost secret passion of her father's. You'd have to know him well to be aware of it. It was not the sort of information that you picked up in the *Financial Times*.

'I was in the Royal Academy the other day,' he said now that he had established his credentials. 'I gather that you are making a programme about *The Triumph of Bacchus*.'

'We're considering the possibility.'

'I have to say I'm disturbed to hear it. The situation is delicate. Interference from the media could upset the balance.'

'I don't intend to interfere, Minister.' Patricia's eyes had narrowed slightly at this turn in the conversation.

'It might be taken as such.'

'By whom?'

'By anyone entrusted with the dirty business of trying to retrieve that scrap of canvas in one piece.'

Patricia adjusted the position of the watch on her wrist then straightened the long white glove beneath, smoothing the material right the way to her upper arm. The operation required her full attention. 'Are you saying that you want this business kept a secret from the public?'

'Not at all. I'm asking only that you keep us informed of your intentions.'

'So you can control them?'

'Not necessarily. We may even be able to help.'

'If you have objections, why don't you voice them on the programme rather than behind its back?' Gus enquired.

Patricia turned around. She hadn't realized that Gus had returned and had been standing listening to the conversation for the last few minutes.

'If you want to impose restrictions you'll have to make it official.' Gus touched his glasses as he spoke. They were the large black-framed ones impregnated with little glittery chips that should have warned anyone that although he liked a party he was not to be crossed. 'I'm not having my staff muffled unless there's a good reason.'

'Do I know you?' Barraclough eyed him testily.

'Gus—Gus Armstrong.' He held out his hand and the broad smile flashed on his face; the two were programmed to come together. 'I'm controller of programmes at Vanbrugh.'

'Then let me make it clear I'm not trying to muffle what you are doing.' He gave a slight jerk of the head, as if invoking the crowded room as his witness. 'I wouldn't be here if that's what I wanted.'

'That's not how it looks from this side of the fence.'

'Then I'm not explaining myself very well.'

'Try giving it another shot, Minister.' Gus spoke with the affable manner that he only assumed when he knew he couldn't lose. Barraclough wasn't backing down however.

'You work in the public interest, Mr Armstrong. That's the nature of the media. But I think you'll agree that the public interest is not best served by having that painting destroyed.'

'I'm glad someone sees it that way.'

'It's my misfortune that I must see it from every point of view, Mr Armstrong. And ultimately the safe return of *The Triumph of Bacchus* is the only thing that matters. I must question anything that threatens it.'

Gus was about to speak but Patricia put her hand on his arm. 'No, Gus, he's right. We should talk about this.'

'Why did you say that?' Gus asked as they were leaving.

'I thought he had a good point. There's no sense in us making an unnecessary nuisance of ourselves.'

'It's our job to make a nuisance of ourselves.'

Patricia held the collar of her fur coat to her throat, so that its softness touched her cheeks. 'You don't believe that, Gus.'

They crossed the road to where his car was parked. It had started to rain, a soft drizzle that settled on her hair and shoulders where it glistened like sequins.

'You should have left the talking to me,' Gus told her.

'You were antagonizing him.'

'If a politician asks you to lay off you don't agree; you start digging around to find what he's trying to cover up. It's the first rule of journalism.'

'I don't think he was trying to cover anything up.'

'Of course he was.' Gus unlocked the door and leaned across the roof. 'I don't know what he's up to but he knows more than he's letting on. We might have found out what it is if you hadn't been so damned soft.'

'You don't really care what happens, do you, Gus? Whether or not that painting gets destroyed doesn't matter to you provided it makes good television.'

'That's what we're paid to do.'

'Not when it's irresponsible.' They were shouting at each other now. 'What's going on out there is real, Gus. Can't you get that in your thick head? It's not a charade put on for your benefit.'

'If that's how you feel maybe you're in the wrong business.'

'Maybe I am,' she said furiously. Slamming the car door shut she ran across the street and waved down a passing taxi. Before she could get in, Gus caught her by the arm.

'Where the hell do you think you're going?'

'Home.'

'I thought we were going on somewhere.'

'I'd rather go home, thank you Gus. Or do I need your permission for that as well?'

'Get back in the car.' His grip on her wrist was hurting her but she wasn't going to give him the satisfaction of showing it.

'Would you let go of me, please?'

'Not until you behave yourself.'

'I'm cold and I'm wet.' The words came out slowly and deliberately, each one frosted with ice. 'My dress is getting ruined out here and if you don't mind I want to go home.'

Gus stared at her, as though seeing her for the first time. 'Jesus, Patricia.' The rain was coming down heavily now, plastering his long hair to his forehead. 'What is it with you? You bonk your way to the top and then think you can turn into some sort of nun. Is that it?'

'How dare you say that!'

'It's the truth. You're not interested in the business. You just want to screw the system and everyone along with it to make sure you come out on top.'

'God, you can be patronizing.' With a quick twist of her wrist she broke free and turned to the taxi driver who'd sat watching this confrontation with studied indifference and said, 'Will you take me to Tite Street, please.'

'Take you wherever you like, darling.'

Chapter 9

Vanbrugh Films is one of those tall modern blocks that are made from a sleek combination of brick and smoky black glass with a few circular windows thrown in to show that it is designed by an award-winning architect. It stood on the southern side of the Thames on a site provided by the Luftwaffe slum-clearance project. From the upper floors there was a good view of Tower Bridge, which presumably meant that the bridge had a good view of it in return. All things considered, Shaughnessy reckoned the film studios had got the best end of the deal.

He came through the revolving doors sideways, pushing the glass panel with his elbow to protect the huge bouquet of flowers he was carrying.

'Patricia Drew?' The girl on the reception desk repeated the name. Then she looked at the flowers and beamed a dull comprehension on to the situation. 'If you leave them here I'll see she gets them.'

Shaughnessy checked a paper in the canvas shoulder bag he carried and shook his head. 'I need a reply.'

'Hang on.' She picked up the phone, clamped it into her shoulder, and fixed her gaze on the middle distance.

A career in the media wasn't everything it was cracked up to be.

The foyer was black carpeted with the spotlights in the ceiling directed towards the glass cases that contained the various awards the film studios had won. On the walls were large photographs of their leading celebrities: confident, trustworthy faces of those who've learnt how to smile sincerely into the camera. Patricia Drew's was amongst them. It was a studio piece with an immaculate hair-do and carefully arranged lighting. There wasn't actually a diamond flash on her teeth but there might have been. It was that kind of picture.

'You can take it up.' The receptionist put the phone down. 'Second floor, at the end of the passage.'

Shaughnessy nodded towards the photo as he signed the daybook with the name of a stylish flower shop that he invented at that moment. 'What's she like?'

The question provoked a minor struggle in the girl's mind. She was undecided whether to pass on her private views of a superior or claim some sort of acquaintanceship with a star in the face of a stranger. In the end she compromised. 'She's OK, I suppose. Bit of a cow when she doesn't get what she wants.'

He took the lift to the second floor. The door of the programme office was open. A secretary was seated at the desk with her back to him. Beside her was sprawled a young man in a white shirt and slightly less white trousers held up by red braces. His black hair was cropped short at the side leaving a tuft above that might have been raised by an electric shock.

'I'm looking for Patricia Drew.'

'Join the queue,' he replied amiably. There is no class distinction in the media. Flower boys are treated with the same engaging insolence as film producers.

The secretary swivelled round in her chair. 'Are those for Patricia?'

'That's what the label says.'

'How lovely. I wish someone would send me flowers like that.' She wore a brightly embroidered jacket and a gold necklace. Her voice was thinly disguised Home Counties. 'I'm afraid she's in a meeting at the moment.'

'Patricia's always in a meeting,' the tufted boy said as though this were some particularly revealing observation.

'I'll wait if that's OK.' Through the half-opened door beyond Shaughnessy could see a superbly furnished inner office. This was the border line, he guessed, the divide between anonymity and fame over which everyone in this over-crowded business hoped to step. 'I was told to give them to her personally.'

'She may be some time. She's with the Head of Programmes.'

'You got back, then?'

'Yes, thank you,' Patricia said evenly.

Gus was sitting behind his desk, his jacket off. Beneath his suntan he looked pale and tired.

'And the dress?'

She turned from the window. 'The dress?'

'You seemed concerned about it last night. In the rain.'

'Oh that, I see…Yes, it's all right.'

Outside a barge was making its way downstream. Through the double-glazed window the steady heartbeat of its diesel motor was clearly audible. Gus swung round in his chair and studied it as though it were a secretary who had butted in without knocking.

'I made you, Patricia,' he said suddenly. 'Did you know that?'

She didn't reply.

'It was me who discovered you and it was me who promoted you. Without that you'd never have made it. I sometimes wonder if you realize that.'

'Yes, Gus,' she said. 'I realize it.'

'You've done well. Hell, everyone knows that. You're our top show. But that's down to me as much as you.'

'What are you trying to say?' Patricia asked sharply. She was feeling bad about her behaviour last night but she didn't want to be given a lecture by Gus.

'Take a look at these.' He pushed a piece of paper towards her.

'What is it.'

'The ratings on your last series.'

'I've seen them,' she said quickly.

Gus picked up the sheet and studied the figures with lazy interest.

'They're down. Not much, but a significant drop just the same.'

'It was a repeat.'

'That's true. All the same it's a warning. Ideas—even good ideas—need to be updated from time to time.' He dropped the paper back on the desk. 'We must put our heads together, you and me, see if we can't freshen things up.'

'There's nothing fundamentally wrong with the series.'

'Maybe not. But still, there's no harm in talking things over, is there?'

'No,' she said carefully. 'I suppose not.'

As she returned to her office she found Jules waiting for her. 'Can I have a word, Patricia?'

'Is it important?' she asked patiently. Jules worked on the principle that the closer you stayed to the presenter of a programme the greater your chances of advancement.

'Five minutes.'

'Oh, Patricia—' Suzie called after her. 'There are some flowers for you.'

Patricia turned, her hand on the door handle. She hadn't noticed the other man in the office. He was standing in the corner, leaning against a filing cabinet. On it was propped an enormous bouquet of flowers.

'Are those for me?' she asked, taking and cradling them in her arms. Flowers were a common enough event in her line of business but she could never escape a little thrill of pleasure at their arrival. Reaching under the cellophane covering she extracted the envelope. Written in the card inside were the words: 'From an admirer'.

'Do you know who this is from?' she asked over her shoulder.

The blonde-haired man had followed her through into the office and was looking around himself. He shook his head. 'I'm just the delivery boy.'

It flashed across her mind that they could be from Gus, a roundabout way of apologizing. But it was unlike him to be so enigmatic. If he'd sent her flowers he'd make quite sure she knew who they were from. Feminine intuition wasn't something in which he put much faith. 'You didn't see who bought them?'

'Most orders are phoned in.'

Patricia often had couriers and drivers from delivery companies in her office. They tended to be uneasy in her presence, the younger of them occasionally took the opportunity to ask for her autograph. But this one kept his distance. 'Are you waiting for something?' she enquired.

'I was told to get an answer.'

Patricia handed the flowers to Suzie, telling her to put them in water, and sat down at her desk. For some reason she found his indifference annoying.

'There's no question to answer,' she said archly.

'In that case I'll be off.'

Shaughnessy went up to the next floor and walked down the passage, thumping his way between the fire doors, until he found an office that was deserted.

It was a dismal little space where, judging from the functional desks strewn with paperwork, three members of Vanbrugh Films' staff were condemned to pass much of their adult life.

Sitting down at one of them he picked up the telephone and tapped in a number that he'd memorized. The venetian blind on the window was hitched up at one end. Through it he could see the back of some large Victorian building, a brewery maybe, or some sort of factory. There were vents in the roof and iron fire-escapes serpentining downwards. In between was a patch of wasteland into which a few cars had crawled to park between the weeds and the rubbish bins and the remains of a heating system that had been left there to rust.

'Scotland Yard. Can I help you?' The voice that came on the line was matter of fact.

'I'd like to report a bomb.'

There was no comment, not even an acknowledgement of the statement, just an imperceptible click as the line was redirected to somewhere deeper within the system.

'Good morning, sir—' Whoever it was that picked up the call sounded friendly, glad to have the monotony of his day interrupted.

'There is a bomb in the basement of Vanbrugh Films.'

'Might I ask who it is I'm speaking to?' You had to hand it to him. It wasn't a question, just the desire to put things on a personal basis.

'Vanbrugh Films.' Shaughnessy didn't want confusion. 'I'm speaking of the central office on the Thames.'

'How do you come to know this, sir?' Somewhere the relays would be working overtime trying to trace the call. In the old days it used to take three minutes to make a contact. Shaughnessy didn't know what it was now but you could bet your granny's back teeth it was a great deal less than that.

'It's timed to go off in twenty minutes,' he said and put down the phone. Propped against the typewriter was a postcard. It showed two monkeys on ice, the larger grasping the other from behind. Across the picture was scrawled the words: 'Bugger me, it's your birthday.'

He picked it up and turned it over. The police would respond to his call; they couldn't afford not to. Earlier that year a bomb had gone off in Victoria station although the police had been given a few minutes' warning. The newspapers had crucified them, not an experience they'd want to repeat.

The door opened and a girl looked in. Seeing him there she stopped in surprise. 'Oh, sorry,' she said, 'I was looking for Andrew…'

Shaughnessy put the postcard back in position. 'I've been waiting for him myself.'

'You don't know where he is, I suppose?' She was looking round the office, in case he happened to be hiding, when the fire alarm went off outside.

'Jesus Christ!' she said, pulling back and looking up and down the passage. 'What's that?'

About two and a half minutes, Shaughnessy guessed. Roughly the time it takes to look up the number of Vanbrugh Films, put through a call, and bang the notion into someone's head that there's a bomb ticking away in the bowels of the building.

He went out into the passage where office doors were popping open, the occupants appearing with the sheepish expressions of those who sense they're about to have their routines terminally disrupted.

On the way downstairs the alarms suddenly cut off, leaving his ears ringing as they adapted to the silence. Above it he heard a detached voice speaking through a megaphone. He glanced out of the stairway window. Three police cars had arrived, spilling uniformed officers. One of them was standing almost directly below him, head back, face obscured by the bell of the megaphone as he advised the occupants to leave the building as quickly as possible.

With people pushing and barging around him, he made his way to the gents. It's not surprising the police switchboards get plagued with false alarms; it's a big reaction for a single phone call.

Going into one cubicle he partially shut the door and sat on the lavatory cistern, his feet on the seat so that they wouldn't be visible from outside.

The thunder of running feet had diminished. There were only one or two now and they were moving more slowly. It would be the police, he guessed, checking that the place was empty. He could hear their voices as they went from room to room.

The outer door to the gents burst open. There was a moment's silence in which Shaughnessy pictured the officer glancing around the little room, taking in the empty basins, the unlocked doors. And then the creak of the spring as it closed again.

He left it five minutes before venturing out into the deserted passage and making his way back to Patricia Drew's office. The PCW screen on her secretary's desk was still awake, the coffee percolator near by trickling out steam. Curiously it reinforced the girl's presence in the room as strongly as if she'd been there herself.

Behind the door were two metal filing cabinets. He checked through them but they were stuffed with correspondence, all neatly headed and arranged in alphabetical order. Nothing to do with the programmes themselves. Sliding the drawer shut he went next door.

He opened a door in the fitted cabinet. It was filled with rows of box files and video tapes that had been subjected to the same regimental sense of order.

Pulling out one entitled 'The Triumph of Bacchus. *Project notes and pilot script'*, he took it over to the desk and searched through the contents until he found the thick brown envelope he was looking for. It contained twelve X-ray plates. He laid them out on the inlaid surface, assembling them together to form the complete picture. Then shuffling them back together again he took them outside.

Further down the passage he found a box room. It had a single overhead light and no windows; stacked on the shelves were what looked like bundles of stationery. Shutting himself in, Shaughnessy took the sheaf of large black envelopes from his bag and laid them out on the floor. On top of each one he placed one of the X-rays.

Standing up, he familiarized himself with the exact geography of the room, the position of the twelve plates on the floor, before switching off the light.

In the sudden and complete darkness that engulfed the room, he crouched down and opened the black plastic envelopes. In each one was a single photographic plate. He positioned an X-ray on its face, holding it in place with the paper clips he had brought in his pocket, before reaching up to the light switch.

He flicked it on for a second and then off again.

The exposed photographic plates he returned to the envelopes, sealing them tightly and tucking them back in his bag. The contact prints that the brief flash of light had created would be in reverse, the X-rays acting as a negative, but a photograph of the prints would return them to their original state. Conveniently, he could use the piece of celluloid directly as a slide.

On the way back to the office he paused to listen, senses alert. Somewhere below he could hear voices—clipped, efficient-sounding voices, the sentences kept short, the information passing economically.

Shaughnessy wasn't sure of the procedure. His message must have been put through to the anti-terrorist squad in Scotland Yard, who'd call in the services of a bomb disposal team, but quite how they operated he didn't know. Sniffer dogs, probably. When he'd rung, Shaughnessy had hoped that they'd wait to see whether the bomb went off at the promised time before moving in. It would be sensible. But by the sound of it, sense wasn't one of the requirements of the job. He hoped they were well paid for it.

He put the X-rays back in their envelope and slipped it into the box-file. Before leaving he looked through the other papers. There were a number of newspaper clippings, most of which he had himself, the transcripts of what looked like interviews, and several drafts of a shooting script. Of more interest was a thick report from Lloyd's. From what he could gather from a quick glance over the front page, it was an assessment of the previous ransoms: the places and methods that had been used. Across the top someone had written, 'Hope this is of some help to you—thanks for lunch.'

Shaughnessy went to the door and listened. The voices were closer now. But if they'd started in the basement they'd work their way upwards methodically, wouldn't they? Combing each floor in turn. That would take time.

Switching on the photocopier in the secretary's outer office he ran the report through it, lifting the cover, turning the pages, concentrating on the sheets that fed into the exit tray with each pop of the flash bulb, blocking the approaching voices from his mind.

When the last page had rolled out he put the box file back in the cabinet and left. At the head of the stairs he stopped dead in his tracks, drawing back from the banisters.

Standing on the floor below was a member of the bomb disposal team, the padded bulb of a helmet on his head, his body squat and shapeless in its flak-jacket. He was speaking into the short-wave radio clipped to his lapel and barring the way out as efficiently as an electric fence.

It's at moments like this that a sudden flash of lateral thinking can save the day. Unfortunately it wasn't one of those days. The best Shaughnessy could come up with was to creep up to the floor above and make his way towards the rear of the building, carefully closing the heavy swing doors after him to prevent them flapping. Noise carries a long way in an empty building.

An emergency exit led out on to an iron balcony but it was of no help to him. Through the reinforced-glass pane he could see down to the ground below where one of the police cars was visible. Around it small groups of people stood around like dispirited football fans waiting for the match to start.

As he continued upstairs, searching through the ribbons of passages, he thought of those wretched laboratory mice who are put into mazes where they scurry around in rising frustration until they finally despair and give in, huddling in a corner to be caught. It was not a pleasant image at that moment.

A door marked 'Maintenance: no admission' was unlocked. Beyond it was a short flight of concrete steps and another door, steel framed and functional with a push-bar catch. Shaughnessy thrust through it and found himself on the roof of the building.

After the claustrophobic, over-heated corridors it was suddenly fresh and open out there, the breeze ruffling his hair in greeting. He walked to the edge of the parapet and looked down over the city. It was a breathtaking view, the cloud cover low, dragging wisps of rain along the horizon.

He sat down, resting his back against the giant head of a ventilation duct and felt his pulse rate slow as he drew the cold air into his lungs. No one would follow him up here. The police weren't looking for the bomber; they'd presume he'd left long before. It was the bomb itself they were after and that wouldn't have been planted on the roof where it would cause no damage.

Taking the notes he'd copied from his bag he glanced through them. Some of the relevant passages had been underlined, he noticed, and into the margins Patricia Drew had added comments and observations of her own. He studied the handwriting. It was clear and cerebral, the letters well formed and identical in size.

Until that moment Shaughnessy had assumed that the only true threat to his ambitions would come from the police, but as he looked at these neat, premeditated notes—every *t* crossed and *i* dotted—he realized that here was a new and possibly dangerous opponent that he hadn't included in his calculations.

Chapter 10

The day after his visit to Vanbrugh Films was one of the two Saturdays in the month in which Shaughnessy, in accordance with the calculations of the court and his ex-wife, was granted access to his children. He took them to lunch at the Roland, where they sat in a corner and had glasses of Pepsi and frozen pizzas that had suffered the trauma of feeling their molecules accelerated in a microwave oven; a gastronomic adventure made all the more exciting for the two boys by the fact that the Roland was just the sort of place Angela disapproved of them visiting when they were with their father.

In the afternoon he took them back to his flat and fired up one of the steam engines, in this case a beautiful scale model of a triple-expansion marine engine that he had spent six months restoring.

After he had delivered them back home that evening he called in on Edward Zadec. His studio, as he preferred to call it, was in a basement flat in Battersea, a depressing house in a street shaded in the daytime by the railway track and illuminated at night by the self-service garage on the corner.

Edward was cooking his dinner when Shaughnessy came in, energetically jiggling a frying pan over the gas cooker in a display of culinary skill. Rolling around the hot oil were two sausages.

'They're shit,' Edward told him. 'Breadcrumbs and offal with no flavouring worth mentioning. But you can do a lot with them if you know how. It just takes a little finesse.' He was an acquaintance of Scobie's, an occasional visitor at the Roland, and usually the last to get in a round.

In his prime he must have been a small man but now his seventy or so years had shrunk him to cockroach proportions. During his life he had bummed his way around Paris and Vienna, making a living as an artist and photographer, but his voice still carried the hardened consonants of his native Czechoslovakia.

'Have you done the pictures?' Shaughnessy asked but the old man didn't appear to have heard him.

'You fry a little bacon and garlic in the oil first. That's the trick. The flavour works its way into the meat. The English don't understand that.' He lowered the gas, bending down to examine the numbers on the plastic knob on the cooker, before wiping his hands on a dish cloth. Age had drawn the skin tight over his face. It gave him the gaunt, reptilian appearance that all refugees seem to share; the look of a derelict building.

'Yes,' he said, 'I've done the pictures.'

He went through into the darkroom, carefully adjusting the door after him so that Shaughnessy couldn't see in. Probably because it was also his bedroom, the acidic stench of developing fluid mingled with the warm smell of sheets and discarded clothes.

To mark his departure, the frying pan suddenly spat hot oil which ignited on the cooker in a little fireworks display of sparks.

'Is Scobie still trying to screw that red-head?' Edward called through the door.

'Maybe. He's using her as a model.'

'He shouldn't do it. He'll only embarrass himself. I told him he should leave that kind of thing to the young men. They don't know shit but they can do it three, four times a night. That's what girls want, you know. No finesse, no quality, just a good shag. Scobie can't compete any more. He should realize that.' There was a lot of spite in the old man.

Shaughnessy looked round the room that was at once living space, kitchen, and office. There was a bare patch in the carpet in front of the armchair. A fragment of glass had been knocked out of the corner of the window and replaced with a piece of cardboard. Pinned on the wall, in place of any other decoration, were hundreds of photographs. A younger version of Edward, dark haired and smoother featured, appeared in some of them along with faces that looked vaguely familiar.

'I knew them all,' he said, coming back and seeing where Shaughnessy's attention was fixed. 'Braque, Sartre, Hemingway—I knew them all in the old days.'

He threw a sheaf of prints down on the table, held the slide he had made of them up to the light to check it before handing it to Shaughnessy. 'It's come out well.'

The plates, in this mounted negative, had been assembled together into a composite picture, the thick underlayers of lead white pigment showing up pale and ghostly like bones beneath their covering of flesh.

'Did we agree on sixty pounds?' Shaughnessy asked.

Going over to the cooker, Edward began pushing the two sausages around the pan. 'Oh yes.' He wanted to get back to the old days. 'You'd be amazed at the people I've known in my life. Someone should write a book about it. I've known them all.'

'They should. Probably make a bestseller.'

He turned around, searching Shaughnessy's face to see if he was being mocked. 'It would,' he agreed stiffly. He gave the pan another shake, like a mother punishing a delinquent child and put it back on the heat. After a moment he said, 'Those are X-rays, aren't they.'

It was a statement rather than a question which gave Shaughnessy the option not to answer. He didn't.

'I couldn't think what they were when I first made the proofs. It was only when the image reversed in the negative I saw it. They're X-rays of a painting.'

'I'm doing some work for a client.' Shaughnessy tucked the slide into the pocket of his shirt.

'That's what I told myself. Tommie will be looking into the background of a picture for someone. He knows a lot about these things.' Reaching up to the cupboard he took down a small jar of herbs and sprinkled some on the sausages, flicking his hand up and down in quick, precise gestures then brushing it clean on his trousers. Above the acrid smell of the oil came a sweeter perfume that Shaughnessy recognized but couldn't identify off the top of his head.

'But that's not any old painting, is it, Tommie? X-rays don't show you much of what's on the surface but I couldn't help noticing that they look like that Titian there's been all the fuss about.'

'Which Titian is that, then?'

'Don't give me that crap, Tommie.' There was a glint of malice now. He'd staged this conversation and didn't need Shaughnessy screwing up the timing at the last minute. 'You think you can talk your way out of anything but I can read the underlayers of a painting as well as anyone. Piss about as much as you like but I know what that is. I was looking at pictures while you were still wetting your bed.'

'And what's it to you?'

'More than sixty pounds, Tommie. I don't know what you're wanting with that slide but it's worth more than sixty pounds.' With a small knife, Edward carved a wedge from one of the sausages with rapid sawing motions and put it in his mouth.

'Taste good, does it?' Shaughnessy asked.

'We should talk about this, Tommie.'

He kept the knife in his hand, Shaughnessy noticed. It might have been chance or it might have been that Edward was frightened that he was going to be attacked.

'What's there to talk about?' he asked.

'I heard you lost that smart job you had up in the West End.'

'You hear a lot of rumours in this city,' Shaughnessy said. For no reason, it occurred to him that the sweet-smelling herb in the pan was rosemary, which was why it had been transmitting such powerful images of roast lamb and Sunday afternoon with the papers. 'I was talking to a man the other day. He was telling me about a tacky little racket that went on in Vienna after the war. Someone had found a way of photo-etching copper plates and was using it to knock out American dollar bills. They weren't much good by the sound of it, no bank would have been fooled. So he was stupid enough to try passing them off in the Russian sector. They fell for it. I suppose they didn't get to see the real thing too often. Made himself quite a pile on the black market before the comrades rumbled him and he had to make a bunk.'

It wouldn't be true to say that the words hit Edward. In fact he made no movement at all. Just stood where he was, turning the knife around in his hand.

'Where did you hear this?' he asked.

'He told me his name but I don't remember it.' Shaughnessy had moved closer so that he stood over the old man. 'Zemlinsky, was it? Or Zempinka? Something like that. I dare say Interpol would know if you asked them. They have long memories.'

Edward still made no movement but he was thinking, reassessing the situation. His eyes darted about the room, hard and bright as ball-bearings, grasping at familiar objects as though they would offer him some solution.

'So that's the way of it, is it, Tommie?' he said bitterly, throwing the knife aside. 'I thought you had come to me because you could trust me to do a good job. But I see I was wrong. You came because you could take advantage.'

Shaughnessy took out six notes and dropped them on the table by the cooker. 'Sixty quid, that's what we agreed, wasn't it?'

'I don't need your money,' he said. 'I do all right for myself. I don't need you coming here, prying into my life with your insinuations. You think you're different from the rest; you think you can get ahead of the crowd. But you can't.' His words seemed to restore some of his self-respect for he bared his teeth in a smile. 'They'll get you; you see if they don't. They'll get you and they'll grind you down like they do with everyone else.'

Shaughnessy picked up the prints and nodded towards the smoking pan. 'Your dinner's burning.'

In the telephone kiosk on the corner he put a call through to Collins. When Shaughnessy arrived an hour later he was waiting for him on Hungerford Bridge, leaning on the metal guardrail, staring up the Thames.

'You'll have to be quick,' he said irritably. 'I'm due in the Festival Hall in twenty minutes.'

'I didn't take you for a music lover.'

'Bach.' Collins felt obliged to justify his taste. 'It has a precision to it that I can appreciate.' He was of no great height but he managed to convey an impression of considerable density, as though a much larger man had been compressed into his polished brogues, his perfectly creased trousers, and correspondingly uncreased trench coat.

'What is it you wish to see me about?' he asked.

'I had some pictures made by a photographer. He suspects what I'm doing.'

'Were they necessary, these pictures?' Collins hadn't looked at Shaughnessy once since he arrived but kept his gaze fixed on the river as though this might prevent any formal connection between them.

'They're necessary. I have stalled him for the time being. I doubt whether he'll try going to the police but there are other ways he might try using the information.'

'What do you expect me to do about it?'

'I thought you should be warned.'

Attached to the handrail of the bridge was a little engraved plate identifying the various buildings and ships along the river. Collins squinted down one of the arrows, the street lights along the embankment illuminating his face. On his upper lip he sported a moustache, or rather the carefully tended patch on to which a proper moustache could be fitted on ceremonial occasions. Above it was a trilby hat which he wore, neither on the back of his head like a ticket tout nor cocked forwards like a second-hand car salesman, but firmly about his ears as befits one who keeps his umbrella rolled tightly, who keeps his back straight and chin up, who demonstrates his appreciation of Bach by pronouncing his name with the correct accent.

'When I last saw you,' he was discovering the position of the Nat West tower for his general education, 'I thought it was understood that you wouldn't be in touch again until this business is over.'

'You can invent what rules you like. My only concern is that the painting is finished on time.'

'What stage has it reached at present?'

'It's not started yet.'

Collins was coming to terms with the location of Cannon Street station as he heard this. He looked up in surprise. 'Is that wise?'

'The gathering of intelligence is as important as any other stage. A military man like yourself should know that.'

In all their meetings, Collins had never mentioned his training or background although it couldn't have been more obvious if he'd worn a regimental insignia on his breast pocket and performed close-order drill for Shaughnessy's benefit, but he chose to treat the insight as a regrettable breach of security and smiled tightly.

'I wouldn't know,' he said, glancing at his watch. His voice became brisk. 'I must go. In the mean time I'll see what can be done about this photographer friend of yours.'

'His name is Zadec, Edward Zadec.' Shaughnessy gave him the address in Battersea which Collins noted down with a propelling pencil.

'There is one other thing,' Shaughnessy said as he turned to leave. 'I shall be wanting more money.'

Collins twisted the tail of his gold pencil, withdrawing the needle of lead, and replaced it in his upper pocket. 'You've already been offered a good wage.'

'It's not enough.'

'What has changed to make you say that?'

'It's a much bigger job than we anticipated.' In practical terms it was true. Shaughnessy had never envisaged having to copy a painting of such complexity. But what had prompted the demand for more money was simpler and more personal, an idea that had been poised in the back of his mind for some time ready to be pushed over into consciousness. He didn't want his children asking, as they had that afternoon, if he was going to be poor for the rest of his life. That was the truth of it. He didn't want to end his days in a basement flat pasting pictures of himself on to photos of the Parisian intelligentsia to lend his life a glamour it had never deserved.

'How much are you asking?' Collins enquired.

'A million.' It was over twice the original fee that he had been offered for the job and Collins knew it.

'That's preposterous.'

'A million or the picture doesn't get started.'

'You realize this is nothing less than blackmail?'

'Blackmail's an ugly word,' Shaughnessy replied. 'Unless you happen to be the one benefiting from it. Then it takes on a certain beauty.'

'I can't allow it.'

Shaughnessy knew that Collins was in no position to bargain. 'Just pass it on,' he told him. 'Give me a ring when you have an answer.'

'How much do you know about Titian?' he asked the following morning.

Scobie was hunched in front of a portrait of an elderly woman, trying to improve the drawing of the hands which on his own admission looked like two bunches of bananas crawling off her lap.

'Titian?' He put his brush down to consider. 'He was Venetian, sixteenth century. His colour influenced Rubens.'

'Is that it?'

'He must have had a beard.'

'But what do you think he was like underneath it? If you'd met him in a drinking house off the Rialto, how do you think he would have talked? How would he have behaved?' Shaughnessy was standing before the easel. The X-ray of the painting was projected on to the canvas, the jumble of brushstrokes glowing greyly in the morning light. As he studied them he was trying to picture the artist's personality, his frame of mind as he worked.

There's an element of play-acting in a forgery. It's not so much the picture that must be copied as the painter. When he first worked on Scobie's paintings it had been easy enough because he knew him. He had been able to stand beside him and mimic his gestures: the fidgety movements of his brush, the way he dodged in and out of the canvas like a timid boxer. Once he had the feel of that he had been able to imitate his style without much difficulty.

But with Titian this was not possible. There was no one to watch, no one to copy. The only evidence of the man's personality was in the marks left by his brush.

'I don't know anything about him,' Scobie admitted.

'He was in his early fifties when he painted *The Triumph of Bacchus*, possibly slightly older. You can't be sure; the old goat couldn't remember exactly when he was born.' Shaughnessy was talking to himself rather than to Scobie, piecing together information. 'He had worked for every major patron in Italy except the Pope and in the last few years he'd been introduced to Charles V who was just about the biggest cheese around when it came to commissioning paintings.'

Taking a clean brush he began to trace out the paint strokes of the drapery around Bacchus's shoulders. Coloured pigments are transparent, only lead white is opaque and stands out in the X-rays.

'He was at the peak of his career. The Emperor had just made him a count. Not bad for a peasant boy from Cadore.'

Placing the tip of the brush on the canvas Shaughnessy followed the line of one white brushstroke, at first slowly, discovering the twist of the wrist, the sweep of the arm, then more rapidly, judging the pace with which it had originally been slapped on to the canvas by the italic of its calligraphy.

The length alone was astonishing, as was the speed and confidence with which it had been applied. For an instant, as the brush sliced across the canvas, Shaughnessy touched the artist who had first created it, felt his arrogance, his desire. 'Jesus Christ,' he said, standing back from the canvas, 'he must have been on top of the world when he made this.'

He tried some of the shorter strokes in the fold of Ariadne's gown.

These were continuous, a single zig-zag of paint that ran down the picture. He tested each movement in turn, letting his arm memorize the gesture. When he put them together it was like the slashing of a rapier. Errol Flynn in the last reel of the film.

'He created the picture as he went along,' Shaughnessy said. 'Can you imagine that? There were no drawings, no studies, none of that pissing about with preparations that the others went in for. He invented the thing while he was working on it.'

'They have no fear,' Scobie said, 'great artists: they make the picture in their heads. The paint just follows the thought.'

Shaughnessy stood back a little, holding the brush out at arm's reach. In that position he found the movements of the arm came more easily; he could give them the scale they required.

Scobie put down his palette and came over to watch. 'Manet, Velasquez, Picasso, they were all the same,' he said. 'They didn't have to think about paint. They just told it what they wanted and let it do the job for them.'

Shaughnessy ran the palm of his left hand across the canvas as though feeling for the build-up of paint. 'There has to be a process,' he said thoughtfully. 'If Titian made no preparatory studies he must have had some way of working the picture out. A sequence of events.'

'Makes you sick when you see what they could do.'

'Watch this,' Shaughnessy told him. He scrabbled the dry brush across the canvas, mimicking the construction of lead white on Bacchus's shoulder, then moving it further up the canvas he carved out the rough shape of the head and the sky behind. 'This is how the first lay-in of paint went in. I thought he would have started with just a translucent stain but it's solid: lead white worked into west Venetian red. Black added into the darker areas.'

Scobie took out his tin of tobacco, rolled a cigarette, and latched it to his lower lip. 'What of it?'

'At this stage it's just a huge abstract arrangement. Hardly any variation of colour.' He stabbed at the canvas with the brush. 'Only these central figures and parts of the foreground have been defined at all, the rest is just a patchwork of tones. He probably doesn't know yet whether they are going to be trees or figures or whatever. He's just thinking it out in terms of composition, balancing the masses of light and shade.'

'How do you know the white is put in at this stage? It could have come later.'

'It's there from the start. I can see it in the cross-sections. I couldn't understand what it was doing there when I first saw it. But it's very simple. Titian sorted out the tonal arrangement of the picture before anything else. One problem at a time.'

'So when did the colour come into it?'

'In the next phase, I should think. When this underlayer was dry. I can't be sure until we get there but my guess is that he ran it over the surface quite thinly to keep the translucency and then built the individual forms directly into the wet paint.'

Scobie took the cigarette from his mouth and held it in his fingers while he made vague passes at the canvas. He could only test out the possibility of a technique by acting it through. 'Do you think it'll work?'

'I think so.'

'Jesus Christ. It's the weirdest thing I've ever heard of.'

'It's a sort of organic process.' Shaughnessy was only partly understanding what he was saying himself. 'He devised a composition around the main figures, then floated colour over the surface and let that suggest the other forms to him.'

'He must have developed it more after that.'

'From there on I should think it's more conventional: dry scumbles and glazes.'

Scobie puffed smoke as he considered what he was hearing. 'Are you trying to tell me he had no idea of what it was going to look like until he'd finished?'

'That's the way of it. It has to be. The painting is sketch, study, and finished picture all rolled into one.'

'Well if that's how he did it, he's welcome to it,' Scobie said with some feeling. 'It'd scare the pants off me.'

'Me too.'

'Can you get the same effect?'

'God knows. All I can do is run it through and see how it comes out at the other end.'

'You're going to try imitating a lunatic technique like that?' He spoke as though Shaughnessy's last grey cell had migrated to a warmer climate for the winter.

'I have to. If I don't follow the same technique I'll never get the right effect.'

They were interrupted by the telephone. Scobie picked up the receiver and handed it over to him. It was Collins.

'I've passed on your request,' he said.

'And they accept?'

'They do.' Collins sounded disappointed to be on the losing side of the deal, although he can never have thought it would be otherwise.

'I need an advance,' Shaughnessy told him.

The demand gave Collins the chance to reassert himself. 'No advances,' he said flatly. 'The arrangement will be the same: payment on completion of the job. Nothing before.'

'You got the money, then?' Scobie said as he put down the phone.

Shaughnessy nodded. He should have been over the moon but he wasn't. The painting hadn't even been started yet. All the problems were still ahead. Celebration would come, he had no doubt of that. But this wasn't the moment.

'They're still refusing to cough up anything on account.'

'Why ever not?'

'They don't want to leave a trail. No money, no link; that's how they see it.'

On the marble washstand that he used as a palette, Shaughnessy mixed burnt umber with a small quantity of terra verte and laid it on to the canvas with a knife, speckling the surface with large dabs of paint. Damping a cloth with turpentine he rubbed the colour together, working it into a fine even stain.

When he'd reduced this to the colour of weak coffee he switched on the projector, the blinds open so that the

X-ray glowed weakly on the canvas, and laid in Venetian red, a deep brick red that flowed quickly into the wet paint beneath.

For this first assault on the picture he worked with a six-inch house-painter's brush which he'd strapped to a longer shaft, the bristles cut to a soft-pointed filbert shape. Following the faint image of the X-ray he modelled the central figures and the vague blur of the background before taking a smaller brush and building up the thick lead-white lights, rehearsing each stroke in front of the canvas before putting it down.

For five hours he worked in silence, his mind locked on to the task, unaware of anything beyond the rectangle of the painting. By the time he finished the bare white canvas had been transformed into a violent, swirling mass of hot colour. As he'd said to Scobie, it was practically an abstract, clouds of red and brown underscored with black and lit by brilliant flashes of white. Vibrant, majestic, thrilling in its scale and energy. Only the figure of Bacchus himself was identifiable, the rest falling away to ghostly suggestions. A dream landscape, half forgotten, half remembered; intangible and evocative. One of the most exciting sights Shaughnessy had ever seen.

Standing back, he examined it in detail, going over each part in turn, occasionally reaching forwards to make small adjustments.

When he was satisfied, he cleaned the brushes and the marble-topped table. Then he went down to his flat, threw himself down on the bed, and slept for six hours.

Chapter 11

'We should be thinking of the future,' Joe Rawson said. He was the head of Light Entertainment at Vanbrugh, an urbane man in his fifties with a fleshy face and wide mouth into which the stub of a cigar fitted comfortably for much of the day.

'You're an asset now,' he told Patricia as he ate. 'You've made your name, broken into the business. That's the hard bit done. But now we should be looking ahead.'

'What do you have in mind?'

Joe dabbed at his mouth with a napkin. 'Your series is a class act, right? It's got style. But what's it take to make— six weeks', two months' research per hour, is it? That's an expensive way to make television.'

'It needs that,' she said patiently. She wasn't going to be bullied by the likes of Joe. 'These are important issues we're looking into. We have to get our facts right.'

Across the table, Gus was watching her closely, his eyes slightly closed as he tried to gauge her reaction. He had flown in from a two-day drip to LA only that morning but he showed no visible sign of jet-lag. In fact he was glowing with health and energy in his pale grey suit, his hair pulled back tight over his head emphasizing the hard bone structure of his face that she had found so devastatingly attractive when she'd first met him.

He had reserved the table by the fireplace in the dining room of the Chelsea Arts Club. It was the best, in his opinion: out of the main thoroughfare but in a good position for catching the waitress's eye. It was the kind of detail Gus thought about. He smiled at her. 'What they're trying to tell you, honey, is that you work too hard.'

'On my side of the business we could use a girl like you.' Joe waved his fork up and down to indicate his train of thought. 'You've got glamour, good looks, great legs. It's a waste to keep you locked away in current affairs. I always said so to Gus.'

Patricia smiled disarmingly. It wasn't Joe's fault that he talked of her as though she was a piece of meat that must be weighed and priced and stuck up in the window for sale. He talked about everyone that way. It was Gus who was to blame. She'd sensed a plot from the moment she'd arrived but it was only now that she was beginning to see where it was coming from. She pushed back her chair. 'Shall we go through and have some coffee?'

'Of course we'd need to put you in the public eye first,' Joe said as he followed her out into the passage. 'Get them used to you. But that's no problem. We can get you on a few quiz shows, show your face in the right places. Leave it to me. I'd have suggested it before but I didn't realize you were available for this sort of work.'

'Didn't Gus tell you?'

'No.'

'How very remiss of him.' She smiled icily at Gus. 'But it's not the only thing he doesn't tell people.'

THE TRIUMPH OF BACCHUS 137

The bar in the Chelsea Arts Club is a large, rather gloomy room with that atmosphere of well-loved down-at-heel traditionalism that characterizes most sought-after British institutions from its schools to its legal system. It has bare floors, tables with tin ashtrays, and a snooker table at which Scobie and Tom Shaughnessy were playing at that moment.

Shaughnessy didn't particularly want to be knocking snooker balls around in the afternoon but he had nothing better to be doing. There are times when oil paint must be left to dry.

He had experimented with various siccatives to accelerate the process but none of them had the effect he wanted. In the end he had resorted to using an alkyd white in these initial stages of the painting. It's a modern, chemically produced paint, smoother than lead white but with the advantage that it dries at something like ten times the speed. He'd thickened it with ground glass to get the texture. It was breaking the rules he had set himself but what else could he do? Time was ticking away.

In the last twenty-four hours he had restructured the under-painting, building in the 'pentimenti'—the little alterations to the design that Titian made as the picture went along. At the same time he had been able to clarify the central figures and rework the areas of sky, defining the cloud formations and the aerial perspective in gradations of ochre. But the painting now needed thirty-six hours to dry completely.

He chalked the tip of his cue. 'Red in the top left pocket.'

They had established a rule over the years that the player must announce what he intends before taking his shot. It made the game more skilful and discouraged Scobie from hitting the balls as hard as he could on the off-chance that they went down somewhere regardless.

'What day was it that you saw Edward?' Scobie asked now as the red dropped in. He was scanning the table, his eyes screwed up in the smoke of his cigarette.

'Saturday, wasn't it?'

'I've been trying to get in touch with him. There's some pictures he was doing for me but he never seems to be in.'

'Maybe he's got a job out of town.' Shaughnessy hadn't told Scobie of what had passed in his last meeting with Edward, or that he had handed the problem over to Collins. For that matter he had very little idea of what might have become of him. He pointed his cue across the table. 'Yellow in the side.'

'I don't think so.' Scobie watched the yellow ball nudge off the cushion. Perching his cigarette on the side of the table, beside the burn marks made by a thousand others over the years, he moved around the table, searching for an angle of attack. 'He should have been round at that college where he teaches today but they haven't seen him all week. It's not like him to miss out on anything that earns. Besides he doesn't get work out of town these days.' He tapped a pocket. 'Red in this one here.'

'He'll show up in a day or so.'

'My guess is he's avoiding the tax inspector.'

'Does he pay any tax?'

'Not much, that's why they check on him.' Scobie had been sawing the cue across the table in preparation as he spoke. He now took his shot and missed. 'Buggeration.'

The ball was poised not six inches away from the corner pocket. Shaughnessy tapped it with the cue ball, watched it roll towards the pocket. It was dead on line. But before it could drop in, a finger reached across the table and stopped it.

He looked up. 'What did you want to go and do that for?'

Patricia Drew didn't answer immediately. Picking up the snooker ball she walked round the table towards him. 'I didn't think you'd mind if I stopped you there.'

'It was going in.'

She tossed the ball in her hand, briefly considering this possibility, and then rolled it away across the table where it could cause no more trouble. 'I hadn't realized that flower boys had the time to hang around here playing snooker.'

'I only work part time.'

'So I gather.' Her expression hadn't moved since she'd stopped the game but she was watching him intently as though waiting for him to set the tone. 'May I ask your name?'

'Shaughnessy—Tom Shaughnessy.' He didn't lie. There were too many people in there that knew him. But he could see her assessing his answer, wondering whether to believe him. 'You can check at the bar,' he said. 'They know me.'

'Oh, I shall,' she replied and turning on her heel she looked around the room. 'But first I need to talk to you.'

'There's no one stopping you.'

'I mean somewhere private.' She nodded towards the garden. 'Out there, for example.'

In summer time the garden of the Chelsea Arts Club is filled with sunshine, bright dresses, and jugs of Pimm's. Now it was a scene of mouldering vegetation. She opened the door, turning the key and giving the lower part a kick with her foot.

Shaughnessy sat down on one of the garden benches and wondered where the hell she'd jumped from. 'So what is it you want to say?'

'You rifled through my office.'

'I brought you some flowers.'

'Please don't try to play games with me, Mr Shaughnessy.' She had remained standing since they came out, avoiding the suggestion of intimacy that sitting beside him might have implied. But now she turned and looked down at him angrily. 'The police taped your voice. I recognized your accent straight away.'

He didn't have an accent, not the soft brown roll that he had been brought up with, but he knew that there was still an empty space in his voice where it had been. It wouldn't have been hard to identify. The rest she would have worked out for herself. 'I needed to see some of your material.'

'Have you any idea of the trouble you caused with that sort of irresponsible trick?'

Shaughnessy shook his head. Only a woman would scold him for the effect before she'd questioned him as to the reason for it. But she was coming to that.

'What did you want to see so badly?'

'Your files on *The Triumph of Bacchus*.'

The directness of the answer took some of the steam out of her attack. She hesitated. 'For what reason?'

'I don't have to answer that.'

'I can't see you have any option.'

'It's your involvement, Miss Drew. I wanted to get some idea of why you are taking such a keen interest in the misfortunes of these paintings.'

'I'm making a programme about them,' she replied primly. 'But you were obviously aware of that before you came.'

Shaughnessy ran his hand across the armrest of the bench. It was green and slightly damp; everything in nature returns to its original state in time. He slapped the palm clean. 'There are a great many subjects for programmes. I have to ask myself why you chose this one in particular.'

'Are you suggesting that I'm connected in some way?' She sounded incredulous, not so much that he might think it of her, but that he should have the effrontery to say it.

'Whoever stole these paintings had a remarkable degree of inside knowledge, particularly of the financial involvement of the insurance syndicates.'

'And that you think could have come from me?'

'You have connections in the City; channels of communication not open to many. It's not impossible.'

'That's ridiculous.' There was a note of impatience in her voice. 'I only started to pay attention to these thefts last week—three days after *The Triumph of Bacchus* was stolen.'

'So I discovered.' He shrugged as though the whole thing were of no importance. 'It was just a process of elimination.' She hadn't asked him yet for whom he might have performed this feat of piracy but he could see that as she stood before him, twisting the gold necklace around one finger, she was trying to work it out for herself.

She must be frozen, it was a savagely cold afternoon and she was wearing a flimsy dress of grey silk to match those amazing eyes, but she gave no indication of discomfort. To have done so would probably be a sign of weakness in her mind and Shaughnessy had a strong impression that weakness, either physical or mental, was something that this girl didn't permit herself.

'It seems I've been slow off the mark,' she said after pondering for a while. 'I thought that I was the one to be making enquiries but I see that in doing so I've put myself under suspicion.' She smiled tightly at her own naivety. 'I should have guessed.'

At a table in the bar Gus sipped at a glass of Armagnac as he watched the conversation in the garden. He was not able to hear what they were saying but from their attitudes he judged it was some sort of argument. The man was sitting forwards on the wooden bench, his hands between his knees while Patricia stood before him, stiff-legged and erect.

It was almost twenty minutes later that they parted. She didn't shake hands with him, he noticed. That in itself was significant. She was generally punctilious about such social formalities. As she came in, he drained his glass and stood up.

'Who was that?'

'A contact of mine.' Her tone was evasive as she looked around the room. 'Where are the others?'

'They've gone back.'

Taking this as a lead she went and got her coat from the cloakroom. As he helped her on with it, his hand touched her arm and he felt her shivering with cold. He eased her hair clear of the collar and spread it across her shoulders in the way she liked. 'Is he going to be any use to you?' he asked.

'I don't know.' She tied the belt, knotting it tightly.

Her white Mercedes was parked down the road. It was three years old but the car-park attendant at the studios kept it shiny clean and running smoothly for her. She drove up into the Brompton Road in silence, her attention fixed on the street and the pedestrians passing on the pavement beside her.

She was looking wonderful. The cold had put a flush of colour into her cheeks and her lips were slightly parted. But to Gus sitting beside her in the confined space she was remote and somehow unreal, like the statues in that damned museum in Athens she'd dragged him round.

'He struck me as a rough sort of diamond, your contact.'

'Rough diamond?' His words pulled her out of her reverie. 'Did you think so?'

'Hard to tell from where I was sitting.'

'I found him rude and rather arrogant.' She turned down into Beaufort Street, putting her foot down so that the car surged forwards. As she slowed again at the lights she seemed to unbend slightly and taking her eyes off the road she looked at him. 'He has been checking into my motives. Can you believe that?'

'Motives? For what?'

'For making a programme about *The Triumph of Bacchus*. It appears I'm on some list of suspects now.'

'Who does he work for?'

'Customs and Excise. At least that's what he said.' She chewed at her lower lip. 'Does that sound right to you.'

'I guess they'd be in on the act. Apart from that it's hard to say. They're a secretive crowd.'

'That's what I thought. He could be working for anyone. You can't tell.'

'How do you come to know him?'

'I've met him before,' she said vaguely. They were heading up the King's Road.

'Could you drop me in Sloane Square,' Gus said, 'there's someone I must see.' The someone was a new discovery of his, a sleek brunette who he'd recently spotted as she delivered the weather reports on daytime TV. He liked her style: she'd worked her way up from the bottom, starting as a researcher and taking the breaks when they came. He had some ideas he wanted to talk over with her. The meeting he'd fixed was in the foyer of the Dorchester but he didn't want to be seen arriving with Patricia. That would be counterproductive.

'This do you?' She had drawn in by the tube station, the car pointing back towards the river.

'That's fine,' he said. 'I'll see you later.' Patricia switched off the engine. She sat quite still.

'I'm not going to let you do it.'

'Not going to let me do what?'

'Cancel the series.'

Gus had the door open to get out. He closed it again. 'Who said anything about that?'

'No one. But that's what you were thinking, wasn't it?' She folded her coat over her legs, smoothing it flat with her hand. It was a small occupation to stop her having to look at him. 'I know you, Gus. I know the way you work. All that talk at lunchtime. You're paving the way to telling me you're closing it down.'

'Why should I want to do that, for God's sakes?'

'I don't know. But I imagine you have your reasons.'

He should never have asked the other two along. They'd handled her wrongly from the start. Joe Rawson understood the business well enough but he was a blundering ox when it came to women. He'd talked to Patricia as though she were a pre-fluffed bimbo. Gus had watched the hackles rise. 'Honey, I created the series.' His voice was reasonable. 'It's our best product. Nothing on earth's going to make me scrap it.'

'I'll fight you, Gus. You realize that?'

'We were just talking over a few ideas. There's no harm in that. Christ, I thought you'd jump at them.' He leaned over and kissed her but she made no response.

'I know what you're doing, Gus.'

'I just want what's best for you. Trust me.'

'How are you feeling?'

Scobie stumped down the gallery steps in his slippers and dressing-gown. There was a scarf round his neck, giving him the appearance of an elderly undergraduate. He'd caught a cold from somewhere and had spent half the morning lying in bed.

'I'll survive,' he said grumpily. From which Shaughnessy was meant to understand it was going to be a close-run thing. He watched as Scobie made himself a cup of tea, pouring in a medicinal slug of whiskey. He didn't look too ill but then Scobie took viruses very seriously ever since a bout of coughing had put him in hospital. But that was back in 1938 and it had been pneumonia, not a cold.

'Are you fit enough to do something for me?'

Scobie came back, mug in hand, and looked at the unfinished painting on the easel. 'How's it going, then?' he asked. He took a mouthful of tea. 'God, that's better. Yes, I guess so, provided it doesn't involve running around in the fresh air or jumping into frozen rivers. What do you want?'

'Count the number of grains of ultramarine in this photo.' He gave him one of the cross-sections of paint that he had taken from Schalk's studio. 'Then the number of white ones.'

Scobie put the print down on the table, peered at it for a moment before giving a grunt of disgust and shambling off to find his reading glasses. 'What do you want to count them for? They're not going to run away.'

'It's the pitch of the tone I'm after. As I see it, ultramarine's a constant colour. If I mix it with the right proportion of white it should come out at exactly the same density of colour as the original.'

Scobie sneezed, adding a groan of his own afterwards to indicate what a painful experience this had been. 'I suppose you're right.'

'It's the only way I can think of for getting an accurate

match,' Shaughnessy said. Dipping his finger in turpentine he rubbed it across one comer of the painting, testing the white paint to be sure it was dry.

'What's the time?'

'About ten thirty.'

'I should give Marjorie a ring. She's meant to be coming round this evening for a sitting. I'm not sure I'm going to be up to it. I didn't sleep a wink last night.'

'You made up for it this morning,' Shaughnessy said, going through into the kitchen. 'I should let her come just the same, ask her to bring a nurse's outfit with her. That's always been your favourite, hasn't it?'

'Shut up, I'm trying to count.'

Shaughnessy took the ultramarine from the sink. He'd ground it two days before and put it on a sheet of glass underwater to keep it fresh. With a palette knife he scooped part on to the marble washstand, placing a smaller pile of lead white some ten inches away.

Scobie tossed the photo away across the table. 'Sixty-five, I make it—give or take a few grains—to twelve white.'

'That's about what I thought.' He mixed the two pigments, using a measuring cup he'd borrowed from the hotel kitchens, cleaning the palette knife on a piece of newspaper after each operation. This initial mixture he divided into two, adding a further measure of white to one, separating it again and adding some more. This gave him three precisely graded tones of blue.

Like many artists, Titian started working his colour from the background, beginning with the sky. Shaughnessy had ground the paint with a fast-drying oil—linseed cooked with lead-white pigment—thinning it until it was just translucent so that now as he spread it across the canvas the ochre ground glowed through the blue, lending it a warm enamelled intensity. Along the lower parts where the sky met the sea and distant hills he scraped the canvas with a knife, letting the underpaint shine out more firmly, resetting the paint with the ball of his thumb.

After a couple of hours he stood back and studied the effect. It still looked strange, the trees and figures in the foreground pale and insubstantial against the brilliant blue sky. But it was right. He knew that. The technique he had calculated so carefully over the last few days worked and he felt the satisfaction of a mathematician who has cracked the system of a code.

It was while he was working in the dead-colour to the painting later that afternoon that Patricia Drew rang.

'Jesus, it's her,' Scobie said, holding his hand over the receiver. He hadn't bothered to brush his hair that day and it stuck out from his head in octopus tentacles.

'Mr Shaughnessy?' she asked as he took the phone.

'Speaking—'

'This isn't your number, is it? I was told it was the address of a Mr Woods.'

'I called round.' He'd come up with better answers in his time but she let it pass.

'I was thinking about what you said yesterday. It seems to me that we both want the same thing.'

'In what way?'

'You want to know who stole *The Triumph of Bacchus*. So do I.' Scobie was clearing the table of plates and mugs. Not something that usually bothered him but it gave him the opportunity to hang around. 'It seems to me that it would be better if we pooled our information,' Patricia went on. 'Fighting each other isn't going to help.'

'I've already seen everything you know,' he told her. 'And frankly it doesn't amount to much.'

There was a moment's silence, while she digested this. When she spoke again her voice was cool. 'I have contacts. As you yourself said, Mr Shaughnessy.'

'So I did.'

'There is a dinner tomorrow night. I wondered whether you would like to accompany me. Several of the people involved with the recovery of the paintings will be there.'

'That might be interesting.'

'It's in the Middle Temple,' she added. 'Do you know where that is?'

'Roughly.'

'Black tie. It's obligatory.' She paused as if expecting him to object. 'You'll have to hire it if you don't already have it.'

'What time?'

'Eight thirty. I'll meet you by the entrance in King's Walk. And please get there on time, I don't want to hang around in the cold.'

Chapter 12

There were twenty or more guests assembled in the handsome first-floor room in the Middle Temple, the women's jewellery glittering in the subdued lighting. Men often complain that formal dress is dull but the unrelieved black is there to ensure that the ladies are the centre of attraction. It compensates them for being pushed out of the room as soon as dinner is over.

'Quite a bash,' Shaughnessy said as they came up the stairs. 'What's it in aid of, then?'

'It's been arranged so that representatives of the Italian government can meet the Lloyd's syndicate who insure *The Triumph of Bacchus*. They're worried about the way the situation is being handled.' Patricia turned around as she spoke, allowing the waiter to lift her coat from her shoulders.

'You mean they're pissed off that Lloyd's won't pay up?'

'That's exactly right.'

'And in the mean time it all has to be done up to look like a dinner party, does it?'

'It does.' She glanced Shaughnessy over but he was looking surprisingly respectable in a sober dinner jacket and plain white shirt, his fair hair brushed. His face had a battered old-suitcase look about it that couldn't be described as good looking but it had character none the less. 'And don't call it a bash in front of Gerald Barraclough,' she added as they went in. 'He won't like it.'

'He's the one pushing out the boat tonight, is he?'

Patricia nodded as she accepted a glass of champagne. Across the room she could see Trevelyan in conversation with the Italian Ambassadress, a handsome black-haired woman in a clinging red dress that showed off her well-preserved figure. Barraclough was with another group over by the open fire. He raised his glass and nodded to her as she came in.

'How did you get me in on the act?' Shaughnessy asked.

'I told him you work for the Civil Service,' Patricia said. 'That's not a secret, is it?'

'Not to anyone you've been speaking to lately.' Shaughnessy looked at the tray the waitress was offering. 'No chance of anything stronger is there, love?'

She shook her head.

'Pity,' he said to Patricia. 'Someone once told me that champagne is white wine that a frog's farted in. I can't get the possibility out of my mind.'

She smiled icily. 'Yes, well it's probably best if you try saying as little as possible this evening.'

'Patricia!' Trevelyan had torn himself free of the Ambassadress and came over to her. He was looking flushed, his collar slightly too tight so that a vein throbbed in his neck.

'I hear you're the guest of honour tonight,' she said, leaning forwards and offering him one cheek to be kissed.

'More like the sacrificial lamb,' Trevelyan said as he did so.

'I saw she'd cornered you already.'

'She was just sending out feelers, trying to work out who's going to pay the bill if their painting ends up on the junk heap.'

'And who is?' Shaughnessy asked.

Trevelyan turned, noticing him there for the first time. As their eyes met it seemed to Patricia that a tiny spark passed between them. Then it was gone again.

'Me, for a start,' Trevelyan said quietly. 'Do I know you?'

'This is Tom,' Patricia put in. 'Tom Shaughnessy.'

'Pleased to meet you.' Trevelyan offered his hand. 'May I ask what brings you here tonight?'

'Patricia asked me along.'

'He works for the government,' she put in quickly, stalling any suggestion of a more personal relationship.

Trevelyan gave a quick smile. 'When I hear that I've found it best to ask no more. Will you excuse me?'

'Do you know him?' Patricia asked as Trevelyan melted back into the crowd.

'Should I?'

'No, I just wondered. He seemed to recognize you.'

For dinner, the guests were ushered through to the oak-panelled room next door. It was lit only by silver candelabra and the shaded spots on the rows of portraits.

'Did I see you coming in with the lovely Miss Drew?' the woman on Shaughnessy's right asked.

'I've been helping her with some research.'

'How interesting. I didn't realize she was allowed out without Gus.'

'Gus?'

The lilac-painted eyelids lowered. 'Gus Armstrong,' she clarified. Her name was Margot Latchman and she wrote a social column for one of the papers.

'Very tanned with long hair tied back in a pony-tail? Tends to smile a lot?' Shaughnessy described the man with whom he'd seen her leaving the Chelsea Arts Club.

'Mr Charisma,' she agreed. 'I sometimes wonder what expression he'd put on if he liked someone. You don't know our Patricia that well then, I take it?'

'It's purely professional.' He glanced across at Patricia. She was looking very fetching in a long dress of black lace, tight at the waist above full skirts that kept her feet invisible as she moved. Her hair was up to expose the curve of her throat around which was a black velvet choker with a pearl brooch. That, and a pair of matching earrings, was the only jewellery she was wearing that evening. At that moment she was leaning forwards, her elbows on the table, listening attentively to the man opposite.

'Thomas Sutcliffe,' Margot followed his line of vision. 'He was the art historian who verified the painting in the last ransom.'

'I read about it in the papers,' Shaughnessy said. Across the table, the Ambassadress was deep in conversation with Trevelyan again, her long hands moving fluently in response to her words.

'I don't suppose you are part of the negotiating team, are you, Mr Shaughnessy?' Margot enquired innocently. It was clearly nettling her that he wouldn't clarify his role there that evening.

'What makes you think that?'

She paused to consider. The candlelight was knocking fifteen years off her but she had to be the wrong side of fifty: thin and pale skinned, with that languid, Pre-Raphaelite beauty that used to be popular around the drawing rooms of Bloomsbury. 'You have the look of a man who is going to play an active rather than an administrative role in this affair.'

'I don't know much about ransoms.'

'No?' She sounded disappointed but not entirely convinced.

Unclipping her bag she took out a packet of Silk Cut. 'Do you mind if I smoke? I find it helps to irritate people.'

'Is that useful in your line of work?'

'Essential.'

As the blue smoke curled from her cigarette Barraclough shot her a glance of disapproval across the table. Detestable woman. Why could she never resist drawing attention to herself? He would never have dreamed of inviting her had not some form of Press presence been required. The Italians didn't just want to get their wretched picture back; they wanted to be seen trying to get it back. Honour had to be satisfied.

Barraclough regarded his role that evening as that of an entrepreneur. He was there to bring people together, make sure the right ones spoke to each other. The seating plan had been worked out with that purpose in mind. The only unknown had been this Irishman that Patricia insisted on bringing along. Barraclough had been watching him. It was the hands that interested him most. They were large and strong but they held the wine glass with the delicacy of a girl's. Craftsman's hands, and don't try to tell him otherwise; every Yorkshireman can recognize a craftsman's hands when he sees them. He was talking to the Latchman woman at present. Without waiting for a pause in their conversation Barraclough butted in. 'I hear you have your own theories on this business, Mr Shaughnessy.'

'Everyone's entitled to his opinion.' The reply came back as pat as though he had been waiting for it.

'And yours is that information is being leaked from a high level. Is that right?'

'I can't see what other possibility there can be.'

'You'll have to explain yourself.' Barraclough thrust himself back in his chair as he spoke so that his chin rested on his chest, the bow tie invisible beneath his jutting jaw. On the advice of his tailor he wore a waistcoat with a gold watch-chain stretched between the pockets rather than a cummerbund which was inclined to ride up on men of his girth. He waited for the reply.

'How did this organization know when the painting was going to be moved?' Shaughnessy asked. 'How did they know the route sufficiently far ahead to have a van ready?'

'They could have found that out for themselves.'

'But in doing so they'd have left a trail behind them. Questions can always be traced back to their source. The information had to come direct from the top level.'

'You mean it could have come from someone sitting round this table now?'

'It could have.'

'That's a dangerous accusation, Mr Shaughnessy.'

'I'm not accusing anyone.' Again Shaughnessy smiled back at him. 'You asked me my opinion. I gave it.'

✿ ✿ ✿

In deference to the Ambassadress, the ladies didn't leave when the port decanters were put on the table. But on Gerald Barraclough's suggestion the guests were invited to change places. Shaughnessy moved down to the end of the table where Thomas Sutcliffe was sitting. Prematurely balding with small round spectacles, he seemed happy to encourage his image of academic benevolence by wearing a stiff wing-collar and boiled shirt with pearl studs. And he showed no disinclination to talk of the part he'd played in the recent ransom.

'It was very dark,' he explained. 'I could hardly see a thing.'

'How did you manage to see the painting?'

'He shone a torch on it.'

'There was just one of them, was there?'

Sutcliffe considered his answer. 'I only saw one. There could have been others, of course.'

'Can you not give a description of him to the police?'

'Most of the time he kept the torch on my face so I couldn't get a look at him. But I have the impression he was wearing a mask.'

'What, a moulded mask?'

'No, knitted. A sort of balaclava helmet. It's hard to be sure.'

A few places away, Patricia was impressing the whippet-thin Cultural Attaché with her fluent Italian. She was laughing a lot, in the way people do to show they can follow the fine nuances of a language. Shaughnessy turned his attention back to Sutcliffe. 'Did he check the diamonds?'

'Yes, indeed. He took one or two out and examined them.'

'Do you think he knew what he was doing?'

The question remained unanswered for at that moment a commotion broke out at the other end of the table.

Shaughnessy learned later that a package had been delivered with instructions that it should be handed to James Trevelyan. He had opened it to find a small box which now lay on the table. In it were the ashes of a piece of paper. From the few charred remains that had not fully burnt it was possible to see that it had once been a watercolour.

'What was it?'

'A painting,' Patricia said as they walked downstairs. 'A watercolour by David Cox. It was stolen this morning.'

'And Trevelyan insures it, right?' While Patricia was putting on her coat, she had spent a few minutes alone with Trevelyan. Shaughnessy had left them to it. He guessed she would learn more without him there.

'Poor man,' she said. 'He's very upset. If he doesn't agree to pay the ransom on *The Triumph of Bacchus* they'll take another and another until he gives in. There's no way of stopping them.'

'He's going to have to give in,' Shaughnessy said. 'They've got him by the short and curlies.'

'At least the Italians have got what they came here for.'

'Perhaps they arranged for it to be taken.'

'You say that and you'll make yourself more unpopular than you are already,' she said drily. She paused in the doorway and looked out into the darkness. 'I suppose you want a lift now?'

'It would be a charity.'

'In that case you can fetch the car,' she said, taking the keys from her bag and giving them to him. 'It's round in the next courtyard. A white Mercedes.'

It was a beautiful piece of machinery, powerful and smooth running. A real lady's car. As he climbed out to let her take the wheel he said, 'It's a question of whether he could resist it.'

'What do you mean?'

Shaughnessy went round to the passenger seat and got in beside her.

'Sending that picture round in a box. It's a sort of practical joke, isn't it? And on the whole people who play that sort of trick like to be there to see how it turns out.'

Patricia headed up into the Strand. She had taken off her satin shoes to drive. 'You're convinced someone close to these pictures is responsible, aren't you?'

'Not convinced, but I know a reputable bookmaker who'd give you two to one that whoever's been nicking those pictures was there tonight.'

'It wasn't very clever taunting Barraclough like that,' she said, after thinking about this for a while.

'I didn't realize you were listening.'

'Everyone was listening.'

She dropped him by the side of Inkerman Mansions. They said good night, brief words in parting, and he walked down the narrow passageway behind the building. It was after one and the lights above the doors were out but he knew the way from long experience. He was feeling slightly light-headed. A mixture of wine and spirits, that was the problem. It always had that effect on him. As he was fumbling his key into the lock a voice behind him said, 'You've given us a lot of trouble, Tommie.'

Shaughnessy turned around. There were two of them. You can always recognize the bastards of this world. They come in pairs.

'You didn't tell us you've moved. Didn't tell us you've left that grand house of yours.' It was Sylvester, the bouncer from Shanghai Lil's. Shaughnessy couldn't make out his features in the dark but he knew the voice.

They had been waiting in the shadows by the dustbins but now they moved out into the passage, blocking his exit. They wore black suits but he could see the white triangles of their shirts gleaming as though they were luminous. The man beside Sylvester was taller. No one Shaughnessy could identify but that probably wasn't surprising. They'd have sent someone who didn't know him. It was easier that way.

He was trying to work his way round behind, but Shaughnessy stepped to one side to block him. Keep everyone in view. That's the first rule in an uneven fight.

'Rinaldi's not pleased with you,' Sylvester said. 'Not pleased at all. You took something that belongs to him.'

They have to talk like that, don't they? These brain-damaged gorillas. They have to go through this laborious ritual of explanation.

'I was going to pay it back,' Shaughnessy said. Sylvester wouldn't believe him. He didn't believe it himself but that wasn't important. Speaking released the tension in his stomach, gave him the brief breathing space in which he stepped forwards and kicked the taller of the two in the groin.

The principle was good but in the darkness he missed the target. His foot hit the man on the hip. It can't have hurt much but he had the grace to give a grunt and crash backwards into the dustbins. Maybe he was just being polite.

To prevent a repeat of this trick, Sylvester rushed him. His head down, arms out on either side. Shaughnessy was thrown back against the wall. Before he could break out of the grip, Sylvester had put two good punches into his body. He must have been carrying something heavy in his hand for the fist went through the wall of his stomach muscles as though they were rice paper.

The other was on his feet again. As Shaughnessy doubled over he landed on top of him and they went down in the alleyway together—just as well he hadn't hired the suit from Moss Bros. Sylvester kicked at him, aiming at his face. He rolled with the force of it, his arms locked around his head. There was a roaring in his ears, the fetid smell of damp and drains in his nostrils. He felt a sudden pain in his ribs as Sylvester turned his attention to the larger target of his chest.

The roaring continued but now it was coming in a series of intermittent blasts. With a sudden flicker of awareness, Shaughnessy realized that the sound wasn't in his head. It was coming from further away. The horn of a car. He twisted round; looked up the alleyway.

Holy Mother, there it was: one wheel on the pavement, the headlights shining against the brick wall.

With a heave, he kicked his legs over his head and struggled to his feet. Picking up the dustbin that had been adding percussion effects he hefted it at Sylvester and ran for his life. As he burst out of the end of the alleyway, the Mercedes was already reversing backwards, its tyres screeching on the road. He could picture the note of complaint on the residents' board tomorrow.

'Get in!' she shouted. 'Get in! Get in!'

It's easier said than done with a moving car. He ran round the back and threw himself in the opened door, landing diagonally across the seat. Before he could sit up she had changed into first gear and let in the clutch.

It was hard to say what Sylvester's friend intended. As he came out of the alleyway he spread himself across the bonnet as though trying to clean the windscreen but it's not easy to do that on a car that can do nought-to-sixty in under six seconds and he spun aside into the road.

'Oh my God,' Patricia cried, 'have I hurt him?'

'He'll feel terrific again in the morning.' Shaughnessy hung on to the dashboard as she swerved left into the main road without waiting to see if anything was coming.

'Are they following?' she was still shouting.

'Not unless they've got rocket-powered roller skates.'

'Who are they, for God's sake?'

'Some people I know.' Shaughnessy was only just getting into an upright position. His ribs were telegraphing sharp jabs of pain into his chest, making it difficult to speak.

'If I hadn't had to turn the car at the end of the street I wouldn't have seen you.'

'You're a brave woman to stop like that.' He meant it too.

'Don't worry. If one of them had come out of that alley first I'd have been off like a scalded cat.'

Shaughnessy combed his hair out of his eyes with his fingers. They came out with blood on them. Patricia put her foot down, clearing the lights at the King's Road as they turned red. She glanced to one side.

'Are you all right?'

'I'll make it,' he said. 'Provided you don't start telling any of your side-splitting jokes.'

A thought struck her. 'They were wearing dinner jackets.'

'Yeah, well, they were probably sore because they didn't get an invitation to the party.'

'What were they doing there?'

'It's a long story.'

'Not one with a happy ending, by the sound of it.' She turned through small side streets and parked by a tall building. Then getting out she examined the wing of the car. 'There's a dent,' she complained.

Shaughnessy walked round and looked at the dimple in the white paintwork that was causing her such distress. 'A panel beater can fix that. While you're about it you might see what he can do with my ribs.'

Straightening up, she inspected him in the light of the street lamps. Then she glanced back in the direction they'd come, coming to a decision. She gave a little sigh and said, 'You'd better come in.'

He followed her upstairs. The building was about as different to Inkerman Mansions as you can imagine. The passages had thick red carpets and chandeliers. There was a cheerful uniformed character in the hallway and the temperature was tropical but then her neighbours probably didn't bicker over service charges. Too uncivilized. They'd discuss them at a cosy little residents' party.

Her flat was on the second floor. It was split-level and very chic with pale coloured walls and furnishings to match the modern paintings. With a rustle of lace she went down into the main living space and ran back the tape of her answerphone. When she turned round she gave a little cry of alarm.

'Not there!'

Shaughnessy paused in the act of sitting down on one of the cream-coloured chairs.

'Those have just been cleaned,' she said, 'I don't want you putting bloodstains on them.'

She was all heart. On her insistence, he went to the bathroom and inspected the damage to his body work. It was more than a dent to the wing. Sylvester's foot had cut his forehead along the hair line and planted two livid red bruises on the side of his chest. By morning they would be black. Shaughnessy pressed them gingerly. One rib was cracked, maybe two. He washed himself as best he could, shaking his head and hands dry rather than use the towels. They looked as though they'd just been cleaned too.

When he returned to the living room, Patricia had covered the sofa with a rug. Beside it was a blanket. 'You'll have to sleep here,' she said.

'Haven't you got a spare room in this place?' It was a gibe but like everything else he said she was determined to take it at face value.

'I have. But I use it as an office.' She looked around the room, checking that everything was in place. She was still wearing her fur coat, the collar turned up so that the lower part of her face was covered. 'It's quite comfortable,' she added. 'I've slept on it myself.'

'It'll be fine.' Shaughnessy threw his jacket down on the armrest and sat down. The muscles in his side were beginning to stiffen and the movement hurt but he didn't show it.

'Is there anything you want?' she asked.

He shook his head.

'I'll say good night then. My PA is coming in at nine tomorrow morning so I'll need you out of here by then.'

The bedroom door closed behind her. Shaughnessy lay back on the sofa. He didn't feel like sleeping, in fact quite the reverse. The adrenalin was still humming through his veins giving him that sharp-eyed, vital sense of wellbeing that every creature experiences in the aftermath of danger.

It must have been twenty minutes later that the bedroom door opened and Patricia re-emerged. She went into the kitchen. Through the hatch he watched her open the fridge and pour herself a glass of water. She appeared to have forgotten his existence but he knew this water routine was a prelude. He lay still and waited. She came through into the living room and looked at him.

'You're lying to me, aren't you?'

'What makes you say that?' Her hair was brushed out around her shoulders again. He preferred it that way. Beneath it she was wearing an ankle-length nightdress, a smooth unblemished sheath of silk.

'You don't work for Customs and Excise,' she said. 'I don't believe you work for anyone except yourself.'

Shaughnessy nodded towards the bedroom. 'You keep a register of government employees in there, do you?'

'Government officers don't get mugged in back alleys,

Mr Shaughnessy. And they don't make impertinent remarks at the dinner table.' She was holding the glass of water out to one side and jiggling what looked like a couple of tablets in the other. Apart from that she was standing quite still waiting to see if he was going to contradict her.

Shaughnessy swung his legs down on the floor. 'It's hard to know exactly how they do behave, isn't it?'

'Who are you?' she asked.

'Just someone trying to make a living.'

'You'll have to explain what you mean by that.' She was speaking with studied politeness, reserving judgement until the trial was over.

'There's a half-million-pound reward going for anyone who can recover that painting.' He gave a shrug as though the rest were obvious. 'I want it.'

'Is that why you went through my files?'

'That's about the long and the short of it.' He wondered if she had any idea of the effect she was having on him in that nightdress. It was smooth as water and a deep golden colour to match her hair. She probably had matching sheets next door so that she would be completely camouflaged in bed if anyone was thinking of ravaging her. Which in that outfit was the first thing they were going to be thinking about.

'Why do you think I shouldn't ring the police here and now?' she asked.

'Because it would be spiteful.'

'How's that?'

'I'm doing nothing different to you, except I don't have half the back-up you have. You can't blame me for using my initiative. You'd have done the same in the circumstances.'

'I'm not working for my own greed.'

'Oh really. Don't tell me—you're a secret Buddhist.'

'Besides, initiative is not the word I'd use for it.' She took a sip at the water and throwing back her head she clapped her hand over her mouth, swallowing the tablets. Then she went back into the kitchen and put the glass in the washing machine. 'Would you like a drink?'

'I thought you'd never ask.'

She consulted the drinks cabinet. 'What do you like?'

'I don't suppose you've got any Irish whiskey?'

'Only Scotch.' She poured two glasses. 'I never know the difference. Do you want ice?'

'Just as it comes.'

She handed him the glass and sat down on the chair which he'd recently tried to impregnate with blood, drawing her feet up on to the cushion. He had the impression that the trial was not over, just temporarily adjourned.

'So,' she said. 'Rather than helping me this evening, it seems I've been helping you.'

'Why else do you think I turned up?'

'I don't know.' She took a sip of her whisky. There was only a film of it on the bottom of the glass, enough to keep him company. She was full of those things that nice girls are brought up to do. 'I assumed you had your reasons. I also assumed they'd be honest. I was wrong in both.'

'Should you drink that stuff on top of pills?' he asked.

'They are only mild. Something to help me sleep. I saw you were talking to that wretched Latchmann woman.'

'She was filling me in on the local gossip.' He wondered what it was that kept this girl awake at night.

'I bet she was,' Patricia said with some feeling. 'I suppose she's going to write one of her acerbic little pieces in the papers tomorrow.'

'Does it matter to you?'

She looked down into the base of the glass. 'Not really,' she said, 'except I didn't tell my producer that I was going to be there.'

'He has to know about these things, does he?'

For a moment he thought she was going to confide in him but she changed her mind, and tossing back her head she drained her glass.

'It's more complicated than that,' she said lightly. Getting to her feet she put the glass in the kitchen. 'I must go to bed now. It's late. I'll see you tomorrow.'

Chapter 13

Scobie was reading the papers and eating breakfast at the same time, clamping the piece of toast in his teeth when he turned the pages. As Shaughnessy came in he dipped his head and peered over his reading glasses. 'Oh my,' he said. 'Look what the cat's brought in.'

'I love you too.' Shaughnessy threw his jacket down over the end of the table, the bow tie after it. He wasn't at his sartorial best, he'd grant him that, but he could do without the chirpy cockney humour. His mouth felt as though a juggernaut had been parked in it all night and his neck was stiff. He was getting too old for sleeping on sofas, even if they were Peter Jones's best with Chinese-silk cushions.

'You didn't come back last night.'

'I got as far as the door. A couple of Rinaldi's boys persuaded me not to go any further.'

'You don't have to tell me. You woke the whole neighbourhood.'

'I didn't see anyone coming to lend a hand.'

'I thought it was those cats again. It wasn't until this morning I guessed what was going on.' Scobie said throwing down the paper, suddenly angry. The old fool had been worrying, Shaughnessy realized. He made himself a cup of coffee and sat down opposite him.

'It was nothing,' he said.

Scobie studied his face. 'You look a mess.'

'It'll mend—'

'They'll be back,' he said. 'You realize that?'

'I'll send him the money. It's come through at the bank. I'll send it to him, plus a bit of interest. That'll keep him happy.' He went over to the easel and took the cover off the painting.

It was huge and magnificent and for a few minutes he stood and admired it. He'd made giant strides in the last two days. The dead colour was complete so that the trees, the figures, and the landscape were all established in large flat areas of brilliant paint. It looked like the finished picture made from pieces of cut-out cardboard.

'They were hanging around the Roland last night,' Scobie said. 'Dave told me he'd seen them.'

'I'll send him the money, OK?'

Scobie gave a grunt and took his plate and cup into the kitchen.

'How did it go last night, then?' he asked when he emerged. Shaughnessy described how the watercolour had arrived during dinner. Scobie listened in silence.

'And if Lloyd's doesn't pay up they'll take another and then another, is that the way of it?'

'That's about it.'

'It had to happen eventually,' Scobie said.

At eleven in the morning, the gaming room of Shang-hai Lil's was a squalid enough sight. With the floor empty, the lights turned up on the debris of the night before, there was a seediness that took Patricia back to dawn at those May Balls when the magic withers with the rising sun and faces that had been glowing are suddenly pale, lipstick smudged, eyes tired.

In the corner of the room three croupiers were play-ing cards, bottles of Budweiser opened on the table. One of them gave a low whistle as she passed. It wasn't a com-pliment, just a reflex action but it was enough to make her wonder whether it might not have been wiser to have brought someone else along with her.

She followed the doorman up a flight of stairs. Through an opened door on her left she caught a glimpse of the monitoring room. It was lined with TV screens like one of the sound studios in Vanbrugh. A comic-strip maga-zine lay on the floor. On its cover was a man with an enor-mous green torso and the head of an insect. For some rea-son she felt vaguely offended that Tom Shaughnessy should have worked in this place.

Rinaldi's office was at the end of the passage. The door was padded with red mock-leather. As it opened she took a step forwards and stopped. Except for a flickering shaft of light the place was in complete darkness.

'Come in, Miss Drew.' Rinaldi's voice beckoned her on.

She could hardly see him, only the movement of his hand as he waved her towards a chair.

'You'll have to forgive me,' he said as she groped her way into it. 'This is a little hobby of mine. I don't get time to myself in the evenings. I like to make up for it in the mornings.'

He was watching a film. Now that she was in the room she could see the screen. It was one of the old black and white musicals. There was no music at that moment but she could tell it was a musical from the bouncy way the actors moved.

'It's good of you to give me your time,' she said. For an awful moment back there she'd thought he was in bed.

'You are in television yourself, I'm told?'

'That's right—' Her eyes were growing accustomed to the light and she could see him more clearly.

'So how can I help you?'

'You had someone working for you recently called Shaughnessy—Tom Shaughnessy.'

'Did I?' Rinaldi wasn't committing himself.

'The chef at the Shropshire Hotel told me he worked here until about a month ago.' There was another man in the room, she realized. He was standing behind her operating the projector. She shifted slightly in her seat. She didn't like having people behind her back.

'What of it?' Rinaldi asked.

'I want to know about him: who he is and what he was doing before he came here.'

It hadn't been hard to trace Shaughnessy. While she was tidying away the rug and blankets that morning she happened to pick up his jacket. The label inside belonged to the Shropshire Hotel. He must have borrowed it from one of the waiters. The rest had been easy. She'd often dined in the Grill Room of the Shropshire; she knew the head chef well. When she'd rung him he'd been happy to pass on what little he knew about his porter—or ex-porter, as it turned out. Rinaldi was going to be another kettle of fish.

'I don't know anything about him,' he said flatly.

'You must have references for your staff, some idea of who they are and where they've worked before you take them on.'

'What he did before he came to me is not my concern.' Rinaldi said. He was wearing a dressing-gown with a high satin collar. On the desk in front was a tray with the remains of his breakfast. 'You ask a lot of questions,' he said. 'I don't like that. Tom Shaughnessy worked for me for a few weeks and then he moved on. That's all I know.'

'Was he sacked?'

'No, he handed in his notice.'

'Then why did you try to have him beaten up last night?' she enquired sweetly.

'It's news to me,' Rinaldi replied. He gave a little smile. They both knew what he was doing. Some smart-arsed solicitor had told him that he was always safe as long as he denied everything. He was just carrying out the order.

'I was there, Mr Rinaldi,' she said evenly. 'I saw it happen.'

The figures on the screen had formed into the shape of a flower and were folding and unfolding themselves in time to the music. Somewhere in the back of her mind she registered that this was *Gold Diggers of 1933*; one of the classics.

'Then you are also probably aware that he owed me money,' Rinaldi said, taking his eyes off the dancers.

'I'm not aware of how much.'

'A great deal.'

'You say you know nothing about this man but you're prepared to lend him money?' Patricia didn't go as far as to sound sarcastic but if the Governor of the Bank of England's post fell vacant she was letting him know that she wasn't recommending him for it.

Rinaldi shifted round in his chair. He put his hands together, the two thumbs lifted, and regarded her thoughtfully. Then he turned towards the projector. 'Take a hike, Sylvester. I'll call you when I want you.'

The man left the room. As his bulk silhouetted in the doorway she recognized him from the night before.

'Is he in trouble?' Rinaldi asked when they were alone.

'What makes you say that?'

Reaching across he took a piece of red plastic from the drawer of the desk and tossed it down in front of her. 'Do you know what that is?'

'It's a gambling chip.'

'It's a fake gambling chip,' he corrected.

She picked it up and examined it in the half-light. 'Are you telling me that Shaughnessy made this?'

'Someone did. He came to me about ten days ago asking for money. When I wouldn't give it to him he passed off some of those on the cash desk.'

'How many?'

'Fifteen. About five thousand pounds' worth. He got one of the girls to pull it for him or we'd have stopped him at the door.'

'Did he say what he wanted the money for?'

'He told me he had a scheme worked out but he wouldn't say what. I couldn't help him if he wouldn't level with me, could I?'

'No,' she said. 'I suppose not.'

Rinaldi seemed pleased that she saw it his way. He sat back in his chair and spread his elbows on the armrests. In the dark she could see the whites of his eyes glimmering. 'He was a nice boy.' He sounded faintly aggrieved. 'Different to the others here. I had him on the bar when he first came but that was a waste. The punters liked him, you see. He was well spoken, educated. I moved him out to the door. That's a good job. You can pick up easy money at the door. But he never intended to stay. I could tell. He had another life out there somewhere. It was just a matter of time before he went back to it.'

On the screen a troupe of girls with strong legs and crinkly blonde hair was dancing. 'Petting in the park—bad boy…' their voices sang in chorus while their button-over shoes clattered along with the rhythm.

Patricia waited. When Rinaldi offered nothing more she asked, 'How do you know this?'

'Small things he said. People he talked to…'

He knew something. She could see it in his eyes, in the slight smile as he watched her but he wasn't letting on.

Opening her bag, she took out her chequebook and spread it on the table. 'I'm going to pay you what you are owed, Mr Rinaldi. In return I want you to tell me what you know about Tom Shaughnessy.'

'Like I said, I don't know anything about him.'

'Five thousand pounds was it?'

Rinaldi watched her writing. 'It was more than that,' he interrupted. 'Five thousand was just an approximation.'

'How much more?' She wasn't going to haggle with this man.

'I can't remember exactly.'

'Shall we say six thousand?' She wrote in the figure before he could up the going rate further and tearing out the cheque she held it up for him to see.

'It was only a feeling I had,' Rinaldi told her, 'nothing solid I can pass on.' He sounded as though he'd been put in an unfair position, offered a bribe he couldn't accept.

'Give it a try.'

'There was someone in here one night who recognized him,' he said after a while. 'I saw them talking together.'

'I imagine a lot of people here got to recognize him.'

'No, this was different. He knew Shaughnessy from the past, seemed surprised to see him. I heard him say so to his friends afterwards.'

'Do you know him?'

Rinaldi's eyes were on the cheque. His tongue licked out, ran round his mouth. 'Beaumont,' he said deliberately. 'George Beaumont. He's a regular here.'

'Do you have his address?'

'It's in the book. But you don't have to bother with that. He works in Christie's. You'll find him there.'

Patricia put the cheque on the desk and stood up. 'Good,' she said. 'I'd like one of your staff to show me out now please.'

'This is dated a week from now,' Rinaldi complained. He had the cheque close to his eyes like a specialist examining a rare document.

'You are going to leave him alone.' Patricia was putting her pen and her chequebook into her bag. 'If I hear that you've threatened him again I shall have it cancelled immediately. Do you understand me?'

The door opened. The blunt figure who had been called Sylvester stood waiting. Rinaldi put the cheque down on the desk top. 'I never said I did anything to him.'

She blinked as she came out into the street. The bad weather of the last few days had cleared away. The sky was clear, Sévres blue, with high cloud, and the air was cold on her cheeks and legs.

She walked round into Regent Street, glad to be out of that stinking hole. Her heart was still pounding and she paused for a moment, leaning back against a pillar-box.

'Are you all right?' a woman asked.

'Yes, fine,' she said and smiled brightly to show she meant it. 'I just felt a little faint.'

It was a reaction. She knew that. She had frightened herself back there in Shanghai Lil's. It was the darkness, the flickering light. Crossing the street, her hands in the patch-pockets of her coat, she walked down towards Christie's. She'd been intending to take a taxi but the exercise suddenly felt good.

George Beaumont was in his mid-thirties. He had fair hair, white skin, and that look of innocent bewilderment that often comes to those brought up on nursery food and nanny's aphorisms.

'Tom Shaughnessy,' he said. 'Yes, he worked here for several years.' He wore a Harvie & Hudson shirt beneath the three-piece pinstripe and there were tassels on his black slip-ons. He stood in the hallway of Christie's fiddling with his biro.

'We were thinking of asking him to help us with some research. I was wondering whether you could tell me a bit about him first?'

'About Tom? Oh sure.' Beaumont did some more of his drum-majorette tricks with the pen and put it away in his upper pocket. 'Why don't we go over the road?' he said. 'I'm dying for a wet.'

'That sounds a good idea.' She assumed he meant for a drink not a liberal member of the Tory Party.

'This is for some programme, is it?'

'That's right.'

'What'll you have?' he asked. The pub was warm and crowded with that bubble of light-hearted conversation that goes with executive pre-prandials and avocado sandwiches.

'White wine, please.'

'What type?'

'Is there a choice?'

'There's Chablis,' he said. 'That's Algerian wine. Or there's Soave, that's Algerian wine with lemon juice in it. Or there's German Reisling, that's the same as the others with a sugar lump.'

'I'd better have Chablis.' She laughed at his description and he smiled back at her shyly. He was wet as yesterday's lettuce but impossible to dislike. While he went off to the bar, Patricia sat at a table by the window and wondered how the accounts department was going to take to a six-thousand-pound expense slip. In her first series that was as much as the budget for an entire programme.

'You couldn't have picked a better man,' Beaumont told her as he returned. He put her wine down on the table, carefully arranging a mat beneath it. 'Tom was a wizard with the paintings, taught me everything I know.' He gave a little laugh and cocked his glass at her. 'And I mean that as a compliment. Cheers.'

'Why did he leave?' she asked.

'I don't know. He was doing well, really well I mean. There was talk of making him a director. Then he just left.'

'He didn't give a reason?'

'None. But he didn't talk about that kind of thing. He talked about everything else—he's Irish after all—but not about himself much.' Beaumont gave a little chuckle and drowned it in gin and tonic. 'I don't think he liked the job much. They had the devil of a job getting him to wear a suit. He used to turn up with a top that didn't match the trousers and so on. But he was a genius with paintings. He could recognize an artist's style at a glance. It was like he was psychic. Steam engines too.'

'Steam engines?'

'He had this thing about model steam engines,' Beaumont said. 'He used to buy them at auctions and do them up. There were always bits and pieces of them lying around his desk. Then he'd sell them again. He liked doing that. I think it was the Irishman in him. He preferred making a bit on the side to earning his real salary.'

Patricia sipped at her drink. 'What makes you think he didn't like his job?'

'It was things he used to say,' Beaumont explained, then amended it. 'More like the way he said them. It's hard to explain. You had to know him.'

'I think I can imagine.'

'He had a sort of contempt for the whole business.' Beaumont was trying to put his finger on it. 'When he had a picture by a complete unknown he'd sometimes invent a name for the artist. And he'd add titles into the catalogues, long titles with quotes from Victorian poetry. It amused him to play games like that. He had a whole family of artists that he invented in the end. People believed him. They're in the dictionaries now: dates, biographies, the lot.' He paused, suddenly embarrassed. 'I'm sorry, I can't believe you want to hear all this.'

'No, please,' she said. 'I'm fascinated.' And she was too. This was the first time she'd discovered anything real of Tom Shaughnessy.

'The place isn't the same without him, I can tell you that.'

'Do you know what he's doing now?' she asked lightly. She couldn't resist the test but as she expected Beaumont shook his head. 'I've no idea.'

She smiled in private satisfaction. Men never split on each other. It's the code. 'He's probably working somewhere else in the art world.'

'Not if he has to wear a suit he won't be.'

Chapter 14

In the nineteenth century the big paintings that went on exhibition at the Paris Salon were called 'machines'. It was just a word. But like so many of those words, it wasn't inappropriate, as paintings have a great deal in common with machines. They work to a system. The colour, the line and form have to be harnessed together to make it work in much the same way as the component parts of an engine. It might have been for that reason that Tom Shaughnessy understood them so well.

As he worked on *The Triumph of Bacchus* he was constantly making new discoveries. Small things: the way the movement of an arm was reflected in the swirl of a dress, the way the colour of a jewel was picked up and repeated across the canvas. There was an ingenuity to the painting that fascinated him.

'Look at this,' he said one afternoon. He pointed to where a bonfire was burning in the distant mountains. There was a trickle of smoke above and three figures standing around it. They were no bigger than ants.

'He's invented that bonfire to get a touch of red paint into the blue of the mountains,' he said. 'It's how the whole picture works. Wherever there are warm colours he puts a cold one beside it, wherever there are cold colours he finds a reason to put in a note of warmth. It keeps the whole thing alive.'

Scobie peered at the minute detail. 'You'd hardly notice it there.'

'It's just the logical conclusion to the sequence.'

Over the last few days he'd come to understand the painting in a way that you would never achieve by standing and looking at it in a gallery. In the past, when he had copied old master paintings, he had told himself he did it for the money, or the satisfaction of knowing that he could fool those who should know too much to be fooled. But there was more to it than that. He copied a picture because he wanted to know it, deeply and intimately, as he had known the places where he had been brought up, as he had known the bodies of the women he had loved.

He was becoming a little obsessed by the thing. He knew that.

When he wasn't actually working on it he thought about it constantly, calculating the techniques he would use. Before going to sleep he would lie awake mentally rehearsing what he was going to do the next day. Much of the procedure he had now resolved but there were aspects of the painting that still evaded him.

'It's that silvery appearance of the women's flesh,' he told Scobie a few days later. 'It's there in every Titian but I can't for the life of me work out how he did it.'

'It must be something that makes the colour cold. Have you tried using a very dark red lightened with a great deal of white? That would cool it off.'

'It comes out too chalky.'

Scobie took a pull at his beer. They were sitting by the window in the Roland. It was dark outside. A wind had sprung up, occasionally rattling the glass panes to remind them that it was winter. 'Is it that important?' he asked. 'Can't you just fudge it?'

'Not for anyone who knows anything about Titian. It's very distinctive. The whole quality of the painting is in the colour.'

'I'm damned if I know how it's done, Tommie.'

'I'm beginning to run out of new techniques to try.'

Scobie took his glass from his lips, keeping it close so that it could be reinserted at a moment's notice and studied him. 'You should take a bit of time off, Tommie. You look knackered.'

He felt it too. The lethargy that comes when only the mind has been exercised was beginning to grip him. He slept hard at night but woke with a stiff neck and a headache that lingered half the morning.

'I just need a bit of fresh air,' he said. 'I might go for a run later.'

'You don't like running.'

'The alternative is to join one of those posh squash clubs but the membership takes nine months to come up, which slightly defeats the purpose.'

Getting to his feet he went over to the bar. 'Any chance of anything to eat, Dave?'

'Kitchen's closed after ten.'

When you've had nothing but a piece of cheese and a couple of biscuits all day that's not a good answer. 'How about some sandwiches?'

'I'll have a word with the chef.' Dave put his head round the door. Chef was just a smart word he liked to use for his wife who performed the necessaries with the frying pan and sat in the back room watching television in the meantime. When he returned he said, 'I could do you egg and chips if you like.'

'Throw in a sausage and you've got a deal.'

'I'll bring it over.'

Shaughnessy went back to the table. A group was playing darts, shouting out the scores loudly when they were high, only mentioning them when they weren't.

'I see you put some work into that portrait of Princess Di,' he said to make conversation. Scobie had been in low spirits that evening, drinking with the steady dedication that comes to men who are thinking about something they want to forget.

'I knocked a bit of sense into it last night,' he agreed. 'I might have got it finished if Jean hadn't shown up.'

'Jean?'

'She walked in while I was working.'

'What prompted that?'

'The usual,' he said flatly. 'She wants money.'

Living on his own the way he did it was easy to forget that Scobie was married. In all the years Shaughnessy had known him he had only met his wife twice, a straight-backed woman with a commanding appearance as he remembered it and a strange way of nodding her head while you were speaking as though she already knew what you were going to say and didn't believe it.

'Any reason in particular?' he asked.

'She says the car needs repairing but I reckon she saw

that article in the *Evening Standard*, thinks I've had a windfall, and has come round to see if she can get her hands on a bit of it.'

A week back a portrait by Scobie had been unveiled in one of the livery halls. It had warranted a few lines in the Press.

'How much does she want?'

'Two thousand quid.'

'Expensive car repair.'

'I haven't got it,' Scobie said. 'Christ, if I had that sort of money I'd have loaned it to you when you asked. You know that.'

'What are you going to do?'

'I told her to go to hell. Not very subtle.' Scobie stared across the pub in recollection. 'I don't know, I could try to get an advance from the artillery I suppose.'

For all his rantings on the subject, Scobie needed his marriage if only to give himself the chance to be rebellious. He had once told Shaughnessy that what hampered his career as a young man was that he'd wanted to be an artist more than he wanted to paint pictures. A difficult wife was part of the necessary paraphernalia as much as the beard, the pictures of sugar-frosted nudes, and the frequent, and nowadays generally futile, attempts to seduce the model. But, beneath the bluster the old fellow seemed genuinely distressed and so Shaughnessy said, 'I could lend you a thousand.'

'Could you?' Scobie lowered his glass and looked at him with new interest. Then he waved the idea away. 'You need that money more than me at the moment.'

'It's up to you. I could spare it if it would help.'

Scobie thought about it for a few minutes before accepting. 'I'll pay it back in a week or so.'

'Think of it as rent on the studio.'

Dave came over with his supper. As he was eating, Scobie said, 'You haven't just been working though, have you?'

'How's that?'

'Last night. You were out.'

'Is that a crime?'

'You were with Patricia Drew again, right?'

'Any objections?' Shaughnessy paused, the fork in midair. Scobie appeared to have several objections but he was keeping them to himself.

'That's the second time.'

'Third if you count that dinner at the Middle Temple.'

'You're playing with fire,' Scobie said gruffly.

'Maybe.' He pointed the fork at him. 'I've always been an arsonist at heart.'

'He worked in Christie's for six years and left suddenly with no explanation,' Patricia told the two men. 'He was doing well—probably due for promotion to the board of directors—and then he threw it away. That was two months before the first of these paintings was taken.'

Barraclough gave a little grunt to indicate that he took the point. He was sitting with his elbows planted on his desk. The jacket of his blue pinstripe was off, the felt braces digging into beefy shoulders.

On the last two occasions that Patricia had spoken with him they'd met over lunch in a restaurant but this time Barraclough had insisted she came to his office. She had the impression he wanted the event put on a formal footing, the fixture logged in official diaries.

'It's an interesting coincidence of dates,' he said bluntly. 'But I can't see it's more than that.'

'Since he left he has had a few part-time jobs, none of them connected to the art market. He's just drifted about.'

By the high sash window, David Ambrose was staring down into the street as he listened. Without turning from the view he said, 'He openly told you that he wants the reward the Italians are offering, did he?'

'At first he said he worked for Customs and Excise. I wasn't sure whether to believe him. When I challenged him he changed his mind and said he wanted the money.'

'I would have thought he'll be lucky to get it.' Barraclough gave a little burp of humour.

'He's convinced he can trace it before the police.'

'He seems convinced of a great number of things.'

There was a knock on the door. They looked round. It was Barraclough's secretary with a tray of tea. She put it down on the desk and withdrew in silence and a whiff of scent.

For a moment Patricia thought Barraclough was going to ask her to be mother. He looked at the tray and then at her but he thought better of it. Pouring out three cups, his left index finger planted daintily on the ivory knob of the silver pot, he handed them around.

'How did you come to meet this man?' Ambrose asked. He took one sip at his tea and put the cup and saucer down on the mantelpiece. He had spent some time adding lemon and stirring the contents but he didn't actually want the tea. He was just going through a formality. 'I'm sorry, you've probably been over this with Gerald.'

'He came to the studios and went through my files when no one was in the office.' She didn't tell them of the bomb hoax. It would only be a distraction.

'You realize he could be doing exactly what he says,' Ambrose remarked. He gave a quick smile to acknowledge that it was bad manners to contradict a lady. The smile didn't touch his eyes.

'I don't think so,' Patricia said. 'The reward he was talking about was only offered last week. Whatever he's doing has been planned for some time.' She gave him back his smile as she spoke, a perfect mirror reflection: white teeth and no warmth.

'Do you think he is involved with the theft in some way?' Barraclough asked.

Patricia didn't answer immediately. She'd put a lot of thought into the question. Every instinct in her body told her that Shaughnessy was concealing his true intentions. And yet there were aspects of his behaviour that she couldn't explain.

'I'm sure he wants something other than the reward money,' she said carefully.

'But is he resourceful enough to have carried off these ransoms?' Barraclough asked. 'It's a considerable undertaking.'

'Yes, I think so. He's very capable.'

Barraclough drank his tea. The cup was bone china but in his huge fist he managed to make it look like a mug.

'Have you seen him since that dinner?' he asked.

'Yes.'

She didn't know why she'd allowed herself to go out with Tom Shaughnessy. It was foolish and very short-sighted. There was no future in it and she had already resolved not to see him again. He was using her, she was sure of it, searching for feminine weaknesses to exploit. But when she was with him she felt excited, invigorated. He made her laugh and if she was honest with herself she found him dreadfully attractive.

Barraclough was watching her with interest. 'What did you do on these occasions?'

'We went round the National Gallery one time.' She gave a little shake of her head. There was no need to explain herself. 'He's extraordinarily knowledgeable about paintings. I know a lot of people who have studied art but he is quite different. It's as though he knows them.'

'You're impressed.'

'Yes, I am.'

'Because a boy from the back streets of Dublin can become knowledgeable about such things?' The gimlet eyes bored into her.

'No, because he is so…in tune with his subject. It's very rare.'

Barraclough shifted in his chair. 'It sounds as though Mr Shaughnessy is wasting his talents. You've told the police, I assume.'

'I have. I think they found it rather circumstantial for their liking. That's why I thought I should keep you informed.'

Ambrose glanced at his watch and held out his hand. 'I must go,' he said. 'Good of you to keep me informed,

Gerald. No, don't get up, I'll see myself out.' He turned back to Patricia. 'I'd be interested to meet this Mr Shaughnessy. Maybe you could arrange it? Why do you smile?'

'I hadn't intended to see him again.'

'That would be a waste,' he said. 'Your relationship with this man is extremely valuable. You must encourage it.'

Chapter 15

'I can't believe she's going to do it,' Scobie said. 'I just can't believe she would be such a bitch. I mean, where am I going to live? Where am I going to work, for God's sakes? If I can't work I won't have any money at all and where will that get her?'

It was a lot of questions to answer at once. 'Did you tell her you were sending some?' Shaughnessy asked.

'Of course. I told her a thousand quid was on the way and I'd send on the rest as soon as I had it but she wasn't listening. It was going up for sale and that was final.'

'It could be a threat.'

'Do you think so?'

Shaughnessy didn't think so for a moment. The announcement that Scobie's wife was putting his studio on the market hadn't come in the heat of an argument. It had been conveyed formally in a solicitor's letter that morning. There was an ominous certainty about it. But he didn't want to depress the old fellow, so he said, 'It's possible.'

'She's sending an estate agent round to value the place.' Scobie didn't sound convinced either.

It was Friday afternoon. They were in the Steam Museum on Kew Bridge. Normally the machines wouldn't be running but maintenance work was being carried out on the Eames & Amos compound engine. It was now turning over, slowly and majestically, with that wonderful silence that was shattered with the invention of the combustion engine.

On the balcony above Shaughnessy's two boys were leaning over the railings to view it from a different angle. They were due to go away to stay in the country for the weekend. Shaughnessy wasn't sure where but it must be somewhere pretty grand to warrant the afternoon off school. Angela couldn't be there to pick them up from the station so he had done it, bringing them here to this favourite haunt in the meantime.

'But can she just sell it like that?' he asked. 'Without your agreement?'

'That's the worst of it. She can. It belonged to her father. I've never had it changed into my name.'

Shaughnessy had only the vaguest of biographies of Scobie's marriage but he knew that his wife was the daughter of his drawing master at the Slade. Scobie had got her in the family way on a sketching trip to Dorset after the war and for that he had found himself in church twice in quick succession: once for a hasty marriage and then again for the christening of a boy who later disappointed him by becoming a highly paid advertising executive.

'She thinks I'm rolling in the stuff,' Scobie complained. 'Just because she sees I've got a few commissions on hand she thinks I'm coining in the cash and hiding it under the bed.'

'It's a fair assumption.'

'She's an artist's daughter, for Heaven's sakes. She should know how hard it is to making a good living out of painting.'

'Is the train running today?' Jamie asked. He arrived at that moment with his younger brother, both breathless from charging around the museum.

'I don't know, you'll have to ask.'

Scobie watched them tear away again. 'It's just spite,' he said. 'If Marjorie hadn't been in there when she arrived I don't think she would have done it.'

'You weren't up to your tricks, were you?'

'The chance would be a fine thing. I was working on that damned portrait.'

'It's hardly grounds for divorce.'

'Jean knows all about models. She's the daughter of one herself.'

Was she, by God. Shaughnessy watched the heavy beam lifting and falling on its Doric columns. It was a beautiful piece of machinery, the product of a golden age when every question could be answered, every problem solved. Steam lifted away from the wooden-clad cylinders, floating up past the window.

'That's it,' he said.

Scobie looked round the room. 'That's what?'

He pointed to the wisps of steam. 'Do you see how the colour changes as it goes up the wall? When it's in front of the shadows it looks almost blue, then when it reaches the window it turns brown.'

'Tindell's effect,' Scobie said.

'You know it?'

'Of course. The colour of any semi-translucent surface is affected by the tone of the ground beneath.' He recited the scientific theory. 'In the old days when a woman wore a white veil over her face it made the skin beneath look slightly bluish.'

'You've known this and you didn't tell me?'

'You didn't ask. What's so great about it?'

'It's what I've been looking for,' he said. 'That's how those flesh tones work in the painting.'

It was after five by the time they dropped off the boys and got back to the studio. Shaughnessy switched on the spotlights and took out one of the studies he'd made earlier. It was of Ariadne's forearm.

'I've been trying to modify the colour,' he said. 'That was the mistake. It's two tones of the same one. The lighter floated very thinly over the other.'

He mixed the pinkish colour of the flesh, making an identical match with the study. Then he added a small quantity of white. Thinning the paint with linseed until it was wet and runny on the palette he spread it across the flesh of the forearm.

At once the colour appeared to cool, turning to the delicate silvery colour.

'It's just like the steam,' he said. 'The moment a darker colour shows through, the temperature lowers. If I rub away some of the paint the undertone becomes dominant again, the flesh turns slightly darker and slightly warmer, and that automatically produces the turning plane. Glaze that with burnt umber and you'd have the full shadow.'

Scobie was looking at it in something approaching wonder. 'That's the damnest thing I've ever seen,' he said.

'I thought you knew about it.'

'I've seen it in nature: smoke and mists and so on. I've never seen anyone try to make paint do the same. How do you think he discovered it in the first place?'

'Who, Titian? He probably put on the wrong colour one day and rubbed it off and saw what happened.'

Removing the cover to The Triumph of Bacchus, Shaughnessy held up the scrap of canvas. 'There,' he said. 'See how it makes the colours around glow.'

'Can you adapt the real thing without major changes?'

'I've just got to drop the flesh colour by a tone and then lift it again. It won't take long. Now that I know what to do I can put it in pretty quickly.'

A voice behind them said, 'Oh, I do beg your pardon.' They turned around.

A young man had come into the studio. He stood poised by the door, uncertain. 'I'm frightfully sorry,' he said, 'I didn't realize anyone was in here.'

There was a moment's silence. Then Shaughnessy asked, 'How did you get in?'

'I was given a key. I assumed the place was empty.' He was a thin young man in his twenties with those weak, pinched features that mothers like to call sensitive.

'What do you want?' Shaughnessy asked.

'I've come to look the place over; measure it up for our brochure. But I can come back another time if you like.'

'No, it's no problem,' he said. 'We didn't know you were coming.' He moved away from the easel.

'It is the right place?' The young man was shuffling through his briefcase. 'Mrs Woods…She asked us to put the place on the market for her. I am in the right place?'

'You are.' Shaughnessy took the papers he was offered and put them down on the table away from the main studio.

'I called in on the way back from work,' the young man said. Over his shoulder Shaughnessy saw Scobie fitting the cover back on the painting.

'How long will it take?'

'Just a few minutes. I just need to check the place over, take a few measurements and that's it.'

As he flitted about the studio with his tape measure, Scobie drew Shaughnessy aside.

'Did he see it, do you think?'

'He must have. The question is whether he knows what he's seen.' Going over to the dresser Shaughnessy took out the bottle of whiskey. 'Can I give you a drink?' he asked.

The young man put his head out of the kitchen. 'It's a bit early for me, actually.'

'If you're on your way back home…I'm sorry I don't know your name.'

'Dodds.'

'A nip of whiskey is just what you need on a night like this. Keeps out the cold.'

'It is pretty parky,' Dodds agreed, taking the glass he was offered.

'A place like this,' Shaughnessy asked, 'is it worth anything?'

Dodds sat down. 'Oh, absolutely. These converted Victorian studios go for a lot. Cheers.'

'Converted?'

'Well, of course it will have to be opened up. A new kitchen and bathroom to begin with.'

'You can't do that to it,' Scobie said, joining them at the table. 'This place has been used by artists since it was built. Hayward Scott-Jones used to work here.'

'Did he, by God?' Dodds was impressed. 'Who's he?'

'A portrait painter in the thirties,' Shaughnessy said, refilling Dodds's glass. 'Quite well known in his day.'

'Oh, really?' he said. 'I don't know much about art and all that I'm afraid.'

'But you reckon the studio will get a good price, do you?'

'Oh, a hundred and twenty grand no trouble at all. If you don't mind dropping a bit lower I could shift it in a matter of days. It's got character, that's the important point: gallery, wood-panelled walls.'

'You noticed the panelling.' Shaughnessy was amazed by his observation. 'I'd never have seen that unless it was pointed out to me.'

'First thing I saw when I came in.' Dodds gave a quick feminine smile. He was feeling more relaxed now. The whiskey had raised two spots of pink on his cheeks.

'It's extraordinary how people see different things in a room,' Shaughnessy went on. 'You spotted the panelling. That's because you're trained to look at the fabric of a building. Now I'm an art historian. The first thing I see in a room are the pictures. But I'll bet you hardly even glanced at them.'

'Not at all.' Dodds didn't want to be written off as a philistine. 'I saw them too. Jolly good they look. Did you do them then?' he asked Scobie.

'Most of them.' Scobie was contemplating the fate of his studio.

'The picture on the easel for example,' Shaughnessy said. 'Did you see what that was?'

'Gosh, let me think.' Dodds was entering into the spirit of the game now. 'It's bluish, isn't it.'

'It has a bit of blue,' Shaughnessy agreed. 'With some naked-looking people.'

'Just one.'

'Are you sure?' Dodds went and looked at the painting. 'Oh, yes,' he said. 'So it has. I could have sworn there were more.'

'Deceptive, isn't it?'

Dodds gave a little frown. 'It's odd,' he agreed.

'Let me give you a refill.'

'I'm not keeping you from anything?'

'It's good to have the company.'

Chapter 16

There are theories as to what is the fastest way to be woken up. Some say it's with an alarm clock, others from a sudden drawing of the curtains. But there's nothing to beat a glass of water in the face, as Shaughnessy discovered the next morning when it hit him.

He sat up with a jerk, water running down on to his chest. For a moment he was wide awake, senses alert. Then the dull thud of the hangover swept over him and he lay back with a groan.

'Holy Mother and all the saints. What did you have to do that for?' Speaking wasn't easy. During the night his tongue had turned into a small furry mammal that didn't have much room in his mouth to manoeuvre. He rolled over into a sitting position, his feet hitting the floor with a crash.

'I tried shaking you but it didn't have any effect,' Patricia said. She sounded disapproving. Putting the glass back in the kitchen she came and stood in front of him.

Shaughnessy straightened up, combing his hair from his face with his fingers. That was a mistake, the light got into his eyes and made a nuisance of itself.

'Do you always sleep on the sofa?' she asked.

'It's the fault of the architect,' he told her. 'He designed the bedroom too far from the door. If he'd put it a bit closer I'd have made it.'

He opened his eyes and looked up at her. She was dressed in a stylish tweed jacket and blue jeans tucked into soft suede boots. Around her neck was a silk scarf and her hair was tied back in a pony-tail. He'd seen people like her in advertisements on the back page of *Country Life*.

'I'd better make you some coffee,' she said. 'You don't have any Coca-Cola in the fridge I suppose?'

'I don't have a fridge.'

'It's the best thing for a hangover.' She had that brisk tone that women assume in the face of masculine weakness.

'You have the same problem, do you?'

'It's the glucose,' she said. 'It gets the metabolism going. And no, but I have three brothers.'

Getting to his feet he went over to the kitchen and leaned on the side of the door. The kettle was boiling. Patricia was bending over the sink to clean a cup. God, she was a sight for sore eyes, even for eyes that weren't sore come to think of it.

'How did you get in?' he asked.

'Your door was open. It wasn't difficult. Shouldn't you be getting ready? We're due in the country in an hour.'

'Which country?'

She smiled despite herself. 'We've been invited down to the country for the day. Didn't I tell you?'

'No, you didn't.' She might have been invited down to the country, he couldn't believe he had. 'What do we want to go there for, it's full of mud and stinging nettles.'

'The fresh air will do you good. Now if you don't hurry we'll be late.'

He took a bath and then shaved in cold water. It's one of the best ways to clear your head. She had a cup of coffee and a couple of aspirins ready when he emerged. They must have been hers, he didn't have any in the flat.

As they came out into the street she ran her hand along the wing of her car. 'Look,' she said with satisfaction. 'Good as new and it didn't cost me a penny.'

'How did you manage that?'

'The attendant in the studio car park did it for me in his spare time.'

He could believe it. Men will do a great deal for a smile of gratitude from a beautiful woman. It's a substitute for a deeper and generally more complicated relationship.

They headed out west on the Hammersmith flyover. It was a clear, cold morning, the sunshine glowing on the trees along the river bank.

'You'll have to map-read when we get to Winchester,' she told him.

'Don't you know where we're going?'

'I know where we're going, not how to get there.'

She was in one of her logical moods. It was best not to comment on the situation. He stared out of the window and wondered why he had to be taken down to the country for the day. It wasn't for his health.

She asked, 'What was the celebration last night?'

'A friend of mine is leaving the block,' he said vaguely. 'We were having a few for old times' sakes.'

'Is that Mr Woods?'

He looked at her in astonishment. 'How did you know?'

'That was the number that I had the first time I rang, remember?' She smiled at her cleverness.

Shaughnessy thought: It's all there. Everything she sees and hears is filed away in that head of hers.

He ran his hand round the back of his neck, massaging the muscles. The one consolation was that if he was feeling rough it would be nothing to what that estate agent was feeling. The last they'd seen of Dodds had been when they bundled him into a taxi at one in the morning. They'd had to go through his wallet to find his address. He'd forgotten it—just as he'd forgotten everything else, with luck.

'You made it then,' Ambrose said, coming to meet them. 'Good to see you. Had trouble getting out of London, did you?'

'There was a bit of traffic on the motorway,' Patricia agreed. She shook hands with him, at the same time reaching up to give him a peck on the cheek. An interesting combination, Shaughnessy observed: half social, half business. Rather what he'd thought.

'But you managed to find us?'

'We followed the sound of the guns.' They were standing in this enormous field, frost following the pattern of the shadows. The drive must have just finished. Dogs were wagging about picking up fallen birds, the guns had assembled by the trailer. In the distance the beaters were emerging from the woods and trickling away to the left.

'Do you shoot, Mr Shaughnessy?' Ambrose asked as they joined the other guests.

'I have done a little.'

'You should have brought a gun.' He wore a green Loden cape over his shooting suit. It was held in place by cross-straps so that it could be pushed back off his shoulders when he swung the gun.

'That would have made it rather expensive.'

Ambrose caught his meaning because he said: 'Ah yes, well, maybe I could have lent you one. It hasn't been a bad day so far.'

'For you or the birds?'

Ambrose gave a quick smile. It was just a spasm, as though an electric current had been run momentarily through his facial features. 'Do you object to blood sports, Mr Shaughnessy?'

'How can I?' he said tonelessly. 'I've always been turned on by girls in leather mini-skirts.'

Ambrose ignored his flippancy. 'I've always consoled myself that nothing creative has come from a non-military nation.'

Shaughnessy waited until he had moved away to talk to his other guests before saying, 'You realize who he is?'

'Yes,' Patricia replied. 'He's the chairman of a Lloyd's agency.'

'Not a Lloyd's agency—*the* Lloyd's agency.'

There was a glint of malicious pleasure in her eyes. 'I thought you'd like to meet him.'

'I was hoping James Trevelyan might be able to join us today,' Ambrose told them at lunch. It was held in a large barn overlooking the valley. On the far side stood a Queen Anne house, red brick and white stuccoed windows, half cloaked in beech trees with a swath of lawn flowing out below. There are bits of Hampshire that were created to have houses like that standing on them. It's hard to imagine what the countryside looked like before they arrived.

'But he had other plans,' Ambrose went on. 'I have a feeling his wife might have been some influence there. I'm not sure she takes to this sort of sport.'

She wasn't the only one, Shaughnessy observed to himself. He'd spent the morning standing in one freezing field after another watching the pheasant population being thinned out. He drained the glass of Bloody Mary that had conveniently been put out in the entrance when they came in.

'Hair of the dog?' Patricia enquired.

'Beats Coca-Cola.'

The other guests were sprawled around them on the hay bales, discussing the day's sport, apologizing for poaching shots off each other's heads. A handsome woman in knee breeches and a dashing trilby hat was dispensing stew from a casserole that had been kept warm in a straw box.

'This is delicious,' Patricia said dutifully as she ate.

'You must tell Octavia,' Ambrose replied. He had hardly eaten himself. 'I sometimes think she gets a little tired of the endless routine of shooting lunches.'

A black Labrador came across and nudged against

his hand. He stroked its ear affectionately for a moment before moving away to talk to his other guests. He was a good host, keeping conversation flowing, adding small self-deprecatory anecdotes of his own when there was a gap. But beneath the surface he was hard as granite, Shaughnessy could sense it.

That morning, to keep his mind off his toes, which were suffering the same fate as Captain Scott's expedition, he had watched Ambrose shooting. You can learn a lot of a man from the way he handles a gun. Some snatch at the shot, others lack the coordination to aim straight. But with Ambrose it had been effortless: the gun rising, following through and bringing down the bird with an ease that comes from practice and the perfect control of mind and body. Not a man to confront in business.

As they came outside after lunch Ambrose said, 'This must be rather dull for you, Mr Shaughnessy. Why don't you take my place for a while?'

'I couldn't do that.'

'It would be a help, as a matter of fact. I have to go back to the house for a few minutes. I don't want to leave a gap in the line.'

'If you're sure.' The beaters had returned and were milling about awaiting orders while the guests finished their port and clambered back on to the trailer.

Shaughnessy took the gun that Ambrose offered him and held it up, running one hand down over the engraved sidelocks. It was a Purdey, one of a pair to judge from the gold plate on the stock.

'I'm number four at present and we're moving up in twos—you probably know the form.' Ambrose took off his cartridge belt and gave it to him. It carried No. 6s in green plastic casings.

'Green cartridges,' Shaughnessy said. 'Are those lead-free?'

It was an old joke which possibly explained why Ambrose didn't appear to hear it.

'If you'd like to get in the Land-Rover,' he said, 'I'll give you a lift.'

'Isn't Patricia coming too?' Shaughnessy asked as they bumped up the track. The sun had thawed out the frost and the ground was now sticky with mud.

'She wanted to walk with the beaters,' Ambrose replied. He changed down a gear and made a grimace. 'Actually, I asked her to walk with them. I was rather hoping we could have a chat.'

'Any particular subject?'

Ambrose flicked on a smile that said he knew bloody well what it would be. 'Patricia tells me you have a lead on the theft of *The Triumph of Bacchus.*'

'I have a few ideas.'

'Enough to earn yourself this reward the Italians are offering?'

'I think so.' He spoke flatly, letting Ambrose make the running. If he wanted something he was going to have to ask for it.

'Isn't that being rather optimistic, Mr Shaughnessy? We have one of the best teams of negotiators working on the case, along with both the Swiss police and the British. What makes you think you can succeed where they haven't?'

'Maybe they're looking in the wrong direction.'

Shaughnessy held the aluminium bar above his head as the car slewed to one side.

'I was wondering whether there isn't a way we could help each other on this.'

'I can't think how.'

Ambrose glanced out across the fields. When he spoke again he came at the subject from a different direction. 'What would your response be if I suggested you work for us?'

'Negative, I imagine.'

'It would mean a guaranteed fee rather than the faint chance of a reward. A smaller figure, I'll grant you that, but more reliable.'

'You mean you'll pay me to tell you what I know?'

'That's putting it rather crudely.'

'What makes you think I have anything worth buying?'

The car had come to a halt at the crest of a hill. Ambrose cut the engine. In the sudden silence he said, 'I think you know something about these thefts, Mr Shaughnessy. Something that you're hiding from the police. I want to know what it is and I'm prepared to pay for it if necessary.'

Shaughnessy climbed out of the car. He opened the breech of the gun and dropped two cartridges into place.

'If you've brought me all the way down here to say that, you've wasted your time. There's nothing I have that could be of the slightest use to you.'

Chapter 17

The M3 motorway was heavy with traffic. Everyone who had a reason to be out of London that day had apparently chosen this moment to return. He tried the observation on Patricia but she killed it before it could develop. To stall any further attempts at conversation she put on a tape. It was Rachmaninov; the third piano concerto. He'd had her down for Mozart, something elegant and tidy rather than this restless music. But maybe it just happened to suit her mood. He should think himself lucky it wasn't Wagner.

He tried a more direct line of question. 'Why did you ask me along today?'

'David Ambrose wanted to meet you,' she said. 'That's understandable, isn't it?'

'I suppose so.' Shaughnessy looked out of the window as another conversational gambit bit the dust. Before leaving, Patricia had spent some minutes in conversation with Ambrose. She'd been uncommunicative ever since. He nodded towards the blue road sign ahead. 'Turn off at the next exit.'

'Why's that?'

'There's something I want to show you.'

She shot him a glance. For a moment he thought she was going to refuse but she flicked on the indicator and dropped into the slow lane.

'What is it?' she demanded as they came down the slip road.

'You'll see when we get there.'

He directed her to a village some ten miles away. On the far side a narrow lane led up the hill. After half a mile it widened suddenly into a deserted yard.

'Is this it?' Patricia asked. There was a note of anxiety in her voice as she peered through the windscreen.

'Park over there,' Shaughnessy said. He pointed to a low red-brick building that was visible in the headlights. It had the blank, shuttered look of a place that hasn't been loved for some time. The ground was rutted and uneven, weeds poking up through areas that had once seen tarmac. Slowly she bumped the car across the surface bringing it to a halt with the bonnet buried in a patch of nettles.

Further along was a large shed, one of those prefabricated affairs of corrugated iron that farmers put up to wreck the rustic appearance of the countryside. Shaughnessy took the key out from beneath a stone and showed it to her.

'High security,' he said.

It was pitch dark inside with the peculiar silence which only comes to large enclosed spaces. He switched on the lights. They were fitted over the work benches and hardly illuminated the place but in the gloom it was possible to see the bulk of ten or more steam trains. They were rusting and delapidated, packed tightly into the shed like cattle waiting for market. The nearest stood only a few feet away, its drive wheels towering above them.

'My God,' Patricia said in a whisper. 'They're enormous. I never realized they were so big.'

'Have you never seen one before?'

'No, I don't think so...not up close. Only toy ones.' She touched the piston rod.

'That's a Pacific 4.6.2,' he said. 'Powerful machines. When they moved off the wheels used to spin on the track. It looked like someone was grinding knives down there.'

Patricia followed him round the back of the train, crossing the track quickly as though walking behind a horse that kicked.

'It's not going to move,' he assured her. 'That thing hasn't gone anywhere under its own steam for thirty years.'

'What is this place?'

'It was one of the old branch-line stations that got the axe in the sixties. It's used for restoring these things now.'

The train he took her over to see was slightly smaller than the others, with a large central drive-wheel and a high dome in the boiler casing.

'This one's special,' Shaughnessy said. 'The Achilles class 4.2.2. Fifty of them were made at the end of the last century but only very few have survived.'

'Why do you keep saying those numbers?'

'It's the combination of the wheels—four little ones up the front, then the two big drive wheels, and another couple behind it.' He ran his hand along the rusted spoke of one wheel. It was solid and substantial: forty-nine tons of cast iron, half of it resting on the central axis. 'Can you smell anything?'

Patricia gave a tentative sniff. 'No, I don't think so.'

'That's because it hasn't been working for seventy years. When it's finished it'll have a particular smell—hot oil, paint, and grease. There's nothing quite like it. It's not a combination of different smells but a single one.'

'I know—like the smell of stables.'

'I guess so.'

Patricia was looking around at the huge silent machines. Women aren't usually interested in engines the way men are but she seemed impressed. 'Are these all yours, Tommie?'

'Only three of them. And together they make up everything I own in the world. I bought them last year just after the divorce. We'd sold the house, you see. I put my share into these. All I need now is another hundred thousand apiece to do them up.'

'Is that what it costs?'

'It's nothing to what they are worth at the other end.'

'Couldn't you borrow it from the bank?'

'I could. But I can't see the point of working myself to death just to make some banker rich.'

'You have to think of it from the banker's point of view.' She gave a little smile. It wasn't much but after the stony silence of the car it was a transformation.

He pulled himself up into the driver's cab. It was small and rudimentary, the firebox opened, the controls cramping the space. He touched them in the dim light that fell through the rectangular window.

'They didn't use pressure gauges in those days. If the thing was going to blow up there was no warning.'

'Maybe that was just as well,' Patricia said. She had clambered up behind him and was brushing the rust off her hands. From the way she was standing he gathered she was trying to decide which was the cleanest area of the cab.

'This one's going to take an age to do up,' he said. 'Everything's welded together with rust. It needs to be stripped down and rebuilt and that takes time and a lot of money.'

'But half a million quid's worth of reward would help, right?' She had cocked her head to one side and was looking at him thoughtfully. 'That is what you've brought me here to tell me, isn't it?'

'Half a million should see me through,' he agreed. 'But it's not the reward money I'm after. You must have realized that. I'm being paid for this one independently.'

She didn't say anything.

'What's the matter? Don't you believe me?'

'How can I believe you?' There was a note of exasperation in her voice now. 'I don't know what you're talking about. Who's paying you?'

'James Trevelyan.'

'To do what?' she asked.

'To find *The Triumph of Bacchus*. What do you think?'

She leaned back against the side of the cab, her hands pressed into the pockets of her jeans. Her eyes searched his face. 'Are you telling me the truth?'

'I am.'

'Promise?'

There was a childlike innocence to the question. He held up two fingers of his right hand. 'Scout's honour.'

She didn't like the flippancy of that. 'If you're working for Lloyd's why does no one know about it?'

'Because no one has been told. It's been between Trevelyan and myself.'

'So why are you telling me?'

'Because it's safer that you know the truth of it. For the last few days you've been digging around behind my back and coming up with all the wrong answers. It's making my life very difficult.'

'Is it?' She didn't show any sign of remorse.

'The one thing I don't need at present is David Ambrose and his cronies breathing down my neck.'

Patricia had found a rust-free zone of the cab and perched herself on it. She was still looking at him with those clear eyes. 'You should have told me this before.'

He should. And looking back on it he should have told her the rest then and there. It would have saved him a lot of trouble. But it's easy to be clever with hindsight.

'You've made yourself a dangerous enemy in Ambrose,' she added.

'He seems to be under the impression that I'm holding on to some valuable inside information.'

'No,' she corrected him. 'He's under the impression that you are in this up to your neck. Offering you money was just his way of checking that you aren't what you claim to be. It's my fault in a way; I put the idea in his head.'

'You thought I'd nicked these paintings?'

'I suppose so,' she said. 'I wasn't sure. I wanted to believe you were responsible in some way. It was...convenient.'

'For your programme, you mean?'

She nodded and stared away to where the lights were burning on the work benches. 'I need to come up with something good,' she said after a moment. 'If I don't I could be looking for a job by the end of the year.'

'Are you being serious?'

'Never more so. I had a row with my producer last week.'

'There's nothing new in that, is there?' From what he had learnt of Patricia's work she lived in a constant state of war with Gus Armstrong.

'This one was different,' she said. 'He's taken on a new girl on the programme—a little bimbo who used to read the weather reports. He didn't discuss it with me, didn't even mention it. Just went ahead on his own. He says she's there as my assistant but I know him. He wants to change the image of the programme, give it a new style. It's his way of edging me out.'

'He can do that, can he?'

'Gus can do what he likes,' she said bitterly. 'He's distantly related to God.'

'But you must be valuable to them.'

'The ratings were down on my last series. They're still higher than anything else they make, but they were down. That's given him the opportunity to step in.'

Shaughnessy was slightly shocked. He'd thought of Patricia's career as part of her, an extension of her personality.

'We had the most God-awful row,' she said. 'It was terrible. He called me everything under the sun; told me there was no room for stuck-up cows in the media. The worst of it was that we were in one of the recording rooms when it started. Half the studio was listening. It was really...humiliating. Now he's frozen all the programmes that aren't actually being made at present.'

'So this one about *The Triumph of Bacchus* has got to be good.'

'It's got to be sensational.' She crossed her arms, hugging herself as though suddenly chilled to the bone.

'Are you cold?' he asked.

'A bit.'

He took a flask from his back pocket and held it out to her. 'Try some of this.'

She unscrewed the cap and sniffed at the contents before taking a swig, her hair spilling back from her face. He could see the glint of a pearl in her ear and the soft hairs on the nape of her neck. 'That's good,' she said. 'Is it Irish?'

'As St Patrick.'

She took another mouthful and handed it back to him. 'What is the difference between that and Scotch?'

'Irish whiskey has an *e* in it, Scotch doesn't.'

She smiled, dropping her eyelashes as though suddenly noticing how close they were in the cramped space of the cab. 'Aren't Es the preservatives we're meant to avoid?'

'Probably,' Shaughnessy said. 'My grandfather used to drink it and he lived to be ninety-four.'

'Do you always have to make a joke of everything?' she asked. 'Always.' She'd put her head up towards him as she spoke. He kissed her on the lips. For a moment he felt her respond. Then she pulled back. There's a time and a place for everything and he guessed this wasn't either.

'I don't believe you were ever a Boy Scout,' she said as she moved away from him.

'I was too. The court martial was a mistake. The scout master told us to chock up the flag pole; we thought he said chop it up.'

She gave a shake her head but this time she was laughing. 'Oh God, you're a despicable man, Tom Shaughnessy. I should never have let you bring me here.'

'We could get a take-away pizza.'

'I hate pizza,' she said.

It's hard at the beginning; there's so much you have to discover about the other. Patricia had waited until they were in the Talgarth Road before suggesting they went back to her flat for dinner and it took them the rest of the Cromwell Road, the queue at the lights beyond the flyover, and the slow crawl up the Earl's Court Road to agree on a Chinese take-away. She made a vague offer to cook something herself and dismissed it before he could accept. Her cooking was lousy, she told him. There had been a moment in her life when she had had to decide between a course on fine art or cordon-bleu school and her dinner parties had been the victims ever since.

'What do you want to drink?' she asked when they reached her flat.

'I don't know what goes with Chinese.'

'Rice wine, but I'm right out of it.'

He assumed she was joking but you can't be sure with girls who have fitted kitchens of stippled blue to match the saucepans that don't look as though they've ever seen action.

Shaughnessy crouched down to put the foil containers into the oven, forming them up into a well-drilled platoon. Behind him he heard the creak of a cork leaving the bottle.

'White wine,' she said. 'It'll have to do.'

She knelt down in front of him and held out the glass. As he took it she put her hand on his cheek. Her eyes were large and round. She had untied her hair when she came in and it fell across her shoulders, glowing in the light of the oven door.

She looked at him intently, then reaching forwards she kissed him, her lips just brushing his, and sat back again. She glanced aside at the oven. 'What temperature have you put it on?'

'A hundred.'

'How long will it take to warm up?' she asked.

'About fifteen minutes.'

She sipped at her wine and put the glass back on the ground. Her lips were wet. 'If you set it at fifty would it take longer, do you think?'

'A lot longer.'

She turned the knob round and stood up. Reaching out her hands she drew him up after her.

When they reached the living room she stopped him and disappeared into the bedroom, returning with a duvet in her arms. He guessed her intention.

'On the sofa?'

'Do you ever sleep anywhere else?' She was standing close to him, her hips pressed into his. He undid the buttons of her shirt and, as it fell open, his hands went inside, cupping her breasts, feeling the hardness of the nipples in his palms. Putting her arms around his neck she pulled him down on the sofa.

For a long time afterwards they lay together listening to the sound of their breathing. Then she lifted herself on one arm, her hair spilling over her face and touched the bruises on his chest.

'Do they still hurt?'

'Only when you poke them.' The duvet was wrapped round them like a loose tourniquet.

'I cracked a rib a couple of years back playing polo. It took ages to mend.' She traced out the sullen purple marks with her fingers as though they were rare hieroglyphics. 'Have you heard anything more from those men?'

'I paid them off,' Shaughnessy said. 'I owed them some money. That was what they were getting so ratty about. Now they've got it they've decided to give me a reprieve. Why are you looking like that?'

'Nothing,' she said. 'It just reminded me of something I must do tomorrow. Are you hungry?'

'Starving.'

'Me too.' She slipped off him. 'No, you stay there. I'll get it.' She came back from the kitchen with a tray. Arranging mats on the coffee table she laid out the containers.

'I think we've got someone else's order,' she said as she took off the lids.

'It'll probably be better.'

She tested some of it, picking out small pieces and eating them. He hadn't realized until then how erotic the sight of a girl wearing nothing but a pair of chopsticks can be. It's not the kind of thing you'd guess without seeing it.

'Don't you want some?' she asked.

'In a minute.'

She nibbled at a spare rib then licking her fingers she came and knelt beside him. 'If I tell you something do you promise not to be angry?'

'That depends on what it is. If you want to tell me you've forgotten the finger bowls I'm not making any promises.'

'It's not that.' She spoke quickly as though she was worried. 'They searched your flat.'

'Who did?'

'Loss and Security Assessment.' It was the name of the negotiating team who'd presided over the ransoms. She watched him for his reaction.

'I thought something like that might be going on,' he said. 'It was too much to hope that Ambrose had asked me down there just to thin out the bird population.'

'That's why he went back to the house after lunch. One of them came down to see him.'

Shaughnessy found the wine bottle and filled their glasses. He wondered if the British public with their breakfast eggs and their touching faith in democracy had any notion that private armies were financed and directed from offices in the City.

'They're welcome,' he said. 'There's not much they're going to learn from rummaging through my laundry bag.'

'I didn't know they were going to do it.'

He drank some wine. The chill had worn off and it tasted warm and aromatic in his mouth. 'What do you know about them?'

'Loss and Security Assessment?' She put back her head and considered. In the light of the curtained window he could see the silhouette of her body. 'It was started about four years ago by a man called Fothergill. He's ex-SAS, about thirty-five, very efficient.'

'You've met him, have you?'

She shook her head. 'No, I only know him by reputation. He's handled a lot of kidnap cases around the world, usually successfully. It's an impressive record.'

'Strange then that he hasn't managed to recover these paintings in that case.'

'He will do.'

'Why do you say that?'

'He's convinced he'll get them this time. Trevelyan told me so the other day.'

Chapter 18

Sunday morning and London quiet as a mouse. As Shaughnessy crossed the King's Road it was looking strangely provincial with the boutiques closed and the teenagers who cruised them still in bed. He cut up into the residential streets above where curtains were drawn and fat newspapers stuffed into letterboxes. A building had recently been demolished. Scraps of wallpaper and a couple of cast-iron fireplaces were suspended on the one remaining wall. On the second floor someone had scrawled the words, 'Thanks for the stay, sorry we didn't clean the toilet.'

It was just after nine when he reached Inkerman Mansions. He took a bath, shaved, and went up to the studio. Scobie was out of bed but still in his dressing-gown. He'd never had to conform to office hours in his life—one day was much like another—but for some reason he insisted on a lie-in on Sunday mornings.

'Don't look so disapproving,' Shaughnessy said as he came in. 'I was on the sofa again.'

'Serves you right.'

Shaughnessy made himself a cup of coffee and searched for something to eat. He'd had a croissant before leaving Patricia's flat but that hardly counts as breakfast; a croissant is just a bit of wind wrapped in pastry.

'Where did you get to yesterday?' Scobie asked.

'I was down in the country shooting pheasants.'

There was a silence in which Scobie decided that he didn't want to know the reason for this. All he said was, 'Did you bring one back?'

'Not a feather.' The old goat must have been able to see that he hadn't got one. A cock pheasant isn't the kind of thing you can carry about your person unnoticed.

The gallery stairs creaked as Scobie went up to dress. When he returned he had put on corduroy trousers and a white roll-neck sweater that must have spent its youth on the Atlantic convoys.

'I knocked this up for you.' He showed him a scrap of canvas on which he had painted a gradated tone of pink. Over this he had laid a lighter version of the same colour, thinly washed on so that it had been modified by the underlayer into a range of subtle variations.

'Good man,' Shaughnessy said. It seemed an age ago that they were discussing the problem of the flesh tones.

'That's the one you want,' Scobie said. He had pencilled a circle around one area.

'You checked it, did you?'

'I painted it in the National Gallery alongside the Titians.' His voice suggested he had spent his time profitably, unlike some he could mention.

The skin tone of the women's bodies was crimson lake with about a fifteen per cent of yellow ochre. He mixed more than he needed, adding white until it matched the undertone that Scobie had marked on his study. He then divided it into two. Half he set aside for use later, the rest he applied directly to the canvas.

It was not a difficult task, but as with every other stage of the painting the touch had to be right. He kept the paint thick, dragging it over the tooth of the canvas with a soft round brush. Starting in the centre areas of the body he spread it out towards the edges, letting the paint break as it approached the contours. Unlike earlier artists, Titian didn't stress the outlines of the figures. He modelled them in colour and light alone and let the hard edges evaporate.

Pinned on the side of the canvas was a reproduction of Titian's self-portrait—the late one in the Prado. It showed the artist's face in profile, the skin loose, eyes hooded and distant. He liked to have it there as he worked. It helped him to live the part.

It was around mid-morning that he stood back to examine the result. Behind him Scobie was reading the newspapers, the pages spread out on the floor around his chair.

'There were some people looking round here yesterday,' he said. 'The place hasn't been on the market for twenty-four hours and the vultures are in already.'

'Were they interested?'

'Full of ideas. They were going to tear the guts out and turn it into an enormous greenhouse by the sound of it. But I think the stairs put them off. Makes you sick, doesn't it? They spend a fortune on exercise bikes and rowing machines and the bastards are frightened of walking up six flights of stairs.'

'You had everything well covered up, I assume.'

'Of course.'

'You realize we're going to need somewhere else?'

Scobie rumpled the pages of the newspaper together and stood up. 'I know. I was thinking about that. There's Gerry Lampton's place. He never uses it these days. I could give him a ring.'

'Where is it?'

'Down off the King's Road; Glebe Place.'

'Won't he be hanging around all the time?'

'No, he lives down in the country nowadays; paints those flabby little watercolours of his.' The phone rang. Scobie picked it up and passed it across to him. 'It's for you.'

'Collins here.'

He didn't have to give his name. Shaughnessy recognized the voice straight away. It had that short, clipped tone that comes to men who do press-ups in the bathroom.

'I need to talk to you.'

'And now you've had your wish come true.'

There was a moment's silence in which Shaughnessy pictured the pursing of Collins' lips, the orange moustache pushing up into his nostrils.

'Holland Park,' he said. 'Do you know the statue of Lord Holland?'

'I can find it.'

'I'll see you there.'

'What, now?'

'No, not now; in exactly the time it takes you to get there.' It was Collins' turn to make a joke. It was only a little one but you have to remember that when it came to jokes he hadn't had much practice.

There was a cold front pushing over London. The sky was clear and almost colourless, exposing that tricky winter sun which sparkles warmly on trees and grass and drops the temperature below freezing.

Shaughnessy walked right round the park before he found the statue of Lord Holland. It was at an intersection of two paths in the woods.

Collins was sitting on a bench near by. He was dressed in scarf and overcoat, the trilby set at its correct angle on his head. In his hand was a bag of breadcrumbs with which he was feeding the pigeons. It takes years of training to teach a man to blend into his surroundings in this way.

He glanced at his watch as Shaughnessy joined him. He hadn't given a time for their meeting but he probably wanted it for his report sheet.

'How's the painting coming along?' he enquired.

'Well enough.'

'Good.' Collins elongated the word to show that he was indicating encouragement rather than praise.

'I was held up on some technicalities but they're solved now. I'll have it done in a day or so.'

'When will it be ready to use?'

Shaughnessy hadn't wanted to commit himself to a date but he could see the end now. 'Ten days.'

'That's December 12th,' Collins calculated. It didn't sound as though this suited him.

'What's the problem? Have you got something else fixed for that day?'

'It's cutting it fine. We could be hearing from the other side any day now.'

'That's the earliest I can do. You'll just have to stall for time if they contact you before then.'

Collins stared at the bronze statue of Lord Holland. He was an amiable-looking old cove who had lived in an age when it was fashionable to write dates in Roman numerals. You could read his name but you needed a classical education to know when he'd died. Collins slipped his hand into his upper pocket and drew out a passport. 'This is for you.'

It was one of the brown Mickey Mouse affairs that's only good for a year. The photo inside was one that Shaughnessy had given them some months back. It showed him wearing thick-rimmed glasses with his hair dyed black and looking like a raddled version of Buddy Holly. It was issued in the name of Anthony James Fanshaw.

'Fanshaw? What sort of name is that, for God's sakes?'

'Don't forget to sign it,' Collins said. 'And practise the signature in case you have to do it again. Shall we walk?'

He got to his feet without waiting for a reply. Shaughnessy tucked the passport away in his overcoat and followed him. It was damned cold. He could see his breath pushing out ahead and then streaming away behind. 'Did you get the list I sent you?'

'Yes I did.' Collins pointed the tip of his umbrella towards a clump of bamboo. 'They've built a Kyoto Garden since I was last here. Did you know that?'

'Did I know that they'd built it? Or did I know that they'd built it since you were last here?'

'No one told me about it.'

'Really? I must take a look.' Did Collins expect to be kept informed of every change in the London parks? Or was he expressing some deeper grievance at the impermanence of the world around him?

'Yes, I got your list,' Collins said. 'But I still have no clear idea of how you are intending to conduct the ransom.'

'I'll tell you what you need to know when I get back.'

'You'll tell me every last detail when you get back.' Collins corrected his phrasing with the mild manner of a schoolmaster who's heard it all before. 'We can't give you the back-up you need unless you give us your full co-operation.'

'I don't need back-up.'

'We work as a team. You know that as well as I do.'

Shaughnessy paused in the pathway. 'Let's get one thing straight. It's your professional reputation that's at stake here and Trevelyan's career. But it's my skin and that's become very precious to me over the years so we'll play this my way. I'll tell you what I want and you'll do it. No questions, no second opinions. That way we'll make a great team.'

Collins was still holding the bag of breadcrumbs. He took a piece out and held it in his hand. For a moment Shaughnessy thought he was going to eat it but he put it back. Then going over to the litter bin he dropped the bag inside.

Shaughnessy said, 'All I need you to do is to get those things I wrote down and put them in place.'

'Do I take it that you are making some alterations to your original plan?' Collins slapped his hands together to remove the memory of the crumbs.

'Modifications.'

'It's extremely unwise to make hasty changes at the last minute.'

'There're not hasty and it's not the last minute,' Shaughnessy said. 'Don't look so worried. It'll go like clockwork on the day.'

'I hope so. I really hope so.' Collins didn't like plans that were modified. He liked them to be written down and stamped 'Top Secret' before they were locked in a safe. He said, 'You know you've been put under observation?'

'I can't believe I am at present. You wouldn't be talking to me now if you thought I was being followed.'

'They're being briefed later this afternoon,' Collins said. 'That's why it was urgent that I saw you now.'

'Who's "they"?'

'Loss and Security Assessment. Fothergill's team.'

They came out on to the lawn in front of the house. There was a sign saying 'No Ball Games'. Behind it three men were going through a slow and elaborate dance which Shaughnessy took to be the preparation for some martial art. They didn't look like Eastern warriors, more like yesterday's hippies who've discovered a new meaning of life to replace the one they've just worn out.

'Which way are you going?' Collins asked.

'Down into High Street Ken.'

'I'll leave you here in that case,' he said, but neither of them made any attempt to part. The smoke from a bonfire crept across the lawn behind them. Collins said, 'They're very good.'

'I'll see what I can do.'

'You'll have to.' Collins gave a little smile that told him he'd warned him a thousand times. 'This was of your making, Shaughnessy. It was you who wanted it this way.'

'How can I contact you in future?'

'Ring me,' he said. 'From a phone box. I'll find a place we can meet.'

'We can have a party,' Scobie said. 'Once it's sold we can have a party; kick the place to bits.' The idea seemed to give him some pleasure. He stood back from the easel and looked around the studio, picturing the damage a few bottles of Scotch could inflict on the decor once they had got inside his friends. He was painting a still-life of a lemon in one corner of a piece of oil-paper. Whenever Scobie was depressed he made minute studies of objects.

Holding up the brush he said, 'I remember when Eddie Frazer left his studio we had a bender of a party. It was back in the sixties. Everyone was there: Duncan, Dominic Richards, Potty Jones. That was a party. Dominic woke up on one of the girders under Battersea Bridge. He'd been sleeping there all night but the moment he came round he rolled over and fell into the river. The police pulled him out with a boathook. I always thought there was a moral in that.'

'No parties,' Shaughnessy said.

'So long as you're unconscious you're safe. It's when you wake up that things turn bad.'

Shaughnessy was preparing burnt umber on the marble slab, blending it with drying oil. 'No parties until we get this finished. Nothing to draw attention to the place. It's bad enough that we have the upwardly mobiles trying to nest here without your friends moving in as well. And as from now you don't know me outside the studio.'

'Don't know you at all?' Scobie asked. Outside the window seagulls were tumbling around in the wind on the mistaken assumption that Chelsea was a small harbour on the Cornish coast.

'I'm just a neighbour who moved in a few months ago.'

'I hate that sort of play-acting,' Scobie complained. 'I'm no good at it. At school I never got beyond being a shepherd in the Nativity plays.'

'I'll keep out of the Roland for a bit so you won't have to give an Oscar-winning performance.' Shaughnessy was working on the body of Bacchus. It had been modelled in thick scumbles of earth colours: yellow ochre mixed with lead white dragged over an under-layer of burnt sienna. Now with a wide sable brush he added a glaze of umber. Without the addition of white paint it was translucent, a rich stain of brown that darkened the existing colour but didn't obscure it. Initially he put on more than he needed, dropping the skin tone to a chocolate brown. Then he began to remove it with a rag, lifting the light out of the surface like a sculptor carving his forms. In places he scraped the tooth of the paint with a knife so that the glaze caught in the crevices, creating complex half-tones on the border between light and shade.

In the face he worked with a smaller brush, developing the fine nuances of the features. With the paint still wet, he added touches of solid colour into the eyes.

The human eye is built something like a car headlamp. When light strikes it it makes a sharp reflection on the outer surface. It then passes behind the pupil and strikes the inner cone of the iris so that the brightest colour appears on the opposite side to the light source. It is this that lends eyes their appearance of clarity. But in the case of Bacchus there were small additional lights in the near side also, weaker and redder, which gave them a hypnotic stare.

On the teeth he added small highlights, drawing the paint out on the palette and leaving it to dry for an hour so that it was stiff when he put it on, tearing slightly at the pull of the brush.

Later that afternoon he bicycled down to an off-licence in the Fulham Road and bought a bottle of red wine. It was Bulgarian Cabernet Sauvignon. Good stuff. Five years back it was unheard of, now there isn't a supermarket that doesn't carry it. They must have had a lot of it around before they started exporting.

On the way back he took the scenic route, weaving his way through the streets of white stuccoed houses. In a straight stretch of road Shaughnessy pedalled backwards and the chain came off his bike. He spent some time putting it on again and wiping his hands on the patch of grass at the base of a cherry tree. A blue Ford passed him. When he reached Inkerman Mansions the same car was parked further up the road. He'd also seen it at the off-licence.

And that's once too often for coincidence.

Chapter 19

By Wednesday evening the picture was finished and the paint dry. Shaughnessy sat on a stool in front of the canvas and studied it for over two hours. Inch by inch he went over it, checking the drawing of the figures, the intensity of colour, the texture of paint, the touch of the brush, in short everything an expert would be looking for when he first saw it.

When he had finished Scobie did the same.

'What do you think?' Shaughnessy asked when he was through.

'It's good.'

He nodded. It was dark in the studio, the smoke from Scobie's cigarette going through a belly dance routine in the hard white light of the twin spotlights.

'We'd better have it off the stretcher, then.'

Scobie had built a shallow container for the finished canvas. It was similar to the one they'd used to cover it, only larger to cater for the extra area of canvas that had been wrapped around the back.

They cranked out the nails and laid the picture in this flat coffin, smoothing it down over the base and securing it there with waterproof tape.

'I never thought you'd get it so good,' Scobie said.

'Neither did I.' Now that the job was done Shaughnessy felt drained and somehow detached from the whole business. For weeks his mind had been centred on this one task. Without it there was nothing to fill the space. It was like losing a favourite pet.

He mixed a bucket of sculptor's plaster and poured it over the painting, moving around the perimeter and keeping the flow even so that none spilled out. It moved sluggishly across the painted surface, slowly obscuring the brilliant colours. He smoothed it with a piece of wood, working the plaster into the corners of the container.

Scobie said, 'I hope you're right about this.'

'It's the best way.' He straightened up and looked at the slab of damp plaster that encased the picture. 'Don't move it until it's dry.'

'I know that.'

'And for God's sakes don't let it crack.'

'I'm not an imbecile. Leave it with me. I know what to do. You go off and play your games, I'll handle this.'

Shaughnessy went downstairs. When he reached his flat he stopped. There was a strip of light beneath the door. He put his hand on the knob. It was unlocked. Slowly he pushed it open.

The living room was empty, the windows closed. A quick glance round but nothing was out of place. There was a movement in the kitchen. He stepped into the flat quietly, leaving the door open.

A figure emerged. 'I was wondering when you were getting back.'

'Patricia. How did you get in?'

'You leave the key on the ledge outside. I couldn't help noticing last time I was here.'

Shaughnessy closed the door. 'I mean how did you get in from outside?'

'I just walked in. They're watching you, not me. Don't look so shocked, I didn't let them see me.' She tossed the dishcloth aside and with a flourish she picked up the long scarf and fur hat that was lying with her coat on the sofa. 'Disguise,' she said dropping them again. 'Aren't you pleased to see me?'

'Surprised would be more accurate.' He kissed her lightly on the lips. She looked at him reproachfully. He gave her another with slightly more gusto. 'Yes,' he said, 'I am.'

She detached herself and went back into the kitchen. 'There's some dinner in the oven.'

'I thought you couldn't cook.'

'Not made by me, silly. I got it from Sansovino's.' She opened the oven door to check progress. The smell that wafted out must have given the kitchen an inferiority complex.

Shaughnessy said, 'You can't take food away from Sansovino's.'

'You can if you talk to Giulio nicely. He's saved my life at times. Have you got any wine?'

'There's a bottle of Bulgarian lighter-fuel in the cupboard.'

'It's freezing,' she said, taking it out and holding it against her cheek.

'You'll have to stick it up your jumper for a while.'

She peeled off the foil, swearing under her breath as one of her nails was damaged in the operation. 'I tried warming a bottle of wine in the microwave once. It made the most terrible mess. This should be allowed to breathe for a while.'

In the event they drank it while it was still suffocating, along with wafer-thin slices of carpaccio, linguine alla vongole, and a green salad. Afterwards they made love and lay together in the small bedroom. The lights of the alleyway below made orange patterns on the wall that jigged about whenever anyone passed.

'There'd been some hiccup in the market.' Patricia was telling him about how she started in television. 'It had gone up or down in a hurry, I can't remember which. The midday news wanted a comment from the Stock Exchange. I was the only one in the office free at the time and so suddenly there I was splashed across ten million screens. After that they kept ringing me. The media's like that, once they've got your name they hang on to it.'

'And Gus saw you and thought, "That's the one for us"?'

She knelt on the bed, wrapping the duvet around her shoulders like a shawl. 'He took me out to Le Gavroche and suggested we set up a financial programme. He was doing his masterful act, ordering things that weren't on the menu and then sending them back again. I thought he was a real pillock. He kept saying it would be a great success with a huge audience.'

'It was, wasn't it?'

'Eventually. I don't think he believed it at the time. He just wanted to make a pass at me.' There was a clanging of dustbins and the sudden screech of cats in the alleyway below.

'So why did you accept?'

Patricia held up her hair and threw out the other arm in an imitation of a Hollywood publicity picture. The duvet parted, showing off her breasts to their best advantage. In a husky voice she said, 'I wanted to be a star.'

'Seriously.'

'Seriously.' She put back her head and studied the ceiling for a while. She looked very beautiful with that expression of concentration on her face. 'I don't know,' she said. 'I wanted to do something on my own. I felt a fraud in the City. Everybody knew I was my father's daughter. There were always contacts and strings to pull.'

'Handy just the same.'

'Whenever I was offered a new job I could never decide whether they genuinely wanted me or whether they were just hoping I was my father in drag.'

'It's a very convincing act if that's what it is.'

'In the media these things didn't matter. There weren't any strings. Anything I achieved was mine, mine, mine.' She spoke with sudden fierceness, slapping her palms down on the duvet. Then another thought came to her and she smiled. 'Gus wanted me to change my name. He suggested adding my mother's and making it doublebarrelled. But Kotopolous-Drew doesn't sound very good, does it?'

'No, it doesn't. Is your mother Greek?'

'My grandmother was. She kept her name when she got married. It's very complicated. I'm three-quarters English, a quarter Greek, and an eighth Italian.'

'That adds up to more than one person.'

'There's more to me than meets the eye,' she said slyly.

'Quite a bit gets there.'

She curled up beside him again, wrapping the duvet around their shoulders. 'The real reason Gus wanted to change my name was that it didn't sound grand enough for the programme. He's such a snob. Under all that working-class-boy-made-good nonsense he's a crashing snob. My father was furious.'

'Because Gus wanted to change your name?'

'No, because I had given up my job in the City. We had a terrible row about it. He thought I was having an affair with Gus to punish him.'

'Weren't you?'

She took his upper arm and held it to her cheek like a teddy-bear.

'It wasn't so premeditated. It just happened by itself.'

'A flirtation that got stuck in a rut.'

'That's right,' she said seriously. 'That's exactly what it was.'

'Are you going to leave Vanbrugh?'

'Maybe.' She rubbed the tip of her nose. 'Actually, I don't know what I'm going to do.'

'With your qualifications you could open a Greek take-away.'

She took a swipe at him but he caught her wrist. 'Never hit a man who isn't wearing glasses.'

'Why not?'

'He could have contact lenses.'

'You talk such nonsense,' she said. 'I've never known a man talk such nonsense as you.' The last words were lost as she buried her face back in his neck.

'You could go to one of the other channels, couldn't you? They must be itching to have you.'

'I could,' she said, turning her head on his chest. He could feel her body beside his, warm and strong. 'But it must be on my terms. I'm not going to go crawling to them because I've been kicked out of Vanbrugh. I want to make something really good before I leave. You've no idea how hard I've been working in the last few days.'

'Is this on the art thefts?'

'They're going to be begging for me when I've made it. You'll see. It's going to be the best one I've ever done.'

At seven the next morning Shaughnessy went up the street and bought a newspaper. It gave Patricia the opportunity to slip out of the building unnoticed. She left a note propped against the kettle and the cap of her lipstick on the bathroom floor.

Shaughnessy packed a few things into a ruck-sack and strapping it to the back of his bicycle he pedalled up into the Gloucester Road. It was a cold morning. He felt his lips begin to stiffen and the raw sting of pain in his nostrils as he breathed. Crossing the end of High Street Kensington he went into the park.

Flocks of Canada geese stood by the edge of the Round Pond with the resignation of commuters waiting for a train. The sun was coming up behind a bank of distant clouds, seemingly daunted at the prospect of warming this frozen landscape.

As he freewheeled down towards the Serpentine he looked around himself. A woman was exercising two grumpy Pekineses; further away someone was jogging his way towards that elusive healthiness that is required of the modern executive. Apart from them the place was deserted. Private cars are not allowed in the park and a man can't keep up with a bicycle for long.

He was alone.

Without hurrying he made his way along the lakeside, letting himself out at the Knightsbridge entrance. Padlocking his bike to the railings of a bank, he took the tube to Heathrow airport.

There were three women at the British Airways check-in desk. Shaughnessy couldn't pin-point their nationality from their accents but they came from a country where it was acceptable to all talk at once and hold up the queue while they argued over the small print of their tickets. The flight to Geneva was delayed by half an hour. He changed two hundred pounds into Swiss francs and wandered around the shops where you can buy socks and aspirins and pieces of silky underwear if you don't already have them.

After an hour he went and sat in the satellite departure lounge and listened to Domingo singing *La Bohème* on his Walkman. Mimi's consumption had reached the critical point when the flight was announced and they were ushered on to the plane.

At ten thousand feet the clear ultra violet light shone through the oval window and breakfast arrived sealed in a plastic module. Beside him a businessman was making diagrams of his marketing strategy. Shaughnessy sat back in the chair and tried to work out in his head how to ransom a multimillion-pound painting.

Chapter 20

In Montreux Shaughnessy changed from the Paris-Milan train on to the MOB. It has a cog between its drive wheels which pulls it up into the mountains with a satisfying growl. The seats are varnished wood, the fittings functional, but it somehow conveys a sense of nineteenth-century luxury.

There was snow on the ground. At first it was the non-gregarious type that stands around in isolated patches. It wasn't until they reached Chateau d'Oex that it became solid and the compartment was sterilized with its clean white reflections. A group of girls from one of the finishing schools clambered aboard. They were talking excitedly in French, smoking cigarettes and waving away the smoke before the conductor came while the windows misted over from the warmth of their bodies.

He got out at Gstaad. It's famous as the resort where celebrities live, although they're an endangered species nowadays. Instead the place is filled with tourists looking for them. A taxi took him the four or five miles up the valley to the village of Gsteig. It was dark by the time he arrived, the street lights turning the snow to orange sorbet.

He went into the Baren, a large carved building in the centre of the village which the postcard firms like to photograph on clear days. Inside it was crowded. There was that all-pervasive smell of cooking cheese and the temperature was hot enough to bring on a nosebleed.

In one corner of the room two men were arm-wrestling amidst a group of spectators. One of the contestants was tall and dark haired, wearing a brightly coloured jumper pulled back to the elbow to expose a forearm knotted with tension. His opponent was shorter and broader. On the anorak hanging over his chair was the circular insignia of a Berg-führer.

As Shaughnessy went over to watch, he seemed to be gaining the advantage. A slight push had moved his opponent round in his seat. His arm leaned back a few degrees. He gave a grunt of exertion, the cords in his neck standing out like violin strings, and gave way. There was a murmur of approval from the crowd.

'Can I have a go?' Shaughnessy asked in English.

The victor looked up. He had blonde hair and small eyes of pale grey. As with many mountain men, the features of his face were pressed into a broad face that showed no sign of malice. Without speaking he set his elbow on the table once more and opened his hand.

Shaughnessy sat down opposite, and rolling up his sleeve he positioned his arm carefully alongside the other's, setting the elbow directly below the hand to give it maximum leverage.

At first they applied only a light pressure, building it up gradually, matching each other's strength so that their hands remained quite still. The blonde man was looking straight into his eyes, calm and unworried, sure of his superiority.

Shaughnessy concentrated all his energy into his hand, draining the rest of his body. After a minute had passed he could feel the muscles of his forearm beginning to ache.

The other watched him placidly.

Putting everything he had into the effort, Shaughnessy moved his opponent's hand a few inches to the left. Then he felt the grip tighten, his arm was pushed back into the upright position again and then backwards, toppling over slowly and majestically like a falling tree.

The blonde man sat back in his chair and flexed his hand. 'You're flabby,' he said.

'I hoped that you'd get weaker as you get older.'

'I have,' he said, 'but so have you.' His name was Dieter Hauptmann. Shaughnessy had known him for eight years, ever since Dieter had been given the thankless task of teaching him to ski.

Picking up his glass, Dieter touched it against his and said, 'Cheers,' in what he took to be an English accent. 'It's good to see you.'

Dieter looked at him searchingly and then slapped his hands down on his thighs as though he couldn't believe who it was he was seeing. 'How long are you in town?'

'A couple of days.'

'Are you fit?'

'I've been walking up six flights of stairs every day.'

He nodded seriously. 'Flabby,' he said. 'That what I thought. Where do you want to ski?'

'Downhill.'

Dieter smiled and repeated the word. It was one of his favourite lines. Ski-instructors are rather like sergeant majors. Once they have come to terms with a good joke they stick with it. 'Bending and stretching exercises, that's what you need. Knock the fat off you. Where are you staying?'

'At the Viktoria.'

'That's good. We can start early.' Dieter spoke with the jerky rhythm that comes to those who try to convert Suisse-Deutsche into English.

'What's the snow like now?' Shaughnessy asked.

'Not bad for December. This time last year there was none at all. But we need a lot more to make a decent foundation. The trouble is the moment it snows all these people come up and scrape it off. It never gets time to settle down properly.'

There was a burst of music. Shaughnessy looked round to see who was playing but it was coming out of a hi-fi speaker concealed in the timber beams. Dieter pointed at the table in front of him. 'Have you eaten anything yet?'

'Not since I came off the plane.'

'You should eat,' he said. Food was important to Dieter. There hadn't been much of it around when he was a child. Summoning the waitress he ordered a plate of grison, the hard altitude-cured meat of the Swiss Alps, schnitzel mit rosti for two, and a bottle of Fendant. It's a Swiss white wine from the Valais that doesn't travel well. In England it tastes sharp and acidic with a slight tingle in the aftertaste as though it hasn't fermented properly. Here in the Alps it is fresh and clean and makes you believe you are a great downhill racer.

'You remember that evening on the Wassengrat?' Shaughnessy asked as they ate. 'The others had all gone down because it was cold and we stayed on in the restaurant and played cards until it was dark.'

'I remember. You lost twenty francs.'

'I want to do it again.'

'What? Lose twenty francs?'

'Ski in the dark.'

Dieter lifted his glass to his lips and looked across the room. There was a low smog from steaming cooking, cigarette smoke, and damp ski clothes. A few couples had started to dance, padding around in an ungainly way in their snow boots. 'Any reason?' he asked.

'I wasn't particularly good at it.'

'Holy shit, you were dreadful. Fell over a hundred times.'

'The drinking hadn't helped. Gravity gets more of a grip on you when you've been drinking. I'll try it on mineral water this time.'

'You English are crazy bastards,' he said.

'I'm Irish.'

Dieter nodded slowly as though this was what he had said. 'Nice guys but hopeless at the skiing.'

'We invented it.' Shaughnessy temporarily accepted English nationality.

'You invented cricket, but you're no good at it.'

'That's why I need the practice.'

'Did you not know that he was leaving the country?'

'No,' Patricia said. 'He didn't tell me.'

'He booked the ticket over the weekend so it was no last-minute impulse. He must have been planning it for some time. I'm surprised he didn't mention it to you.' Ambrose leaned over the balcony and looked down at the main floor of Lloyd's. It was 11.30 a.m. and trading was in progress. These days there are computer screens, satellite communications, and vast sums of money at stake but fundamentally Lloyd's is a market place. Forget the stainless steel and smoky glass for a minute; forget the young blades who clamber around the old-boy network, and it's a street bazaar. The only things missing are the knife fights and the beggars. Which is not to say that they're not there; it's just that they're not so easy to recognize.

'When did you last see him?' he asked.

'Last Wednesday. Please don't go on about it. You've made your point. I saw him on Wednesday and he didn't tell me he was going abroad. That's all I know.'

'I'm sorry, I didn't mean to imply anything. I was hoping you might be able to cast some light on his motives.'

They came down the escalator. The mechanics of the thing were exposed so you could see what made it rattle.

'He flew into Geneva on Thursday morning and took the train out to Gstaad. Our own team tracked him to Heathrow airport and then handed over to the Swiss police. They have been keeping an eye on him for the last two days.'

'How very efficient of them,' Patricia said. She glanced back over her shoulder at her shoes. Escalators are death to high heels.

'He did his best to give them the slip. Before leaving he bicycled round Kensington Gardens until he'd dropped the tail. Fortunately our men guessed what he was doing and contacted the airports. We picked him up again at Heathrow.'

What was he doing? she wondered. He must have a reason for going to Switzerland like this. But why hadn't he told her?

'For the last two days,' Ambrose continued, 'he's been skiing with a private instructor called Hauptmann. Shaughnessy has known him for some years. They are quite close.'

'Has anyone spoken to this man?'

'I doubt whether he's relevant. One of the plain clothes officers got into conversation with him last night. He knows nothing more than that they've been skiing together. Shaughnessy rang him about a week ago and suggested they spend a couple of days together.'

Ambrose was looking at her hands. She realized they were shaking and put them behind her back.

'I'm sorry,' he said. 'This appears to have come as a shock to you. I assumed you already knew.'

He didn't assume anything of the sort. He had called her over to Lloyd's to break the news in person so that he could see how she reacted. She hated him for it. There was a lot of malice in this man, gift-wrapped in old-world politeness.

'Where is he now?' she asked.

'That's the problem. We don't know. He succeeded in dropping the tail. I imagine that plain-clothes officer who spoke to Hauptmann had his size fourteen police boots showing. Shaughnessy guessed he was under observation and gave them the slip.'

'If the painting is still in England he has to come back for it.'

'Oh yes.' Ambrose wasn't concerned. 'We'll pick him up again.'

After they had parted, Patricia walked back to her car. There was a ticket on the screen. Crossly she stuffed it into the glove compartment and put a call through to Suzie at the office. From her she got Trevelyan's phone number in Lloyd's.

'Tom Shaughnessy?' He sounded dubious. 'I don't think I know anyone of that name.'

'He works for you.'

'Not here he doesn't.'

'Privately. He told me he works for you privately. Please this is very important, you must tell me.'

'You must have made a mistake, Patricia. I don't know anyone called Tom Shaughnessy.'

Patricia felt the first clutch of panic. Did he use another name perhaps? 'He was at that party in the Middle Temple. I introduced you to him: tall, fair haired.'

There was a moment's silence on the line and then Trevelyan said, 'But he was with you, Patricia, not with me.'

'You've never seen him before?'

'No. I'm sorry, Patricia, I don't know where you've got this idea from but he's nothing to do with me.'

'Damn him!' she said. 'Damn him to hell!' She kept her voice down but the words hissed across the table with a greater ferocity than if she had shouted them.

'It's hard to believe,' Suzie said unhappily.

'He must have thought I was so gullible,' Patricia said. 'Lapping it all up, believing every word he said. He must have thought I was the biggest idiot on earth.' She threw back her head and stared up at the fan slowly revolving on the ceiling as she pictured the scene.

They were in an Italian restaurant close to the London Wall, elbows on the table, heads close together in the way women do only when they have intimate confidences to exchange.

Suzie had never seen Patricia in such a state. Angry, often enough, frustrated by inefficiency or stupidity, frequently, but nothing like this. When she'd burst into the office an hour ago she'd been on the verge of tears.

As if in response to her thoughts Patricia sat back and said, 'What we need is a bottle of something to cheer ourselves up.'

She summoned the waiter and put in an order for Bollinger in her immaculate Italian, flashing him a dazzling smile as he withdrew. Suzie wished she had this kind of style. When she broke up with her boyfriend a year back it had been with a lot of sniffling and red-rimmed eyes. Patricia had thought she had a cold and packed her off home for the day.

'He actually said he was working for Trevelyan, did he?' Suzie asked after it arrived.

'Yes, he actually said it. He took me to a railway siding and showed me a lot of rusting junk and said he wanted the money to do them up. And I took it like a sucker.'

'It's incredible.'

'He probably made the whole thing up as he went along. He must have laughed himself sick afterwards.' She studied the rising bubbles in her champagne as though they were a new life form she'd discovered. 'He was so damned plausible, that's the worst of it.'

'He must have been,' Suzie said quietly. She didn't like to say it but Patricia let men use her. It was the one paradox in her nature. She was shrewd in her dealings with other people until it came to personal relationships. Then she threw it all away and let her heart govern her head. Gus had used her for years now, although Patricia never seemed to realize it. There had been times when Suzie had felt like screaming at her. When they broke up it had been the best thing that could have happened to her. Now she had let this new man walk all over her.

'He recognized him.' Patricia grabbed another detail from her mind. 'Trevelyan recognized him. I'm sure he did. That's why it seemed so plausible that they were working together.'

'When was this?'

'At that do which the minister put on. When I introduced them to each other I could have sworn they recognized each other.'

'What are you going to do now?'

'What do you think?' Patricia retorted. 'I'm going to nail his head to a stick where everyone can see it.'

Chapter 21

After Patricia left the restaurant she drove down to Fulham with a renewed sense of purpose.

A documentary is built something like a pyramid. From a broad base of facts it narrows to a single point. In the last week she had done much of the work for the programme but that single focal point had been missing.

Now she had found it again.

The traffic was heavy and it took her forty minutes to reach Inkerman Mansions. But she had no trouble getting into Shaughnessy's flat. She'd been worried that he might have taken the key away with him but it was where it always was: above the door frame.

Ambrose's team had already been through the flat with a fine-tooth comb. It was unlikely she was going to find anything that they had missed. But she knew Tom better than they did. There was just a chance she could find something they'd overlooked.

But after half an hour she gave up. Going outside she locked the door, pausing for a few minutes to consider. There was nothing in the flat to give her a lead. She'd have to dig deeper. No man could live in a vacuum. Somewhere there must be a link.

'Are you looking for Tom?' a voice asked her.

She turned around. The voice belonged to a red-headed girl about her own age—maybe a bit older now she looked more closely. She was coming down the stairs.

'Do you know where he is?' Patricia asked.

'I haven't seen him around,' the red-head said. She had glossy skin that looked as though it had been polished. Her dress was red, a dangerous colour with her hair. The two were fighting like tomcats.

'You don't know when he's coming back, I suppose?'

The red-head shook her head. 'You could ask Scobie, I suppose. He might know where he is. Bit of a law to himself our Tom, tends to come and go as he pleases.'

'Scobie?'

'Scobie Woods. He has the studio upstairs. I was just collecting a few of my things. He's having to move out.'

'Is he there now?'

'Not at present. Poor dear, he's in such a tizz trying to get his things together.'

Scobie Woods! The name suddenly registered in Patricia's mind. He was an artist—of course. How could she have been so slow. She'd seen his portraits in the Mall Gallery.

'It's his wife,' the red-head was saying. 'She wants him out so she can get her hands on the money.'

'Did you say his studio?'

'A crying shame. I mean where's he going to work in future? Yes, it's his studio.'

'I'd be interested to see round it,' Patricia said as they went downstairs. 'If it's up for sale, that is.'

'Oh, it's up for sale all right. The estate agent's board's outside.'

There were three above the entrance to the passageway. The one Patricia wanted said: De Luxe Studio/Penthouse for Sale.

She hurried back to her car and threw herself across the seat, her legs draped out across the pavement like an advertisement for ladies' stockings as she phoned the office.

The estate agent they sent round was a walking barometer. His nose was red from the cold and registering a slight sniffle. His eyes were moist, the lips a faint tinge of blue that stood out against his white cheeks like the beginning of a bruise.

As he shook hands with Patricia he made a belated attempt to upgrade his image, pushing his hair from his eyes and straightening his tie. His collar was soft, the edge frayed. Poor little mite, she thought, he needed someone to look after him.

'It needs modernizing, of course,' the estate agent—who introduced himself as Dodds—told her. He led the way upstairs, producing a key from his pocket. It was attached to a crumpled label. 'But it would make an ideal pied-à-terre. Perfect for someone such as yourself.'

Patricia wasn't sure whether he meant it was ideal for an unattached young lady such as herself or ideal for holding the wild media orgies that he probably imagined she threw.

Dodds rapped on the studio door with the knuckle of one finger. Putting his ear to it, he listened for a moment, and then rapped again the way doctors do to diagnose minor ailments.

'I don't think anyone is in,' Patricia said.

'You can't be too careful. Sometimes they're in even when the door's locked.'

The studio had the warm smell of linseed oil and paraffin. The floor was cluttered like a junk shop but the huge studio window gave it a sense of scale.

'It's lovely,' Patricia said.

'It's only been on the market a few days but there's been a lot of interest. The price is low, you see. The owner is looking for a quick sale.' Dodds eased himself into his sales pitch.

'I mean it's lovely as it is,' Patricia said. There were canvases stacked against the wall. She lifted a couple back and looked at the painted surfaces. They were portraits, upside down.

'The owner's quite a well-known artist,' Dodds informed her in case she hadn't guessed.

'You met him, you said?' She put the canvases back in place and flicked the dust off her hands.

'When I came round to measure up for the brochure. He was in here working on a picture with his assistant.' Dodds opened his mouth to say something further and then closed it again. His Adam's apple jumped up from the collar and hit the underside of his chin like one of those fair-ground machines that tests your strength. After it had fallen back, he tried again. 'It was rather embarrassing, actually. I thought the place was empty and just walked in. They were pretty sore about it.'

'Artists can be temperamental,' Patricia said soothingly.

'Oh yes, I know that. It was all right once I'd explained who I was. We got on fine after that. We even had a few drinks together.'

'He must do very well for himself if he has an assistant. Not many artists have assistants nowadays.' Patricia was looking the place over as she spoke.

'I don't know whether he was an assistant,' Dodds said. 'He could have just been a friend. He was very knowledgeable about pictures.'

Patricia went into the tiny kitchen. The gas cooker had been put in around the same time as they discovered gas. The cupboard doors were loose and there were short burn marks on the white-painted worktop where cigarettes had rested.

'Which picture were they working on when you came in?' she asked as she came out. It's hard to pump someone for information without them noticing. But Dodds was one of the rare exceptions.

'This one here.' He pointed to a large picture standing on its side against the wall.

It was a picture of the red-headed girl wearing baggy Persian trousers and pointed shoes. She was lying back on yellow cushions, breasts bare and brassy, the eyes glazed with a distant dreamy expression. It looked as though she had been laid out with a left hook in the third round.

Dodds asked: 'Are you interested in art, then?'

'I know what I like,' she replied vaguely. And this didn't qualify.

'At least I think it's the one,' Dodds said. The Adam's apple was trying to ring the bell again. 'I'm not too sure…'

Patricia looked at him. Unhappy memories had come out of his mind and were running around his face. 'Not sure?' she asked.

'It seemed to change as the evening went on.'

'I don't understand.'

'When I first came in it looked sort of greenish, then after I'd seen it more carefully it sort of changed...' Dodds was listening to his own explanation and realizing it didn't sound too good. 'My fault I guess. I'm not used to drinking whiskey, you see. And I had a bit of a cold at the time...'

'You poor thing,' Patricia said. 'Was this on the Friday before last?'

'That's right. How did you know that?'

'I think I know the assistant in question,' she said grimly.

Dodds took the news philosophically. When it came to brightness he was a novice glowworm but he was beginning to sense that she wanted something other than a rundown studio.

Patricia smiled at him winningly. 'I'd like to bring someone round to look at this place. An interior decorator.'

'Oh yes, sure.' He was back on firm ground again. 'Any time you want me to open it, just give a ring.'

'I don't want to take up your time, I'm sure it's valuable. Maybe I could just pick up the key from the office?'

'We're not supposed to do that really.'

'It must be such a nuisance having to leave the office every time someone wants to measure the windows for curtains.'

'It is actually.' Dodds was drowning in Patricia's smile. 'Oh, I don't see why not. It's not as if you're going to nick anything.'

'Tomorrow morning, perhaps?'

'That should be fine.'

She had the heater on and Alfred Brendel playing the Chopin nocturnes on the radio as she drove back along the Embankment. The traffic was as bad as before but she didn't notice it.

'That's where it's been all this time,' she said as she came into the office.

Suzie followed her through into the next room. 'What's been there? The painting?'

'Where better to hide a painting than in a studio?'

'Is it still there do you think?'

'I don't know,' Patricia said. 'I doubt it. But I'll know for certain tomorrow. Where did those flowers come from?'

'They arrived just now.'

The bouquet was lying on her desk. Patricia opened the envelope without disturbing them and plucked out the card. From Suzie's expression she guessed she'd already taken a look.

The card read: 'Missing you—'. Beneath it was the name of a hotel in Venice.

'When did they come?' Patricia asked.

'About half an hour ago.'

Patricia tossed the card back on the cellophane covering. 'What's he expect me to do?' she asked crossly. 'Drop everything and run half-way across Europe to see him?'

Suzie didn't reply. She waited to see if anything more was coming but Patricia had turned away to the window.

It was dark now and the lights of the far shore turned the water to molten lead. A oil freighter was passing, its low slung deck almost awash. Patricia watched its navigation lights gliding along above.

'Oh, damn him,' she said. 'Get me on a flight to Venice as soon as you can, Suzie. What's the time now?'

'Ten past four.'

'Give me an hour to get to Heathrow. Anything after six will do.' She pulled on her rain coat.

'When will you be back?'

'Tomorrow,' she said opening the door. 'I won't be late. Cancel anything I have early in the morning.'

'Do you want me to book you a hotel?' Suzie called after her, but Patricia was already gone.

Chapter 22

Someone once told her that Venice airport is amongst the most dangerous in the world. The plane has to clear the Dolomites and then drop like a stone on to a runway which reaches out into the sea. Come in short and it hits the mountains, overshoot and the passengers find themselves disembarking by rubber dinghy.

Patricia read her magazine as they made the approach and tried not to think of it. She heard the clunk as the wheels locked down, the sudden roar of wind as the wing flaps grasped for support. There was a sickening moment when the plane seemed to stop in the air. She concentrated on the page. It was only when they touched down and were taxiing across the tarmac that she realized she was studying an advertisement for condoms and quickly turned the page.

From Venice airport she took a taxi out to the city. The address that Shaughnessy had given her was a hotel in the maze of streets between San Marco and the Rialto Bridge. One foot of the tall red stuccoed building stood in a piazza, the other in a narrow canal. The water was sullen in the street lights, pieces of polystyrene, empty bottles, and scraps of wood floated between the moored boats. A black plastic bag of rubbish was setting off towards the Grand Canal.

The foyer was long and narrow. A group of tourists sat round a table to the left. On the other side was the reception desk where a man leaned on the counter. He had a bald head and plump jowls. There were bags beneath his eyes the size of hot-water bottles and he was staring across the marble floor with an air of infinite sadness.

The sight of Patricia gave him a much-needed tonic. He looked up at her and then toppling forwards he checked her legs.

'Signor Shaughnessy?' He pronounced the name with some difficulty.

'He's staying here.'

He consulted a ledger and then ran his fingers along the pigeon holes behind, stopping at a key. It was attached to a piece of brass the size and shape of a mooring buoy.

'He's out.'

'Is that a note he's left?' Patricia asked.

The receptionist removed the scrap of paper and looked at it with suspicion. 'Patrizia Drew?'

'That's me.'

'It's for you,' he said, passing it across the counter. 'You're English, no?'

'That's right.'

'I think so.' He confirmed it for her. 'You have nice English hair, nice English legs.'

She assumed it was a compliment and smiled at him, showing her nice English teeth. 'Where's the Scuola San Antonio?' she asked.

The question hit stony ground. He thrust out a lower lip that was wet and red and thick as a piece of steak.

'The Scuola San Antonio.' She showed him the name written on the note. 'He says he's gone there. I need to know where it is.'

The receptionist drew out a map and consulted it. His shirt was clean but the vest beneath carried the battle scars of a recent encounter with tomato sauce. He ran a thick finger over the streets, stabbing the page when he found the Scuola. It was over on the left bank of the City, not far from the Frari.

'It's shut,' he said with sudden authority. 'To the public. Only the members are allowed in.'

'I'd better go and see for myself.' She moved away but his voice held her.

'Do you want a room?'

'Are there any free?'

'Of course.' The melancholy was settling on him again. His eyes became tired. 'It is winter. Foreigners: they only like to see Venice in the summer. In the winter they stay at home.'

'I'll see when I get back.'

She walked to the Rialto Bridge, past the small bright cafes where espresso machines wheezed and people with nothing to do behaved as though they were in a hurry to get somewhere. Past smart shops—the modem fillings of ancient cavities—that were shut up for the night; past narrow alleys where the neon lights didn't want to go.

The Scuola San Antonio wasn't one to advertise itself. It was up a small side street. The door was of heavy black wood, studded with nails and set deep into a crumbling wall. There was one window alongside. It wasn't big enough to climb through but was covered by a wrought-iron grill in case anyone was thinking of trying.

She dragged on the bell pull but it didn't appear to work. In the darkness she found a buzzer and tried that. The street was deserted. Water dripped in the silence. The canal at the end of the street winked at her and a cold draft felt her legs as it passed.

The door opened a few inches and a man's face appeared. He had black hair and the look of someone who only opens doors so he can slam them shut again.

'Is this the Scuola San Antonio?' Patricia asked. The name was carved above the door but she felt it best to start with questions to which she already knew the answer.

'Si,' the face replied.

'I've come to see Mr Shaughnessy. I believe he's here.'

The face disappeared and the door opened a few more inches. Patricia stepped inside. The hallway was in darkness, the real liquorice darkness that comes with shuttered windows and oak panelling. The receptionist at the hotel was right. This place was shut to the public. The air was stale and heavy with the smell of damp and decayed plaster overridden by the sharp biting perfume of disinfectant.

'If you'd like to follow me,' the face said.

He led the way up the carved staircase to the first floor where a yellowish light glimmered from a yellowish chandelier. There were paintings of forgotten naval engagements on the walls and an oriental rug spread across the crooked marble floor.

The face went to a door at the end of the passage, knocked, and opened it, standing aside to let her pass into what looked like a library. A coal fire licked orange light across shelves of ancient books that reached up to the ceiling. There were deep leather armchairs that had passed the age of retirement and an enormous cradle-globe, tobacco-brown and mounted on brass legs. Standing by the fireplace were two men.

One was elderly with white hair as light as spun sugar. He was dressed in a black suit that was probably tailormade but with his fragile, bowed figure, the plain white shirt and black tie it gave him the air of a night porter.

The other was Tom Shaughnessy. He was leaning against the mantelpiece, a glass in one hand. As Patricia came in he looked around.

'Patricia.' The corners of his eyes crinkled as he came across to her. 'You got my message, then?'

She took her hand out of her pocket. In her fingers was the scrap of paper the hotel receptionist had given her. 'Do I get a prize for winning the paperchase?'

'I didn't know when you might arrive. As a matter of fact I didn't know whether you would be coming at all.'

'How could I refuse?' she asked coolly. Without waiting for a reply she brushed past him and flashing out a smile she offered her hand to the elderly man. 'How do you do. My name's Patricia Drew.'

'It's an honour,' he replied. To her surprise he spoke in English with only a suggestion of accent in the precision of his vowels.

'This is Professor Barbieri,' Shaughnessy told her. 'He's the director of the Scuola.'

As they shook hands the old man placed his left hand on top of hers. It was dry as an autumn leaf and not much heavier. 'May I get you something to drink?' he asked politely. 'We have some rather good Madeira, if I say so myself.'

'That would be lovely,' Patricia said.

'The Scuola has the best cellars in Venice,' Shaughnessy said as Professor Barbieri poured Madeira from a cut-glass decanter and gave her the glass.

'Cellars is just a figure of speech in this city, of course. Anything below ground-level would be buried in mud. But we are fortunate enough to have a great deal of space in the building which my predecessors have used to our advantage.'

Patricia took a sip of Madeira. It was warm as rocks that have been baking in the sun. 'That's delicious.'

The Professor smiled and his eyes closed. Not one lid but a succession of folds closing down like the shutting of a camera's aperture. 'You are probably wondering where it is you've been brought,' he said. 'But I'm sure the name of the Scuola San Antonio is not unknown to you.'

'I must admit I'd never heard of it until a few weeks ago.'

The Professor went across to the table and refilled his glass. 'But now no doubt you know us as the owners of *The Triumph of Bacchus*. Can I give you some more wine, Mr Shaughnessy?'

Shaughnessy shook his head. He went back to the fire and leaned against the mantelpiece.

'We have always prided ourselves in our anonymity,' the Professor said, replacing the glass stopper and setting the decanter on its silver tray. 'Now this unfortunate incident has brought us into the public eye. I fear the situation will never be the same.'

Shaughnessy said, 'When the painting is returned, the Scuola has offered it to the city. It will be put in the Academmia Gallery.'

'It's the only way.' The Professor gave a little shrug. 'If we have it back here again we will be subjected to a stream of visitors. We have never denied access to the painting, you understand, but in the past very few knew of its existence. We were rarely disturbed. Now all that is changed. Perhaps it is for the best. We shouldn't try to hold these things for ever.'

'Did it hang in this room?' Patricia asked.

'Up there. Above the fireplace. Four hundred years it hung there. No one had touched it since the day Titian put it in place. It's said that Napoleon wanted it but someone told him to do so would bring him bad luck. And so he left it.' The Professor permitted himself a little laugh, a shaking of the shoulders that made no sound. 'It's one of the few advantages of our reputation.'

'What is it you do here, Professor?' Patricia asked.

'Astronomy.' He pronounced each syllable with care as though she had suddenly been struck deaf and was relying on lip reading. 'The Scuola was founded in the fifteenth century to study the movements of the stars. There is a viewing platform on the roof. But over the centuries the science developed out of all proportion and we couldn't compete. So gradually we ceased to study astronomy and turned our attention to the astronomers themselves. It's a fascinating subject, Miss Drew. Alchemy, necromancy, the myths and traditions of astrology, that's our field. Venice has always attracted those seeking alternative views of the world. We simply recorded their ideas.'

There was a knock at the door and the janitor appeared. 'There is a call for you, Professor.'

'Ah,' he said. 'You'll forgive me for a moment. Help yourselves to more Madeira if you wish. I will not be long.'

As soon as he'd gone Patricia put down her glass and moved away from Shaughnessy. She went over to the globe and studied it in silence.

'There's only one phone in the building,' Shaughnessy said after a while. 'And that's right at the back where it won't disturb anyone.'

Patricia's entire concentration was on an area around the southern Antarctic. 'Why did you send me those flowers?'

'I wanted to see you.'

'It was very childish.'

'You didn't have to come.'

She turned to him. Her face was perfectly still, the pupils of her eyes a pin-prick in the centre of the blueness. 'I spoke to James Trevelyan this afternoon.'

'So I gather—'

'He's never heard of you.' Somewhere in the room a clock was ticking away.

'You put him in a difficult position,' Shaughnessy said. 'Ringing him like that demanding explanations. What did you expect?'

Patricia didn't reply. She stood with her feet together and her hands in her pockets, her face half hidden by her hair.

'He had people around him.' He risked a suggestion of reproach. 'There was no other answer he could give you. Particularly since he'd seen you hanging around Lloyd's earlier.'

'He told you this?'

'He rang me at the hotel after you'd called.'

Patricia tossed back her hair and moved further down the library, browsing along the lines of shelves. 'What were you doing in Switzerland?'

'Arranging the ransom. What do you think?'

'Are you trying to be funny?' she asked sharply.

'Never more serious. The ransom has to take place in Switzerland. The only part I know is the Alps, so that's where I went. And before you work yourself into a lather, no, I haven't got the real thing. It's a fake.'

She looked at him with eyes that would have bored holes in a safe door. 'I think you'd better explain yourself.'

'Most of it you already know.'

'Then just give me the interesting bits,' she said. 'The bits that tell me not to walk out of here and go straight back to London.'

So he told her. Right from the beginning this time, nothing held back. It took him over fifteen minutes but Patricia listened without interrupting.

'Oh, God,' she said when he was through. 'That's it, is it? You must be out of your mind. You'll get yourself killed.'

'I don't think so.'

'No? But there's every chance, isn't there? Why on earth do you want to do it?'

'For the money. I told you. I need the money to do up those steam trains I showed you.' The answer sounded lame.

'They're that important, are they?' She looked at him in amazement. 'I can't believe you're prepared to risk your life to mend a few rusty trains.'

'They're important to me,' he said stiffly. 'Restoring those things is the only future I have. Is that so difficult to understand?'

'I don't know,' she said, 'I really don't know.' She gave a shiver and moved closer to the fire, holding out her hands to the warmth. It was the nearest she'd been to him since she came in. 'This copy of yours,' she said after a while. 'That's been made by Scobie Woods, has it?'

'No, it was made by me. Scobie just lent me his studio.'

'Where did you keep the painting?'

'On the easel, tucked behind another.'

'That's what I thought,' she said to herself. Putting one hand on the mantelpiece she stared down into the fire. Shaughnessy let her take her time. Flames are a good place to collect your thoughts. Without looking up she asked, 'What am I to you?'

He didn't reply.

'Someone to play with, is that it? Someone to use when it suits your schemes?'

'I didn't lie to you, Patricia.'

'No?' Her voice was low but there was bitterness in it. 'You just spread the truth out so thinly that no one can see it.' With an abrupt movement she looked up at him. Her eyes were large and wild. 'Why didn't you tell me about this before? Why didn't you give me some idea what you were doing instead of leaving me to find out like this?'

'You came up on me too fast,' he said. 'I would have told you when the time came.'

This wasn't good enough for her. 'Do you know what it's like to find out the hard way?'

'It was my mistake,' Shaughnessy said. 'I thought I'd ditched those guys who were following me. I went into the park and ran them around. But somehow they hung on.'

'I know. David Ambrose called me over to Lloyd's and filled me in on every detail. It really gave him a thrill telling me how naive I'd been.' She brooded on the memory for a moment and then straightened up, letting out her breath in a sigh. 'Oh, Christ, Tommie, if I'd had a gun then I'd have shot you dead.'

'It's just as well I wasn't invited along.'

She found a tight smile from somewhere and tried it on. It didn't stay in place for more than a second. 'This scheme of yours, will it really work?'

'I don't know,' he said and that was the truth of it. 'It's worth a go.'

'It sounds like madness to me.' The anger had gone from her voice. 'Have you really made a copy?'

'All by myself.' He drained his glass and laid it on the mantelpiece. Patricia came a little closer and touched his hand.

'I didn't know you could paint,' she said.

'Didn't you? Everyone can do something. Of course, I couldn't have done it without you.'

'How's that?'

'You had the X-rays I needed.'

'I did?' She didn't catch his drift.

'They were in the file in your office. I borrowed them from you.' She smiled, this time it was a real smile that touched her eyes.

'You really are a very despicable man,' she said. 'I don't know why I love you.'

At that moment the door opened and Professor Barbieri came back into the room. He made no sound. Seeing them together he paused. 'I'm so sorry,' he said in his polite voice. 'You have things to talk about. I should have realized. I'll leave you.'

Patricia had moved away from Shaughnessy when he came in. She gave a shake of her head and said, 'He was just explaining what brought him here.'

For those with a good arm, the restaurant they dined in that night was just a stone's throw from the Rialto Bridge. It was after midnight when they left. Outside, it was cold. Steam from the kitchens crawled up the wall. Patricia turned up her collar and gave a shiver.

'How did you meet James Trevelyan?' she asked as they walked up towards the Grand Canal.

'I copied some paintings for him a few years back. It was for a big country house up in the Midlands. The cost of insuring them had become pretty hefty and the owners hadn't a bean between them and so they gave them to the Walker Gallery—or flogged them, I can't remember which. James got me to make some copies to hang in the house.'

'That's a good idea,' Patricia said. A man was loading cardboard boxes on to the side of the canal. Two of them toppled over and landed in the water but it didn't seem to worry him.

Shaughnessy said, 'It was open to the public, you see. The guide book said there were paintings by Turner and Reynolds and so they had to be there.'

'Did anyone notice the difference?'

'Not that I've heard of. But no one in England looks at the pictures on the walls of private houses anyway. It's bad manners. We're going the wrong way.'

'No, this is right.'

'The hotel's further back.'

Patricia turned around so that she was walking backwards in front of him. 'Yours is,' she said smugly. 'Mine's this way.'

'You've got a hotel fixed?'

'Of course. You don't think I was going to stay in that fleapit of yours, do you? I rang from the restaurant. Why do you think I was away so long?'

'I didn't like to ask.'

'We need somewhere to talk,' she said.

'Do we?' He stopped in the street. She stood in front of him, eyes bright, breath pouring out in the cold air. 'What do we need to talk about?' he asked.

'About this ransom.' She seemed amazed that he should ask. 'I need to know how you are going to do it; how it's going to work. I can't help you unless you tell me everything.'

'I don't need you to help me.'

'Are you joking? Of course you do. If I don't help you you're going to wind up in terrible trouble, Tommie.'

Chapter 23

Patricia woke in the early hours of the morning. The room was in darkness. At the far end were two high windows and a stone balcony beyond. None of it looked familiar. For a few minutes she lay quite still, drifting contentedly on the edge of consciousness as she searched her memory for recognition. Then the events of the night returned to her. With a thud of realization she rolled over in bed and groped for her watch. It was four thirty. Tommie was still asleep, she could hear his breathing on the pillow beside her.

Pushing back the bedclothes she slipped out of bed. Putting on her dressing gown she went across to the window. The glass was cold and misted with her breath as she looked down the Grand Canal. It was still night. The sky was black but in the street lights she could see the lacework of the buildings and the sluggish movement of the water below.

She had hardly slept. Most of the night she had lain awake arranging the scattered thoughts in her mind, herding them into an ordered plan. She was no longer the girl she'd been when she first visited Venice: the silly, headstrong eighteen-year-old who'd walked around with a copy of Mallarmé in her pocket and her mind crammed with romantic nonsense. She'd left her behind with the puppy fat and the Afghan coats. Her mind was cold and logical—she'd trained it to be that way—and as the small hours had dripped away she had reached the decisions she needed. She knew now what she had to do.

Behind her Shaughnessy stirred in his sleep. She went over to the bed and looked down at him in the darkness. For a moment she had a wild impulse to slip back into bed, to cling hold of him as she had the night before, and let the rest of the world go to hell. But it was no good. If she allowed herself any weakness now she could never go through with this.

She picked up the telephone from the bedside table. It was on a long extension lead so that it could be moved around the room. Taking it through into the bathroom she closed the door as far as it would go and sat down on the edge of the bath. The tiled floor was cold beneath her feet. In the glimmer of light from the bathroom window she could see the phone lying on her lap. For over a minute she sat and stared at it. Then pushing the hair from her eyes she dialled 9 and waited until she had an outside line before adding the rest.

The connection came almost immediately. She could hear the phone on the other end trilling; pictured it lying on the white bedside table beside the Patek Phillipe clock and the notepad which he kept to jot down ideas that came to him in the night.

'Come on, come on,' she shouted in her head.

Maybe he wasn't there. She pushed her legs out across the floor and looked at them. They'd once been described as the best in the business. Here in the cold, dark bathroom they looked like two dead fish.

A click at the other end as the receiver was lifted. There was a long silence and a voice blurred with sleep said, 'Yes, what is it?'

'Gus,' she said. 'It's me.'

'Patricia?' He was groping his way awake. 'What in God's name do you want?'

'I need you to do something for me.'

There were muffled noises as Gus hoisted himself up in bed.

'Speak up, I can't hear what you're saying.'

'I can't speak any louder—just listen to me.'

'Jesus, Patricia, do you realize what the time is?'

'I want you to ring the police.' He wasn't alone. Nothing Patricia could put her finger on but she could tell there was someone else there with him.

'Police? What do you want the police for—Jesus, do you realize what the time is? What are you talking about?'

'Listen, Gus. Just listen and do what I say.' Who was it? That little slag of a weather girl? She said, 'I know where *The Triumph of Bacchus* is hidden. I want you to ring the police.'

'Are you tight, Patricia?'

'This is important, damn you.'

'OK, hold your hair on.' He was listening now.

'Tell them to go round to Scobie Woods's studio. The painting is hidden inside a big picture of a nude.'

'Inside it? What do you mean inside it?' His voice had the strangled sound that came from gripping the receiver in his neck as he scribbled with his pen.

'It's standing by the easel, you can't miss it.'

'OK,' he said. 'Got you. Who's this Scobie Woods when he's at home?'

'He lives in the same block as Shaughnessy. Call the Athenaeum Club, ask for David Ambrose—got that?'

'Sure, I know Ambrose.' Good old Gus, never one to hang on to a name when it could be dropped.

'He'll have the address,' she said.

There was the sound of a sleepy voice in the background, then silence as Gus put his hand over the receiver. He came back on the line. 'Where are you?'

'Venice. I'm leaving now. I'll call again from the airport to tell you when I'll be back.'

'OK.'

She put the phone down.

Tommie was still asleep. She dressed quickly, stuffing her nightclothes into her bag. As she was leaving he turned over in bed and made a small sound with his lips as though repeating a word he'd forgotten. She went back to the bed and stood over him. He had one arm thrown out across the pillow, his hair in his eyes. He looked younger when he was sleeping, she'd noticed it before. The creases in his cheeks were softer, the long dark lashes giving him a child-like appearance.

Bending down she kissed his face and very softly she whispered: 'Stay lucky, my darling.'

Chapter 24

Heathrow airport on a grey morning that hadn't quite got round to raining. Forsyth was waiting for her when she came through customs. He had two uniformed officers with him. They stood in a group just beyond that barrier where the drivers hold up their hand-written placards and watch the passengers go by with the boredom of drunks who've come to the end of the line.

Ambrose was there too, set apart from the others in his long black overcoat and cashmere scarf tucked around his neck. He had a black fedora on his head and that air of aristocratic detachment that insulated him from his surroundings.

Patricia only had to look at Forsyth to know the news was bad. She stopped before she reached them.

'You haven't found it.' She said the words for him.

'No luck.'

'I don't believe it.' She stared at him in horror. 'It must be there. Did you look where I said? In the back of the painting on the easel.'

'We looked there. We looked everywhere else. There's no painting: nothing, zippo.'

'It has to be.'

'Oh, it has been,' Ambrose put in. 'The canvas on the easel was just a shell that he used to hide it.'

'Very neat,' Forsyth said. 'A very neat little job. But it's gone now.'

'And Scobie Woods?' she asked.

'Him too.' Forsyth gave a hunch of his shoulders as though he were taking on an invisible rucksack. 'But we'll run him in in time.' A woman with a loaded trolley pushed past, jostling Patricia aside.

'We'd better get out of the way,' he added. 'Have you got any other luggage?'

'Only this bag.'

They headed towards the exit. 'Oh, yes,' Forsyth said. 'I've sent out a description of Mr Scobie Woods. Someone will pull him in.'

'We won't have to wait that long. Shaughnessy will lead us to him when he returns.'

'When will that be?'

'Sometime later this morning, I should think. It's going to take him a while to get going. I made certain he has two separate hotel bills to pay before he can go.'

Ambrose was walking in step with them. He didn't ask her to clarify this last remark. He just gave one of his little smiles and said, 'Will he not be surprised that you left so early in the morning?'

'I told him I had to get back for a meeting. He doesn't suspect anything.'

'Good.' The word was a purr of breath in his throat.

As they came outside a sharp-tempered wind caught them, tugging at the skirt of Patricia's raincoat. She glanced at the clock. It was nine twenty. The day had hardly started and already she felt exhausted.

They drove into London in Ambrose's royal-blue Rolls. He sat in the back beside her, his hat on his knee, his gloves carefully arranged in the brim. Forsyth was in front. He had sent the squad car he'd come in back on its own and now leaned round on the leather seat. With a quick, expert movement he took out a packet of Benson & Hedges from his front pocket and flicked one up. A glance from Ambrose that would have had lesser men reporting sick with frostbite stopped him.

Ambrose opened the window beside him a crack. 'Why did Shaughnessy call you over to Venice in such a hurry?'

'To try to talk me into thinking he was innocent.'

Ambrose said, 'Ahh.' He said it softly and reflectively, with the satisfaction of a man who has found the last piece of a jigsaw puzzle which had fallen on the floor.

'He realized he had been followed to Switzerland,' Patricia said. 'And he needed to come up with an explanation. So he summoned me over to Venice and tried to sell me a whole pack of lies.'

'But you weren't falling for them?'

'No,' she said quietly. 'Not this time. He managed to fool me once. He's not going to do it again.'

She let herself into her flat. The living room was in semi-darkness. Dropping her bag on the coffee table she drew back the curtains, running her hand down the material to straighten the folds.

As she was turning towards the bedroom a voice behind her said, 'Who's been a clever girl then?'

It was Gus. He sitting in the armchair by the fireplace, legs crossed, arms stretched out on either side.

'What are you doing here?' she asked. He must have been sitting there in the dark waiting for her.

'I thought someone should be here to welcome you home.'

Patricia moved away. She opened her travelling bag as though there was something in it she needed. Gus watched her.

'You got back quicker than I expected.'

'I had a lift from David Ambrose.'

'Now there's an operator,' Gus said, going into the kitchen and opening the fridge door. 'When I rang him I thought he'd bite my head off. But no way. He was up and about, can you beat that? Five in the morning and the guy's already got his show on the road.'

The light of the fridge was on his face, giving his suntan more credit than it deserved. He took a bottle of champagne from the ice box and felt it in his hands. 'This hasn't had time to chill properly.'

'You're not going to open it, are you?'

'I didn't think you'd be back for at least another half-hour. Yes, I'm going to open it.'

'What's there to celebrate?'

Gus had hoisted out two glasses, holding them in one hand by the stems without letting them touch each other. He practised these little skills.

'Dear Patricia,' he said. 'Always the puritan.' The playful smile was still in place but she knew Gus. He was here to talk business. Everything else was just stage production. 'What we're celebrating,' he said with unscratched humour, 'is the way you've put the finger on this son of a bitch Shaughnessy.'

'He hasn't been caught yet.'

'I know, Patricia. I know.' He put down the bottle and held up his hands, surrendering in the face of superior forces. 'You're still mad at me for pissing on your fireworks. But I know when I'm wrong, OK? I should have listened when you first came up with this. You've got a nose for these things.'

'I'm not mad at you,' she said. 'I'm tired and I've had a long journey so if it's all the same with you I'm going to have a bath.'

'Be my guest.'

She marched through into her bedroom and closed the door. As she undressed she heard the report of the champagne cork and then the clink of glasses being loaded on to a tray at the beginning of a journey. Holy saints, he might be thinking of bringing it through into the bedroom. He was in that sort of mood. Throwing on a dressing-gown and tying the belt she went back to him.

'Ah,' he said, looking up from the task of pouring champagne. 'I always preferred you in something loose.'

She didn't want to drink but she took the glass he offered. He raised the other to her and took an experimental sip. Then he said, 'So tell me all about it.'

'There's not much to tell. Shaughnessy's coming in to London later today. The police think he'll lead them to the painting.'

'And you don't?'

'No,' she said. 'He's far too crafty for that.'

Gus put his glass down and stood in front of her. Putting his hands on her shoulders he adjusted the collar of her dressing-gown. His voice was soft, coaxing. 'Do you know where this painting is, Patricia?'

'I don't need to know where it is. Shaughnessy's going to bring it to me.'

'Why should he do that?'

'So that I can take it to Switzerland,' Patricia told him. She had the lazy, contented smile of a cat on her lips. 'I persuaded him that it would be better that way.'

'And he fell for it?'

'Of course—he trusts me.'

Reaching down, Gus parted the lapels of the dressing-gown until it revealed the cleavage between her breasts. Then stepping back he studied the effect in satisfaction. 'And the police know nothing about this?'

'Nothing. I didn't see why they should be given everything on a plate.'

With one hand she closed the front of her dressing-gown and taking the glass of champagne through to the kitchen she poured it down the drain. Gus leaned on the partition counter and watched her.

'They think Shaughnessy's working alone,' she said, upending the glass on the draining board. 'They've no idea how deep it goes. When I broadcast my programme it's going to raise a stink that won't blow away for months.'

Gus gave a snap of his fingers. 'What are we talking about? Fifty minutes?'

'Ninety.' He was referring to the programme length. 'I need space. There's a lot of background information to lay out.'

'Prime-time viewing—eight, eight thirty in the evening.' Gus was practically salivating over her words. 'How quickly can you deliver?'

'Straight away. As quickly as I can put the tape together.' Patricia glanced around the kitchen, checking that everything was tidy. Then she looked up at him. 'The only question is who I make it for.'

Gus held his hands up, thanking some invisible god of deliverance for his foresight and said, 'You're making it for us, Patricia.'

'Not necessarily.'

'You're under contract.'

'I'm under contract to make a documentary about art theft. Once Shaughnessy is arrested it will be a straight news story and that's public property, Gus. Anyone can have a shot at it.'

'I'll have to put that to our lawyers.'

'By the time they've fiddled around it will be too late.'

The reality of this hit Gus pretty hard but it didn't dislodge the smile. The teeth were just as white, the laugh lines just as deep.

'Don't press it, Patricia,' he said lightly.

'I'm giving you first refusal. That's fair enough, isn't it?'

'This is blackmail, you realize that?'

'Call it what you like, Gus. If you want this one it's yours, but it has a price.'

He held her gaze for a moment. Then he took an apple from the bowl of fruit and tossed it in his hand. 'OK,' he said, 'what do you want?'

'My show back.'

Gus gave the apple another aerial view of the kitchen and caught it in one hand. He studied its freckled green skin as though he might see his reflection in it. 'Is that it?'

'No interference with the production, no editing of the material. Just as it was the way before.' She smiled up at him sweetly. 'And of course no assistants to take the load off my shoulders.'

He gave a shrug. 'If that's the way you want it. I'm not sure she was right for the job anyway.'

Patricia was all concern. 'Oh dear,' she said. 'Does she have headaches, Gus darling?'

'Don't get sarcastic. It doesn't suit you.'

'I'm sorry,' she said. Brushing past him she went into the bathroom and turned on the taps.

'Where were you last night?' Gus asked from the doorway.

She added bath salts from a crystal jar and felt the water with the tips of her fingers. 'In a hotel in Venice. I told you.'

'Were you with Shaughnessy?'

'Of course,' she said evenly. 'You don't think I got that kind of information by talking to him on the telephone, do you?'

Steam was rising. The air carried the sharp crystalline smell of lilac.

'You did that just to make this programme?' Gus asked.

'I thought that's what you'd expect.'

'Jesus, Patricia,' he said quietly. 'I'd forgotten what a bitch you can be.'

Chapter 25

It was around eight when Shaughnessy finally made it home. He switched on a few lights around the place and lit the gas fire before going through his mail. Someone wanted him to seize on the chance of a lifetime in the Algarve, another offered a huge discount on fitted bedrooms. He dropped it all in the wastepaper basket and thought of going round to the Roland but the idea didn't appeal. Instead he made himself some supper and watched television before going to bed.

It might have been the film, or the combination of whiskey and tinned sardines, but he didn't sleep well. He'd set his alarm clock for five thirty but by the time it went off he was already awake. He clambered out of bed, took a bath and shaved. The face in the mirror looked as though it had had a bad night. He splashed cold water over it and rubbed it dry with a towel.

Tugging on a few warm clothes he went outside and bicycled up towards Marylebone in the dark. First the cold numbed his fingers, then his upper thighs where the material of his trousers was pressed tight against his skin. Finally it dug in deeper and made his teeth chatter. What they were telling him was that he should trade in this old bone-shaker and get a car with a nice fan heater.

The Langley Hotel is modern. It has big glass doors that see you coming and open on their own and receptionists who don't know how to wipe the smile off their faces. It may have something to do with the price of the place.

The staff entrance is up one side. Concrete stairs led down into the kitchens. Shaughnessy pushed open the swing doors. Only a few of the overhead lights were on.

Jake didn't hear him come in. He was standing over a mechanical mixer that was slowly pounding dough. The sleeves of his white tunic were pulled back to the elbow and there was flour on his hands and wrists.

'How's it going?' Shaughnessy asked.

Jake looked up. He had a round face with reddish skin and precious little hair above. He gave a wink and said, 'Morning, Tommie.' With a deft movement he cut the power on the mixer and the grinding noise died away. The silence made the hotel kitchens seem suddenly larger and more empty.

'I was expecting you yesterday,' he said.

'I got held up.'

'Points failure at Acton? That's what you used to say, wasn't it?' Jake had worked with Shaughnessy at the Shropshire.

'Something a bit further away,' Shaughnessy said. 'Any problems this end?'

'None. I don't think anyone even saw it. Want some coffee?'

'If you have any going. What's this you're making in the cement mixer?'

'Danish pastry.' Twisting the stainless-steel container off, Jake set it down on the worktop. He washed his hands in the sink, flicked off the water, and dried them on his apron. From a percolator he poured a cup of coffee and pushed it towards Shaughnessy. 'It's all very continental here: croissants and Danish pastries and all the rest of that crap. English breakfast comes extra. There's milk in the fridge if you want it.'

'I'll take it as it comes.'

'Rough night, was it?' Jake grinned. It was the expression that came easiest to a face like his. 'We'd better get this thing of yours out. The others will be along in a minute.'

He went across to the bread oven and cranked open the door. The heat rolled out to greet them. Taking a wooden paddle he slipped it under the slab of plaster. It was lying at the base of the oven, scarcely noticeable down there beneath the wire shelves.

Together they lifted it down on to the floor.

'I'll leave you to it,' Jake said, closing the doors again. He went back to his dough.

After three days in the oven the plaster had darkened to a deep brick colour. The surface had cracked into fissures and it was hot as a new loaf of bread.

Shaughnessy broke it up with the handle of an iron chopping knife, picking out the larger pieces and sweeping away the rest with his hand. Gradually the painting emerged, the deep colours shining through the plaster dust. He wiped it clean with a rag and then touched its surface.

The paint had shrunk as it dried. It was no longer the thick fleshy material he had buried in wet plaster. Now it was hard and brittle, the different layers compacted into each other. Shaughnessy ran his finger tips over the canvas, probing, exploring the terrain.

It felt right. The pigments wouldn't have oxidized in the way they would over four centuries but it had taken on the feel of an old master painting.

He sat back. It was not so much satisfaction he felt as relief. This was the moment he had dreaded more than any other. If this part had failed there would have been no going back, no way of correcting the mistake. This had been a one off.

Lifting the canvas out of the wooden container he rolled it up loosely and went back to where Jake was working.

'You through, then?' he asked without looking up.

'I need a brush to clean up the mess.'

Jake was breaking small lengths of dough from a long roll and curling them on to a baking tray. The movements of his hands were quick and extraordinarily skilful. 'Leave that to me,' he said. 'I'll do it when you're gone.'

He wiped his hands across the front of his apron and went next door. He returned with a key. 'It's on the third floor,' he said. 'Go up the stairs over there. There's a lift. It'll take you straight up.'

The room he had reserved was at the back of the building. It's not hotel policy to allow the staff to use the amenities—as they like to call them—but it happens just the same. There had been a sous-chef at the Shropshire who'd kept the key to a room on a more or less permanent basis for clandestine meetings with one of the wine waitresses.

Shaughnessy shut the door and switched on the lights. The bed was turned down ready, note-paper laid out on the desk beside the kettle and a wicker basket filled with sachets of coffee and camomile tea.

Opening the wardrobe door he tucked the rolled canvas into the corner. Then he went back into the passage and locked the door. On the brass knob he hung the 'Do not disturb' sign.

Back in the kitchen he found Jake sweeping up the remains of the plaster. Shaughnessy put the envelope of money down on the table beside him.

'What do I owe you for the room?'

'Forget it,' he said. 'I've got a sort of understanding with the receptionist.' He tucked the money away in his tunic.

'I'll see you around then.'

'Yeah, take care, Tommie.' He propped the brush against the wall. Shaughnessy went down to the kitchens. As he reached the door Jake called after him.

'Got anything for Kempton Park on Saturday?'

'I don't even know what's running.'

'OK,' Jake said, 'just asking. I like to ask all the Micks I know and then bet on something they haven't recommended. It narrows the odds.'

There are some important bones in the Natural History Museum. They belong to dinosaurs that died out forty million years ago—or is it four hundred million years ago? Anyway, it's well before living memory.

Shaughnessy sat on the bench and stared at the skeleton of the Diplodocus. It's enough to send a chill down the spine until you discover that it's a phoney. As are all the others. One toenail is real, the rest is a plaster cast. Fakes come in all shapes and sizes in London.

Sometime after midday he left the museum and walked down into Chelsea. He had lunch in a pub, one of the new breed of pubs with barmen in waistcoats and soft drinks that come out of something which looks like a shower head. When he had finished he went through into the Gents. It was not much bigger than a telephone booth with two cubicles and a stand-up urinal. Above it was a small window about head-height from the ground.

There are probably dignified ways of climbing out of a lavatory window but if that is so he didn't find one. He came through head first, landing in the alleyway outside with a crash that knocked the wind from his lungs and made his two broken ribs lodge a formal complaint.

He picked himself up and looked around. The alleyway was a dead end. In one direction it led out into the street beside the pub, in the other it was blocked off by a garage. There were stacks of cardboard boxes and the remains of a motorbike that would have been more at home in the Natural History Museum.

Shaughnessy climbed up one flight of a fire escape and dropped on to the roof of the garage. He went to the far end and lowered himself down into a mews yard. It had brightly painted doors with coach lamps and led out into a residential street. From there he took a bus down into the King's Road.

There are parts of London that are practically hidden. Generations of development have grown up around them until they are completely obscured. It would take an aerial photo to realize they existed at all. Gerry Lampton's studio was in one of these.

A door in a high brick wall led through to a passage-way. At the far end it opened unexpectedly into a large garden. The studio was a lean-to affair of wood and glass along one wall. In architectural terms it was about as so-phisticated as a potting shed. Shaughnessy opened the door without knocking.

Scobie was stretched out asleep in a wicker chair. There was a newspaper opened across his face. At the sound of Shaughnessy arriving he pulled it down and stared at him.

'What the bloody hell have you been playing at?' he asked. There was no smoke but the question came out like a shot from a gun.

'I don't know,' Shaughnessy said, 'I hadn't realized I was playing at anything.'

Scobie levered himself into a sitting position and scratched his scalp with his finger tips so that the hair stood on end. 'Are you trying to screw this up intentionally? Or is it a natural genius of yours that you just can't control?'

'Hang on. What's all this in aid of? Did you get out of bed on the wrong side or something? Where's the "How did you get on in Switzerland, Tommie? It's good to see you back"?'

'Don't give me that crap,' Scobie said. 'The police were round in Inkerman Mansions Yesterday. Early—six in the morning. Turned the studio inside out, then your flat. Doz-ens of them.'

'Ahh.'

'Yes,' Scobie agreed getting to his feet. 'Ahh.'

'You heard about it then?'

'Heard about it?' His eyes bulged in disbelief. 'They made such a racket you could have heard about it in France.'

'But you weren't there presumably.'

'No, I wasn't. If I'd been there I wouldn't be here now, would I? I rang Bill Wainwright yesterday. He told me they'd been through the place like a dose of salts. Not just the blue-bottles either. Special Branch were there and all the rest of the plain-clothes bastards: asking questions, poking their noses in places they don't belong.'

'Just as well you weren't around,' Shaughnessy said lightly. He swung his jacket over the gallery steps banister.

'You picked up the painting then?'

'Yes, I've got it.'

'No problems at the hotel?'

'None,' Scobie said. He rubbed his eyes and then removing his hand he aimed one bony finger at him. 'You know who's behind this, don't you?'

'Patricia.'

'That's right,' he said, 'Patricia bloody Drew; Patricia "I don't care who I screw to get a story" Drew.'

Shaughnessy sat on the steps of the gallery. The windows were dirty which made the place unnaturally dark. Beyond them he could see up the unkempt garden. Rose bushes that had once been trim sprawled like barbed-wire defences, the lawn was tufted with overgrown grass.

'I can't think why she's done it,' Shaughnessy said.

'You knew she'd turned you in, did you?'

'I rang Trevelyan this morning. He gave me the gist of it.' Shaughnessy ran his hand over his face, then combed his fingers into his hair and left them there as he looked up at Scobie. 'Is there anything to drink in this greenhouse of yours? I've just had a pint of lager that has appeared in so many adverts it had gone flat.'

THE TRIUMPH OF BACCHUS 291

'There's some whisky in the kitchen.'

There was some but not much: a half-bottle of Bells with an inch in the bottom. He poured it into a glass and put some away. 'I can't think what got into her.'

'A bellyful of spite, that's what's got into her.' Scobie was looking around the watercolours pinned to the wall of the studio.

'I told her what I was doing. Why couldn't she believe me?' Scobie forgot the watercolours and stared at him. 'You told her?' he asked. 'When was this?'

'The day before yesterday.'

'You were in Switzerland.'

'Venice, to be more accurate.' There was no point in tiptoeing around this one, Scobie was going to have to know the full story. 'I asked her over.'

'And poured out your soul to her?'

'You could say that.'

Someone had taken Scobie's batteries out. He stood stock-still for a moment. Then he threw his arms in the air. 'Oh, that's lovely, that is,' he roared, stumping away across the studio. 'That's all we bloody needed. Thanks very much, Tommie. This bitch starts sniffing around so you tell her everything she wants to know.'

'She was on to us, Scobie.'

'So you decided to make life easier for her and give her the evidence. A bottle of Chianti, the Grand Canal by moonlight, and you shoot a million pounds out of the window. That's brilliant.'

Shaughnessy didn't say anything. What could he say? It was dangerously close to the truth.

'I hope she was good,' Scobie said. 'I hope she was

bloody marvellous in the sack because she comes damned expensive.'

Shaughnessy drained his glass. 'Are you going to belly-ache all day or are you going to show me where you've put the painting?'

'It's there,' Scobie said.

'What's done is done, OK? It's not the way I wanted it but it's too late now.'

The painting was hanging on the back of the door, zipped into one of those plastic covers that women use to store long dresses. Shaughnessy unrolled it on the floor.

'Have you taken a look at it?' he asked.

Scobie was standing by the window, looking up the garden. His head was down, hands pressed into his pockets. 'It looks good,' he said without turning round.

In his present frame of mind that was probably high praise, Shaughnessy reflected. 'I think some of the cracking needs to be encouraged.'

'You'll have to repair it afterwards.'

'That won't take long,' he said. 'I've kept samples of all the paint I used.'

'The fire-extinguisher is in the kitchen.'

It was one of the CO_2 cylinders. Scobie had brought it from his studio in Inkerman Mansions.

Shaughnessy carried it over to the painting and un-clipped the nozzle. Holding it close to the canvas he hit the trigger. The gas streamed out with a whoosh, freezing as it decompressed. A crust of frost appeared on the paint-ed surface.

Slowly he worked it across the figures and trees. Then taking a cloth he wiped it clean. The sudden cold had shrunk the paint, opening the cracks around the contours a fraction more, exposing the reddish underpainting. He went back over certain parts, holding the nozzle close, firing the gas in short spurts until he was satisfied.

'There,' he said. 'Four hundred years of decay in a few seconds.'

'I know the feeling.'

Later that night they had a pizza delivered from a local take-away. It saved them having to risk going out into the street. When they were through Shaughnessy took out the painting that Helmut Schalk had restored. Scobie had picked it up some days earlier.

The tear had been beautifully repaired—something of a waste, as Schalk had said, on such a worthless picture.

On the reverse side of the canvas was Schalk's business stamp. It was a circular design made up from his initials. Shaughnessy traced it in pencil then transferred the design on to a piece of linoleum with carbon paper. From this he was able to cut an accurate die.

There had been a number of publicity pictures of *The Triumph of Bacchus* when it had been hung in the Royal Academy. One of them showed the picture being carried into the main hallway by two porters. Conveniently it was the reverse side that was showing. From this photo Shaughnessy was able to calculate the exact position of Schalk's stamp. He taped the piece of lino on to the end of a kitchen knife, tested it a couple of times, before printing it on to the back of his version of *The Triumph of Bacchus*.

'I've just broken the law,' he said. 'Until then this was a copy and there's no law against that. Now it's a fake.'

The studio only had one bedroom, a small space beyond the kitchen. Scobie had set up a camp bed on the gallery for him. It was as stable as a canoe in rough water. After he had switched out the lights Shaughnessy lay with his arms behind his head and looked up at the low ceiling.

Next door he could hear Scobie moving about the kitchen. He came through into the studio. There was a cigarette in his mouth, a pin-prick of red in the dark. For a while he stood looking out into the night with his back to Shaughnessy. Then he said, 'Does Trevelyan know you are here?'

'He has the phone number, not the address.'

'Why don't you ask him to talk to Patricia, explain to her that she's screwing up the whole business?'

'It's too late. She might not take it from him and that would only make matters worse. It's better to leave things as they are.'

Scobie gave a grunt and the cigarette glowed as he drew on it, lighting up his face.

'Besides,' Shaughnessy said, 'it won't be long now. Trevelyan had another tape delivered yesterday.'

'What did it say?'

'*The Triumph of Bacchus* is in Switzerland. They want the money taken to Zurich where they'll contact him again. In the past the ransom has followed within the next twenty-four hours of that.'

'What's he going to do?'

'Ignore it, I imagine.'

Chapter 26

'The police have ballsed up the whole thing,' Patricia shouted.

With an expression that was meant to convey amusement, Gus watched her pacing the floor. He had a glass of wine in one hand to compensate for the temperature of the office which was high enough to have it picked up on the infra red sensors of a passing American spy satellite.

'I thought that was what was expected,' he said.

'Yesterday he went to some hotel at six in the morning then sat in the Natural History Museum. Now he's vanished completely.'

'What do you mean, completely?'

'He obviously knew exactly what was going on and dropped the tail the police put on him as soon as he got the chance.'

Gus sipped at the wine. 'But wasn't this what you wanted? I thought the whole point was that he was going to come to you.'

Patricia didn't reply. She stood at the window, staring down at the view with one hand on her hip. Gus watched her for a moment and then a smile spread across his face.

He gave a low whistle. 'He didn't come through, right? The deal was he would ring you and he hasn't.'

She still didn't say anything.

'Holy shit, honey, you're in it now.'

'They must have spooked him,' she said angrily. 'If they'd just left him alone he would have come to me, I know he would.'

'But you didn't tell the police that's what he was going to do, did you? You didn't let on that you had schemes of your own so you can't blame them for what they've done.'

'I've got to find him.'

'Damned right you have. You foul this one up and you can whistle for any future contracts with us.'

She shot him a black look but Gus ignored it. He'd seen too many in his time to be impressed.

'What was Shaughnessy doing in this hotel?' he asked.

'He went to see some friend of his about getting a job there.'

'At six in the morning?'

Patricia gave a shrug. 'That's when he came on shift. It sounds a bit odd but I can't see what else he could be doing there.'

'This must be a new experience for you,' Gus said.

'What? Tracing a man?'

'Screwing up.'

Patricia took a couple of his smoked salmon sandwiches, wrapped them in a paper napkin, and tucked them into her pocket. 'Yes,' she said as she stormed out of the room. 'Well, don't start writing my obituary yet.'

She ate the sandwiches as she drove down to Fulham. The meeting she'd attended in Trevelyan's office earlier that afternoon had been brief and to the point. David Ambrose had been there as had Detective Inspector Forsyth. Of greater interest to her had been the presence of Fothergill, the head of Loss & Security Assessment, a lean figure with the quick, watchful eyes of the predator.

The estate agent's office she was looking for was in the Fulham Road. Dodds was nursing a cold at his desk but as Patricia swept in he scrambled to his feet.

'Miss Drew.' He held out his hand. It had recently been holding an overworked handkerchief and so she decided not to take it.

'I need your help,' she told him.

'Of course. You want another look round Scobie Woods's studio.'

'No,' she said. 'I want Scobie Woods.'

'Want him?'

'I want to know where he is.'

'I see, yes. That's confidential information, Miss Drew.' The smile on Dodds's face flicked on and off like a gas cooker on the blink. 'We're not supposed to reveal confidential information about a client.'

'I thought his wife was the client?'

'Yes, she is, but still…' His voice trailed away in search of an explanation. 'It's a matter of trust and all that.'

'I don't think you need worry about betraying his trust, Mr Dodds,' Patricia said briskly. 'Scobie Woods and the assistant you saw with him are engaged in one of the largest art frauds of this century. I need to know where they are.'

Dodds sat down slowly and put the handkerchief to his mouth as though he was about to cry. 'Art fraud?'

'They are holding *The Triumph of Bacchus*. It was in Scobie Woods's studio until yesterday. You saw it there yourself.'

'Oh, my God—'

'Now, do you know where he has gone?'

'Yes—well, no. I don't know where he is but I might have a phone number.' Galvanized into action, Dodds opened a drawer and began rummaging through the papers. 'He rang and gave it to me the other day—in case the studio was sold.'

'You don't have the address?'

'No, only this.' He fished out a scrap of paper and showed it to her. 'It looks local.'

Patricia went back to her car and put through a call. Then she waited half an hour, killing time by wandering around the shops, before making another. This time it was to Inspector Forsyth.

'Can you trace an address from a telephone number?' she asked.

'No trouble.'

'Then we've got him.'

Chapter 27

'Why does it have to be you?' Scobie asked. He sat on the end of the bed and watched Shaughnessy packing clothes into a ruck-sack.

There wasn't much he needed for this trip. He was only going to be away for forty-eight hours at the most. Most of the space in the small ruck-sack was taken up by a thick skiing anorak and a pair of Gore-Tex gloves. Beneath these were two cassette recorders and a number of tapes.

'Because I'm the only one who knows how to finish it,' he said.

'You were commissioned to make a copy of the painting. That was all. And you've done that. Your part is finished. Let someone else risk his neck over there.'

'Oh yes? And who do you have in mind?'

Scobie waved his hand as though this was immaterial. 'One of Collins's men. They're trained for that kind of thing.'

'They're paying me to do it.

'You're not interested in the money,' Scobie said scornfully. 'You're already getting more than you expected. And you stand a good chance of picking up that reward from the Wops on top of that. You've got money coming out of your ears.'

Shaughnessy zipped up the ruck-sack and carried it through into the studio. He didn't want to talk about this any longer but Scobie followed him to the doorway.

'You want to go through with it, don't you? That's the truth of it. You want to be the one to ransom that damned picture.'

'It has to be me. That's all there is to it.'

'Bollocks. You just can't bear the thought of anyone else handling your precious painting, can you?'

'I don't care who handles it.'

'You're obsessed by the thing.'

'That's not true,' Shaughnessy said mildly.

'What is it then? You want to be there when they look at it, is that it? Painting a fake isn't enough for you; you have to see some half-baked expert being taken in by it too.'

'Look, Scobie, I don't like it any better than you but there's no other way. They all know that I have the painting. They're all watching to see what I do. It has to be me.'

Scobie hadn't moved from the doorway. The cigarette in his hand had gone out. 'Go on then,' he said loftily. 'If that's the way you want it, you go off and get your neck broken.'

Shaughnessy dumped the ruck-sack on a chair, unzipped the side pocket, checked for passport, tickets, and cash. 'It's not the way I wanted it. If there was a way out right now I'd take it. But there isn't. I'm stuck with things the way they are.'

Scobie put the cigarette to his lips and found it was dead. He threw it away across the floor. The sound of it hitting the back of a canvas was minute but in the silence of the studio it could have been a lead bar dropping.

'You know what you're doing, Tommie?' he asked after a moment. 'This ransom. You do know how to get away with it?'

'It'll be a piece of cake.'

'You reckon so?'

'Would I take the risk if I wasn't pretty certain I was going to come out of it in one piece?'

'Yes, you probably would.'

Shaughnessy hefted the ruck-sack on to his shoulder. It was one thing sounding confident; it was quite another feeling it. He gave a nod of his head. 'I'll see you when I get back.'

Scobie made no answer. From somewhere beyond the high brick wall that isolated this tiny patch of London came the wail of a siren. Shaughnessy opened the door.

'Tommie—'

He turned back.

Scobie stood in the middle of the darkened studio. There was a frown of concentration on his face as though he was trying to find words for something that was bothering him. Then he gave up the struggle and brushed it away with a flap of his hand.

'I'll see you when you get back.'

Shaughnessy let himself out into the street. The wail of the siren was closer now. He walked away in the opposite direction. The gate to a basement flat was open. He went down three or four steps and shut the gate behind him.

He didn't have long to wait. From his worm's eye view through the railings, he saw the squad car draw up at the garden door. A second one arrived moments later. They spewed uniformed police into the street. Amongst them was a plain-clothes officer in a blue anorak.

Patricia was the last to get out. She was wearing a long black overcoat with the collar turned up, her hair spread out across her shoulders. Her back was turned to him so he couldn't see the expression on her face at that moment.

She was standing back, hands in pockets, watching the police as they broke the lock on the door. They disappeared inside but she still stood waiting. What was the matter? he wondered. Was she frightened of finding him in there? It was only when one of the officers came back out that she ventured down the passage.

Climbing back into the street, Shaughnessy walked up into the King's Road without looking back.

'He's gone.'

'How long ago?'

'I don't know,' Scobie said. 'An hour, maybe longer. He's well away from here by now, that's for sure.'

The uniformed officers were combing through the rooms at the rear of the studio. Scobie watched them with contempt. He was sitting in the wicker chair as he had been when they first burst in, his feet thrust out in front, a tin of tobacco on his lap from which he was rolling a new cigarette.

'Be my guest,' he called out. 'Search the place, tear it to shreds if you like. You won't find him here.'

Patricia had never seen him before but he was much as Shaughnessy had described: a bear of a man—part prophet, part tramp, like one of those Velazquez paintings in the Prado.

She had hung back when the police moved in and now stood just inside the entrance, her head down so that her fair hair fell across her face.

Forsyth was getting angry. 'Does he have the painting with him?'

'Painting?'

'Please don't try to be clever with me, Mr Woods. You know perfectly well what I mean. Does he have *The Triumph of Bacchus* with him?'

'Oh no,' Scobie said. He had decided to play his role for high comedy. He put the cigarette in his mouth, lit it and smiled through the smoke. 'That left here days ago.'

'How is he getting it out of the country?'

'I really couldn't tell you. Second-class post I should imagine. It's very reliable.'

'You'll find it helps to co-operate.'

'I am co-operating. I'm telling you everything I know. And that amounts to practically nothing.'

'Excuse me, sir—' One of the police officers put his head round the kitchen door.

'Could you take a look at this.'

Forsyth went next door. Scobie Woods sat back in the chair and puffed at the cigarette. Then he looked round at Patricia as though seeing her for the first time.

'You must be feeling very pleased with yourself, young lady.' Patricia kept her eyes on the ground. The affected humour had gone out of Scobie's voice.

'Why did you have to do it?'

'Do what?' she asked steadily.

'Run him in like this. What has he done to you that gives you the right to treat him in this way?'

'What did he do?' Patricia repeated bitterly. 'He didn't have to do anything to me. He's a criminal.'

Scobie threw back his head at this word. 'Oh, I see,' he said as though some deep mystery had been unravelled before his eyes. 'And you're judge and jury all rolled into one, are you? You decide when a man is guilty?'

She was in an impossible position. The old man hated her for what she was doing. There was no way out. 'He's swindled money,' she said defiantly. 'Not just a few hundred pounds—millions. You would just overlook that, would you?'

Scobie got to his feet. It was a remarkably quick movement for a man of his age. He came close to her. 'Of course I overlook it. Tom Shaughnessy is my friend.'

'And that puts him above the law?'

'Do you know the meaning of friendship, Miss Drew? Does it come into the calculations that go on in that clever head of yours?'

Patricia took a step away from him. She didn't frighten easily but he was a scary old devil. 'It's a strange friendship that encourages a man to commit a crime.'

'He trusted you.'

'Trusted me?' She spat the words back at him. 'Tom Shaughnessy didn't trust me. He tried to trick me into helping him. Just as he's tricked you into helping him, if you stopped to think about it.'

'Do you blame a man for trying to get on in the world?'

Forsyth came back into the studio with two of the uniformed officers. Patricia glanced at them and then back at Scobie.

'There's no excuse for stealing,' she said under her breath. It sounded unnecessarily prudish in her own ears.

'The money came from an insurance company. That's what they have it for. They expect to lose it. It doesn't hurt anyone.'

'If that's what you think you're more of a fool than I thought,' Patricia said, and turning on her heel she walked out of the studio. Her cheeks were burning. She hadn't expected to be confronted by the old man like that. It was not an experience she wanted to repeat.

Back in the street she wandered aimlessly around the pavement as she waited.

'He's gone then?'

She turned around. It was one of the police drivers who'd spoken. He was sitting in the squad car, one arm resting along the side of the opened window.

'Yes,' she said. 'He's gone.'

Forsyth came out of the door in the wall. He nodded back in the direction of the studio.

'We'll take him in and get a statement.'

'Will you learn anything from him, do you think?'

'Probably not,' Forsyth said. 'The old bastard has decided to be as obstructive as possible. Fat lot of good it will do him.' He stared up the street. His lips and nose were red from the cold as though they had been dusted with rouge.

She could understand his anger. It had been so close. A few hours earlier and he could have wrapped up this whole business. As it was they were as far from finding him as they'd ever been. 'I imagine there's a good chance you'll pick him up when he tries to leave the country.'

Forsyth shrugged. 'We might. It depends when he left here. Woods says it was an hour ago but he's probably lying. It could be either earlier or later than that. Take your pick. If it's earlier we must face the fact that he has probably already skipped it.'

Patricia didn't say anything. She'd come to much the same conclusion.

'We've contacted the Swiss police,' Forsyth said. 'If we don't get a fix on Shaughnessy in the next few hours I'll have to hand over to them.'

Patricia turned at the sound of the garden door opening. Scobie Woods emerged, escorted by a couple of officers. He left with bad grace but no trouble, sitting in the back of the squad car with his arms folded, eyes fixed on the road ahead.

'I'll be sending on what information we have,' Forsyth said as the car passed. 'I'd welcome it if you could give me as much as you can.'

'Of course—'

'Perhaps you could come back now and give us a statement?' Patricia didn't want to go anywhere where she might be confronted by Scobie Woods again. 'I've left my car up by the Fulham Road,' she said. 'It's on a meter.'

'Hop in. I'll give you a lift up there. We can talk on the way.'

It was growing dark as the car swung out into the King's Road. Forsyth unzipped the front of his anorak and gave a jerk of his shoulders as he sat back. It was a gesture of possession as much as a search for comfort. This was his car, just as it was his case—for a while.

'You've no idea where he intends to carry out the ransom?'

She shook her head. 'Nothing positive. He wouldn't say what he had in mind.'

'If we could get some fix on it beforehand it would make all the difference. We could get people in place, seal off his escape.' Forsyth placed his hands on his widespread knees and gave another jerk of his shoulders.

'I don't know where it's going to happen,' Patricia said. 'But I think I might know where he's going to go afterwards.'

Forsyth looked round at her. 'You do?'

'Possibly. It might be nothing.'

'Tell me.'

She paused, uncertain. 'When I was in Venice with him he said he'd meet me somewhere further down the valley after he had got the money.'

'Did he say where?'

'No, but before I left I went through his wallet. There was a phone number in Switzerland. I rang it the other day. It's for a hotel in Rougemont. That's a few miles outside Gstaad.'

'Why didn't you tell me this before?'

Patricia smiled thinly. 'Because I didn't think he was ever going to get this far.'

'Do you think he'll still go there?'

'Why not? He doesn't know I have the address.'

❀ ❀ ❀

The London Library is set in one corner of St James's Square. It is not open to the public. Like the clubs that surround it, it is only open to subscription paying members.

Shaughnessy showed his card at the desk. It had arrived in the post three days earlier.

'You'll have to leave your luggage here, sir,' the librarian told him.

Shaughnessy handed over the ruck-sack. It had never been called luggage before. 'I'm looking for the section on military history.'

He was directed down to the basement. The stairs were metal and the air was thick with that aromatic smell that comes from books that have been locked away for too long. The rooms were in darkness but in one a single light was illuminating a row of shelves. Shaughnessy groped his way towards it.

Collins was standing beneath the neon strip, a book opened in his hands. 'You're late.'

'I didn't realize it was a formal occasion.'

'You have some explanation, I presume?'

Shaughnessy tipped the book up so that he could see the title on the spine. 'I thought I'd give you the chance to learn a bit more about *Napoleon's Egyptian Campaign*.'

Collins put the book back on the shelf and ran his hand along the others, smoothing them into line. 'The police have taken Scobie Woods in.'

'I know.'

'But from your late appearance here I gather you

managed to extract yourself in time.' Something in the tone of his voice suggested this was the one unfortunate aspect of the event.

'I heard them coming.'

Collins didn't appear to be listening. 'You've made a mess of this, Shaughnessy. Right from the start you've made a mess of the whole business.'

'I thought things were going rather well in the circumstances.'

The circumstances were evidently what Collins was complaining about. He pulled a quick smile. Not really a smile, just a shift of the facial features to demonstrate the principle of a smile to novices. 'Is that what you think, Shaughnessy? Is that how you see it? Then it might interest you to know that Trevelyan wants to call it off.'

'For what reason?'

'They're on to you.' Collins was getting some pleasure from laying out the facts. 'The hounds are snapping at your heels.'

'You're a terrible pessimist. The painting will be in Switzerland within the next few hours and I'll be there by tomorrow. What more do you want?'

'In the mean time they've taken in Woods. And what's he going to tell them?'

'He's going to tell them that I'm a fearful crook who's been stealing paintings and hiding them in his studio for the last year. That's why he hung around waiting for the police to arrive.' Did Collins understand nothing? he wondered. His aim had always been to create confusion, to keep the opposition guessing. That was never going to be done by hiding away in a dark garret.

'The painting's in Switzerland already, is it?' Collins asked. To say that he spoke with more respect would be overstating the case but his manner had thawed by a few degrees.

'It's on its way.'

'Is it good?'

'It's a shade better than a painting by numbers, if that's what you mean.'

'No.' Collins had some more precise distinction in mind. 'I mean is it good, very good—good enough to fool a real expert?'

'Why do you ask?'

'They've put that Austrian restorer on the case. He's going to be looking it over before the money is handed across. I'm told he could recognize that painting with his eyes closed.'

'Who's idea was that?'

'David Ambrose's, I believe.'

'I thought it might be.' Ambrose—every time it was Ambrose. Never taking over control but always there, nagging away in the background like a hole in the tooth.

'You don't seem surprised.'

'It was always going to be that way,' Shaughnessy said. 'If it hadn't been Schalk it would have been someone like him.'

There was a sudden clanging of footsteps on the metal stairs next door. This hadn't been a stupid place to meet, he realized. No one could approach unnoticed. Collins waited until the intruder had moved away into one of the further rooms before saying, 'You realize you're on your own, Shaughnessy? If you get caught red-handed you're getting no help from us. There's no link that you'll ever manage to prove: no money has changed hands, no contact has been made. If the Swiss police feel your collar you'll take what's coming to you.'

It was a charming way of putting it. Shaughnessy took out a piece of paper and gave it to him. 'I'll be wanting this.'

Collins raised his eyebrows as he read. 'For what reason?'

'Because I want to stay alive.'

'It might take more than this,' he said frostily. 'Does it have to be Kevlar? I could lay hands on one of the Bristol models more easily.'

'Anything, provided it works on the day. I must go now. I'll see you in Switzerland.'

'And what do I tell Trevelyan?' Collins didn't like to admit it but he was just the messenger. And they've been known to get shot if they bring bad news.

'Tell him to hold on to his hat and hope that the Good Lord is on our side.'

'You intend going through with it, then?'

'Of course,' Shaughnessy said. What else could he say? What else could he do, come to think of it?

'Aren't you forgetting something?' Collins called after him. He took a bunch of keys from his pocket and tossed them over to Shaughnessy. 'It's a green BMW. You'll find it parked across the square.'

Collins was a grouchy little man with the impish good humour of a broken bedstead but his saving grace was that he carried out his orders to the letter. The car he'd arranged for Shaughnessy had been hired in Geneva. It had left-hand drive and Swiss registration plates just as he had requested. After weeks of pedalling a bicycle round London in the perishing cold, it was like travelling in state.

He switched on the radio and tuned into Radio 3 and thought of the accusations that Scobie had made before he left. It wasn't true that he wanted to see whether he could fool an expert with his copy of *The Triumph of Bacchus*. That suggested the whole project had been nothing more than a dangerous practical joke from the start. But then neither was his own claim that no one else could do the job for him true either. It was more simple than that. More simple and more fundamental. He wanted to earn the money he was getting. That's what it boiled down to. Like his father and his grandfather before him, Shaughnessy had a deep-rooted belief that he had to work for what he earned. Good old Catholic guilt. You can't beat it.

Taking the A217 out of London he drove to Gatwick airport and booked into the Penta hotel. That evening he lay on his bed with the two cassette recorders beside him piecing together a tape from the television. It was one hell of a job. The next time someone told him he was a film editor he'd show him some deference. The job took him over three hours. It would have been longer had he not been given some of the previous ransom tapes from which he could extract passages.

At six the following morning he handed the finished article over to a motorbike courier and then collecting the car from the underground car park he drove down to the south coast.

Chapter 28

'Assuming he left immediately he could be anywhere by now,' Forsyth said. He took the tape out of the cassette player.

'Have you checked the flights out of Gatwick?' Trevelyan asked.

'We're doing it now but I doubt whether we'll learn anything useful. He's almost certainly travelling on a false passport and even if he's not he had a four-hour lead on us.'

The tape had been delivered to Trevelyan's office at ten past nine that morning. He'd rung the police immediately he'd come in, which was about fifteen minutes later. But that still gave Shaughnessy enough time to have taken any one of the Saturday morning flights into Switzerland. And that was assuming he was heading there directly.

'You're certain it was Shaughnessy who made it?' he asked Forsyth.

'The description fits. The driver said he was tall, fair haired. He can't be sure about the accent but you tell me Shaughnessy's is not strong.'

'Almost imperceptible.'

'He paid in cash and signed in the name of a Mr S. Rocco. That's the name he gave the hotel also.'

'Sounds like him.'

'It was him,' Ambrose cut in. He gave them the tolerant look that he reserved for those whose education has been rudimentary. 'San Rocco. He's a fifteenth-century saint. You often find him in Venetian paintings. He's usually depicted as a man dressed in travelling clothes.'

'You think it's his idea of a joke?' Forsyth couldn't see the funny side of it himself.

'Not a joke, Inspector. I think it's Shaughnessy's way of telling us he has left the country. Which is why we must ask ourselves whether he has.'

Forsyth didn't blink but there was that kind of pause. 'You reckon it could be a trick?'

'He clearly wants us to assume he's gone. But on that tape of his he says he'll contact us outside the Bahnhof Hotel in Gstaad at eight p.m. tomorrow night. That's thirty-six hours from now. Why the delay? We could be there by this afternoon.'

'You mean he's travelling by land?'

'It's a possibility. I should certainly warn the ferry services along the coast to be on the alert.'

'But why should he want to go overland when he could have flown?'

'Possibly because he's carrying an eight-foot painting.'

There was probably a time when Portsmouth was a charming naval port bristling with masts. Now it's a huge shapeless desert of concrete linked together by motorways. Shaughnessy parked in the underground car park of a hotel and checked into a room. It had four stars which meant there was a television and a bidet in the bathroom but he hadn't a use for either of these at present. It was the basin he wanted.

From his ruck-sack he took out a bottle of hair-dye. He'd used it twice before so he was getting the hang of it now. It was a gel that had to be worked into the scalp and then left for a bit to take effect. He wandered around the room without disturbing anything while he waited. After fifteen minutes he washed the stuff out again and dried his hair with the device that was built into the bathroom wall.

A change of hair colour has an extraordinary effect. It not only changes your appearance; it alters your entire ancestry. With nutbrown hair Shaughnessy no longer looked Irish. A bottle of patented beetle juice and centuries of Gaelic blood was wiped out at a stroke. He brushed his hair back close to his head and added a pair of thick-rimmed glasses and he was someone else. He wasn't sure who, maybe a salesman—someone with all the insurance policies you could want and a clean shirt on the hanger in the back of his car.

Going back downstairs he dropped the key at the reception desk. He didn't bother to pay. This wasn't the kind of hotel that rented rooms for half an hour. The very suggestion would be insulting.

He drove down to the ferry terminal and joined the queue of cars that were filing in through passport control. The whole place was lit up like a Christmas tree. Above the low buildings he could see the superstructure of the ferry towering above them, its bows opened like some primitive insect waiting to devour its prey.

The queue wasn't moving. He cut the engine and getting out he walked up towards the barrier. There were three men in the brightly lit office. One was sitting at the window, thumbing his way through the passports, checking the faces of the drivers against the pictures in his hand. Another sat beside him. The third stood behind. He wasn't interested in the passports. He was staring through the window at each car as it passed.

They were looking for him. The bastards had guessed how he was travelling and were waiting for him. Was his disguise good enough, he wondered, as he got back in the car. It would fool the casual observer, but would it be good enough to get past someone who was on the lookout for him?

A movement made him look up. A figure was coming up the queue of cars towards him, glancing at the vehicles on either side, checking the registration plates.

As he came closer Shaughnessy sank down in the seat to give himself the appearance of a shorter man. He should have worn a hat, that makes a difference in the dark.

The man had seen his car; he was coming straight towards him. He can't be looking for me, Shaughnessy told himself. He can't know I'd be here at this port, waiting to catch this ferry. It must be chance. He looked away. Keep calm, don't look ruffled. The worst thing to do in these situations is to give any sign of reaction. You're a businessman going over to the Continent for your firm. You're bored, slightly impatient.

THE TRIUMPH OF BACCHUS 317

There was a knock on the window. It seemed to go right inside him, hitting the pit of his stomach.

He wound down the window.

'Is your name Shaughnessy?' the man asked.

He didn't answer. There wasn't an answer he could think of giving at that moment.

The man put his face forwards a degree. 'If you'd like to get out of the car, please, sir.'

Chapter 29

It was pretty damned cold outside. The man's face was raw, his lips chapped. Warm breath streamed out of his mouth and went off somewhere in a hurry. Reaching into his breast pocket he drew out a plastic folder and flicked it open.

'Securicom,' he said. 'I've been told to take this car on board the ferry.'

It took Shaughnessy a few moments to comprehend what he was saying. Securicom—that was Collins's outfit. He sat back and let his heart catch up on the beats it had missed.

'If you'd like to get out, sir,' the man repeated. He spoke in that flat tone that driving instructors spend their lives perfecting.

'Holy mother,' Shaughnessy said as he climbed on to the tarmac. 'You had me worried there.'

'Sorry, sir. Didn't mean to alarm you.' He gave a little grin which suggested he knew bloody well what effect he'd had and enjoyed it. 'Security's been boosted up there. We thought it might be better if you went on board by foot. It's someone in a car they're looking for, not a pedestrian. I've got this for you.'

Shaughnessy took the ticket he gave him.

'You'll find the way on board over there,' the man said as he got in behind the wheel. 'Have a good journey.'

Score one up for Collins, Shaughnessy thought as he walked up the gangway. All along he had told him he'd need his back-up and he was right. He'd try to remember to be a shade more grateful in future.

Shaughnessy had never been a good sailor and he spent most of the night on deck while the ferry bucketed its way across the Channel. Sometime before midnight, on the far side of the French customs, he retrieved his car and headed south.

By midday, beneath a sky as bleak as a dentist's waiting room, he reached Geneva and turned on to the motorway that runs along the lake. A few miles beyond Château Chillon he left it again and started the slow climb up into the mountains. It had been snowing since he was last here. The snow-line was further down the valley than it had been. He didn't know whether that was an advantage or not.

Over the Col de Pillon the snow was several metres deep and the car passed between smooth white walls that had been carved out by the snow-ploughs. By this time he had the window open and the radio belting music into his ears as, apart from the brief stops for petrol and a stretch of the legs, he had been driving non-stop for fourteen hours. He was stiff and tired and his face felt as though it were made of cake icing which would crack at the slightest movement.

A mile before Gsteig he turned off the road on to a track. It ran downhill between fir trees to a small barn. Shaughnessy parked his car on the far side where it couldn't be seen from the track. Getting out he hobbled over to the double doors on legs which had forgotten their purpose in life. The key was where every key should be: above the door lintel. He opened the padlock and went inside. In the old days it would have been centrally heated by cattle, straw, and manure. Now it held a few pieces of farm machinery and smelled of diesel fuel.

At the far end was a ladder that led up into the loft. In the light of the single window in the roof he found what he was looking for: a canvas bag hanging from one of the rafters. Unfastening the strap he laid the contents out on the wooden floor.

It was all there: a portable telephone, not one of your yuppie slimline affairs but a good solid military model, a rubber-bodied torch, a pair of handcuffs, and a gun wrapped in oil paper. Score up another point to Collins.

The gun was a standard-model Walther PPK. He pulled out the clip but as he expected it was empty. That had been part of the deal: he could have a gun but no ammunition. The Swiss police wouldn't be sticking to the same rule. They knew nothing about the conversations that had gone on behind closed doors earlier that year and wouldn't get to hear of them either if things went wrong. As Collins had said, he was on his own in this one.

Packing it all back in the bag Shaughnessy took off his anorak, wrapped it up as a pillow, and lay down on the wooden floor. In his time he'd slept on water mattresses, in four-poster beds, and once, on an ill-advised trip across the Bay of Biscay, in a hammock. But none of them had felt as comfortable as these wooden boards did now.

He didn't know how long he'd been asleep when a sound jerked him awake. It was the door below opening, a noise no louder than the striking of a match but enough to have the adrenalin breaking the speed limit through his veins. Rolling over he gently slid the canvas bag away out of sight and got to his feet.

There was a creak from the ladder. Shaughnessy stepped behind the opened hatch so that the intruder's back would be to him when it appeared.

'Tommie?' It was just a whisper, slightly apprehensive. Then another step up the ladder. 'Tommie, are you there?'

Patricia's head, prettily decorated by an Hérmes scarf, poked up through the hatch, looking round 180 degrees without seeing him, and paused.

Stepping forwards he caught her by the arm. She gave a yelp of surprise as he helped her up the last few steps.

'Did anyone follow you?' he asked. Her arms were locked around his neck so he found himself speaking to the top of her head. It wiggled from side to side in reply and he felt the rub of her cold nose against his neck.

'Sure?'

She pulled back and looked up at him. Her eyes were sparkling. 'Dead sure. I stopped and checked twice on the way up.'

'Have you got it?'

'It's on the car.' She let go of him and headed back down the ladder, keen to show him her handiwork.

Parked beside his own BMW was a Fiat, not the kind of machine Patricia would normally be seen dead in but, as he learned later, she'd borrowed it from the hotel manager in Gstaad. Strapped to the roof rack was a ski-bag.

'Did anyone comment on it?' Shaughnessy asked as he undid the clasps.

'Barraclough did. He was pretty sarky about it too: asked me when I thought I was going to get the time to go skiing.'

'Barraclough? What's he doing here?'

'He wanted to come. That's how I got here too. He had a private jet to take him up to Saanen. He gave me a lift in it.'

'When did he arrive?'

'Lunchtime. Scared me to death. Have you ever been in one of those things? We were that close to the mountains all the way, and then we just dropped out of the sky on to the runway. I thought I was going to faint.' She was speaking in a sort of breathless rush as she lifted the ski-bag down to the ground. He offered to carry it but she took it inside on her shoulder. At the foot of the ladder she propped it against the wall and went on up. She was wearing a shiny blue ski-suit which stretched in all the right places and a pair of those shaggy snow boots. Shaughnessy passed the ski-bag up to her and followed.

'Have you had a look at it?'

'No. I wasn't sure whether I should.' It had been sitting in her flat for the last two days and, from the tone of her voice, the temptation to have a peek had been almost irresistible.

Shaughnessy undid the zip and pulled out a pair of skis. Beside them was a plastic tube, a length of drain-piping as it happened. In it was the rolled canvas.

He spread it out on the floor. Patricia knelt in front of it, her hands clamped on her temples to stop her hair falling into her eyes and studied it in silence. After a few mo-

THE TRIUMPH OF BACCHUS 323

ments she touched the surface and then sat back. Her face was serious. 'You did this?'

'All by myself.'

'But it's old. I mean it doesn't just look old; it is old.'

'Bits of it really are. The rest is younger than a bottle of Beaujolis Nouveau.'

'It's incredible,' she said. 'I thought it would be a good copy. Like a photo. But this is the real thing. No one could tell it was a fake.'

'Unfortunately there's one person who can.'

'That restorer, you mean?'

Shaughnessy nodded. 'Schalk. He knows the real thing like a child.'

'Maybe.' She understood what he meant. 'He's a strange fish, isn't he?'

'You've met him?'

'He was there at lunch just now. He didn't say a word. It's as though he's in a dream. I tried to talk to him but nothing came back.'

'Where are you staying?'

'At the Park Hotel.'

'The Palace was full, was it?'

'Yes,' she said. 'It was.' She had missed the irony in his voice and looked at him now with a strange expression on her face. 'How long does it take for that muck to come out?'

He'd forgotten that his hair was still dark brown and slicked back in his salesman's look. 'It's rather becoming, isn't it? I'm thinking of keeping it.'

'Over my dead body.'

'Pity. Who else has turned up apart from Barraclough and Schalk?'

'Trevelyan arrived about an hour ago. And Fothergill's crowd are around but I haven't seen them. They're staying down in the town somewhere.'

'Ambrose?'

'Not that I know of.'

'How did they react when you got back from Venice?' Over the last few days their conversations on the phone had been short and to the point. Only essential information had been passed.

'It was easy.' She leaned forwards and grinned at him in satisfaction. 'None of them questioned me at all. I don't think they even stopped to consider it. Ambrose thinks I'm the bitch of the century, of course, and Trevelyan has been avoiding me like the plague. I was round at his office the other day. He looked as though he wanted to shrink into his shoes. He was terrified I was going to blow the whole thing out of the water.'

'How about Gus?' She'd been worried about him. Of all of them, Gus knew her best.

'He was no problem. I hit him with so many demands that he didn't have time to wonder whether I was telling him the truth. Scobie was the worst. He was in that studio when the police arrived.'

'Did he go at you?'

'Skinned me alive.' Her face was suddenly serious. 'He's never going to forgive me, is he?'

'Who, Scobie? Of course he will. You don't know him. It's all wind with Scobie. He'll sulk for a bit and then forget it.'

'Are you sure?' She sounded less than confident.

'He'll get over it. You'd better get going now. What reason did you give for going out?'

'I told them I wanted to see a friend over at Saanen.'

'Do you have a friend in Saanen?'

'Of course I do—several.' She sounded hurt that he should ask. They went back to the car. Shaughnessy took the bag containing his ski-boots out of the back. Patricia watched him. Her face was suddenly pale. He dumped the bag in the boot of his car. 'I'll see you later then.'

'Oh God, Tommie,' she said quietly. 'This is going to go all right, isn't it?'

It wasn't the moment to discuss the subject. They'd been over it time and again that night in Venice. All they could do now was hope and pray—if prayers worked up here in the mountains.

Patricia didn't ask again. Instead she put her arms around his neck and squeezed him hard. Then quickly she got into her car and left.

He watched it disappear up the track. Going into the barn he rolled up the canvas and tucked it in the ski-bag. He strapped it to the roof rack, put everything else in the boot of his car, and drove back up to the road.

The cable car up the Diableret mountain is at the head of the valley. He'd passed it earlier that afternoon. It's an extraordinary feat of engineering, one of the longest unsupported spans of cable in Europe. Above it towers the peak of the Wilderhorn, a crooked pinnacle of rock that stands out above the ice fields like the conning tower of a gigantic submarine. As he approached now it was silhouetted against the evening sky with a few wisps of cloud feeling their way around the base.

He parked and locked the car. It was going to stay there for the next few hours but with its Swiss registration plates it shouldn't arouse any interest. Putting on his ski-boots and swinging the ski-bag over his shoulder he walked across to the ticket office.

There were only a few others going up. Shaughnessy stood by the window and watched the ground vanishing away beneath them as the cab swung out across the valley.

It took twenty minutes to reach the first station. Beyond that there are two shorter lifts that stretch up to the glacier. Shaughnessy stepped out on to the platform which cantilevers out from the mountain face. Beneath him the valley was laid out like a road map, the first lights beginning to twinkle in the dusk. A chalked message above the exit door told him the last lift would be at four thirty. That was twenty minutes from now.

Outside he took out his skis. The bag was still rigid from the plastic tubing inside. He locked it into the rack by the restaurant door. There's not much theft up in the mountains—anyone who can afford to live in the Gstaad valley doesn't need to nick a pair of skis—but the Swiss never miss out on a source of revenue. Putting five francs into the slot he removed the tag and zipped it into his breast pocket. Then stamping his feet into the bindings of his skis he headed down the slope.

It was a narrow track that snaked between the trees. Shaughnessy snow-ploughed along it for fifty yards until he was almost directly below the cable-car station before stopping. He fiddled with the binding on one foot, letting the others pass by. It was getting late, only a few figures were left on the slopes and they were all heading down now. When the path was clear in both directions he took off the skis, put them over his shoulder, and walked down into the trees.

❀ ❀ ❀

The hotel receptionist smiled politely as Patricia came into the brightly lit foyer.

'Did you find your friends, madame?' he asked.

'I did, yes.'

'That is good. The car you ordered has arrived,' he added. 'You'll find it outside.'

She signed the form he put in front of her and hoped it was for something with a bit more kick to it than the second-hand Fiat he had let her use in the mean time. Ordering coffee to be sent to her room she went upstairs and ran herself a bath. The knock on the door came while she was still submerged in scented water. She threw on a bath robe, wrapped a towel around her wet hair, and flicked open the catch on the door.

'Just leave it inside,' she called out as she went back into the bathroom.

'Patricia—'

She turned around.

It was David Ambrose. He stood in the doorway. 'I'm so sorry. Am I intruding?'

'No—no, of course not. Come in.' She wrapped the bath robe more securely around herself. 'I thought you were the waiter.'

'Ah yes, I see—' He closed the door behind him.

'I didn't realize you were here.'

'I arrived about an hour ago. I called round on you earlier but I gather you had gone out somewhere.' Ambrose looked around the room quickly and keenly as he pulled off his gloves. He had made no concessions to his recent change of environment. Beneath his black overcoat he was wearing a chalk-stripe suit and polished black brogues which clearly hadn't been allowed to make contact with the snow.

'I went over to see some friends of mine.'

'Ah yes, quite.' His heart wasn't in the subject. Strolling over to the window he looked out at the view.

'Did you want something?' Patricia asked. She felt like adding: or do you make a habit of bursting into a girl's room whenever you feel like it?

'I gather you have given the police some valuable assistance.'

'Have I?'

'Concerning this ransom. You have an idea where Shaughnessy may be trying to get to afterwards.'

'Oh that. Yes, it's just a possibility.'

Ambrose turned from the window. His eyes were two blue chips of ice. 'You didn't think to tell me also?'

'I didn't—no. I assumed they would pass it on to you themselves.'

'I need to keep the negotiators fully briefed, Patricia. Every small detail could be useful. If you have something that might be of help you must let me have it.' There was a flatness to his voice. She'd thought he was uneasy in her room but she realized now that he was angry: angry to have been deprived of this information, angry to have had to come searching for it.

'I'm sorry,' she said. 'I didn't realize it was so important.'

'Unfortunately the police take a slightly narrow view of this whole affair. They seem to think they are the only ones involved. It was quite by chance that I discovered you'd had this conversation with them at all.'

'It was just a thought I had.' She wasn't going to be reprimanded by him. 'It may be nothing at all.'

'Let me be the judge of that,' Ambrose said quietly. 'Where is it he intends to go?'

'A small hotel. It's further down the valley.'

From his pocket Ambrose took out a map of the area. Sitting down on the bed he spread it on his lap. 'Show me,' he said. 'On this.'

'It's on the Saanen-Moser road.' Her finger traced the route on the map. 'There—just after that bend in the road.'

'Does it have a name?'

'The Gasthof Adler.'

'And you think he will head there?'

'Yes, I do.'

After Ambrose had left, she threw on some clothes, tied a scarf around her damp hair and walked down into the town. Just off the main street she found a telephone booth, shut herself inside and put through a call.

It lasted less than thirty seconds. When she was finished she padded down the street to Charlie's bar. Trevelyan was sitting by himself at a table in the far corner. He looked up at Patricia in surprise.

'Do you mind if I join you?' she asked.

He paused an instant, long enough to take in the expression on her face, before saying: 'No, please do.'

She ordered a cup of hot chocolate and warmed her hands on it when it arrived. Trevelyan was drinking brandy.

'Nervous?' she asked.

He nodded.

'Me too.'

It was a long wait in the darkness. For the first hour Shaughnessy sat on the base of a large outcrop of rock that shielded him from view and pictured what was going on in the cable station above. He knew the routine the staff went through as the place was closed down for the night. He should do: he'd sat in the restaurant on the first floor and watched it often enough.

First the two upper lifts were stopped and the piste-control skied down checking no one was left on the slopes. They usually stopped for a few drinks and a chat at this mid-station before heading on down into the valley.

Tonight was no different. Just after five he heard them pass by on the track, their skis rattling on the freezing snow. One of them must have been smoking a pipe: he caught the sweet aromatic smoke a few moments after they'd gone. Fifteen minutes later the cable car went down taking the last of the cooks and ski-lift attendants. There would only be one guard left up there now. He spent the night in the cabin beside the restaurant ready to open the lift in the morning.

After the cable car had disappeared out of sight, Shaughnessy stood up and stretched himself. It was a clear night, which was no bad thing as far as he was concerned, but without a blanket of cloud any warmth there might be in the mountains had vanished. It was freezing cold, two or three degrees below zero at a guess, but at least there was no wind.

Twice he went for a walk along the mountain side, partly to get his circulation going and partly out of boredom but the rest of the time he sat on the rock and stared down into the valley. It was strangely peaceful. He didn't think of what he was about to do. That seemed remote, more like a memory than an impending event.

Patricia had brought him some food: bread rolls and cheese. It was all she'd been able to get from the dining room at the end of lunch. He rather wished she'd added something to drink. He'd made a decision to keep off the alcohol during this operation but if a small bottle had been included he wouldn't have had the heart to turn it down.

At seven thirty-five he stood up and stretched himself. Taking out the Walther PPK he tucked it into his waistband. The handcuffs he put in his left pocket. He was already wearing the black woollen balaclava; he had put it on earlier to keep his face warm.

It had taken him only a few seconds to ski down to this spot but it took him over fifteen minutes to trudge up again. Without skis his feet kept breaking through the crust of snow and sinking in up to his knees. By the time he reached the cable station he was sweating hard beneath his anorak and thick seaman's jersey. He paused to catch his breath. There was a light on in the first-floor cabin and a trickle of smoke coming from the stack above but apart from that there was no sign of life.

Shaughnessy laid his skis down on the ground by the entrance to the cable car and then retrieved the ski bag from the lock-up rack. It was common enough for people to leave their skis up here for the night rather than haul them the five miles back to Gstaad. He unzipped the bag and put the rolled canvas in its plastic tube by the door to the control-room.

The steps up to the cabin were of galvanized metal. He tip-toed up them—as far as you can tip-toe in ski boots—placing each foot down slowly so that it made no sound. In the event he needn't have worried: the guard had the TV going full blast and wouldn't have heard if an avalanche had hit the place.

Taking the gun in his right hand, Shaughnessy turned the handle of the door, felt it give a fraction. Standing back, he kicked it open with his foot.

The security guard was making his dinner, leaning over the gas cooker in the far corner of the room. He half turned in surprise as the door burst inwards, his mouth opening to speak. Then he saw the gun and froze: a wooden spoon in one hand and an expression of idiot incomprehension on his face.

They stood by the entrance to the Bahnhof Hotel and waited. There was very little conversation, just the occasional brief remark. Patricia had known more cheerful gatherings at a funeral.

In the street light she could see Fothergill over by the entrance to the railway station. Two of his team were with him: hard-looking men in dark clothing, the type who would shoot first and not bother to ask questions afterwards. Near by a couple of police cars were parked, the uniformed officers chatting quietly amongst themselves. They, of everyone here, seemed the most relaxed.

Gerald Barraclough stamped his feet on the ground. 'Shouldn't be long now,' he said to her.

'No,' Patricia agreed mechanically. She looked at the clock on the station platform. It was ten to eight. Was that right? It seemed to have been ten to eight for a long time now. She peeled back her glove and checked her watch. It also said ten to eight.

'Why here, of all places?' Barraclough had a flask of brandy in his hand. He took a swig and offered it to Patricia.

'No thank you. I don't know why.'

Ambrose was further along the pavement, his hands in his pockets. He walked away a few paces as though measuring out some precise distance, turned on his heel and came back again.

'No TV cameras, Patricia?' he enquired. 'I thought you'd be here with an army of media men.'

'That would hardly be practical.'

'No, I suppose not.'

Fothergill had already outlined the procedure. When the call came one of his men would be accompanying Helmut Schalk to the rendezvous. The car they would use was standing ready by the hotel entrance. The rest of them must wait behind, under the supervision of the Swiss police, until it was thought safe to move up closer.

It was hard to tell what Schalk felt about his role in all this. He was sitting on the steps to the hotel, his hands clasped between his knees, an expression of distant contemplation on his face. Trevelyan had tried talking to him earlier but given up the challenge and moved away.

Barraclough nodded towards the track. 'You don't think he is thinking of using the train, do you?'

'It's possible,' she said.

'Well, I wish he'd get on with it. It's getting damned cold out here.'

Shaughnessy stepped out of the doorway into the bright light of the cabin. The gun he held at chest height, his left hand clamped on his right wrist. The fetid warmth of the room wrapped around him like a hot towel.

'Do you speak English?' he asked.

The guard's attention was fixed on the gun. He was a short, broad-shouldered man with hair like an old kitchen scourer and blue eyes that showed signs of animation but not much in the way of intelligence. He lifted his head and nodded. 'Yes,' he said. 'A little.'

'I want you outside.'

The man didn't move. It was possible that he had been bragging about his linguistic skills. Shaughnessy twitched the barrel of the gun towards the door.

'Outside!'

With resignation the guard turned back to the cooker and dropped the wooden spoon into the saucepan. Everyone acknowledges that a man with a gun in his hand must be obeyed. It's one of the unwritten laws of our time. Only a few try breaking it. Unfortunately this was one of them. As he let go of the spoon he grabbed hold of the saucepan and hurled it at Shaughnessy.

He realized what was happening the moment he saw the guard swing round but that was a moment too late. The pan hit him on the shoulder as he ducked. Through the balaclava he felt a flash of pain on his cheek as scalding liquid splashed across his face. Then the guard was on him.

Dropping his head he had charged across the short distance that separated them. He must have been fourteen stone and travelling at some speed. Shaughnessy took the full force of it in his chest. The momentum lifted him from his feet and slammed him back against the door frame. What breath he had been storing in his lungs for the purposes of supporting life and limb was jettisoned in one go.

The guard held him around the waist in a bear hug and seemed intent on trying to squeeze out what little air he still had. In retrospect he probably realized that this was his first mistake. It left Shaughnessy with his arms free.

Lifting the butt of the gun he brought it down on the back of the man's shaggy head. It should have been enough to have laid him out cold but skulls are built solidly in the mountains. The guard gave a grunt and loosening his grip he staggered back a couple of paces, still doubled up.

It gave Shaughnessy a momentary advantage. Kissing good-bye to Anglo-Swiss relations he brought his knee up into the man's face. He fell back against the table. There was a crash of breaking glass as a bottle hit the floor but the guard didn't go with it. Throwing out his arms he steadied himself.

'Hold it right there,' Shaughnessy shouted. 'Hold it right there or I'll blow your head off.'

The guard gave a shake of the head in question, either as a sign of refusal or to clear his senses, then without a second thought he lunged at him again.

One bullet, Shaughnessy thought to himself. One bloody bullet and I could have this lunatic in the mood to co-operate. It's amazing what a shot into the air can do. But there was nothing. The gun in his hand was about as useful as a water-pistol.

The guard's head was down as he came, his arms held out on either side as they had been the time before. In strategic terms this wasn't clever. Shaughnessy was able to anticipate him. Instead of trying to stop this unstoppable force he stepped aside, took him by the collar and drove him onwards into the wall.

As it happened, it wasn't the wall that knocked him out. It was the storm lantern that was hanging on the wall that did it. The gas canister hit him on the temple. It didn't make much sound but it must have had an effect. The strength went out of his limbs and he fell to the ground in a heap.

Shaughnessy heaved him up into a sitting position. He had landed in the pool of liquid that had been warming on the cooker a moment earlier. It trickled down his face, pale and sticky: chicken soup, by the smell of it.

Taking out the handcuffs, Shaughnessy secured his hands behind his back before he could come round and put in any more objections. By rights he should be dead, Shaughnessy told himself angrily. He had a fake painting in his luggage and no ammunition in his gun but this idiot wasn't to know that. Fighting back had been madness.

Shaughnessy straightened up. His cheek was stinging painfully from the hot soup and his ribs were screaming in complaint. But that was becoming a commonplace these days.

There was a dirty coffee mug in the sink. Shaughnessy filled it with cold water and threw it across the man's face. He came round quickly enough: two quick shakes of his head as though he was sneezing and then a gasp for air. The eyes drifted round the room and focused on him. The expression in them wasn't one that he wanted to see too often.

'Get up,' Shaughnessy said.

The man obeyed without any overt sign of enthusiasm, rolling over on his side and then struggling to his knees. Standing up is a difficult business when your hands are out of commission but the good news was that the fight had gone out of him.

Shaughnessy opened the door and pushed him outside. The cold air hit them. Keeping him two paces ahead, they went down to the control room of the cable car. It was locked. With the barrel of the gun pressed into the base of his skull, Shaughnessy took the keys from the man's back pocket and they went inside. The room was alongside the embarkation platform. It had glass windows on two sides and a view that must have been breathtaking in the daylight. But the scenic beauty of their position wasn't uppermost in Shaughnessy's mind at that moment.

'Sit down,' he ordered.

The guard slumped into the steel-framed chair. With his hands behind his back he couldn't sit up straight. Undoing the handcuff on his left wrist, Shaughnessy locked it to the back of the chair. The man still couldn't sit straight but he couldn't stand up in a hurry either.

Shaughnessy glanced at his watch. It was six minutes after eight.

'The bastard's late,' Barraclough said.

It's what they had all been thinking. As the minute hand on the station clock touched eight a hush of anticipation had settled over the group standing outside the Bahnhof Hotel. Barraclough was the first to break it.

'Where's he got to? He's never been late before. Every other time he's been punctual.'

Patricia didn't need to be told. She felt a sickness in her stomach as she watched the clock twitch forwards one more minute. Tommie had been intending to ring in at eight—not about eight, or the nearest he could manage to eight, but bang on eight. Something must have gone wrong.

A train was approaching, curving down through the town, its wheels singing on the track as it slowed. She watched it draw into the station, the doors thumping open. Only a handful of passengers climbed down. All eyes were turned on to them, scrutinizing their faces as they shambled away. But there was nothing of interest.

Fothergill walked across to the hotel entrance where they stood. 'Well, gentlemen,' he said calmly. 'It looks as though we're going to be kept waiting.'

'You're sure this is the right place?' Barraclough said.

'The main entrance to the Bahnhof Hotel at 2000 hours local time. That's what he said and that's where we are.'

'You're confident that this isn't a hoax, are you, Captain?' It was Ambrose who put the question.

'There's only one way of finding out the answer to that, sir.'

The train drew out of the station again, the lit carriages filing away down the valley. Silence and darkness once more.

'We'll give him a few more minutes,' Fothergill added. 'This is his party.' He paused for a moment and listened.

Somewhere a telephone was ringing.

Fothergill looked around. The sound was coming from one of the public call-booths in the station. Without hurrying, he walked across to the platform and lifted the receiver. After less than thirty seconds he put it down again and returned to them. His voice carried no emotion.

'We have made contact, gentlemen.'

Chapter 30

Shaughnessy had given them eight minutes to reach the public telephone in the village of Feutersoy. He'd measured the distance. By breaking the speed limit and ignoring the safety of pedestrians it was just possible to do it in that time. Which should ensure they didn't spend too long thinking about anything else—such as where he was phoning from.

As he waited, Shaughnessy kept a constant check on the time. Coming in late like that hadn't done anything for his credibility. The organization who'd pulled off the other ransoms had always been smack on time. But then they'd never had to contend with a belligerent security guard who had lost interest in living. Or if they had they'd dealt with him more efficiently than Shaughnessy had managed.

He turned and looked back at the control room. The portable phone hadn't worked in there so he had to bring it out on to the end of the cable car platform. But he could still keep an eye on the guard through the big plate-glass windows. Not that he needed to worry. The guard wasn't thinking of going anywhere. A bang on the head from a storm lantern takes a lot of hostility from a man.

Shaughnessy leaned back against the railings and glanced at his watch. Six and a half minutes gone. He took out his notebook and checked the number although he knew it off by heart. As the second hand swung round to the eight-minute mark he drew out the aerial and dialled.

They must have driven at breakneck speed: the receiver was picked up at the other end before it could ring twice.

'Who is that speaking?' Shaughnessy asked.

'Thornton. Loss and Security Assessment.' He might have driven like a bat out of hell but it hadn't affected the man's nerves. His voice was cool as the first Martini of the evening.

'Do you have a phone in the car?'

'Yes.'

'Give me the number.'

Thornton either had a very good memory or frequently used the car he was driving. He recited the number without going to check it. Shaughnessy wrote it down in his notebook.

'Continue along the Gsteig Road. I'll contact you in a few minutes.' He cut the line and went back into the control room. The guard looked up at him. Shaughnessy pointed to the internal phone on the control panel.

'Get on to the lower station. Tell them to open the lift.' There was a restaurant down there under the cable car so there was always someone to answer the phone.

The guard didn't have to be told twice. He grabbed the receiver and within a few seconds was gabbling rapidly and urgently into it.

Shaughnessy went back outside. He dialled Thornton. 'Where are you?'

'Half a mile beyond Gsteig, continuing up the valley.'

'Drive to the Diableret cable car.' There was no point in hiding his position. The base station would be alive with the news by now. Even as he spoke he could see lights flicking on down there. 'Park directly in front of the entrance. I'll contact you then. And Thornton—no one else. If I see more than one car, the painting burns. Do you follow me?'

'I understand.'

Shaughnessy cut the line. There was a pair of binoculars in the control room. He took them to the end of the platform and trained them on the valley. From where he stood he could see most of the road back to Gsteig. Three cars were making their way up the valley, their headlights swinging from side to side as they took the steep turns. At that moment a fourth appeared. This was the one, he guessed. It was travelling fast, accelerating out of the corners: a trained driver behind the wheel. He watched it approach, occasionally disappearing from sight as it dipped in and out of the fir trees along the road.

At the cable station it swung in and stopped. The lights were killed and two figures emerged. They stood by the car where they would be clearly visible.

Shaughnessy pressed the redial button. He saw one figure duck back into the car and Thornton's voice came on the line. 'We are at the cable station.'

'I can see you, Thornton. I want you to go up and stand beside the cable car. The two of you will wait out there alone. The diamonds will be in your hands and the doors will be closed and locked behind you. Do you understand?'

'Yes—'

'You will need a key to open the cable-car door. That you will have with you before you come out. In the mean time, there is a restaurant in the station. I want it cleared. I want the whole place cleared with the exception of you two and the lift operator.'

'Got you—that's already happening.'

Shaughnessy glanced down through the binoculars. He was right. In the light of the station he could see a small group of people assembling outside in the car park. Into the phone he said, 'Go inside now, Thornton.'

'How will I keep in contact?'

'There is a phone in the cable car.'

It took Thornton less than a minute to collect the key to the cable-car door and the two of them emerged on to the brightly lit platform below. Shaughnessy watched through the binoculars. One of them, he assumed it would be Thornton, was holding what looked like a suitcase in his hand. The other was standing with his arms crossed. That would be Helmut Schalk. It was hard to tell from such a distance but he didn't look too scared by the ordeal.

Shaughnessy went back inside. 'Get on to the station down there. I want one operator at the controls.'

The guard stared at him in incomprehension. Brilliant, Shaughnessy thought. I damage a few of his grey cells and they happen to be the ones that hold his knowledge of the English language. 'Pick up the phone,' he said more slowly. 'Tell them to put one operator in the control room.'

This time it sunk in. 'Ah ja—operator.'

'Just one.' Shaughnessy held up a finger. 'If there are any more you'll be going to the big fondue-pot in the sky.'

A brief conversation produced the result. A figure took the seat behind the control panel below. Shaughnessy picked up the internal phone and told the guard to page it through to the cable car.

While it was ringing he touched the binoculars to his eyes, saw Thornton unlocking the door, getting into the cab, and picking up the receiver. Shaughnessy put down the phone at his end and jerked his thumb at the guard. 'Bring them up.'

The drive motor of the lift was in the lower station. At this end there was just a system of large belt wheels around which the cable was looped and so, apart from a soft thump as the pneumatic brakes disengaged on the support cables, the cab made practically no sound as it glided away. Shaughnessy went outside, locking the control room door after him, and watched it disappear into the darkness.

By now the police would have pin-pointed his exact position and would be trying to formulate some sort of counter-measure. There was no way they could surround the place. Even the most accomplished mountaineer would need two or three hours to reach the station. The only feasible way of getting a force to the spot would be by helicopter but the roar of the engine would give them away.

For the time being he was safe.

Collecting the canvas in its plastic container he placed it on the platform some distance from where the cable car would stop and stood back against the rear wall of the station.

It took another fifteen minutes for them to arrive. The lights were off in the cab: Thornton wasn't going to present him with an easy target as they approached. He'd know that this was the most dangerous moment for them. At a guess they would be lying on the floor.

As the cable car docked, Shaughnessy switched out the lights in the station.

'Open the door,' he ordered.

It slid back. Still no sign of anyone. He was right—they were on the floor.

'Get out!'

The two figures scrambled on to their feet, emerging as twin silhouettes against the clear sky behind. It must be almost impossible for them to see him in the shadows.

'Move out to the end of the platform.'

They reversed back until they stood against the railings. Schalk had his hands on his head. Thornton would have instructed him to do so: it's important to give no sign of aggression in these situations. Putting the aluminium case on the ground between them, Thornton did the same. His face was masked in shadow but he was a capable-looking man who moved with that unhurried ease which comes to those who are confident of their physical ability.

There was silence in the station. Shaughnessy stepped forwards until he was visible in the moonlight. It gave them their first chance of seeing him. It also gave them the chance to see the gun in his hand. He turned it towards Thornton.

'Are you armed?'

'No.'

'Take off your anorak.'

Thornton unzipped the front and very slowly removed it. He held it out to one side and dropped it on the ground. Beneath it he was wearing a dark roll-neck sweater. It was unlikely that there was a gun under there but even if there was Thornton wouldn't try to use it at present. The risk was too great, the consequences too unpredictable. It was later that they would try to nail him, after they had the painting back in their possession.

Shaughnessy held the gun on him. 'Now drop your trousers.'

There was a momentary pause before he obeyed, slipping them down around his ankles.

That dealt with Thornton: he might get pretty damned cold but with his legs hobbled in this way any last hopes he might have of springing a surprise attack were out. Shaughnessy turned his attention back to Schalk.

'Open the case.'

It had two clasps on the front. Schalk undid them and lifted the lid. Taking the torch from his pocket, Shaughnessy shone it on the contents. The diamonds were wrapped in cellophane packets. Each one was sealed and would contain a certificate of its value from the jewellery merchant.

'Throw one of them over here,' he ordered.

Schalk glanced up at Thornton and then taking one out he tossed it down the platform. It was about the size of a bag of toffees. Shaughnessy broke the seal and took out one of the dull rocks.

It's a commonly held misconception that a diamond can be verified by a quick glance through an eyeglass. It's not true. The only certain way of testing a diamond visually is to check its refractive index. The density of a diamond's molecular structure causes it to refract light at a different angle to even the most convincing imitation.

Shaughnessy had been given a light meter for the purpose. He took it out of his breast pocket, positioned the diamond on the glass screen, and peered through the eye-piece. He didn't bother to check the angle of refraction: he didn't know how to do it, and anyway the stones were Japanese 'yellow' diamonds. Together they were worth about thirty thousand quid. But neither Thornton or Schalk knew that. He still had to put on the show for them.

After a moment's examination he replaced the stone and tossed the bag back at Schalk who returned it with the others. Shaughnessy lifted the torch so that it was shining in the restorer's eyes. It was the first time he'd seen him since that day he went to his studio. He'd been struck then by the man's inner calm. He noticed it again now as Schalk stood up, folding his hands above his head.

'Move forwards,' Shaughnessy ordered.

With the beam of the torch in his eyes, Schalk was blinded. Tentatively he stepped towards him, his head slightly averted. After four paces, Shaughnessy directed the torch down at the plastic tube on the ground.

'It's in there. You may take it out to examine it.'

As Schalk knelt down, Shaughnessy stood above him, the gun pointed at his head, the torch directed on to his hands. Briefly he glanced over to Thornton standing against the railings, but he was posing no threat, neither was the guard locked in the control room. The only real danger was from Schalk.

He had unrolled the canvas on the ground and was poring over it. His face was just a few inches from it, his hands on the surface. They were large hands, strong enough to crack walnuts, Shaughnessy remembered from the time of their introduction.

Shaughnessy held the pool of light on the centre of the picture but after a moment Schalk asked him to move it to the right. Then up a few inches.

Holy mother and all the Saints, Shaughnessy said to himself, he's going to check the whole thing. He'd been hoping that with a gun breathing down his neck, Schalk would just give it a quick once over. But the restorer wasn't going to be hurried.

'Put it back on the central figure again, please.'

Shaughnessy felt cold fingers reach out to touch him as he moved the light. He couldn't tell the difference; surely he couldn't tell the difference in the beam of a torch.

It was five minutes before Schalk sat back on his heels. He paused before looking up at Shaughnessy.

'This is not the painting that left my studio,' he said.

From where they were standing, at a bend in the road a mile below the cable station, they could only guess what was going on up there in the mountains.

Patricia gripped the binoculars in her hands until the knuckles showed white. It was ten minutes now since the cable car had docked and the lights went out in the station. At present there was just a little flickering beam. That would be a torch. Twice she thought she had seen figures against the platform railings but it could have been a shadow caused by the thin cloud that was skimming over the moon. It was just too far away to tell.

She stamped her feet to get a bit of warmth into them. 'Come on, come on,' she shouted to herself. What's taking so long? She'd imagined that it would be over in a few seconds: a brief look at the painting, the diamonds passed across, and they'd be coming back again. What were they doing up there?

She dropped the binoculars and looked round at the others. Ambrose and Barraclough were standing by the squad car where the police lieutenant was passing on the scraps of information that were coming over his short-wave radio. From the rapt expressions on their faces they could have been listening to the Test match.

When the call came they had driven to Gsteig and waited. It wasn't until Thornton and Schalk were on the cable car that they had been allowed to move up the valley to this point. The police had sealed off the road on both sides of the station, marksmen had been posted on the hillside above. There was no sign of Fothergill or his team but she knew that they were further up the road too.

'Shouldn't be long now.' Trevelyan had come to stand beside her.

'No—'

'Why's it taking so long?'

'You don't think anything's gone wrong?'

Her face was pale as she turned to him. 'Don't say that, James—please don't say that.'

Shaughnessy held the light on Schalk's upturned face. He could feel the sweat trickling down the ridge of his spine. It was strange because the whole of his body was cold.

'What do you mean?' he asked. To his surprise his voice was steady in his own ears.

'It has changed,' Schalk replied. 'When this painting left my studio it was in perfect condition but now it has deteriorated. The cracking is worse than it was, the paint has been allowed to dry.'

The paint had dried? What was he talking about?

'This is an act of gross negligence, Mr Shaughnessy, for which I hold you personally responsible. You have allowed a priceless painting to be damaged by your greed. It's the altitude, the dry air. An oil painting should never be brought up into this atmosphere. Don't you realize that? It's pure vandalism.'

He was accusing him of damaging his handiwork. Shaughnessy could hardly believe his ears. Schalk was kneeling there with a gun at his head and instead of wondering how to save his skin he was complaining about the deterioration of the paint. What was the matter with the man?

'I'm not concerned with that,' Shaughnessy told him.

'No, I didn't think you would be.' Rolling up the canvas Schalk slid it back into the tube and stood up. Without another word he walked back to the end of the platform.

Thornton paused before asking, 'Do you accept it?'

'Of course.'

Shaughnessy turned the torch on Thornton's face. Reaction was setting in now, he could feel his heart pattering with the sudden withdrawal of adrenalin. Stepping forwards he picked up the rolled painting and tossed it into the opened door of the cable car. Then he drew back to the rear of the station.

'Leave the case where it is and get in.'

He watched the cable car sliding down into the night. It was done. The moment for which he had been steeling himself, the moment for which he had worked non-stop for six weeks, was over. He had passed it off.

Shaughnessy felt elation, a sudden rush of warmth in the belly, but it blew out like a candle flame in the wind. Now was the time of danger. They had the painting. There was nothing to be lost now. They'd be coming after him.

Quickly he transferred the diamonds into his rucksack. It meant leaving behind some of the other kit he had brought but he no longer needed it. Buckling down the cover-flap he went back into the control room.

The guard blinked as the lights came on and struggled up in the chair. His expression was vacant, eyes following Shaughnessy around the room. He might be slow off the mark but he must have realized that his face was now the one unresolved piece of the puzzle.

Shaughnessy let him sweat on it for a while longer. Picking up the internal phone he asked to speak to Fothergill.

The line connected directly to the control room below but they must have tapped into it because an English voice came on almost immediately. It had the short clipped manner of the British Army but otherwise was devoid of expression.

'Fothergill speaking.'

'I'm coming down in the next lift, Fothergill. I want the station cleared down there, do you understand?'

Fothergill understood. He understood also that the balance of power had shifted in their favour. 'It won't work, Shaughnessy.'

He sounded as though he were pointing out a flaw in a cooking recipe. Shaughnessy gave him the facts.

'I have the security guard with me.'

'I am aware of that but it would be in your interest to let him go and give yourself up. You can't get away from here.'

'There is a car parked by the station—a green BMW. When I get down there I shall drive away in it. If I see anyone, if I hear anyone—if I so much as think I hear anyone—the guard dies. Do you understand me?'

'I understand what you are saying but I shall have to discuss this with the police—'

Keep the other side talking, force them to haggle. That was their method and Shaughnessy wasn't having it. He cut him short. 'No more talking. We are coming down now.'

He hung up and went outside. The cable car was approaching. Its lights were off but he could see it in the dark, laboriously crawling up the mountainside. Shaughnessy went to the end of the platform and lay down on the ground.

The humming of the overhead cable changed note as the engine slowed. As it came in to dock, the cab was almost directly below him. It was empty. That was no surprise: it would have been suicide to try using it to mount an attack—at least it would be suicide if he'd had any ammunition in the pistol.

The cable car manoeuvred itself into the station, the bulk of its cab blotting out the moonlight.

The guard showed no sign of resistance as Shaughnessy unlocked him from the chair and bundled him into it. He'd grasped the simple fact that his best chance of survival lay in getting down to the valley as quickly as possible.

'Lie down,' Shaughnessy told him.

He didn't understand. Shaughnessy gave him a kick behind the knees and he fell to the floor. There's nothing like physical violence for improving one's grasp of a foreign language.

He picked up the phone and said, 'Are you there, Fothergill?'

'I am.'

'OK—we're coming down.'

'He must be out of his mind,' Ambrose said as the information was relayed back to them. 'He'll never get away with it.'

'He has one of the cable-car guards with him.' The police lieutenant was listening in on the short-wave.

'He won't make it.'

Barraclough stared up at the night sky. It wasn't possible to see the cable car against the mountains but the sound of its motor just reached them. 'He's coming down now, is he?'

The policeman nodded. He was leaning against the bonnet of the squad car, the ear piece of his radio clamped to the side of his head. Trevelyan walked up the road to where Patricia was standing by herself.

'He knows what's he's doing, does he?' he asked.

She didn't appear to hear him. Her arms were crossed and she was hugging herself for warmth, or it might have been for comfort. 'Yes,' she said after a moment. 'He knows what he's doing.'

It confirmed what he had been thinking. 'I've been rather slow off the mark, haven't I, Patricia?'

'What do you mean?'

'You and Shaughnessy. You've been working together.'

She turned and glanced down the road to where the others were gathered and then back at him. Her face was in the shadow of her hair but he could feel her eyes on him.

'He needed someone to help him,' she said simply.

'But you nearly ran him in.'

She smiled, not her usual radiant smile but a distant relation that has fallen on hard times. 'Nearly,' she said. 'But not quite. I rang him before the police arrived. It looked good though, didn't it?'

'Yes,' Trevelyan said. 'It did.' It had been a guess on his part, an intuitive leap that he had made as he watched her this evening. He still needed time to go back and think it through but he understood now. She'd been his eyes and ears, keeping him informed; keeping him one jump ahead.

'Why didn't you tell me?'

'We were going to at first,' she said. 'We talked about it for hours that night in Venice but in the end we thought it would be easier for everyone if we kept it between ourselves. That way no one had to make any sort of pretence.'

'No one except you.'

'Yes,' she agreed. 'No one except me.'

Chapter 31

On the roof of the cable station the marksman eased the Heckler & Koch HK81 rifle into his shoulder. He was dressed entirely in black, a balaclava pulled over his head so that only his eyes and his right hand were exposed. With his thumb he felt for the safety catch and slipped it off. Through the telescopic sights, with their battery-illuminated reticles for night firing, he watched the cab approach. With the natural sag of the cable it was running in almost level. Straight at him.

To shoot a man who is using a hostage as a human shield is nearly impossible. The slightest inaccuracy and the bullet will reach the wrong target. But with a laser projection system on the sights there was always a chance that the opportunity would present itself. He only had to place the tiny red beam on to Shaughnessy for a second, long enough to squeeze off a round, and the job would be done. If he didn't get that chance there was another marksman on the roof at the back of the building and two more positioned up in the trees above.

Shaughnessy would never see them. He had demanded that the area be evacuated but the first he would know of them would be when the 7.62mm-calibre bullet hit him. And by that time it's too late.

The cable car was slowing down now. Briefly the windows were silhouetted against the snow in the valley. No sign of anyone at them. That was to be expected. The marksman lowered his head and cradling the rifle on his body he slithered back down the steep incline of the roof on to the flat top of the restaurant behind. Set in the step between the two were a row of narrow windows. One of them he had opened ready.

Through it he could see the inside of the darkened cable station. He fed the tip of the barrel through the crack, fixing his aim between the bay where the cable car would dock and the exit door. That way he would have to make only the slightest movement when the time came.

He felt the tremble in the concrete roof as the drive motors wound down. The cab was nosing into the station, its side bumping along the platform. The brakes locked on, the engine cutting out.

There was a sudden and complete silence that gripped the building like freezing air. The marksman slipped his finger down the side of the rifle casing on to the trigger. He increased the pressure of his hand on the pistol grip. When the moment came he wouldn't have to pull the trigger: he would only have to relax the muscles of his finger and it would do the job of its own accord.

From the cab there came a sound. It was a soft thump. Then two more, both rather louder, on the thin aluminium side. A moment's silence and a man's face appeared at the window.

The marksman examined him through the sights. Whoever it was, it wasn't Shaughnessy. This one had shaggy hair and a wide, dishevelled face with blood beneath the nose. He was banging his head against the glass pane, his mouth open as he shouted.

After a few minutes the marksman took the laser projection spot off the man's face. He laid the rifle down beside him and spoke into the radio that was clipped to his anorak.

It was Fothergill who opened the cable-car door. Covered by another who crouched in the doorway, he approached across the ground, wriggling forwards on his elbows. He slid back the door and the guard flopped out on to the concrete platform beside him. The rest of the cab was empty.

Fothergill rolled on to his feet. 'He's not in the cable car,' he said into his short-wave. 'Repeat, not in the cable car.'

He walked to the front of the station and looked out into the darkness. He hadn't really expected Shaughnessy to be on board. It would have been a bad mistake on his part and Shaughnessy didn't strike him as someone who made that kind of mistake.

It was at that moment, far away across the valley, that he heard the sound of a motorbike engine being kicked into life.

For the first two miles Shaughnessy drove with the lights off. Visibility was limited and the icy track forced him to keep the motorbike in a low gear but after the slow run down from the cable car he felt as though he was flying.

Skiing in the dark had been extraordinarily difficult. The clear sky had given him enough light to see the snow, a pale phosphorescent glow on the ground, but he couldn't get any real idea of the surface beneath his feet. Ruts and bumps had hit without warning. Unexpectedly the slope would drop away then suddenly lift again, jerking his legs up, knocking the wind from his lungs like a punch in the stomach. He'd lost count of how many times he had fallen and had to grope for the skis in the dark.

From the cable car he had followed the marked piste, running down between the trees. This was the easiest part, the path was wide and the snow well packed down. Keeping the skis in a shallow snow-plough position he had made good time but he couldn't stay on this route for long: it led down directly to the cable-car station.

After a couple of miles he came to a barn in an open meadow. Here he cut off to the right, keeping low, hugging into the shadows of the trees along the edge. Even at night, the slightest flicker of movement can be spotted in the mountains.

Above him he could see the two cable cars against the sky. They had almost reached each other. He must have been going ten minutes, maybe slightly longer. If felt like an hour.

Leaving the piste he headed down a narrow track in the trees that he had discovered earlier with Dieter Hauptmann. In summer it would be used by shepherds taking their herds up into the pastures, which didn't make it ideal for skiing. Every fifty or so yards there was a sharp bend. In the darkness of the over-hanging trees it was hard to see them. Twice he overshot and found himself floundering in thick snow.

His heart rate was up, his breath painful in his lungs, but he had to keep moving. As soon as that cable car reached the bottom they'd guess what he was doing and fan out across the valley. Maybe they'd already done so. It depended on how many men the Swiss police had sanctioned for the job.

After fifteen minutes and several more falls he emerged from the trees into the valley below. The snow was thinner here and he had to weave his way through broken areas of bare earth.

At first he thought the motorbike wasn't there. For one terrible moment, as he reached the pile of stacked logs that had been the agreed destination, he thought they'd made a mistake. But he found it a few yards down the mountain side: a 500cc scrambler, covered in a tarpaulin. Strapped to the seat was a crash helmet and the Kevlar flak-jacket he'd asked Collins to provide. He put them on. The ruck-sack of diamonds he secured to the back of the motorbike.

The engine fired first time. With his feet out on either side for stability he headed along the valley, snow kicking up behind the rear wheel. He kept the light off but apart from that he didn't try to hide himself: the sound of the engine would already have given him away. What was important was to get as far away as possible before the police could respond.

He glanced back over his left shoulder. The cable station was about a mile away and slightly above him, its concrete frame visible above the tree tops. They must have already discovered him missing from the cable car: the lights were on and even from this distance he could see figures grouped around the open mouth of the building.

Leaving the flat meadow he dived up into the shelter of the trees. The track here was better than the one he'd skied down earlier: wider and firmer. He flicked on the headlights, saw it stretching away in front and accelerated hard. The motorbike surged beneath him, a wonderful sensation of power that momentarily pushed all thoughts of danger and fear from his mind. It was enough to be moving; enough to be getting away.

At the lower end of the valley the track suddenly dropped more steeply. There were fewer trees. Boulders and shattered rock were scattered on either side. He knew that in summer the air here would be filled with the sound of waterfalls. Now they were frozen into silence.

He paused at a turn in the track, breathing hard. Beneath him he could see the lights of Gsteig. Less than half a mile to his left was the road. He couldn't make out any cars on it but that's where they'd be: watching, listening, trying to estimate his position, the direction he was taking.

Shaughnessy cut the engine and let the motorbike freewheel downhill. The animal instinct to run urged him to keep going as he had been, to drive as fast and blindly as possible. But he knew he must resist it. The sound of the engine had been their only real means of fixing his position and even then it would have been vague. Sound carries so clearly in the mountains that it's hard to get an accurate reading of distance from it. He might have been one mile away from them or ten. Now with the engine cut off he would be invisible.

It didn't feel that way. Like all hunted creatures he felt exposed out there in the open, vulnerable, the stars that crusted the sky above him a thousand eyes staring down.

For half an hour he bumped along the track, occasionally getting off to push the machine, until he reached the flat ground behind Gsteig. He could make out the dark-shaped steeple, see the warm lights of the Baren below. There were cars in the road, their exhausts clouding up in the street. They alone would muffle any sound that he made. Starting up the engine he drove along a narrow track between the fields.

This central valley he'd come down into was far wider than the other and he was able to keep well away from the main road. It was only after he had passed Feutersoy that he ventured on to it. Approaching through a belt of trees around a river bed, he waited by the kerb for over five minutes, checking the traffic in either direction but there was no sign of a police car. Pushing the motorbike out into the road, he kicked it into life and drove the last few miles into Gstaad.

The Gasthof Egli was a four-storey chalet on the way out to Rougemont. It had painted shutters, gingham curtains, and heavy carved gables. Only the light orange colouring of the wood suggested it was modern. A blackened cooking pot hung above the door to the restaurant.

Shaughnessy stopped on the other side of the road and watched it for some minutes. Then getting off the bike he walked up to the door. The Kevlar jacket beneath his anorak thickened his body, made movements slow and ungainly, but ultimately he supposed that he looked no different to any other motorbike courier.

Inside the door was a heavy felt curtain that kept out the draught. He pushed it aside and glanced round the restaurant. It was warm and inviting, the smell of cooking, pipe smoke and conversation in the air. A waitress asked him whether he wanted a table.

That's exactly what he did want: a table by the fire, a glass of whiskey, and something to eat. The urgency of that need was like a pain in his belly. But it would have to wait.

'Just looking for someone,' he said, and returning to the bike he headed back in the direction he'd come. At the roundabout on the other side of Saanen he turned up to the left and followed the road that climbed steeply up the hillside. It had been a mistake going into that restaurant. He could feel his hunger gnawing at his stomach. But it wouldn't be long now. When this was over he could sit down, relax in the warmth for as long as he wanted. Maybe there would be time to have dinner with Patricia later. Just the two of them together. That would be good. There was so much to tell her, so much that needed to be talked about. As he came round the corner, the bike heeling over at a forty-five degree angle, he could see the lights of Saanen-Moser ahead.

He wasn't aware of the bullet hitting him, only of a force that threw him back off the motorbike. He saw the machine rearing up above him. The impact followed immediately: the drumming of blood, the scream of tearing metal was in his ears. He didn't feel pain so much as see it as brilliant splashes of orange and yellow that exploded before his eyes.

Then he dropped down through it into silence.

Chapter 32

Shaughnessy had never been in a hot-air balloon but he imagined it must be much the same sensation as this. He was floating above the landscape, or rather he was quite still and the landscape was floating around him. There was sunlight and a wonderful lazy warmth. Sometimes below he could hear voices talking but they were too far away to understand.

He opened his eyes and looked up at the white ceiling. It didn't belong to the dream and he closed them again. 'He's coming round.'

The voice was much closer. Shaughnessy tried opening his eyes again. A man he didn't recognize was standing at the end of the bed. There was a pen clipped in the upper pocket of his white coat. Shaughnessy didn't much like the look of him but after his flight in the air balloon he was in a beatific mood so he smiled.

Someone came between them. It was Patricia. She sat on the edge of the bed and studied him closely.

'Can you hear me, Tommie?'

'Yes,' he said. The word was a fossil that had been in his mouth for a long time.'

'We've been so worried about you.'

The hospital room was small with a plate-glass window along one side covered by a colourless net curtain. Beside him was a bedside table and above it hung some sinister-looking medical kit. There were other people in the room, he realized, but he couldn't see them properly. He asked Patricia where he was but the words came out more like a groan.

'Are you all right?'

'Fine,' he said more carefully. 'At least I was until you woke me up with all your questions.'

He discovered later that his only major injury was a broken arm. The bullet had hit him in the centre of the chest but the impact had been spread by the flak-jacket, leaving him with a bruise the size of a meat plate but no serious damage. His present state was down to the sedation more than the fall from the motorbike.

'I think maybe you should leave now,' the doctor in the white coat told them.

'Would you like that?' Patricia asked.

'If you want my honest opinion, I'd rather you stayed and he left.'

'He's getting better,' Trevelyan said. He came into view now.

With him was Inspector Forsyth whom Shaughnessy recognized by the blue anorak.

'What's he doing over here?'

'You're in London now, darling,' Patricia told him. 'You were flown in last night.'

'And there I was looking forward to a long convalescence in the Alps.'

'The Swiss didn't want you. They're very thankful for what you did and all that but they'd rather you weren't there while questions are being asked.'

'Did you get the money back?'

Patricia nodded. 'Some of it. But they found *The Triumph of Bacchus*. We've just heard they've picked it up.'

'Where was this?'

'In a bank in Zurich. The rest of the money is probably there in a separate account. We'll find it. I've asked my father to help. He's good at getting round Swiss banks.'

It took Shaughnessy several days to piece together the full story but the facts were simple enough. The ambush had been carried out by two assassins, one with a silenced rifle, the other half a mile down the road to give warning of his arrival. When it was done they had collected the rucksack of diamonds and driven it to Zurich. Collins's team had arrested them the following morning when they were depositing the diamonds in the Muller & Weissmann bank.

All this he learned later. For now there was only one question he wanted answered.

'Who did it?'

'Loss and Security Assessment,' Patricia said. 'Two of Fothergill's men.'

Shaughnessy nodded. There was some satisfaction in knowing he'd been right.

'The Swiss police have run the rest of them in now,' Trevelyan told him. 'Picked them up at the border as they were leaving.'

'Any trouble?'

'Not really. It was rather odd, Fothergill seemed to expect it. He was almost philosophical about it. I think maybe he'd realized that there was more to what went on that night than he'd been told.'

'I gather you knew it was them,' Forsyth said.

Shaughnessy glanced over to Trevelyan. 'We didn't know it was them, Inspector, but we guessed it might be.'

'And you arranged all this—the fake painting, the ransom in the Alps—just to test the theory?'

'We wanted to see how they'd react if someone else snatched the money before they could get their hands on it.'

'I see,' Forsyth said in a tone that implied he was only half-way to seeing.

'Right from the start,' Trevelyan explained, 'Tom thought it could be Fothergill's team who were taking the paintings. They had the perfect opportunity. They took the paintings, held them for a few weeks, and then ransomed them back.'

'To themselves.'

'Fool-proof system when you think about it. They made it look pretty good each time but there was no danger of ever getting caught. The whole thing was just a charade. So Shaughnessy here came up with the idea of faking *The Triumph of Bacchus* and claiming the money himself.'

'Just to put a spanner in the works,' Shaughnessy said from the bed.

'He guessed that if he took the money, Fothergill's lot would come after him.'

Shaughnessy smiled sleepily. 'Like a swarm of angry hornets.'

'And the moment they did that we could nick them. The trouble in the past was that they had never showed their

Douglas Skeggs 368

heads above the ground for long enough to get a look. This way we had a chance of flushing them out into the open.'

'Risky just the same,' Forsyth said.

'I employed Securicom, the rival outfit Major Collins runs, to keep an eye on Shaughnessy while he made the copy.'

There was a knock on the door and a nurse bustled in. Sensing she was interrupting a conference she removed herself again. Forsyth waited until her footsteps had receded.

'When this started, you had no idea which painting Mr Shaughnessy was going to have to copy.'

'None,' Trevelyan agreed. 'That was the greatest problem. We were hoping it would be something not too hard to copy. When *The Triumph of Bacchus* was taken we nearly had to call the whole thing off. Faking that seemed impossible.'

'But you kept going.'

'If anyone could pull off a convincing copy of it, I reckoned Tom could.'

'But I needed more time,' Shaughnessy said. 'So James very decently refused to pay the ransom. It drove the Italian government round the bend but it gained us a couple of extra weeks.'

'And a burnt watercolour,' Trevelyan added drily.

Forsyth leaned back against the windowsill. Taking out a note book he made an entry and then wagged the pencil in their direction. 'You've known each other for some time, I take it?'

'About three years,' Trevelyan told him. 'For the last six months we had to avoid any direct contact but we kept in touch through Collins.'

Forsyth glanced over at Patricia. 'And how did Miss Drew get involved in all this?' he asked. 'She wasn't part of the original plan, was she?'

'No,' Shaughnessy said. 'She was a last-minute convert to the cause.'

So far Patricia had been listening to this conversation without speaking but now she said, 'I thought Tommie was the one who'd stolen *The Triumph of Bacchus*. I was absolutely convinced of it. He tried telling me that he was working with James but we got our wires crossed and I still didn't believe him.'

'She'd got her claws into me,' Shaughnessy said, 'and there was no way she was letting go. So eventually I called her over to Venice and spilled the beans.'

'And not a moment too soon,' Patricia added.

'But when you came back you were still after his blood,' Forsyth pointed out. Patricia shook her head.

'No,' she said modestly, 'That was just a bit of show.'

'A convincing bit of show.'

'It had me fooled,' Trevelyan agreed. 'I was scared out of my wits.'

Patricia smiled at him in apology. 'We talked it over for hours in Venice. In the end we thought it would be best if I continued to appear to be hunting Tommie. That way I could work as a…What's the word for those beastly people in M16?' she asked Shaughnessy.

'Moles.'

'That's right. We thought it would be good if I was a mole.'

Even in his drug-induced haze, Shaughnessy could think of no creature which looked less like Patricia at that moment. 'We could never have pulled off the ransom without her. The real weakness in our scheme was that once I'd got the ransom money there was no way of knowing when or where Fothergill's lot would try snatching it from me. Or how they'd do it,' he added as an afterthought. 'Patricia came up with the bright idea of giving them some helpful information. She leaked the route I was going to take when I came down from the mountains.'

'Leaked it to me,' Forsyth said with some feeling. He didn't like being the victim of a deception.

'And to various other people, Inspector. You don't have to feel bad about it. It was the only way we could be sure the news would get through to Fothergill. It gave us some idea where the ambush would take place.'

'Collins monitored the route, did he?'

'He had his team posted along the road out of Gstaad. As soon as the strike came they moved in. The rest was easy.'

Forsyth checked his notebook again. 'Your copy of the painting. How did that get out to Switzerland?'

Shaughnessy could feel sleep creeping over him but he wanted Forsyth to have the whole picture. 'Patricia brought it out with her. In Gerald Barraclough's private jet.'

'That was dangerous. What if he'd found it?'

'It wouldn't have mattered,' Shaughnessy told him. 'Barraclough was in on it from the start. Or at least, he was half in on it. He knew James had commissioned a fake. He didn't know who was making it until after I'd met him one night at dinner.'

'Barraclough knew about this?'

'We needed a bit of political back-up. Just in case things went wrong. Don't bother to check, Inspector. He'll certainly deny it.' Shaughnessy's eyes glazed as he spoke. The doctor took it as the cue to butt in.

'I think that's enough for now, gentlemen. He needs to sleep.'

It must have been what he did because the next thing he knew it was evening. The room was in darkness except for the bedside light. Patricia was sitting in the only comfortable chair talking on the phone. Seeing him come round she rang off and perched herself on the edge of the bed. She was still looking very St Moritz with a white polo-necked sweater beneath her jacket and her hair tied back in a matching white band.

Again she studied him with a serious expression on her face. It's strange being treated like a specimen under a microscope but he was getting used to it now.

'How are you feeling?' she asked.

'Better. This plaster is itching and that's got to be a good sign. What day is it?'

'Monday. You've been out for nearly twenty-four hours.' She reached over to the bedside table and picked up a paper bag. He could feel her weight on his legs. It was good to know they were still there and making a nuisance of themselves.

'I brought some pears,' she said.

'I thought grapes were the approved fruit—no skins to peel and all that.'

'They're not for you; they're for me. I haven't had anything to eat all day. These are for you.' She rolled out four miniatures of Jameson's whiskey. They'd been hidden in her gloves. 'I couldn't bring in a real bottle. There's a dragon at reception who frisks everyone before they get in the door.'

She selected one of the pears and bit into it, putting her hand to her chin to stop the juice running down. 'The doctors in Switzerland said you were lucky to get away without a broken neck.'

'I hadn't expected them to hit me while I was moving. I thought they'd wait until I'd stopped.'

She turned the pear in her fingers, not looking at him. 'Why were you wearing that beastly jacket thing?'

'I didn't fancy having a hole blown in me.'

'You knew they were going to shoot you, did you?'

He could see what she was driving at now. He'd promised her all down the line that he'd be in no real danger. 'Not until the last minute,' he said. 'When Fothergill applied for those lasers on his rifles I had a nasty feeling he was out for my blood and asked Collins to lay in a flak-jacket.'

'You said they'd just snatch the diamonds and run for it.'

'Wishful thinking, unfortunately.'

'I thought you were dead,' she said quietly. 'When they radioed through to say there had been a shot, I though you were done for.'

'I wouldn't have disagreed at the time.' She looked up at him and for a moment her eyes were scalding hot. Then she threw the core of the pear into the waste-bin. 'Don't you ever, ever do that to me again, Tom Shaughnessy.'

'I won't.'

'Scout's honour?'

He raised two fingers of his good hand. She was smiling now but for a moment her voice had been deadly serious.

'Scout's honour,' he said. 'So are you going to give me one of those ridiculous bottles or are they just there for show?'

She bounced off the bed to fetch the glass from the basin. The whiskey tasted good and ran around his veins in excitement, finding places it hadn't been for a while.

'Who were you ringing just then?' he asked.

'The studio.' She busied herself behind his back, arranging the pillows so that he could sit up in bed properly while he drank. 'At this time of night?'

'I've got four days to put together a fifty-minute documentary. That doesn't get done by everyone knocking off at tea-time.'

'How's it coming along?'

'Not too bad, except I need you up and about. You're going to be a TV celebrity, did you know that?'

'I can't wait. Have the newspapers got hold of the story yet?'

'They know the painting has been recovered. What they don't know is what happened to the money. Trevelyan's got journalists camping outside his office.'

'Talking of money,' Shaughnessy said as she sat down again. 'I want you to do something for me: go along to that estate agent's and buy Scobie's studio. I'll get Trevelyan to pass through the money but don't let Scobie get wind of what's going on.'

'Can't you just tell him you've bought it?'

'He'd get in a terrible stew if he thought I'd done it. Best to keep it between ourselves. You must know some way of tying the whole thing up in financial jargon so he doesn't get a whiff of who owns it.'

She gave him one of her aloof smiles that said butter wouldn't melt in her mouth. 'I'll see what I can do.'

It was on the following morning that *The Triumph of Bacchus* was flown into England. By a quirk of mythological images it arrived in the belly of a Hercules transport plane. Major Collins was there at Brize Norton to receive it and with a detachment of Special Branch in attendance the canvas was driven to Lloyd's. It had been agreed that the painting should remain in the possession of the insurers until the money put up for the ransom was returned.

Later that afternoon Trevelyan took it over to David Ambrose. With him was Collins.

'I thought you'd like to see it before it's handed back to the Italians,' he told Ambrose.

'Indeed I would,' he replied without looking up from his work.

Trevelyan glanced around the office. It was decorated in that spartan manner that comes to those brought up to accept responsibility from an early age. At his elbow stood a secretary, a middle-aged woman in a tweed skirt who, like the furniture, was included in the scene for her functional rather than her decorative features.

Gathering together the papers, Ambrose handed them to her and she retreated from the room. The door made no sound as it closed other than that soft gasp of air which freezers give when they are opened. Trevelyan had often wondered whether the office wasn't sound-proofed.

'Not everyday that you get a private viewing of a Titian,' Ambrose said, getting to his feet and pulling on his jacket. 'I should put it down there on the desk.'

Trevelyan moved aside the silver ink-stand and the large leatherbound blotter and unrolled the painting. There aren't many desks that can take an eight-foot by six-foot canvas but Ambrose's was one of them.

He studied it in silence for a while. 'You must be relieved to see it again, James.'

There was the slight jocularity in his voice that he only assumed when he was carrying understatement to the point of absurdity.

'I am,' Trevelyan agreed. Collins had moved over to the window and was staring down at the street below. 'You realize that's the copy you're looking at?' Trevelyan added.

'No,' Ambrose said. 'I didn't.'

'The original's underneath.'

Trevelyan took the top right-hand corner of the painting and peeled it back. Beneath it there appeared an identical section of the scene: ringing blue sky and the outline of distant trees.

'Extraordinary,' Ambrose said. For once he sounded as though he meant it.

'It is, isn't it.'

Ambrose pulled back the upper painting some more so that he could compare the two. 'It's hard to believe.'

'I spent some time earlier today comparing them together. I can't see any difference at all.'

'Are you telling me that Shaughnessy did this without the original to copy?'

'He didn't start work on it until the other had been stolen.'

'But how did he match the colours so exactly?' Ambrose was still baffled by the technical achievement of the painting.

'I'm not really sure. He explained some of it to me but I must admit most of it went over my head.'

Ambrose turned the canvas back some more. 'It's quite a talent he's got there.' He flicked his smile on to his face. 'You should be careful of carrying these two around together, James. They could get confused. It wouldn't be a bad idea to mark the copy in some way.'

'Shaughnessy's already done that,' Trevelyan said. 'He showed me this morning. If you look at that boat in the distance you'll see that the original has only two figures in it. His version has three.'

It was a tiny detail of the painting. The figures in question were just pin-pricks of paint. Ambrose examined them thoughtfully. 'He seems to have thought of every-thing. Shaughnessy's seen them together himself, has he?'

'He came round to the office this morning.'

'How is he?'

'In pretty good condition considering. His arm's going to be in plaster for a while and his ankle's sprained but otherwise he seems fine. The doctors say he's built like a battleship.'

Ambrose nodded as he considered this analogy. 'He took a ridiculous risk. You know that?'

'It was his own decision. He knew what was coming.'

'I appreciate that, but he still deserves to be dead. Can I get you some coffee?'

'Not for me.'

'Major?'

Collins turned from the window. Gravely he shook his head. His self-imposed role there that afternoon was as an observer. Speaking wasn't part of the brief.

Ambrose paused before he spoke again. 'I need hardly tell you how shocked I am by this business, James.'

'Fothergill, you mean?'

'We employed the man. That's what I find offensive. We entrusted the whole business to his organization and he repaid us with this.' He touched the surface of the painting as he spoke as though it were personally responsible for the trouble it had caused.

'We should have guessed, I suppose. Looking back on it, they were in the ideal position to pull a stunt like that. It's ironic, really. We were trying to find a leak in the system and all the time they were getting the information perfectly legitimately. It just never occurred to me that they could be doing it.'

'It occurred to Shaughnessy,' Trevelyan said. 'He reckoned it was possible to get away with a ransom once. To do it twice would be a matter of luck but after that there must be some sort of fiddle.'

'Is that what he said?' Ambrose had raised his eyebrows a fraction as though he found some grain of humour in the remark. 'How very astute of him. He's quite right, of course. But I can't help feeling that he's a degree closer to the criminal mentality than the rest of us. It was his idea to pull this elaborate hoax, was it?'

'More or less.'

'I wish you had felt able to confide in me, James.'

'We didn't tell anyone—'

Ambrose held up his hand. He wasn't blaming him for his decision. 'No, I understand. You were in a difficult position. You did however find the time to tell Miss Drew.'

'She found out of her own accord.'

'A remarkable actress,' Ambrose said. 'I must confess I never guessed she was in league with Shaughnessy.'

'I don't think he could have pulled it off without her help. It was her idea to let slip where he was heading after the ransom. It gave Major Collins the chance to have his team in position.'

'You knew they would try to ambush him, did you?'

'We thought they'd give it a try—provided they were given the opportunity, that is.'

Ambrose smiled. It was the thin smile of a senior officer who can understand a junior's enthusiasm but can't condone it. 'It's probably just as well you never told me, James. I would never have been able to approve such a foolhardy plan.'

'It worked.'

'Indeed it did.'

'What interested us was the exact location of the ambush.'

'Oh, yes?' Ambrose sat down behind his desk again. His voice held only a polite interest.

'It was on the road out to Saanen-Moser. He was heading for the Gasthof Adler.'

'That's where Patricia Drew told everyone he would be going.'

'Not quite. After she came back from Venice several people came to her for information. She told each one where she thought he would go. But in each case she gave a different address.'

Ambrose looked up. 'Why should she want to do that?'

'To pin-point the exact source of information. After he had the money, Shaughnessy went round to each address she'd given. The ambush came as he was approaching the Gasthof Adler. There was only one person who knew that's where he was going and that was you.'

There was silence in the office. Collins had moved away from the window and stood by the door. Ambrose flicked his gaze in his direction and back at Trevelyan.

'Are you trying to imply something, James?' His voice was distant.

'It was you who passed on the information to the assassins who ambushed Shaughnessy.'

Ambrose placed his hands on the desk. For a moment he contemplated this statement. Then he gave a little laugh. 'My dear James, I think you're letting your imagination run away with you. Of course I passed on the information she gave me. Anyone would have done the same in my position. But you're not seriously suggesting that I knew that they were going to attempt to shoot him, are you?'

'I don't know what you were intending,' Trevelyan replied. 'I just can't help wondering why you didn't tell the police afterwards.'

'How's that?' Ambrose sat back and steepled his fingers. His face was concerned—not for himself, but concerned that Trevelyan should be harbouring such thoughts.

'After Shaughnessy was shot you must have known

who had done it. The penny must have dropped. But you didn't think of telling the police.'

Ambrose opened his mouth to speak then closed it again. Trevelyan pressed the point.

'That worries me. Why didn't you tell them that you had unwittingly passed on that information to Fothergill?'

'Does it matter?'

'It does to me.'

'Really, James. I'm beginning to lose patience with this. You have nothing to back up this preposterous theory.'

'I don't, that's true. It's just a suspicion.'

'I'm glad you admit it—'

'But a suspicion is all that's needed nowadays. With the Swiss Bank Corporation, that is.'

'I don't follow you.' Ambrose spoke slowly.

'In the old days,' Trevelyan told him, 'there was no way a Swiss bank would confide the name of its account holders. But that's changed. Now they will reveal it on suspicion of criminal activity.'

Ambrose was suddenly angry. 'Are you telling me that you've taken this ridiculous hypothesis to the Muller and Weissmann bank?'

'I didn't personally. Leonard Drew was kind enough to speak to them for me.'

'You asked him to do that?'

'The Chairman is a personal friend of his, I believe. They were able to confirm that you personally hold a number of accounts at the bank. A search has been made. One of them was found to contain a quantity of uncut diamonds.'

Ambrose's expression didn't flicker. 'I wish you hadn't

done that, James,' he said eventually. 'Bringing in Leonard to do your dirty work, I mean. I've always found it embarrassing to have one's acquaintances involved.'

Trevelyan didn't answer. Ambrose looked across to where Collins stood by the door. 'Am I to understand that your presence here is in some way connected with this, Major?'

'The building is under police surveillance,' Trevelyan said.

'I see.' He sounded faintly offended. 'That was not necessary, James.' Getting to his feet he straightened his cuffs. 'Shall we go, then?'

Collins had opened the door in readiness. As he went out Ambrose turned to Trevelyan.

'You knew, didn't you?' he said. 'You knew it was me from the start.'

'We thought it was a possibility.'

'That's why you made Shaughnessy raise the money for this absurd venture himself. You knew that if the syndicate advanced him money I'd see it in the accounts.'

'It was a risk we couldn't afford to take.'

For a moment the cold blue eyes touched his. 'I had to do it, James,' he said softly. 'You do understand that? We are both victims of circumstance. Myself as much as you. It was nothing personal.'

Chapter 33

'He'd built up massive debts,' Patricia said. They were walking down a narrow alleyway close to the Grand Canal. There was a smell of frying fish in the air and a couple of cats were slinking along the walls in anticipation.

'I thought you'd checked all that.'

'I did, and I didn't find anything at the time, but that's because the investments are all in his wife's maiden name. He owes millions. Much more than he could ever pay even if he sold up everything he owns.'

'Why hasn't it come to light before?'

'It takes time to assess loss and profit in Lloyd's. He knew he was going down badly but he also knew he'd have about three years before it would be called in.'

They paused on the bridge over a small canal. Shaughnessy sat on the crumbling stone balustrade. His right arm was in a black linen sling that matched his suit. It didn't trouble him much, the only thing that still hurt was his ankle. It was just a sprain, the least of his injuries but the one that was making his life hardest. Patricia leaned over the edge and watched the hard winter light playing on the water.

'Why do you think he picked on Trevelyan?' she asked. She'd been over this with him already a hundred times before but it interested her.

'I guess because paintings are the easiest things to ransom.'

'There are other syndicates that insure pictures. He could have hit one of them instead of James.' She was wearing a dark red cape over her black dress, her hair tucked up into a fur hat.

'He could influence Trevelyan, make certain he employed the right team of negotiators.'

'I think he did it because he wasn't one of his own kind,' Patricia said. 'Ambrose had helped him to start up his own syndicate but he was still an outsider to him. When it came down to it, he was disposable.' She flicked some dry stone dust off the bridge and watched it float away. Then straightening up she brushed her hands together.

'Don't move,' she ordered.

'I'm not going anywhere.'

Taking a camera from her bag she stood back against the other side of the bridge and viewed him through the lens. Her programme had gone out two nights before and, as she'd hoped, it had caused a sensation. The viewing figures had been high, the reviews ecstatic. But more important than that, it had been news. All the way over on the plane she had been rifling through the papers, reading out passages from articles that had been lifted directly from the programme as Fleet Street made a belated attempt to catch up with the story. It was a scoop in the old-fashioned sense and he was pleased for her.

It had been a beautiful piece of work, in his opinion the best she'd done. She'd given it no sensationalism but delivered her lines calmly, weaving the separate strands in the complex financial intrigue, letting the story speak for itself.

She pressed the shutter and smiled as she put the camera away. 'You look like one of those veterans from the Great War.'

'All I need are some matches to sell and I'd be set up for life.'

She was relaxed now but for the twenty-four hours before the programme went out she had been a bundle of nerves, pacing the floor, remembering things she could have added, thinking of better ways to have done certain parts. It had been like living with a caged tiger.

'We'd better get going,' she said, glancing at her watch. 'Is your ankle hurting?'

'I can hop the rest of the way.'

As they crossed the Accademia Bridge she pointed up the canal. 'There's a dear little hotel just behind that piazza,' she said. 'We might move there in a day or so.'

They were staying at the Gritti Palace at present but Patricia wanted to move. She had a theory that changing hotels gave one a new outlook on a city. It brought different routes and restaurants and scenes into view.

The state room on the first floor of the Accademia Museum was crowded when they arrived.

'There you are,' Trevelyan said. 'I was beginning to wonder whether you two were going to turn up.'

'I was going to take the vaporetto but he insisted on walking,' Patricia said. 'And he's not good at doing that at the moment.'

'You know my wife, Maggie, don't you?' Trevelyan asked. She was a small woman, pretty with dark hair and a slightly discontented smile.

'You managed to make him bring you along, did you?' Shaughnessy asked.

'I don't like to miss out on everything.'

On the far wall, above the heads of the guests, hung *The Triumph of Bacchus*. Shaughnessy collected a couple of glasses of champagne for himself and Patricia and they pushed through the crush towards it. He didn't know who all these people were, where they came from, or where they would be if *The Triumph of Bacchus* hadn't arrived in town that day. They were part of that wealthy international set who appear in every society magazine: the purveyors of silky smooth small-talk, the bearers of jewellery and sun tans. They are the glitterati, the social tramps. Without them the beaches of St Tropez, the casinos of Monte Carlo, and the ski slopes of St Moritz would be desolate places.

There were faces amongst them that he did recognize. Gerald Barraclough was putting away champagne and staring down into the glass wondering where it had gone. Over by the window Scobie had found a group of ladies eager to lionize him.

'I thought you weren't coming,' Shaughnessy said when he had him alone for a moment.

'I wasn't. But after two days of police tea I needed something to perk myself up.' He was wearing a magnificent green smoking jacket that had first seen smoke in the days of Queen Victoria and for once his hair was brushed.

'Are you here alone?' Shaughnessy asked.

'No, I've brought Marjorie along. She's never been to Venice before.' He spoke under his breath as though he was referring to the initiation into some mystic cult.

'Could be your lucky day then, Scobie.'

'They say gondolas are an aphrodisiac.'

'They are—for the gondoliers. The women usually feel slightly seasick. Besides I think you'll find the price of them has the same effect on you as a bucket of cold water.'

'Really?' He sounded disappointed. 'Maybe I could just hire one and get her to row it. That should do the trick.' He was looking around the room as he spoke, checking for other options should his first one fail.

'You know that bank which has bought the studio,' he said after a moment. 'They're going to let me stay on as a tenant.'

'Sounds good.'

'They must be soft in the head. Do you know how much they want in rent? Fifty quid a week. How about that then? Call themselves financial wizards; they couldn't take money off a baby.'

'I shouldn't look a gift horse in the mouth, Scobie.'

'Oh, I won't.' He straightened his back so that two of the buttons on his shirt front came open and drank some more champagne. 'In fact I'm going to do pretty well out of it. I've rented it out. The estate agent reckons it could fetch four hundred a week.'

'Where are you going to work?'

'Gerry Lampton's place. I talked to him the other day. He never uses it and he could do with someone to keep an eye on the place. I'm paying him another fifty quid. That leaves me with three hundred a week clear profit. I could retire on that.'

Shaughnessy didn't like to point out that he'd been retired for most of his life.

'What are you two talking about?' Patricia asked, coming between them.

'Scobie was telling me about his career prospects.'

She said, 'I saw the Italian Ambassadress was into you just now.'

That was one thing Patricia had been right about: he didn't know who this glittering crowd were but they knew him. The first time he'd met the Ambassadress she hadn't bothered to say a word to him. Now he was an old friend who'd had to be introduced to all her other old friends. 'She wants us to go and stay with them in Sorrento.'

'I know,' Patricia said. 'I've just been talking to her husband. I hope you refused. He's got a very mobile left hand.'

'Do you trust her?' Scobie asked as Patricia moved away again. 'I mean, I know she was just play-acting the other day but she was dangerously good at it.'

'I thought you expected women to be like that.'

'When they've got a figure like hers as well you want to be careful.'

Scobie was beginning to settle in.

'Stick to the ugly ones, eh?'

'At least they'll row a gondola for you.'

It was later that evening that Shaughnessy stood in front of *The Triumph of Bacchus* with Patricia. The room had begun to clear, there was space to stand back on it.

Patricia held her glass in both hands to her breast as she looked up at the towering figure of Bacchus.

'He looks half animal, doesn't he?' a woman behind them was saying.

Patricia caught his eye and smiled. 'Do you think if you hadn't put that third figure in the boat into your version anyone would have been able to tell them apart?' she asked.

The sun was going down outside and the low light struck her face as she spoke, knocking sudden bright sparks from her hair.

'I didn't put the third figure into my version,' he said. 'I put it into the original.'

'How could you have done that?' she asked. Her voice was soft and suddenly serious.

'The other morning when the two paintings were in Trevelyan's office I asked him to get me a cup of coffee. I was left alone with them long enough to put it in.'

'Are you trying to tell me...?' She couldn't believe what she thought he meant.

'This is my picture,' Shaughnessy confirmed it for her. 'It's what Scobie wanted me to do. That was the condition he laid down before we started.'

Her eyes were bright but it was a long time before she asked, 'Where's the original?'

'Back in the Scuola, where it should be.'

'But won't somebody find out?'

'Maybe, maybe not. It depends on how good their eyes are.' Patricia looked up at the mocking face of Bacchus: his mouth open, teeth bared. Behind them the woman's voice said, 'It's strange, but when you look at him you can almost hear him laughing.'